CARTWRIGHT'S CAVALIERS

BOOK ONE OF THE
REVELATIONS CYCLE

Mark Wandrey

Seventh Seal Press
Virginia Beach, VA

Chris Kennedy/Seventh Seal Press
2052 Bierce Dr.
Virginia Beach, VA 23454
http://chriskennedypublishing.com/

Publisher's Note: This is a work of fiction. Names, characters, places, and incidents are a product of the author's imagination. Locales and public names are sometimes used for atmospheric purposes. Any resemblance to actual people, living or dead, or to businesses, companies, events, institutions, or locales is completely coincidental.

Ordering Information:
Quantity sales. Special discounts are available on quantity purchases by corporations, associations, and others. For details, contact the "Special Sales Department" at the address above.

Cartwright's Cavaliers/ Mark Wandrey. -- 1st ed.
ISBN 978-1942936398

This book is the culmination of several years of brain storming by my wife Joy, son Patrick, and myself. I owe them so much already, but now even more for helping this come together. Thanks to Chris Kennedy for publishing it, and to Patty McIntosh Mize and Beth Agejew for editing it.

To everyone who loves mecha, and the sheer boyish destruction we can do with them!

"I watched as the Lamb opened the first of the seven seals. Then I heard one of the four living creatures say in a voice like thunder, "Come and see!" I looked, and there before me was a white horse! Its rider held a bow, and he was given a crown, and he rode out as a conqueror bent on conquest."

— *Revelation 6:1-2*

Chapter One

Jim Cartwright was daydreaming. What else was there to do in school when you were basically done, but they insisted you be physically present the last week? Of course, there were the VOWS, voluntary off-world assessments, but he still had a few hours to try and forget about them. At least he had a nice view of the school grounds. As a senior, he'd managed to secure a window seat in the 12th floor study lounge. If you were watching him sitting there with a slate propped up, its plastic screen full of dates and figures, you'd almost think he was actually doing something school-related.

It was a beautiful spring morning in Indianapolis. Below, he could see a group of rising freshmen taking their orientation tour. The physical education compound – the bane of his existence – was nearly deserted as everyone prepared for events later that day. Across the street, the primary school's playground was full of young children running and squealing in exuberant play, full of excitement that the school year was almost over. Watching them, he couldn't help but find his thoughts slipping back to that period of time in his own life.

It was twelve years earlier, at a school near his family's estate in Dallas. His mother had insisted he attend the local public school, as she believed it would build character. Mrs. Addams was his first grade teacher. She was a tall, stern-looking woman who wore her hair in an almost masculine style – short, slicked back, and parted neatly down one side – and she ran her class in a similarly disciplined manner. Children were expected to sit ramrod straight, their special beginner slates in the proper place on their desks. Students were seated in alphabetical order waiting as patiently as six-year-old boys and girls are capable of waiting. They were about to have their initial exposure to MST, and the excitement in the room was palpable.

Most of his classmates were thrilled to begin. He was...less so. Most of the kids in the room already knew each other from kindergarten, but he'd only entered a public classroom for the first time that morning. On the chubby side, he'd already drawn far more attention to himself than he liked. For young children, different was a thing of instant interest. It could be fun, exciting, or just something to point and laugh at. Jim's extra childhood weight fell into the latter category. The fact that he'd been raised as a privileged child with a tutor until now also meant he didn't really know how to deal with negative attention, so he took it in silence.

"So class," Mrs. Addams had said, making an odd face, "I'm sure many of you would like to grow up to be *mercenaries*."

Jim wouldn't realize until years later the emphasis she put on the word mercenaries had not been a positive one. While she, like all the other teachers, promoted MST as was mandated by the government, like most other teachers, she was far from approving of it.

"Today you're going to meet your primary school MST Facilitator, Major Taylor. Major Taylor works for the United States Government and she will be here throughout your school years to...help you understand your potential future career." The door to the classroom opened and another woman walked in.

A couple of inches shorter than Mrs. Addams, she had ultra-short black hair and deep-set, piercing gray eyes in a face so thin it was almost skeletal. She wore her dark blue Army uniform like plate armor. He only knew she was a woman by the slight swell of her breasts beneath her uniform shirt. Major Taylor walked the same way she wore her uniform – with crisp precision. Her hat remained firmly tucked under one arm as she marched into the room. All the kids sat up a little straighter, recognizing authority as it arrived. This authority clearly outranked even Mrs. Addams, by whom they were more than a little intimidated. Jim took immediate note of the rows of ribbons on her chest. In particular, his perceptive young eyes spotted two ribbons that did not match the others. *I know why you do this job,* he thought with a little smile. He'd recognized service ribbons for two different mercenary companies.

"Good afternoon, class," she said as the teacher gave the new arrival the position at the head of the class.

"Good afternoon, Major Taylor," everyone repeated in the same way they'd learned from Mrs. Addams. A small smile broke the Major's face, almost like a crack appearing in a granite counter top.

"I'm sure your teacher has explained why I am here. MST, which stands for Mercenary Service Track, is your pathway to fame, fortune, and a brighter future for all humanity." Jim remembered smiling. It was the same catchphrase used in TV commercials promoting MST all the time. "There are a lot of exciting classes in your future, and I'm here to help guide you through them. I'll answer any questions you may have and provide you with whatever help you need, should you decide to continue with MST later in your schooling." She looked around the room, seeming to make eye contact with each of them in turn.

"So," she continued, "how many of you think you might want to choose merc service when you grow up?" Almost every hand in the room went up. Jim raised his without thinking. A couple boys further back snickered, and he knew why. "Excellent!" Major Taylor said.

"Now how many of you have someone in your family who has military service?" A few hands went down. "Good, good. And how many are mercs?" Another percentage went down. "Parents who are or were?" A larger group went down this time. Only about ten were still up, Jim included.

"Okay," she said and clapped her hands together. "Can any of you kids with your hands still up tell me what unit your mother or father served with?" She pointed at a girl toward the rear. "You, young lady?"

"My daddy is with the Hellcats," she said proudly to some applause.

"Good unit, you may put your hand down," the Major said with a nod. "And you, son?" she asked another boy.

"Drake's Rangers," the boy said. More applause.

"I had a friend serve with them," the Major replied. "And you, little miss?"

"Triple T," she said. More applause.

"Tom's Total Terrors," the Major laughed. "Tough bunch." The girl smiled as she put her arm down. The Major went around the room and almost stopped before she realized Jim still had his arm up. "Oh, almost didn't see you," she said.

"Hard to believe," one of the boys who'd snickered earlier said. A few others laughed but Mrs. Addams' glare brought almost instant silence.

"Speak up, son! Who'd your parent serve with?"

"Cartwright's Cavaliers," he said in as clear and even a voice as he could. The room was deathly silent, partly because of the name, partly because many were only now remembering Jim's name from when he'd stood that morning and introduced himself in front of the class.

"What's your name, son?" the Major asked, her gaze like dual lasers.

"Jim Cartwright, ma'am." She grunted, almost like she'd been punched.

"Wow," the kid sitting next to him said loud enough that Jim could hear it.

"So, your father would be…" the Major said, letting her sentence trail off.

"Thaddeus Cartwright, ma'am," Jim finished for her, knowing she was pausing to let him prove his claim. Almost anyone in America would know the name Cartwright, but not many five-year-old boys would know the name of its commanding officer.

"So, we have a son of the Four Horsemen here," she said and nodded. Jim felt like he was being examined by a medical scanner. Despite himself, he fidgeted in his seat under her gaze. "Of course, all of you kids know the Four Horsemen were the only merc units to return from the Alpha Contracts, right?" There were noncommittal mumbles from the kids. Most only knew the Four Horsemen were heroes and famous, not many knew why. The Major nodded again. "Well, Jim, tell your father Major Evelyn Taylor, formerly First Sergeant of the Golden Horde, sends her regards. You deliver that message for me." Jim nodded his head; he knew to take such a request seriously, even at his age. "See that you do. Now, let's talk about the MST classes you'll be taking this year."

"Son of a Horseman," the kid next to him whispered, "That's cool!" Jim beamed at him. "My name is Rick. Rick Culper."

"Hi," Jim said back. It occurred to him that his standing in the class had just shifted for the better – and he wasn't quite sure how he felt about that. He'd find through his life that being a Cartwright often worked in strange and confusing ways.

Jim had delivered the message, just as he'd been instructed, that evening at dinner. His father smiled and got that distant look in his eye as he often did when thinking about events long past.

"Tell her Thad says, 'Hi!' right back," he'd said, "and to have a Coke on me." Jim returned that message, and Major Taylor had laughed uproariously, thanking Jim for the message. It was the last time she'd ever smiled at him. As the years went on, and he'd begun to grow in all the wrong ways, the Major became less and less interested in Jim. She always looked at him with the sort of disappointment one reserves for a particularly poor meal you'd paid far too much for. She had retired in his eighth year. Her replacement never gave Jim a second glance.

He'd continued to doggedly study all the academic classes needed to be a merc, regardless of his scores in other areas required for MST success. He'd suffered the barbs and scorn of his classmates. The Great Waist, they called him. Portly Cavalier. Cartwaist's Cavalier, and another hundred they'd come up with, each more stupid and insulting than the last. Through it all, he'd studied, and he'd learned about the service, about merc history (the parts he hadn't been taught at home), and about the galaxy in which they served and its history of combat. When the planetary Aethernet ran out of resources, he went to the Galnet node provided by the Galactic Union.

He learned about the beginning of FTL flight, and the formation of the First Republic (before the Union). He read about the Great War between the two strongest races of the Republic, the Dusman and the Kahraman. The history spoke about how the war spiraled out of control, ultimately embroiling thousands of races and tens of thousands of worlds in the conflict. The Republic's form of democracy proved unable to contain the war, and the final results were cataclysmic.

Eventually the Kahraman unleashed what they believed to be an unstoppable terror weapon upon the galaxy – the Canavar. They were titanic beasts genetically engineered to wreak havoc on property and destroy populations. The planets where they landed were helpless to defend themselves against these monstrous creatures. They were living engines of ultimate destruction. Details were fuzzy, but he read how the Canavar were bred to be resistant to all but the most powerful weapons, yet too agile to be killed from orbit without laying waste to the entirety of whatever civilization lay below.

Somehow the Kahraman were defeated after many years, but much of the galaxy was devastated. It took hundreds of years for many worlds to recover. Many others were left uninhabitable. In the aftermath of the Great War, the Union was born, as were the many guilds which the Union used instead of its old structures. At the core was the Mercenary Guild, with its rules of warfare to ensure such devastation never happened again.

While his fellow students both hated and envied him, he used his elementary school years to learn as much as he could about his future career and about technology – specifically about computers. He loved computers. He had a natural knack for programming and working on the Aethernet. His mother called it an unhealthy attraction.

"Ready for the VOWS, fat boy?"

Jim was jarred back to the real world by the insult, and he remembered where he was. The implants in his brain told him it was 2:30 – time to head to the PE compound. The young man who stood next to him was several inches taller and about 100 lbs. lighter, despite all the muscle and hair. He'd had a run-in with him before, as he had with many of the other merc jocks. Didn't this twit know that he could well be begging Jim for a job someday?

"Sure Brad," he said dismissively.

"Not that it matters, rich fat kid." The jock looked like he was trying to start a fight – something Jim had been adept at avoiding most his life. He'd only been in one, and that was enough of a humiliation to teach him to avoid fistfights at all costs. It wasn't that he was afraid of getting hurt, he wasn't. He just wasn't good at fighting and didn't want to give the other kids one more thing to laugh at him about.

"Piss off, Brad," another student said. Jim recognized Rick Culper's voice without looking up and couldn't resist a little smile. That same kid from his first school day – they'd remained friends the whole time they were in school together.

"I don't know what you see in that loser," Brad said and left without another word.

"Don't let that asshole bother you," Rick said, giving Jim a nudge. "Come on, we're going to be late to the VOWS."

"Ready...set...*bang!*" The starter pistol's report was both old-fashioned and sharp. Each group took off down the track, their legs pumping furiously and arms working as they ran for their lives. The physical tests were something Jim had been dreading for most of his school years. They were the last hurdle of the MST.

"Don't sweat it, Jimbo," Rick said as he strolled into the room, relaxed and casual as always.

"Easy for you to say," Jim said, casting an envious look at his best friend's physique. You could describe Rick as a Greek god, and you wouldn't be doing Zeus or Hercules any disservice. He was just over six feet tall with a chiseled chin, and bright Delft-blue eyes under thick waves of dark brown hair. The muscles on his arms were veined, while his chest and abs looked like they were cut from stone. There was no deviation from that perfection from his lips down to the tips of his toes. His ass was so tight the girls in their class went weak in the knees at the sight of it.

Rick held the school record in almost every athletic accomplishment, including the 100-yard dash they were about to run. He'd spent the last month as Jim's personal trainer, working with him methodically every day after school and on most weekends — at least when he could catch Jim before he sneaked off to avoid training, anyway. Over the course of that agonizing month, Rick had managed to shave two seconds off Jim's best time in the 100-yard dash. He now produced a blazing 15.5 seconds. Rick's best was 8.75 — only a quarter second over the world record.

"Next!" the tester barked and glanced down at his slate. "Caan, Cadley, Cartwright, Culper..." he went on listing the names. Jim couldn't help but hear a few guffaws from the stands full of his fellow seniors, who'd already taken this test and were waiting for their turn at the next. Jim moved forward to the starting line, and put a foot in the blocks while trying to figure out how to adjust the damned jockstrap that had worked its way into the crack of his size-able ass.

Jim glanced up at the tester, a serious-looking retired merc hold-ing the slate and sizing up the candidates – nine boys and two girls. His entire demeanor spoke of barely restrained violence. As he turned, they could all see that one side of his face was entirely synth-flesh, and the eye on that side was a solid bright red that glowed with an inner light. Like so many mercs, part of him never made it home. When he got to Jim the man's eyes narrowed, and he looked at the name again. "Cartwright," he said. "Any relation to Thaddeus Cart-wright?"

"He was my father, sir." The man grunted then looked over Jim again.

"Well, your dad was one hell of a merc." He pulled the starting pistol from his belt. "Ready…"

Thirty seconds later, Jim was lying in the grass 120 yards away gasping and wheezing for all he was worth, still trying to catch his breath. His knees hurt, his hips hurt, his back hurt, and there was a stitch in his side so severe he was sure his guts must be hanging out. Even his man-boobs hurt. He lifted his head enough to look down at his belly going rapidly up and down under the shirt plastered to his sweaty chest. He let his head smack back down. A rock dug into his scalp. Great.

"You okay, Jimbo?" He glanced over to see Rick standing there. The fucker wasn't even breathing hard. Of course, he'd been there almost nine seconds before Jim. For a specimen like Rick, that was enough time to run another dash.

"What…time…" Jim huffed.

"You or me?" Jim just glared. "You did it in 16.25," he told him. Jim blinked away tears. "You staggered off the blocks a little."

"And...you?"

"What does that matter, buddy?"

"Just...tell me." Jim had enough breath back to ponderously lever himself to a seated position. Rick wasn't looking at him.

"Culper!" a familiar, gruff voice yelled. They both turned to see the Merc who'd called their names striding over like he was on a parade ground.

"Sir?" Rick asked.

"You keep that up you'll make a top billet, son." He stopped and punched Rick in the shoulder. It was meant as a brotherly gesture, but it almost knocked the eighteen-year-old off his feet. "Damn fine, son, 8.55 official. Hope you aren't thinking about being a worthless athlete?"

"No sir!"

"Good, your planet needs you." He reached into his pocket and pulled out a coin. It glinted silver in the sunlight. "You give this to the recruiter for Gitmo's Own, tell him Crosser sent you." Rick looked stunned but took the coin. A silver challenge coin, from a veteran merc. Jim nodded in appreciation. Gitmo's Own was a good company, if rather small. Crosser glanced down where Jim was still sitting dejectedly in the grass, his red eye glinting in the sunlight. He half nodded, half shook his head, and marched off.

"Wow," Rick said, examining the coin. Jim didn't have to see it to know what was on the coin. He'd memorized all the Merc logos before he'd been old enough to ride a bike. That one would be a globe of the Earth with a stylized ship's anchor bisecting it and an eagle astride the planet. An ancient symbol of a planetary military unit whose former members formed Gitmo's Own.

"Silver," Jim nodded, "He must have been impressed."

"Yeah," Rick agreed and carefully, almost reverently put it in his pocket.

"You going to use it?"

"You know I won't," Rick snapped and looked down at his friend, a hurt expression on his face. He held out a hand thick with muscles. Jim took it and his friend grunted as he levered him up to his feet. "We're both going to serve in the Cavaliers."

"Sure," Jim said. Down the field, students were mustering for the next test, pushups.

"Come on," Rick encouraged, patting him on his shoulder, "you always do better at this next one." Unable to keep his friend's unabashed good nature from intruding on him, Jim grinned sheepishly and followed him. Rick hurried on ahead to make sure they didn't miss their turn. When his friend wasn't looking Jim slipped his necklace from under his shirt and glanced at it.

A challenge coin, not unlike the one Rick had just received to help him become a recruit, was affixed to a silver chain. Only this coin wasn't silver, it was a dark metal that had a slight bluish tinge to it. It also didn't look shiny, as if the metal had been exposed to some extremes before being minted. The image was of a medieval knight, astride a charger, a banner flowing behind him. His lance was lowered as he charged a prostrate dragon on the ground. Inscribed on the banner was "*Lead the Charge.*" He sighed as he put it away and headed to his next humiliation.

Hours later, Jim returned to the little flat his family rented for him. It was just blocks from the school – an academy carefully selected by the family to maximize his educational chances. His mother still held out hope he might yet make it into the family business from the ground up and continue the tradition, all physical evidence to the contrary. The apartment in Carmel, Indiana, was evidence of that. "The best leadership and physical development primary classes in the country," the school's marketing brochure had bragged. It also happened to have a top-notch Aetherware department, and that was what decided it for Jim.

It had taken him nearly a year, but he'd managed to skim enough from his allowance for the pinplant procedure. These types of implants had come down steadily in price since they first became available, almost a century ago. He'd had to spend some of his carefully saved money to get a forged permission from his mother to get them; his mother would never have signed it. She believed what mercs went through was bad enough. He'd made an excuse during spring break last year, flown to Tijuana, and underwent the implant surgery.

Jim stripped out of his sweaty sweat pants and shirt, then gym shorts, and gloriously dug the jockstrap out of the crack of his ass and the folds between his legs. Sometimes he hated not changing and showering at school. Of course, dealing with the stink of himself all afternoon was not nearly as bad as getting naked in front of all the other guys in the locker room. He stopped on the way through the bathroom to grab his interface device and clicked it in place behind his ear.

In the bathroom he glanced at himself in the mirror – hairless chest, man-boobs, rolls of belly fat, other worse things lower. It was only a quick glance, more out of habit that anything else. A minute later he was in the shower letting the stinging hot water wash away the sweat and grime of the afternoon tests.

As the soap and water did their jobs, Jim closed his eyes and let himself slip into the Aethernet through his pinplants. It was only his own personal node, but he'd been working on it for a year. Building, improving, and creating his own world. A long time ago people would have called it virtual reality. But that was before Aetherware was invented. Inside the Aethernet, his mind linked directly via synaptic relay, was better than reality. Especially his current reality.

As he was drying his considerable body, his relay informed him of an incoming call. When he mentally clicked to answer it, he was surprised to find it was a message and not a live call.

"Jim, it's Mom." Jim shook his head, as if he wouldn't know. The contact ID linked to his mom's GVP – her Global Verified Persona – the second the call came in. "I wanted to call and see how you did on the tests! I know you did great! Look, I'm stuck in Seattle on company business. We've run into a few problems, so I won't have time to come out tomorrow like I had planned. I'm sorry, we'll get this taken care of, and then I will fly out there first thing on Sunday. See you then."

He pondered his mother's message as he dried himself off. After his father died, she had taken over running the company. While not a merc, she came from old money out East; she'd let the company's military leadership run contracts while she managed the money. All indications were that she'd done pretty well. When his father was still alive, she'd helped out as an accountant. Father had insisted. Cartwrights weren't known as the idle rich. So he was left with the mystery of what she would be involved in that was both company business and a big enough problem for her to miss their planned appointment.

He pulled on a pair of sweatpants and a T-shirt and shuffled into the apartment's living room where he kept his rig. He glanced briefly at the only prominent picture in the room – a large 3D Tri-V of his father and himself. Jim had been nine years old, standing on the back of an ancient Drake ACV, armored combat vehicle, holding a laser carbine almost as big as he was. His dad stood a little in front of him, like Jim, looking at the photographer. All around them were members of the Cavaliers waving and hamming it up for the picture, just before a deployment on contract. It was the last time he'd ever seen any of them alive.

The full-body support chair gently reclined as the robotic arm reached out and made contact with his pin-points. Jim felt the momentary disconnection as his biological senses were shut down, and he fell away from the real world, and into the Aether.

* * * * *

Chapter Two

"The seeker-bots are going crazy," the mining foreman chirped. "They've found something!"

Ashattoo turned part of his viewing area away from the slate which displayed the expected yield data for the well, and he turned in the direction of the foreman. The mine on Ch'sis had been almost a complete bust for the Athal, and he was just unlucky enough to be in charge of it. His brood mate had pitched the deal to the Athal Collective. He'd been doing valuable historical research before being transferred to Ch'sis. To be taken away from a job he'd loved and sent to the ass end of the universe had left him with a profound feeling of betrayal.

"What nonsense are you speaking?" Ashattoo spat back. There was only one hour left until feeding break and there was still much to be done. He didn't want to waste time analyzing questionable data.

"The probe shaft you ordered on mine feed nine," the foreman said, using a foothand to smooth the sensing hairs on his side.

"I gave no such order."

"Sure you did," the supervisor insisted. "Yesterday at the research meeting."

Ashattoo looked away from the data in annoyance, giving his complete attention to the foreman, who noticed his annoyance and yet...still persisted.

"You said that a probe shaft on mine nine would provide answers to interesting questions."

Ashattoo's mouth parts fell open, and he spit fluid on the floor. "Fool!" he barked, "I said it would be foolish to sink a probe shaft in nine; it would only answer a question that does not need answering and provide questionable data!"

"I...don't remember it that way."

Ashattoo threw up all six hands in frustration, slapped the slate he'd been reading onto his tool harness, and skittered over to the supervisor who twitched in fear. He used most of his high-attenuation eyes to examine the screen, first noting with horror that the probe shaft had been sunk more than three miles already. At just under 100 credits per yard...it was a disaster.

"Five thousand credits, you grub!" Ashattoo exclaimed in frustration. "You don't listen to what I say, and you waste many thousands of our credits on a probe shaft!?"

"But, look at the data!"

"What could possibly be so interesting?" he moaned. The supervisor pointed at another area of the readout, beside the basic drill data. The seeker robots at the end of the probe looked for certain elements and reported the results back. That data helped steer the probe, and this particular probe was capable of deviating several degrees per yard dug. It was picking up massive concentrations of a particular noble gas. "That is...interesting."

"That's what I said," the supervisor mumbled peevishly.

Ashattoo wondered – what was the chance, on this world of all worlds? They'd harvested modest amounts of gaseous hydrocarbons, enough to make the operation almost worth the expense of the 100-cycle lease, and the Mining Guild didn't sell leases on worlds that had even a minor possibility of being profitable with ease. More than 10,000 cycles ago, Ch'sis had been a veritable treasure trove of various rare gases. Despite the remnants of the white dwarf in the center of its system, though, Ch'sis wasn't found to possess the rarest of the rarest of the rare — a gas so rare it was usually only found in the rocky core of a former gas giant. Ch'sis had been such a planet and had barely survived the supernova that reformed it. After the gaseous atmosphere had been blasted away by the shockwave of its star exploding, only a planetoid less than four thousand miles wide remained.

The intense pressures inside a gas giant were ideal for the creation of exotic elements and the pooling of other more commonly found ones. Deposits of fluorine gas sometimes found deep in the core of such worlds, exposed to the unbelievable radiation of a supernova, resulted in something else entirely — something extremely valuable — and something that was usually found in combination with...

"Xenon gas," Ashattoo said, the light in the operations center glimmering off his multifaceted compound eyes. Was it possible? "Any hint of it?"

"Of what?" the foreman asked.

"Don't be a fool!" Ashattoo snapped.

"No," the other replied sheepishly. Ashattoo didn't really blame him, the very idea of anyone finding a deposit, previously undiscovered, on a world so thoroughly gone over, was unthinkable.

"Press the probe deeper," Ashattoo ordered.

Four hours later Ashattoo flew down the bare-walled corridors of the mining module to his office, using both feet and foothands to speed himself along. He was glad his ancestors had not been flightless, like his species was now outside of the near-zero gravity of the facility. If he'd been forced to walk, he probably would have stumbled all the way there. He was in far too much shock to have navigated by conscious thought.

He activated his main computer and used his security code to compose a message to the Collective. They had to be informed immediately. In minutes the dispatch was completed, using the highest level encryption algorithm at his disposal, and sent out to the jump point. There it would await the next ship to transit through the system. His multifaceted eyes took in the room. Did everything look different? If the discovery played out, it would be different in amazing ways.

All the rest of that day and into the next, Ashattoo set every available robot in the manufactory unit to constructing the extraction, refining, and storage facilities needed to process the incomprehensible treasure sensors had indicated was buried in the gas giant remnant below. As he worked the next day, his slate gave him a routine notification. His message had been relayed to a free trader passing through the Ch'sis stargate in the correct direction. With luck, the Collective would receive his amazing news in a matter of a few weeks. He would not realize the magnitude of the events he'd accidentally set in motion for months to come.

* * * * *

Chapter Three

When Jim returned to his apartment on the afternoon he turned eighteen, he was wallowing in the pit of the lowest moment of his life. He'd had to go to the school to get his final grades as well as the results of his VOWS. His grades were stellar, of course. Even with mandatory physical training dragging him down, he finished with a sliding scale GPA of 4.86, in the upper ninety-ninth percentile.

The VOWS, however, were graded based on a battery of physical and mental tests, with the physical having greater weight in the results, of course. Each category was graded from 100, worst, to 500, best. There were five mental categories and four physical. The mental total was divided by five, the physical by three. Thus the mental range was from 100 to 500, the physical 133 to 667, resulting in an aggregate between 233 and 1167.

To stand even a remote chance of being picked up by a company, a graduate needed to score over 900. Even with a mental category score of 471, just 29 points below perfect, he only managed a combined score of 664. Dead last in his class. The PhysEd teacher wouldn't even look him in the eye when he handed Jim the chip with his VOWS score.

Jim briefly considered swinging by the little startown just outside of Beach Grove to pick up some drugs. Maybe a little Sparkle, to lift his feelings? It was stubborn pride that stopped him. He'd managed to make it through his entire education without resorting to drugs to feel better, despite always being "the fat kid" in his class. Sure, maybe everyone else was destined to be beautiful, but he was going to be running an entire merc company.

It had become harder as his teens hit. He'd been taller than Rick initially. Sure, Rick was thin and athletic, but being taller had meant something, right? Then their growth spurts hit. Rick shot to over six feet, while Jim petered out at around five foot nine inches. As Rick got even leaner, his muscle tone began to arrive. He ate like a horse, and grew the muscles to match. Jim ate sparingly, and grew to resemble a hippo. It didn't seem to matter what he did. Of course, the doctors gave him diets and all kinds of advice, which he tried to follow, but once he discovered the Aethernet, his level of physical activity – and consequently his level of physical fitness – went steadily downhill.

So with the abysmal VOWS score in his pocket, he stared at the cab's control screen and half reached for the Chicago Starport's icon. A one-hour ride on the hyper-expressway. As an extra territorial area, he could acquire anything he needed there for the right price. A function of Earth's joining the Union, the zones around starports were basically not human territory. The laws of the Union stood there, and the Union had damned few laws. The surrounding community was mostly indifferent. Normally a human needed to be twenty-one to enter without an adult escort, but he had a pass. Perk of the family.

Once, in order to impress a girl, he'd taken her and two of her friends in using his pass. They'd acted all impressed, and he'd hoped he might receive certain...considerations in return. They'd ditched him within minutes and showed up the next day with brand new morphogenic tattoos, something that underage girls could only obtain in a startown. Of course, everyone knew the only place to get those was in a startown, and no one else in their school had a pass to get in except him. The girls did him the tiny favor of not directly implicating him, but word got around. Soon others began bothering him to take them to the startown. Not wanting to be used that way again, he refused as politely as he could. One girl slapped his face in the hall after class when he said no. He was once again the school joke, but at least they finally stopped asking him.

Jim sighed and keyed in a mall near his apartment instead. Now that he'd graduated, he'd be heading to Houston pretty soon. The Cavalier's HQ was there, and he had figured doing his management training closer to operations would enable him to actually work a few hours in the company every week. His mother had told him that was fine months ago. The problem was she hadn't returned his calls or emails for a week now. She never left the planet, so there was no way she'd gone on deployment. To his knowledge she'd never even gone up to orbit where the Cavalier's starships were located.

Jim killed a few hours at the mall then went back to his place. When he closed the door to his apartment, he was feeling depressed and hungry. He went to the kitchen first and flash-cooked a meal pack, then headed for the living room and his Aethernet direct connection. He almost missed the envelope on the floor just inside the door. He couldn't remember *ever* getting a physical letter in his apartment in the four years he'd been there. It was large and legal looking.

From the Law Offices of Leo Witwicky, Bankruptcy Attorneys in Extra-Planetary Law, Houston Startown, it read. For a rare moment, Jim forgot about food as he felt his blood run cold. He fell into the seldom used kitchenette chair that creaked in protest. He tore open the envelope and began to read.

A few pages in, he groped around his belly and reached into his front pocket to retrieve a mobile pinlink to his system. He was always careful in public, pinheads often were attacked by purists. That's why he didn't shave his head and get tattoos like many of his fellows.

The mobile link clicked in place and instantly synched with his main system. He could have just hooked up, but it was hard to read in the real world while submerged in the Aether. After chewing through the pages and pages of legalese, he needed the hive-mind to help him make sense of it all.

When he put the paperwork down, he glanced at the microwave meal and probed it with a finger. It was room temperature, just like his life. In his head he summed up what he'd read:

Cartwright's Cavaliers went back to the beginning of the off-world mercenary companies. Founded by James "Jimmy" Cartwright, Sr., shortly after initial contact, it got one of the first one hundred contracts ever signed. Of the companies that signed contracts, ninety-six of them did not survive action. The remaining four became known as The Four Horsemen, partly because they'd seemingly survived the apocalypse, and partly because they all just happened to have horses in their logos.

His father was the sixth owner and director of Cartwright's Cavaliers in an unbroken line of wealth and success that was the most storied of the Four Horsemen. Jim had grown up listening to unending tales of the exploits of the company on a thousand alien worlds. It was his history, his past, his birthright. And it was gone. It had survived thousands of battles across the galaxy, but it had not been able to survive his mother.

After Jim's father died, the company had been left to him, in keeping with both law and tradition. He could not legally serve in the CEO role until he was eighteen, so in the interim his mother had agreed to run the company until he was old enough to take over, which would have been now. Jim had watched her slowly depleting the company's financial reserves, but he'd never worried too much. The contract acceptance and deployment aspects of the company were handled by handpicked officers who'd served with his father for many years.

As he was getting closer to being able to chart the company's future, Jim had visited with their command staff the last time he was in Houston. They'd assured him it was impossible for her to do any real damage. A merc company's real wealth was in its assets, and she couldn't sell or give those away. Tragically, that was only partly true. Pages of affidavits attested to his mother making a number of extremely risky investments, and with her authority as CFO of Cartwright's Cavaliers, she had used the company's name as collateral.

His mother hadn't wanted him to come down to Houston – or to visit him after his birthday – because she'd been fighting her way through a series of appeals in the World Court while the company's combat units were fulfilling a contract off-world. According to the paperwork he'd just read, the appeals were lost, and the company's assets had been seized to cover the debt.

Jim checked his account linked with the company. There were still several thousand credits there, but the account showed as frozen. He couldn't touch it. His rent was due in days. In a panic he slipped into the Aether and checked his private account. It was still there, and untouched. Being very careful to avoid linking it to his company account in any way, Jim logged onto the airline and made a reservation to Houston on a flight leaving in three hours. He then set about tying up his remaining loose ends in Indiana.

An hour and a half later he was back in a cab heading to Beach Grove. He'd ended up spending almost a quarter of his hidden account between the airfare and arranging to have his Aetherware gear carefully packaged and sent to their Houston home. He had two bags with all his clothes and a few personal items – mostly some tech, and a small collection of very precious stuffed animals. Everything else in the apartment had been leased anyway. With no way to pay the lease, he didn't care what happened to it.

At the startown, he checked his bags and went through security. The screeners, obviously ex-mercs, didn't pay him any attention. Terrorists were never fat teenagers. He was at the gate more than an hour before his flight and with time to kill. Not wanting to be seen with a pinlink over his ear in public, he dug out a seldom used slate and looked through the public Aethernet news. It only took a minute to find a story.

"Fall of the Four Horsemen!" read one headline. "Steeplechase of Fraud," said another. "Millions Go Missing," was another. He clicked through a few and read the pieces haltingly. They all told the same story, just with different slants. Large, risky real estate deals. Interstellar speculating. He sighed at that one, his mother always thought his father was a fool for not playing the aliens at their own game. One story even mentioned something about her buying a decrepit old manufactory. Then there was the only publication that treated the demise of the Cavaliers as anything other than juicy fodder.

"One of the Best Is Gone," said the cover of the ancient *Soldier of Fortune*. There was a picture of his father, resplendent in light combat armor, with the gleaming Cartwright's Knight – a logo of a soldier in shining plate astride a warhorse, with his lance tip pointing skyward – on a dropship behind him. The resolution wasn't high enough to read the motto around the image: *Lead the Charge*.

"That one of the greatest merc companies in Earth's off-world service is lost to financial mismanagement is not only a disgrace, it's a terrible blow to the prestige of human mercs as a whole, and ultimately to the planet's economy," *Soldier of Fortune* said. There was a picture of his father standing with Jim, taken many years ago. His father was smiling, holding his deployment duffle bag over his shoulder with one hand and holding Jim's hand in the other as they walked down a corridor in Houston's Startown. His father looked so happy, and so did Jim. A couple passing Jim slowed and wondered why the fat kid sitting by himself was crying.

Two and a half hours later, Jim was trundling down the jetway from the flight into the Houston Startown air terminal. As he walked, Jim noted random things. Posters describing attractions in and around Houston. The long windows of the terminal that showed the near distance where the pointy noses of several orbital shuttles could be seen nestled in their launch cradles. Runway traffic like his flight accounted for mostly short, regional transport anymore. It all seemed so disturbingly normal, unlike what waited for him.

As Jim left the jetway and turned toward the baggage claim area, he caught sight of a gaggle of reporters. Most were conferring with their camera crews, adjusting equipment, or checking their look in a mirror. Some were performing sound checks and referencing their notes. Jim was in the first group off the plane, and when he came into sight, the newsies all sprang into action.

Oh, shit, Jim thought. He knew the fate of the Cavaliers would be big news, partly due to the company's high-profile status and partly because of the nature of what had befallen it. A hundred companies had died over the years, but the vast majority had been lost in the line of duty, not to poor financial management. Jim ducked his head and walked with a group of curious tourists, even slowing as they did while passing the reporters.

"We're here at Houston Startown hoping to catch a word with James Cartwright, once heir of the powerful Cartwright's Cavaliers..." he heard as he went by. Jim risked a glance and saw one of the reporters scanning the crowd with a critical eye. The man looked right at Jim for a split second, and moved on. He almost laughed. They must have been looking for someone like his dad, and Jim looked nothing like his dad. He always thought his build followed the men of his mother's family: dumpy and fat. Luckily the brains seemed to be pure Cartwright.

Realizing none of the talking heads seemed to have been smart enough to access his high school records so they could get a current image of him, he took strategic advantage of a people-mover grinding along with a load of old people and accelerated to his rather plodding top speed. To his great relief, he soon rounded a corner in the concourse, and the reporters were out of sight. He chuckled to himself as he rode the escalator down to baggage claim. There were a few reporters waiting there as well, but all of them were busily accosting anyone who looked remotely like a young potential-merc. In that moment, he was happy not to be one of the beautiful people.

Jim took up a place between a portly old man absorbed in a video on his headset and a trio of teens all looking at a slate showing a basketball game while he waited. After a minute, the carousel beeped loudly and ground to life, disgorging its usual wide variety of bags, parcels, and golf clubs. He had just grabbed his first bag and was watching for number two when someone spoke up from behind him.

"Jimmy?" He jerked visibly, cursing himself. "It is, isn't it? Jimmy Cartwright?" The portly guy next to him turned and eyed him curiously, obviously recognizing the name as well but not from where. Jim turned his head, afraid of some news hound who'd be about to make his life hell. He wasn't expecting a familiar face.

"Hi Buddha!" he said. A second later all 325 pounds of him was swept off his feet in a full body hug by the only fat merc Jim had ever seen.

"James!" Buddha said in his thick Asian accent. "I can't believe you're here." Buddha wasn't really fat, just round. He was as strong as a horse and could run for hours.

"Me neither," Jim admitted. He hadn't seen Buddha for years.

"Look how you've grown!"

"Yeah," Jimmy said dejectedly, trying not to look down at his belly and failing.

"Don't worry about a few extra pounds, kid! Look at me!" Buddha was wearing a shirt that strained around his middle, the sleeves torn off revealing bulging muscles. He lifted a massive arm and flexed, the bicep fairly exploded into prominence. "We can get you in shape, no problem! Some exercise, protein shakes, and lots of pineapple."

"Buddha," Jim said, cutting him off, "have you seen my mom?"

"Elizabeth?" Buddha got a dark look on his face. "Haven't seen her since before the last deployment." Jim extracted himself from Buddha and glanced at the carousel. Naturally, his bag had just slid past and now he had to wait for it to go all the way around. You'd think after more than two centuries of space travel, someone would have devised a better system to claim your baggage than letting them crawl around on a mechanical conveyor. "I guess you're kinda pissed at her, huh?"

"Yeah," Jim said. "You guys were on deployment, right?"

"Yep," Buddha said. "Just made transition from Sigma Draconis yesterday and came down a couple hours ago. We usually have a company bus waiting, but obviously that isn't happening. So, we're all waiting for friends and cabs and shit." Jim nodded as his bag finally came back around, grunting as he pulled it off the belt. He was a little embarrassed to find himself unable to lift the bag without wheels while pulling the other one. "Here," Buddha said and leaned over the bags, "Let me, little buddy." With zero effort, the big merc took both bags under one arm, slung his own massive duffle bag over his shoulder and looked down at Jim. "Got a car?"

"No, I'm low on funds. I was going to grab a cab."

"We can share. You going to the estate?" Jim nodded, and they were off.

After mercs started bringing back ever larger amounts of intergalactic currency, the governments of Earth realized the potential and started slowly raising taxes. A lot of merc companies grumbled, but even now with the tax rate at nearly fifty percent, an average paid contract would net each member of a company thousands of credits a day. Buddha probably made more on a one-month contract than the average American made in ten years. Of course, that was balanced out by the incredible risks to life and limb mercs were often expected to face, but to most of them, it was well worth it.

With vast sums of liquid assets flowing into their accounts, the mercs spent lavishly. Cars, boats, planes, and of course, real estate. Since many liked to stay near Houston's Startown, the center of Earth-based merc contract negotiations, most of the land around the city belonged to merc companies, owners, and contractors. The Cartwright's Cavaliers family estate was a short ride west of Houston – more than 1,000 acres the company founder had bought with money earned during the early days. Back when a handful of credits could buy a stack of gold.

The computer controlling the cab had taken his instructions and Buddha's credit chip, and sent them off at a respectable pace. They merged onto the expressway and soon they were rocketing along at 200 mph, crowded in with dozens of other cars only inches away. Jim suppressed a wincing fear as the cab shot away from startown. Those in the Indianapolis region weren't nearly as fast. But of course Houston was the biggest city on Earth, so they needed to move faster to keep up with demand.

Jim did not want to just sit there like an idiot for the whole ride, but he also didn't want to discuss the company's situation. His anger and disappointment were simmering just below the surface. He'd almost cried once on the plane as he reread the lawyer's letter. The last thing he wanted to do was lose it in front of Buddha – that would be like crying in front of a big brother.

"Any losses on that contract you just completed?" he ended up asking, a much safer subject. Mercs died; it was a fact of life. They considered it a point of pride that they could buy it any day they worked. The mental tests and conditioning a merc went through first verified they could handle the stress, then got them prepared for the reality. Most got truly excited by the prospect of being in mortal peril. It drew them to the job. And some just liked blowing things up, regardless of the species.

"Naw," Buddha said and shrugged, then gave a little grin. "Just a garrison job. The Zuparti thought someone was going to make a move on a huge stash of radioactives they had. Turns out no one knew about it, and they were just being paranoid. Still, we got paid."

Jim had studied the Zuparti. They looked like big weasels and acted like shell-shocked chickens. They walked around in a perpetual state of freak-out, but they were shrewd traders, and that meant lots of merc contracts. Because they were both wealthy and typically had half a dozen merc companies around them eating, smoking, and generally making themselves at home, no one tended to mess with them. Ironically, that only served to further feed their paranoia, making them certain that someday, it would all come apart at the seams.

"About the pay," Jim said timidly. "You'll still get yours, right?"

"Sure, no problem," Buddha said cordially; "we're paid on contract. So we'll all get our contracted share before the fucking lawyers get the rest." Jim nodded, relieved that none of his men were going to get shafted. Then he felt even worse when he remembered they weren't his men and never would be.

The autonomous cab eventually slowed and pulled off the high-speed throughway and onto local roads. Minutes later it was turning onto the family's private estate road where it came to a sudden and unexpected stop. Parked across the road was a Texas State Patrol car.

"Oh," Jim said as the cab informed him, "Road closed. Change destination?" A pair of police officers froze in mid-bite of doughnuts and eyed the cab curiously.

"Guess this is the end of the road," Buddha said with a shrug.

"You take the cab," Jim said and clambered out. One of the officers was approaching to see what he wanted.

"Are you gonna be okay, Jimmy?"

"Sure," he lied and shook hands with the man. "Thanks for the ride."

"No problem," Buddha said with half a smile. "Don't forget, you're a Cartwright. Greatness is in your blood, young man." Jim sat his bags on the concrete driveway and watched the cab spin about on new orders and head down the lane until his thoughts were interrupted.

"You aren't supposed to be here," the officer said. Jim turned around sullenly and looked at him.

"I'm Jim Cartwright, that's my house."

It took an hour to get past the police. First he had to prove who he was, then he needed to provide copies of the legal documents sent by the lawyer indicating he had access to the house. In the end he was escorted by one of the officers who drove him the three miles up to the main house. The compound was comprised of nine buildings in the middle of several thousand acres of real estate. The largest of the buildings was the primary residence; beyond that, there were garages, warehouses, a small private museum, and quarters for both servants and guests. Growing up, most of the employees jokingly called the estate, "The Ponderosa." Jim didn't get the joke until he was in his teens.

He strolled through the pristine, robot-maintained halls of his family home, past a long line of Cartwright patriarchs, both from the merc era and before it. The family dining room was quiet and deserted. His father's vast library, expanded considerably in Jim's youth, was also deserted. The officer followed, acknowledging the difficulty of the moment for the young Cartwright with his silence.

His wanderings eventually took him up on the expansive third floor, made up primarily of the family's personal quarters. There was a small separate living area here, along with a family room, and even, a long time ago, classrooms where the Cartwright children received private tutoring. The Cartwright family had numbered in the dozens in decades' past, not at all like the three individuals who he'd grown up with, now only two. And one was gone, possibly in hiding.

At the end of the hallway was a familiar room – his own. He pushed the door open and found it exactly as he'd left it four years ago. He ran his hand along the desk with its now out-of-date computer. Posters hung on the walls of bands no longer in vogue and merc companies that now lived only in memory and history books. And finally, there was a shelf full of memorabilia.

Opening the closet, he quickly packed a couple things then swept the memorabilia into an old duffle bag. The police officer watched from the door, but said nothing. The court order said Jim wasn't allowed to remove anything of value; as it happened, none of the junk in his room was valuable.

"Anything else?" the officer asked.

"One more stop, please," Jim said, walking two doors down to his parent's room. The door was open. He looked inside and found it bare. The furniture was there, but no pictures, no valuables, nothing. It used to sport a number of very expensive paintings and other art, now all gone. While he thought about it, he hadn't seen any of the other art he remembered from his youth. If half the stories he'd read in the lawyer's brief were correct, those items had been sold at auction long ago. He lingered for another moment, then turned to savor one last long look at his childhood home before he left it, forever.

* * * * *

Chapter Four

Ashattoo skittered out of the trading office both excited and fearful. Four months after the find on Ch'sis, they were delivering the first tanker load to the great trading center of Sakall. The Cimeron region was located just beyond midway to the other side of the galaxy and the Athal's home world. They'd picked Sakall as the ideal distribution point as it was a proactive feint against their adversaries. Well, there weren't any adversaries yet, but they would come soon enough.

As soon as the robotic tanker arrived in orbit, and the manifest data was transmitted to Sakall customs, the process began. He stopped outside the off-world trading office and used his implant to access the Athal data link. He sent a message confirming the sale, as well as the transfer of nearly twenty billion credits to his people's much-needed bottom line.

"You are to be congratulated." Ashattoo turned fractionally so some of the rearmost of his eyes could see who'd addressed him. What he saw sent chills down his thorax. A senior Acquirer of the Besquith stood there, his big black-in-black eyes regarding Ashattoo; his rows of perfect pointy white teeth gleamed in the artificial light. The solid iridium pendant of his Acquirer rank caught the light as well.

"My thanks, Acquirer," Ashattoo said through his translator. It occurred to him he had better play this carefully. "For what am I being congratulated?"

"Oh, now you need not be coy," the Besquith hissed. They spoke in hisses and grunts which didn't require their mouths to open, making Ashattoo quite happy. Many mercenary species were imposing to view. Others, like the Besquith, were truly horrifying. A predator species with huge mouths full of razor sharp teeth, a smiling Besquith was often the last thing a being would ever see. They were one of the few races in the galaxy with a reputation for both combat and trading – a truly frightening combination.

"We are just here doing some trading, same as everyone else on Sakall," Ashattoo persisted.

"Halfway across the galaxy from your home? Rather…inconvenient." The Besquith looked Ashattoo up and down. It did not feel like the huge predator was taking his measure as an opponent, but rather as a meal. Ashattoo pretended to be intimidated. It wasn't hard. If the Besquith Acquirer had been an Athal, he would have laughed at how scared Ashattoo was at that moment. Of course, had the Acquirer been another of his own species, Ashattoo would not have been in mortal fear at that moment.

"Look, Athal, I'm not in the mood for games."

"I can go then?" Ashattoo asked and half turned to leave.

"No," the Besquith said and grabbed one of Ashattoo's wings. The chiton cracked in the powerful grip and Ashattoo gasped in pain. "Everyone on this wretched station knows you just unloaded almost a million gallons of F11, so don't play dumb with me if you want to live."

"It was a fair transaction," Ashattoo cried piteously as he tried in vain to pull away without leaving a wing behind. The Acquirer pulled him closer instead.

"I never said it wasn't, only that I know about it. And if you had a million gallons, you probably have much more where that came from. You will sell it to us."

"You can negotiate for it like every other–"

"What?" the Acquirer demanded, "Like what? Common lower species such as yours?"

"That is not what I was saying!" Ashattoo pleaded, moving his eyes' perspectives around desperately in hope of seeing a peacekeeper. Unfortunately, the usually bustling station hallway appeared all but deserted. He glimpsed some being start to come around a corner and, witnessing what was happening, immediately reverse its direction and leave. Ashattoo knew it was far too much to hope the stranger would summon help.

"Then what are you saying, you pathetic bug?"

"I'm saying…" the Acquirer squeezed harder, and Ashattoo's wing cracked more, "can we negotiate?"

An hour later, he stumbled into his temporary quarters in Sakall station. More like fell into it. He had two shattered wings and was missing a leg. He was mad, and in immeasurable pain. Worse, his species was now in a worse way then he was physically. The Athal had struggled to make ends meet for all its time since first venturing into space and joining the Galactic Union. A small, young species had to scramble to get ahead, and the best way was prospecting for rare elements. Finding a trove of F11 was a coup beyond measure. Having others find out it was in their possession before they had had a chance to properly secure it was a disaster of equal proportions.

Ashattoo went to his travelling case and removed the medical kit. His severed limb had self-sealed, a benefit of his species' biology. What good was a detachable limb if you then bled to death after giving it up? Nevertheless, the wound still required a sealant to keep out infection. The wings were another matter. He used the medical scanner and quickly concluded one was a lost cause. He concentrated and felt the tendons sever almost painlessly. Just like the limb, it was sloughed off. He would replace both losses at his next molting.

After taking an analgesic, he picked up his slate and began writing a communique to the collective. It was difficult, not just because of the pain from his missing limb and wings, but also because he was describing his own utter failure. After all their hard work and luck, this find would be reduced to nothing more than a few percentage points. Sure, it would be millions of credits, but that was no more than most other ventures managed to garner. It took this fabulous find and turned it into a minor footnote in the collective's P&L table.

He was nearly finished with the dispatch when his room's door control chimed, telling him he had a visitor. His remaining wings buzzed furtively, and he cast around the room with all his eyes for anywhere to hide. The space was small and offered only one way out. With a shaking hand, he waved the door's intercom alive and spoke.

"What do you want?"

"Are you the Athal who sold the F11 today?" asked the anonymous voice. It was pre-translated into Ashattoo's voice, which instantly let him know it wasn't one of the dangerous and arrogant Besquith. That didn't mean this new being wasn't dangerous, only more congenial.

"Who are you?" he asked instead of answering the question.

"I am Grislawn, a trader with the Wathayat." Ashattoo thought for a second, then released the door. It swung open to reveal a tall, stout, and furred Cochkala. Beady black eyes regarded Ashattoo from inside an expressive face covered in striped white and blue fur.

Long whiskers quivered as the being sniffed the air. "Thank you for seeing me." Ashattoo calmed somewhat. The Cochkala were not known for violence.

"Say your piece. What does the Wathayat want with the Athal?"

"We are interested in your F11."

"Of course you are. Unfortunately, it has already been sold on the open market."

"A mistake, if you consider the results." With a graceful sweep of a long arm the Cochkala took in Ashattoo's mauled physique. "Are you well?"

"Well enough," Ashattoo replied with a grunt of displeasure he knew would be translated but didn't care. "Again, what do you want of us? I have no more F11."

"You have no more right now," the Cochkala corrected. "We've analyzed a sample and know it comes from a new source, and an unattributed source at that." Ashattoo didn't think he could have gotten more nervous; he was wrong. "You are acquainted with the Wathayat, or you wouldn't have let me in."

"You are well known traders," Ashattoo admitted. "It is also known you have a reputation for acquiring very hard-to-get resources and holding onto them, making them even more valuable." The Cochkala nodded in the universal sign of assent. "You are also the only trading organization that does not limit its membership to a single species. I believe there are four species in your guild?"

"You are well informed," it said with another nod. "Could I ask you a question?" It touched the iridium shield on its chest, a symbol of his office as a Galactic Union trader. "Under my oath, it shall not leave my confidence."

"Ask, but I may not answer," Ashattoo responded cautiously.

"That is fair," the Cochkala agreed. "You have a firm source of the F11, do you not?"

"We may."

"It is considerable, is it not?" No answer. "After all, you would not have brought such a massive shipment so far across the galaxy if you did not have access to considerably more."

"Maybe this is all we had, and we wanted to sell it quickly for a profit," Ashattoo suggested.

"Unlikely," the Cochkala disagreed. "If you only had that much to sell, you would have sold it in smaller lots around the galaxy, and by doing so, avoided the attentions of species such as the Besquith." Ashattoo silently cursed his decision to come to Sakall.

"If we do have more, that is our own business."

"It will not be for long; we know the Besquith have demanded it, and you are in no position to refuse them."

"If you are here to threaten me, I have been threatened more than enough this day," Ashattoo snapped, now too upset to make much of an act of it. "Besides, you cannot demand of me what I already must surrender to another bully."

"What if my offer is better than their offer?"

"Offer?" Ashattoo snorted, spitting fluid on the floor as he did so. "Demanding we hand over the F11, exploration contract and all, for a five percent commission is not an offer."

"The Besquith were only going to leave you with five percent?" The Cochkala asked, followed by a snorting whistle. Ashattoo didn't know for certain, but he suspected the other being was chuckling at him.

"They are strong; they don't hire mercs to do their fighting. They prefer to do it themselves."

"Yes, they are unusual in the galaxy, both thinkers and fighters. Sadistic and merciless."

"You are not helping your case," Ashattoo said, and the Cochka-la spread its hands in surrender. "What can you offer, a higher percentage? It would have to be well worth our while to risk the Besquith's wrath. Even after giving it to you, there is nothing to stop the Besquith from descending on us and laying to waste the entire Athal home world."

"There is one way to avoid that and give us the F11." Ashattoo found himself moving closer to better hear, despite his doubts. "As you know, there are four species in the Wathayat." It paused for a moment and leaned closer. "How would you like to be the fifth?"

Galrath, senior Acquirer of the Besquith, roared in rage and threw the slate across the bridge of his ship. It bounced and ricocheted around the space, making a number of the bridge crew duck or cover their heads. "The filthy insect!" he bellowed and looked for something else to break.

"Please, Acquirer," the captain of the trader vessel beseeched him, "If you damage my ship..."

"To entropy with your cursed ship," Galrath snarled and rounded on the captain, his mouth open slightly, saliva flying as he spun. The captain remained floating just a few feet away, and to his credit, he didn't budge an inch, even in the face of his superior's rage. It was his ship, after all. The unspoken challenge calmed Galrath enough to allow him to get control of himself. He didn't need an honor duel with this one – not now. Besides, he would have no use for a starship beyond selling it, and selling anything so large on the black market would invite unwanted attention from the authorities and others.

The fact that he'd been robbed by the double-dealing Athal was what mattered most right now. "With the damnable Wathayat involved, it's infinitely more complicated."

The captain observed him for a moment longer then returned to his station when Galrath didn't say anything further, confident that, at least for the time being, the Acquirer wasn't going to tear his bridge apart.

Galrath considered. Was it possible to strike at one member of the Wathayat without drawing the ire of all of them? Probably not.

"What about Project K?" the captain asked.

Galrath turned his unblinking eyes on the captain. At first he was angry with the captain for even mentioning what was supposed to be a top secret project – a project, that, should the other great houses and guilds of the Union discover was underway, would likely mean the end of the Besquith in a most spectacular fashion. Perhaps the captain had a point, though; he obviously had a high enough clearance to know about the project, and that meant he had likely been privy to a full security briefing. All it would take was one glimpse of a few images for any sentient species in the galaxy to recognize the goal of Project K.

He scratched his ear with one of his blunt working claws, not one of the sharp ones used for fighting, and thought. If it were done carefully, and in such a way as to avoid wide visibility, then perhaps it was a good opportunity. He reached for his slate before realizing it wasn't there, then spent an annoyed minute searching the bridge for it. He found the machine wedged into a now non-functional instrument panel. The slate was still functional. The bridge crew pretended not to notice, and he ignored them as he began to create a dispatch to central command. If this worked, and Project K had a successful test, he stood to rise greatly in stature.

From the far side of the bridge, the captain watched the Acquirer with keen interest. His goal achieved, he went about his duties.

* * * * *

Chapter Five

He'd sat and listened as the lawyers and the judge droned on and on. Like all the interested parties, he had a lawyer. His father's will had specifically designated the money and property he would inherit, so the judge could not strip him of it just because his mother had screwed the proverbial pooch.

Through his lawyer, Jim had done everything he could think of to contact his mother. The judge had allowed him some funds from the company account to prosecute this effort. His own funds were nearly gone. They'd hired a skip tracer, done extensive Aethernet searches, and contacted every place she'd charged hotel rooms. All of them turned up absolutely no results. Ultimately, they ended up before the judge without her. For Jim, it was the final straw in his relationship with his mother. He felt like an orphan.

The judge assigned to the case was well-respected, skilled, and seemed genuinely interested in Jim's welfare. The Cartwright estate was worth in excess of a billion credits, especially when you took into account the ships, weapons of war, and contracts it held. He'd begun to become confident the company could be spared...until the lead lawyer for the state finished tallying the damage and announced his findings.

"So, Your Honor..." the slick shyster representing the group of creditors was reading from a slate, his thousand-credit suit as immaculate as his haircut, "the total debt incurred by Mrs. Elizabeth

Cartwright-Kennedy in her business dealings and back taxes comes to 612,544,612.12 credits." A stunned silence came over the courtroom. Jim's lawyer had been in mid-drink and froze, the glass halfway to his lips, jaw hanging open.

"I'm sorry," Jim's attorney gasped. "Did you say six hundred million credits?!"

"Yes," the other man said, glancing back at the table full of lawyers representing the collection of clients who had filed suits against the Cartwright estate. "Total of 612,544,612.12 credits." The judge looked down at her slate and nodded before speaking.

"I've reviewed the stats and find them to be in order." She looked down from the bench at Jim and his counsel. "Do you or your client have any objection to these calculations, Mr. Holloway?" The man grabbed his slate and scanned it furiously. Jim cursed under his breath. Hadn't the man even read the briefing? Jim had absorbed it all through his implants and had cross referenced the dozens of suits and claims through the Aethernet. It looked like every company the Cavaliers did business with wanted a piece of the corpse. And all from a series of attempted money transfers his mother had made. The trades themselves shouldn't have cost the company more than a few million, but she'd been leveraging the company's assets for more than two years. It technically exceeded her authority, using the company's name to obtain loans, but that was all moot now that the deals had imploded. The Cavaliers' credit was destroyed, bills could not be paid, and the entire empire had turned into the storied calliope, sneezing and wheezing, as it collapsed to the ground.

"Do something," he hissed at Mr. Holloway, Esquire.

"A moment, Your Honor?" the attorney asked. The judge nodded her head. "The most I can do is to slow this up on procedure," he told Jim. "By not showing up, your mother has driven a stake through the heart of any defense you might offer."

"So you're just going to let them destroy one of the Four Horsemen?" Jim almost cried. "My father – my family – has fought and died for generations to build this!"

"Take it easy," the judge snapped. Looking at Jim, her expression softened. "Son, I understand how difficult this must be for you."

"Do you?" he asked, with thinly veiled sarcasm.

"Yes, I do. I really do. As a corporate law judge I hear a dozen of these stories a week, and some are even more tragic than yours." Jim looked down and sighed. "What's been done to you is tragically unfair, of that there is no doubt. But under the letter of the law, a legal solution must be met." She turned to Jim's lawyer. "Counsel, do you have anything further to say?"

"Not at this point, your honor."

It was late afternoon when Jim left the Houston Startown Federal Courthouse. The entire estate had been placed into receivership. The only concession the judge was able to grant was releasing the freeze on his personal bank account, and the counsel for the debtors objected to even that.

"It is reasonable to allow this young man to hold on to the few thousand credits he has in his personal savings to pay his living expenses. No egregious harm will come to any of you as a result, agreed?" They hadn't, but the judge did it anyway. So he had enough to rent a room in a seedy flophouse a few blocks from the courthouse.

Jim spent some of the money getting a local node in place so he could do some freelance work on the Aethernet as well as look for full time employment. As the week progressed, the formal will was read into record, but that was just a technicality. Thaddeus Cartwright had left various sums to his trusted lieutenants and friends that was to be paid by Jim when he became an adult, all of whom would never see a dime now. The majority of the estate was given to Jimmy Cartwright. He'd get less than nothing, as he'd inherited the debt left over. Vast as the estate was, it was nothing compared to the legion of debtors clamoring for the rotting corpse of the Cavaliers.

He worked the occasional odd job, helping create Aethernet presences, advertisements, applications, or any other work he could get. He had to hustle to keep from dipping into what little money he had left. That also meant he spent most of his waking hours sitting in a chair, pinned in, just working, working, working. When he ate, it was always takeout food as he didn't have access to a kitchen, and even if he had...he didn't cook. After two weeks of this, his clothes were getting snug.

At least once a week he sat in on court proceedings, usually Monday so he could hear the summaries of the week ahead. It felt like an autopsy as he listened to the results of auctions. Accountants were selling off everything his family had worked for more than a century to amass. Luxury items like cars, planes, boats, and the estate were sold to the wealthy or to corporate investors. The mercs' hardware and rolling stock were purchased by other mercs. He was pleased to see *EMS Bucephalus* – the company's Akaga class space cruiser – go to the Winged Hussars. It was good the ship stayed within the Four Horsemen...now three, Jim thought, with a pang of regret. The final sales price actually made him guffaw, especially since the Hussars were the only bidders. The smaller craft and drop ships went dozens of different ways.

As the assets were listed and disposed of, Jim began to wonder what had happened to the family's personal yacht. *Pale Rider* had been in the family for a century. He'd always thought it was a beautiful ship, unlike the boxy warships and commercial transports. Capable of landing on a planet, rare among true starships, his great grandfather had bought it somewhere on the far side of the galaxy and brought it home to convert to a family ship. He'd ridden on it many times but had not set foot on it in several years. There was no mention of it in the will, and he wondered if his mother had somehow stolen it or sold it on the black market.

After an entire month, it was all over. The fire sale had totaled out at just over four hundred million credits and the balance of goods owned by the Cartwright Cavaliers, and by default Cartwright Transglobal (the official corporate entity), was gone. The remainder would take a little longer to get rid of. Largely personal items of limited value, they would be bought by junk dealers.

"Mr. James Cartwright," the judge finally said more than five weeks after it all began. "I'm completing the disposition of your estate."

"I understand," he replied.

"You realize that you are, by law, responsible for the remainder of this debt, under the Inheritance Reform Act of 2020."

"I do, Your Honor." The judge looked down at her slate.

"The total remaining debt is 188,012,801.15 credits. How do you intend to settle this?" Jim's attorney spoke for him.

"Mr. Cartwright is declaring bankruptcy, Your Honor." She nodded, having expected that.

"You could have done that before any of this happened, you know," she said, shaking her head.

"It wouldn't have been fair," he said. "Besides, doing that would have destroyed the name of the Cavaliers, and we'd have lost our charter."

"That's true," the judge said, "but what good is a charter when you have no capital or equipment with which to operate? Who would give a contract to the shell of a company, even one with your name?"

"No one," he admitted, trying and failing to keep a tear from rolling down his cheek. "But our name is all my mother left me that those assholes couldn't sell." He glared at the table full of lawyers, all of whom had made millions off the dismemberment of his life.

"I respect that decision," she said. "This case is transferred to bankruptcy. I assume you have the necessary documents prepared?"

"Yes, Your Honor," the lawyer said, and held up his slate.

"Very well, let's handle this then."

Unlike the case to settle with the claimants against the company, his personal bankruptcy was cut and dried. He'd declared most of what he owned. A few things had been stashed in storage, and they were only worth a few thousand credits, but he was damned if he was going to allow them to leave the family. The inventory and his personal assets were summed up. In an hour, the same judge decided that, considering the level of debt and remaining assets, James Cartwright could not be left in complete poverty as his wealth could not even settle one of the outstanding debts. With the bang of a gavel, it was all over.

Jim left the courthouse with exactly two things that had once belonged to the Cartwright Cavaliers: the corporate headquarters in Houston Startown – bereft of all furnishings and office equipment, of course, but it still had a three-year non-transferrable lease that had been paid for in advance, and the company name, complete with charter. They'd actually tried to sell the name and charter at one point. All 288 currently-chartered merc companies had unanimously refused to bid, and no one who was not currently chartered was allowed to make an offer. That was a Union Mercenary Guild law. It was the lone high point in the entire proceedings. With nothing but empty offices and the company name, Jim returned to his flop to eat pizza, work, and try to create a new life.

* * * * *

Chapter Six

The knocking was insistent and showed no sign of relenting. He rolled over ponderously, the bed frame groaning in protest and eyed the door only a few feet away. The knocking resumed.

"Go away!" he yelled. The apartment in the outer ring of Startown was cheap and came with many undetailed extra features. For example, prostitutes came by at regular intervals, as did drug dealers, panhandlers, and thieves. Luckily he seldom left the little flat. Everything he needed could be delivered. He spent his days in the Aethernet, and his evenings eating pizza. He'd given up worrying about his weight only a week after the conclusion of his bankruptcy.

"Mr. Cartwright?" a voice called through the door.

"Fuck," Jim groaned. One of the blood suckers who hoped there was still some marrow left in the bone had managed to hunt him down.

"I don't have any money left!" he barked. "All the money I have, I earn myself. Go away."

"Mr. Cartwright, I'm not here for your money. It's about the will." Jim got up and went to the door, unlocked all the bolts, and yanked it open. His face was purple with rage.

"The will has been discharged already – what the hell?!" he said, to where the intruder's face should have been, but wasn't. He looked down to see a man who was as short as Jim was round. He couldn't be three feet tall, dressed in a perfectly-tailored suit and holding an expensive-looking briefcase.

"That was the family will," the man said, looking Jim over with casual interest. "Would you mind putting on some clothes so we can discuss this?" Jim looked down and realized somewhat sheepishly he was only wearing boxer shorts.

"Just a minute," Jim said and closed the door. He found a pair of sweat pants and a tee shirt, pulled them on, then opened the door again. The tiny attorney was still standing there.

"May I come in?" he asked. Jim gestured, and he squeezed past.

The rented room had a tiny built-in table and a pair of chairs that slid in and out from the table. Jim moved empty pizza boxes off the other chair and the table. The visitor put his briefcase on the table and hopped up onto the chair not unlike a child would have.

"What's this about another will?" Jim asked. The man opened his case and drew out some legal papers.

"The will that discharged the Cartwright estate was the one we all watched on TV – a painful drama. I'm sorry about that." Jim nodded. "What we have here is an estate will that predates your father's own estate; it goes back to the founders of the Cartwright's Cavaliers." He read off the papers. "James Eugene Cartwright, Sr., established the independent trust to fund a Cartwright Historical Association. You are James Eugene Cartwright, II, are you not?"

"Only when I have no choice," he mused.

"Interesting," the diminutive lawyer said, then returned to his paperwork. "Anyway, as I mentioned, this trust is outside the family's assets. Instructions were to wait for six weeks after the will was completed before this one was executed." He consulted the paperwork again. "The trust was established in order that historical artifacts, relics, and curios of the Cartwright estate would forever be preserved. He, your great, great, great grandfather, had the intention of giving the material to the Smithsonian, but they were not interested in weapons of war and mercenary history. Their words." Jim shook his head. He'd heard sentiments like that from the government all his life. Despite the fact that taxes on mercs paid 90% of all the taxes on Earth.

"So what is included in the trust?" Jim asked. The lawyer slid a paper across to him and began listing.

"The First Horseman Museum, including all assets and grounds. Operational control of the same. The airfield, landing rights, as well as all hangars and facilities. And of course the operating fund of the museum." Jim glanced at the bottom of the page and whistled.

"You're positive all those creditors can't take this?"

"It never actually belonged to your father or his wife," the lawyer said, then handed out another page. "In the will is the option to leave the museum in trust. An appointed trustee ran it. Your father left the trust alone, which is why it is still here. So, I know it's sudden, Mr. Cartwright, but do you wish to assume control of the trust or leave it for your children?"

"So I can just sign and I get all of this?"

"That is correct, Mr. Cartwright." The little man folded the papers and looked at him. "You have seventy-two hours to make your decision, at which point the trust remains untouched." Jim nodded in understanding. "Are you going to wait, or decide now? It doesn't really make a difference to me either way. I'm paid by the trust."

"I think I'll decide now," Jim said.

T he cab dropped him off in the circular drive just outside the main entrance. The building was old and had been built with the intention of thousands of guests a day. A plaque next to the entrance gave some history.

"Houston's William P. Hobby Airport served as the city's principal airport from the 1950s through 1969. After being revamped, it continued to serve the public until 2049 when the Houston Starport began operation, and it was sold to the Cartwright Historical Preservation Society and converted to the museum you see here today."

"I don't know how I didn't know about this," he said as he looked up at the main entrance. A huge representation of the Cartwright Cavalier astride a sturdy warhorse was top center, with the Winged Hussars, Golden Horde, and Asbaran Solutions flanking it. The words, "First Horseman Historical Museum," was displayed in an arch across the top, and, "Lead the Charge," the house motto, was inscribed below the Four Horsemen. Why had his father never brought him here? As he climbed the final stairs, a Tri-V display came alive, and there was the inspiring profile of James Eugene Cartwright, Sr., standing with a wide stance, and a hand held up. "Welcome to history!" And then Jim remembered.

He'd been no more than five the time he came here. His father had brought his mother and him to the museum. Jim had been too young to understand this was his own family's museum – all the displays, all the history...the staff treating him like a little celebrity, his mother hating every minute she spent in this museum full of the instruments of war. They never went back.

Jim looked at the locked doors. It was Sunday, and the museum was closed. He took out a pinlink and clicked it to his interface. Instantly, complicated locking codes appeared in his mind. Jim keyed them in, and the doors obediently slid open for him. He walked through the front doors, which slid closed and locked behind him.

Inside, he walked past Tri-V displays that sensed his presence and came alive. Each was a perfect representation of a director of the Cavaliers, from James Eugene Cartwright, Sr., on down. He made a mental note to have his father added right away. He moved past a gift shop, the main ticket office, and into what had been the old Hobby Airport's main terminal. It stretched for more than half a mile in both directions – one vast space filled with hundreds of displays. Like the small representations of the founders in the entry, many of these detected the presence of a visitor and came to life. Soldiers marched, tanks rolled, drop ships took off and set down over and over again, all in glorious Tri-V technology.

He walked along, taking in this historical banquet spread out before him. It wasn't all computer-generated either. A surprising amount of the memorabilia consisted of actual artifacts. A Boeing B22G Albatross dropship was suspended from the ceiling, wings gracefully folded into orbital drop mode. The plaque proclaimed it as the first B22G ever to fly. Jim knew the rest. The Albatross was the last Earth-designed merc dropship. After that, they were all manufactured off-world. The Albatross had a sentimental place in their hearts. It had distinctly human qualities that no longer existed in dropships because all those now manufactured on Earth were heavily influenced by alien designs.

Further down was a German *Gepard* reconnaissance tank, and next to that a Caterpillar X1000 command and control tank. Just beyond, after a pair of Tri-V tank prototypes, was the Mitsubishi Heavy Industries' Combat Assault System, Personal MK I, or CAS-Per for short. This was the first iteration of a human combat armor –

it had enabled Earth's mercs to stand toe-to-toe with anyone else in the galaxy. It was squat, ugly, and looked like it could barely move. Looks could be deceiving. Jesus, it still had actual blood on it! There was a Tri-V being projected next to the suit showing none other than its inventor, Dr. P. Mauser.

"Hey!" someone barked, and Jim almost pissed himself. "What are you doing in here?" A man who had to be 100 years old was bearing down on him, a huge wrench held in one hand. He wore faded and stained coveralls that might have once been white but were now closer to yellow. His hair was much whiter and just as completely unkempt. It surrounded his head like a hazy halo. The coveralls proclaimed, "Cartwright Historical Preservation Society."

"Easy, old man," Jim said and backed away.

"We're closed, how the fuck did you get in here?"

"I'm the new director," Jim said as the menacing old man closed the distance.

"Bullshit!" be barked. "Prove it."

"I can't if you cave my head in!" Jim said, fetching up against the heavy steel of a very real tank. The man stopped less than a yard away and paused, but the wrench remained poised to strike. Jim slowly raised a hand again to touch his pinlink. He accessed the museum's Aethernet, entered the master control code he'd gotten when he assumed control, and started the lights in the hallways flashing in order. The man looked up in surprise. "Not good enough?" Jim asked. The man looked at him, his eyes narrowing. Jim sent another command to the museum's computer, and the PA system boomed.

"Ladies and gentlemen, please offer a warm welcome to the new director of the First Horseman Historical Museum, Jim Cartwright!"

"Shit," the old man grumbled and lowered the wrench. "Kinda fat for a merc, aren't you?"

"Kind of old and nasty for a caretaker, aren't you?" Jim offered as rebuttal. The man looked at him and squinted. For a moment Jim wondered if he was about to get knocked senseless with the wrench. Then the man laughed, more like a cackle, and shook his head.

"Yeah, you're a Cartwright all right. Knew the last three, and you have the looks, if not the build." Jim just shrugged helplessly. He looked at Jim with a critical eye. "Suppose you wanna move into the living quarters?"

"You living there now?" Jim asked, not wanting to deprive an old man of his home.

"Me? Shit, kid, I look like a high falutin' rich man to you? I have a space down in the restoration department. Lived there since I retired from the Cavaliers."

"What do you do here…I didn't get your name."

"Hargrave," he said and offered a heavily-callused hand. "Ezekiel Hargrave. I'm the head of mechanical restorations. Glorified grease monkey, but I got me the gift of gears." Jim shook the hand. Hargrave's grip was firm but not too strong, and he smiled slightly for the first time as he looked his new boss in the eye. "Decided not to let the museum remain in trust, eh?"

"You heard what happened to the company, right?"

"Who hasn't? Don't worry about it. Things have been worse."

"Hargrave, the company is wrecked," Jim said incredulously. "My mother cleaned us out."

Hargrave snorted. "You still have the name, right?" Jim nodded. "None of the other companies would bid on it?" Another nod. "We mercs look out for our own. Down, but not out. The first Cartwright started with a hell of a lot less than you have right now. He mortgaged his house and sold his Grammie's wedding ring to get the company started." Said like that, Jim didn't feel as bad as he had when he first pulled up outside.

"Well, Hargrave, how many personnel do we have."

"Six," Hargrave said. Jim's eyes bugged out. "Yeah, don't seem like much, does it? But the museum itself is almost completely automated. One supervisor and a programming troubleshooter run it during the day. We have a janitor who keeps the toilets unclogged and mops up kids' vomit. The rest of us maintain the exhibits and handle restoration of new acquisitions."

"You mind showing me around, Hargrave?"

"Sure, boss." Jim was struck by how quickly he went from being threatened with a wrench to being "boss."

"Just call me Jim, thanks."

"As you wish, Jim."

Hargrave took him through the remainder of the museum proper – displays of field-portable medical technology, chronologies of how bivouacs had evolved over the centuries, as well as personal infantry weapons. Several theaters were set up showing repeating features on the Cavaliers, starting with that first contract and ending with the Zeta VI campaign.

Finally, they reached the end of the main exhibit where there was a small automated snack bar flanked by a door showing 'authorized personnel only' which opened automatically at Hargrave's touch. Inside, a hallway led back into the old airport terminal, which now served as space for offices and other facilities. A hallway branched off with a sign proclaiming it, "Collections and Restoration." Hargrave led Jim into that wing saying, "This is where I do most of my work."

The Collections and Restoration area proved far more extensive than it appeared. It had once been the east wing of the concourse, and now it was a cavernous warehouse with dozens of combat vehicles and transports.

"This is amazing," Jim said as he saw all the vehicles.

"This is nothing." Hargrave laughed. As they passed an area called, "Modern Warfare," and moved into, "Earth's Past," it got even more interesting. Old tanks, Tri-Vs of soldiers in uniforms, cases full of guns, and even more aircraft suspended from the ceiling. A British Sopwith Camel hung next to an American Boeing F39 Orbital Shrike, the last fighter Earth ever produced.

"How long has the family been collecting this?" Jim wondered.

"Back before they were mercs," Hargrave said. "The Cartwright who fought in the American Revolution had a small museum in Virginia. That grew over the centuries until the Cavaliers were formed, at which point the trust was created. All through history, your family has grabbed bits and pieces."

Jim stopped where a massive Tri-V was running a panorama of warships, going from wooden-hulled man-of-wars to WWII battleships, and on to the stealth frigates and submersible carriers of the mid-twenty-first century. Just past that display was an incredibly massive gun turret with three barrels big enough to crawl into. A sign proclaimed them as being, "From the Battleship *USS Missouri*, BB-63. On permanent loan from the defaulted Smithsonian Museum." There were many other guns, too, collected from ships of all kinds.

"Hard to believe the family saved all this history."

"This? This is still nothing," Hargrave chuckled. They'd reached a stretch of windows that had been part of the original concourse when it was built. He pulled Jim to a window and pointed at a series of hangars more than a mile away. "Those hangars are all full of preserved history. Over there we have the old Southwest Airlines maintenance buildings." Jim could just make out the winged heart logo in faded paint. "We have ten of the old KX9 *Phoenix* drop ships. When the Cavaliers switched over to the Overlord, they sold all but ten of the *Phoenix* for scrap or to smaller merc companies. But that was twenty years ago. I don't know that anyone is still using them. We planned to put one on display here, eventually."

Jim scratched his chins. "But why keep ten if only one is going to be displayed?" he asked.

Hargrave shrugged and grinned. "I guess curators are kinda hoarders too. They played around with the idea of a living exhibit someday. Take a flight in a real dropship, or something like that."

"They still air-worthy?"

"Oh, more or less," Hargrave said. Now that he was getting used to Jim, he was becoming steadily more congenial. "They need maintenance, but they all dropped here from orbit before going into storage." Jim nodded and thought he'd want to inspect them soon.

"Are all those hangars full of that kind of stuff, too?" Jim asked and pointed to more of the huge buildings south of the ones Hargrave had indicated, and closer to the control tower. "What about those?"

"In there? Oh, shuttles owned by the trust, planes, and a few thousand other unprocessed articles of merc history."

"Wow," Jim said simply. "Anything really cool?"

"Depends on what you consider cool, son. There's some experimental stuff, some that is just historic, and others that are kind of dumb in my opinion. The trust governor picks up whatever he thinks is interesting."

"And who is that? Must be a pretty interesting person."

"I think he is," Hargrave said, "since that person is me." Jim regarded him with a growing feeling of respect. There was a lot more to this crazy old grease monkey than he'd originally let on.

"What about those living quarters you mentioned?"

"Oh, right," Hargrave said and turned out of the restorations shops and down a hall. Jim had a mental map growing of the airport's previous layout and as they descended some stairs and went down antiquated hallways, he knew they were passing under the main runways. "You can get there from the access road behind the airport too," Hargrave said. "It's all industrial buildings there – robotic factories, warehouses, some abandoned old-tech industry. Don't go for a walk without a gun though. It's also gang territory."

"The Startown security doesn't patrol it?"

"Not really. It's rare that people venture out that way anymore. A few guards have been jumped and messed up, so they just avoid the area. Our perimeter defenses are top notch, however. This place was built back before we were a backup field for the starport, way before the city of Pearland was leveled and turned into the landing and operations center of the starport. We're technically still on the list of emergency alternate landing sites, but we haven't been used for that purpose in twenty years or more. The landing system is fully automated and tied in to the starport's main flight and approach control anyway. You ever want to jet up to orbit, we can get approval for that in a matter of minutes."

"Why would I want to go to space? Just to look around?"

"Well, if you wanted to go to another star system or something, of course."

"Hargrave, booking transition is expensive as shit." The old man nodded as they kept walking.

"Sure, but why pay someone else when you have your own ship?"

"Wait, what?" Jim said, stopping and staring in surprise. "The *Bucephalus* was sold in the bankruptcy! The Hussars took it."

"Sure, but the trust has three more ships, all from the Cavaliers' past history." He ticked off on his fingers. "There's the *Prince Rupert*, the first starship the Cavaliers owned. That's an old *KT*-Class frigate. Retrofitted for human use, it sucked, but it was the first ship the company bought after it began to succeed. The *Traveler*, the ship right before we got the *Bucephalus*. *Enterprise*-class cruiser. Your grandfather had it commissioned from the Martian Shipyards based on our planet's own cruisers. Nice ship. It's the one I served on. The Cavaliers tried to sell her several times, but none of the other companies bit. Your old man considered converting it to a yacht, or a bulk hauler, but the costs were too high, so he transferred it to the trust about a year before he died. And finally there's the *Pale Rider*."

"The family yacht?" Jim said, surprised this time. "Damn, I was wondering what had happened to it during the will's execution. When it didn't turn up in the list of assets I thought maybe my mother had stolen it or sold it off – no idea. Either way, I just kept my mouth shut."

"Well, you aren't far off. Your mother did try to grab it. But as soon as she did, the trust's historic clause went into effect. Every Cartwright controlling director has a line written into their will.

Should certain assets of the family come into peril, they are immediately and irrevocably transferred to the trust in exchange for a compensation of one credit. There's a lot more legal mumbo-jumbo, but all well-documented and iron-clad. Your ancestors spent a lot of credits getting that written up. Supposedly, the other Four Horsemen all did the same thing. Like I said, young man, the Cavaliers are down, but not out." Hargrave gave a wink and resumed walking. Jim followed.

"Do the judges and lawyers know about it?"

"Some of it, but probably not all. Lawyers like money. They try to play hardball with one of us, the other Horsemen will make life difficult for them. All four of us have fallen on hard times at one time or another, and all survived. This is just the first time it's been us. But we backed them up when it happened to them, so now they'll be there for us. Jim, you have to know that, without the mercs, Earth would be too poor to afford a pot to piss in."

"Yeah," Jim said, "we learned that in school."

"So you really think we, the mercs, would let the lawyers kill us that easily?"

"Sure seemed that way during the bankruptcy."

"I can see that," Hargrave said. "But it was just a chance to wet their beaks. Keep score, son. You might well have your chance to turn the tables someday. As for the rest of the mercs – trust me, they have our backs."

They finally came to the end of the seemingly endless corridor. Along the way, they'd passed two robots doing maintenance on lighting and electrical conduits. At the end was a doorway with another of those remote identification devices. Hargrave stopped short and took out a slate. He typed on it and waved it at the door.

"New identification," a computer voice spoke. Hargrave looked at Jim and gestured with his head to the door.

"Oh," Jim said, "Jim Cartwright."

"Identified Jim Cartwright, full access to residential quarters." The door slid open.

"Where are we?" Jim asked as they entered a small antechamber. On one side was an exit to more tunnels, and on the other was a manual doorway where stairs could be seen through a window. They stopped in front of an old-style elevator.

"You'll see," Hargrave said and thumbed the control on the elevator. It opened instantly to reveal a plain elevator car. There were only three buttons: B, 1, and 2. Hargrave pressed 2, the doors closed, and they began to ascend. The back wall of the elevator was glass, and Jim turned to watch concrete slide by for several seconds. Then it gave way to metal walls, and a moment after that, bright afternoon Houston sunlight briefly blinded him. While his eyes adjusted, they continued moving swiftly upwards. He looked further past the windows going by and spotted the museum proper and what had once been the terminal buildings. Then he realized where he was.

"The control tower," he said. Hargrave nodded. A second later the elevator slowed and plunged into confinement again, then stopped with a ding that announced their arrival at the top.

"Welcome home," Hargrave said as the doors opened.

The top of the airport's old control tower sat ten stories above the tarmac. Situated above a hangar, opposite the main terminal, the top was three stories of glass-walled rooms totaling just over 3,500 square feet. It had all been converted into a residence with three bedrooms, three bathrooms, and a small gym with a countercurrent exercise pool and sauna. The kitchen, gym, and dining room were on the main floor, one level below the elevator's exit. The floor where the elevator let out held a small foyer, a massive living room, two bedrooms, laundry, and some storage. The top floor, the biggest, held a bedroom which was more like a studio apartment as it not only had a small kitchen, but a huge bathroom with a Jacuzzi tub and dual shower heads. By the time the tour was over, Jim's mouth hurt from smiling. The top floor – the studio – also had an all all-around balcony accessible on all four sides by sliding glass doors. All the glass was transmorphic so the walls could be made transparent, translucent, or be utilized as displays by accessing the controller through an authorized slate. A similar interface allowed him to control the whole building.

"Roof's a landing pad too," Hargrave added, and showed him how to access it via a ladder that ran all the way from the basement via a dizzying climb of more than 200 feet to the roof. "Your dad looked at extending the elevator up there, but the landing pad is barely big enough for a four-person hopper as it is, so nothing was ever done. Most of the time, if you want to go anywhere, just go down to the ground floor and take off from the tarmac."

"This is incredible," Jim said, standing in the sunken living room and looking out the huge bay window overlooking the rest of the airport, and the distant view of starships in their launch cradles. "And it's all paid for?"

"The facility has a 999-year lease for one credit a year. We have to pay for maintenance and upkeep, including keeping the port operational, but the main trust is self-funded. Even if interest rates went to shit, we'd have enough for about 250 years." Hargrave chuckled and told Jim what the current balance was, leaving the younger man agog, at which point the older man laughed even harder. "Your family has dumped a lot of money into this over the last century, all tax deductible. It's one hell of an insurance policy."

"So now I need to put the Cavaliers back together," Jim said, and suddenly didn't feel quite so elated anymore.

"If you want to," Hargrave said.

"It's what they wanted."

"It is," Hargrave agreed, "but you aren't a robot. What do you want?" Jim thought for a bit then shrugged.

"I guess I'm not sure. This is a lot to take in." Hargrave reached over and gently patted Jim on the shoulder.

"Settle in here, take your time. But think on it. The trust will support you here indefinitely." He reached into his coveralls and pulled out a UAAC – Universal Account Access Card – phonetically referred to as a "Yack." Jim took it, noting that his name was already on it, and when he accessed his accounts through his pinlink, there it was. The old man was heading for the elevator.

"Hargrave?" He glanced back. "You were expecting me all along, weren't you?" The man just shrugged, but the twinkle in his eyes was unmistakable. "You scared the shit out of me with that wrench."

"A scare is good for you, from time to time." He called the elevator and stepped in, speaking as the doors closed. "And who do you think sent that midget lawyer? Good touch, don't you think?"

The elevator door closed, and Jim shook his head in amusement. He went to the third floor suite and looked around. The view was stupendous. Just then the ground shook slightly and in the distance a huge starship began to claw its way toward orbit. He reached into a pocket and pulled something out – a stuffed toy. As fate would have it, this one was his favorite. Jim chuckled as he took it over and sat it on the windowsill facing the starport. The bright blue body and wings with multicolored mane and matching tail belied the ferocity of the little equine. Rainbow Dash didn't take shit from anyone.

"What do you think?" he asked it. Of course, the toy had no reply. He chuckled again, as if it had responded. "Okay, let's see what fate brings. Shall we?" The sunlight caught the toy's ancient plastic eyes just right, and they seemed to sparkle in anticipation.

* * * *

Chapter Seven

The planet Slost was a nowhere assignment. Working for the Wathayat was a way to make your fortune, though it often meant boring, long-term assignments handling trades or moving freight. As a trading concern, it was what they did. And Slost, while an important part of the Wathayat's operation, was not generally considered a desirable working station by anyone who ended up there. Afasha could not have agreed more.

He was known among his fellow elSha who worked on Slost as a repeat (and creative) offender in the department of complaining. "This job never ceases to bore me." Like most of his fellow elSha on Slost, Afasha worked on maintaining the station's many complicated pumping, storage, and purification plants. The planet had a marginally breathable atmosphere, even if it did smell like rotten fruit. Afasha crawled a little further into the valve complex and ran his instrument over them, searching for the link.

"You never cease your complaining," his coworker joked. The rest of the team all chittered their agreement.

"I tell you," Afasha said, "when I get my bonus I'm going to get a lease on a small free trader and..."

"And get rich!" the others all chanted, then chirped their laughter.

A passing Zuul supervisor stopped, turned its pointed ears and growled. "Get to work. This pump has been down for an entire day." The elSha all sounded their assent, and the supervisor moved on.

"Why do they concern themselves so much?" Asasha resumed his complaining once the Zuul was out of range. "This pump is ninety-nine percent efficient already."

"Rumors," one of his work mates said. "Riches to be arriving soon."

"It has to do with the Athal joining the Wathayat," another said.

"Only one element could be so valuable that ninety-nine is not efficient enough," Asasha said. "It must be F11."

"You are an idiot," another one said, setting up a robot to trace a pipe's length. "This tank complex can hold millions of gallons. That much F11 would be enough fortune to buy our entire home world!"

"Have you not considered?" Asasha asked.

"What?" one of the others demanded.

"Why the Athal were suddenly invited to join us in the Wathayat?" The others all fell silent. "All our species brought something to the table."

The team worked for some time until the results exceeded ninety-nine percent, as they'd been ordered, then headed back to the station's control room to get another assignment. As they crossed the huge field of interconnecting transfer pipes toward the central control, the group of elSha noticed a transport slowly descending from the sky. It was a huge one, a bulk freighter of the kind that transported massive machinery or mineral ore between the stars.

"The transport has finally arrived," one of them said and pointed a claw toward it.

"A week late," Asasha agreed. "Typical. Now we'll have to work twice as hard to finish off-loading before the next one arrives in two days!"

The transport didn't finish the landing sequence; instead, it stopped ten miles up and hovered. Asasha stopped and stared. That meant something to him, and it triggered a thought. The distance was significant.

The ship was suddenly covered in flashes, and he wondered if they were experiencing a malfunction. Dozens of little darts raced away from the ship in all directions, lancing toward the ground. He thought for a second they almost looked like missiles, a second before the first of them hit their targets, and thunderous roars shuddered through the thick Slost afternoon air.

The first explosions were still echoing as alarms began to sound. More missiles were launched from the freighter, and they streaked toward the ground.

"We must flee to shelter!" one of his assistants screamed, pulling at Asasha's work harness. A missile landed only a few hundred yards away on a defensive station where anti-aircraft beam weapons sat. It blew up with a brilliant flash of light and a cataclysmic explosion. Asasha was knocked from all four feet by the blast wave, even though a reinforcing beam directed most of the blast around him. The same blast wave turned his workmate into a reddish smear on the concrete.

Asasha looked in horror at what had once been his longtime friend as the missile bombardment continued to systematically destroy the installation's air defense. Asasha lurched away from the carnage of his dead and dying team members as he finally remembered why ten miles was significant. It was the maximum altitude a space ship was allowed to be above a planet when using weapons against the surface. One of the Union's most inviolate rules.

He managed to make it to a relatively safe area, an armored observation post above the starport as the transport finished its bombardment and descended toward a landing pad. He had a perfect spot from which to watch as the planet's defenses finally came to life. Unable to stop the landing and caught completely off guard, all the defenders had left were their ground units; however, almost all of the heavily armored bunkers had survived the attack. Dozens of tanks, armored transports, and troops in combat armor were pouring out toward the starport even as the ship fired its massive jets, extended its landing legs, and thundered ponderously to the ground.

"You will pay for those deaths now," Asasha hissed as the defenders, mercs of several species, began to fire heavy cannon at the grounded ship. It was armored to some extent, but its lift engines were quickly disabled, and several rockets reached out to all but obliterate the visible and vulnerable bridge. Whoever these fools were, they'd done damage to the installation, but they would never be leaving.

No dropships were plummeting from the sky to carry more attackers. Something must have gone wrong. While the transport could surely carry hundreds of combat-armored troopers and many tanks, the ship was now surrounded, and enemy casualties would be high for any attempt to break out. The friendly fire fell off, and Asasha guessed the attackers were being offered quarter. Then something strange happened. The side of the massive transport suddenly bowed outward, as if something powerful had crashed against it. Even inside and more than a mile away, Asasha heard and felt the impact. An internal explosion, perhaps? It was repeated, the side of the transport bulging outward precipitously.

The nearest troopers bounced back a few dozen yards on their jumpjets, as the bulkhead was struck yet again, and this time a massive rent appeared in the incredibly thick armor. A hideous scream came from inside the ship, a scream born of hate, rage, and nightmares.

"No," Asasha said and shook his long snout. His tongue slipped out and tasted the air for threats. An arm crashed through the already torn hull of the transport, shattering the superstructure and sending parts of it careening into the waiting defenders. Hundred-ton pieces of shattered alloy obliterated a dozen troopers, crushing them in their armor. One chunk of hull plating landed on a tank and smashed it like a child's toy. "NO!" Asasha cried as a nightmare come to life tore itself free from the hull of the ship that had brought it down to Slost, unfolding the incredible mass that had been carefully tucked into a space that seemed much too small to hold it.

In only moments it came erect. Asasha turned his head up, up, up to watch the terror stretch and scream a feral battle cry to the forces arrayed against it.

Defenders fired their weapons. Cannon, lasers, and missiles tore at the unspeakable horror, lighting explosions across the armored sides and limbs. It responded instantly, bending slightly and sweeping a 50-yard-long limb with impossible speed to destroy a quarter of the arrayed defenders in one titanic orgy of death and destruction. Huge rents were torn in the concrete and steel of the landing structure. Combat-armored troopers were ripped to pieces. Armored transports were torn apart, spilling their occupants like bearings pouring from a broken machine. Tanks were thrown through the air like they were made of paper.

The defenders began to fall back in panic as they realized the ancient terror they were facing. They fired their weapons and drew death to themselves. Asasha knew he needed to tell the galaxy about what had suddenly appeared in their midst. He grabbed his communicator and looked back to the battle, just as a forty-ton tank, casually flicked from the ground by a backwards glancing blow, hit the observation area like a bomb.

* * * * *

Chapter Eight

ESS *Pale Rider* transitioned back into normal space exactly as planned. Jim had been through transition several times, though it had been quite a few years since the last time. Long enough for him to forget the disorientation at reemergence.

"How are we, Captain?" he asked.

"Position and velocity ideal, sir," the pilot replied in his crisp English accent. Captain Reginald Winslow had come with the ship, it seemed. He'd immigrated to the US from Southern England as a young adult and quickly found his way into space. Jim wasn't sure when he'd risen to the level of ship's captain. "We should make orbit in a quarter of an hour." When Jim had gone to Hargrave and announced he wanted to take a trip, the old grease monkey had changed into an almost clean coverall and taken him to the only new hangar on the field. Inside was the *Pale Rider*. One hundred-twenty feet of sleek alien curves, bought by his ancestors on the cheap and worked over several times. It had once been a *Crucible*-class escort frigate, used to help get dropships through orbital defenses. That was many centuries ago. When that generation's Cartwrights had found it, the *Pale Rider* had been floating around an alien boneyard waiting to have its guts ripped out for salvage.

The ship's captain and sole crewman, Reginald Winslow had been sitting in the hangar office looking over technical journals and sipping Earl Grey tea. Jim had met the captain during earlier flights, but only in passing. He usually limited himself to an occasional meal with passengers and then returned to the flight deck and his adjoining cabin. He'd been glad to see Jim and more than happy to take "the old warhorse," as he called *Pale Rider*, up to space and to go wherever Jim wished.

Hargrave had surprised Jim by announcing he was going along as well.

"Been a while since I got myself into the black," he admitted, bringing a tiny carry-on bag that couldn't hold more than a couple pairs of underwear and a toothbrush. "Besides, someone needs to watch your ass."

"That would take at least five people," Jim admitted. While he'd stopped putting on weight after moving to the museum grounds, he'd also not lost any. The stairs in the apartment had helped, as had the fact that he couldn't order delivery pizza. The drivers refused to brave the industrial roads without armed escort. Hargrave had arranged for an industrial delivery service that handled other companies within the zone to make regular deliveries of precooked and frozen meals. Jim had gotten used to them and found most quite tasty. Somehow the older man knew when the fridge was getting empty and a delivery would arrive.

The week in transition from Earth to Piquaw had been mostly in freefall, as thrust was a waste of fuel during the 170 hours it took to transit between transition points and stargates. Jim hadn't forgotten how wonderful it was to be in null gravity. It didn't matter that he was so fat anymore. The only issue was, if he moved too quickly, he tended to create a wave of fat that created unusual and difficult to control movements, so he'd learned to be careful. After that, he soared through the ship like a manatee, as Hargrave had joked. For some reason, when Hargrave chided him about his weight, it didn't feel like the pointless hurting other kids had done at school. And, he often called Jim "Boss," which made him feel good.

They spent a few days in Piquaw seeing the sights. It was a binary system where the secondary had an eccentric orbit and a rare double-gas-giant sub-system. It seemed to Jim that navigating inside the star system would be incredibly difficult, but Winslow took it in stride.

Primarily a trading point between more populous regions and Earth, there wasn't a lot to see. Jim went over to the sprawling trading station that the *Pale Rider* docked at to refuel, located in a deep space Lagrange point. He floated around the zero-gravity docks, saw a few of the passenger transfer areas, and explored the few human-oriented businesses he found. Afterward, he returned to his ship and watched the myriad alien ships coming and going from the station as well as the thousands of transfer shuttles racing back and forth.

"How much is the refueling?" he asked Captain Winslow as they docked, and fuel was transferred aboard.

"Rates for L-hyd are pretty standard at approximately 100 credits a ton," the captain explained. "A ship like *Pale Rider* takes about eight tons for a standard transition. She's a fine girl, and lean on her consumption, so we usually use less." Jim was now fairly conversant in the funds the trust had available. He could fly around the galaxy for the rest of his life at those rates and never burn through ten percent of it. "But we'll need more F11 after about 12,000 hours in transition." Jim quickly estimated this meant the *Pale Rider* needed F11 every seventy transitions.

"How much?" Jim asked.

"Quantity? Well the F11 isotope is degraded by that point. They reprocess it, but you don't get credit because of handling. They siphon it all out and replace it. The *Pale Rider*'s core needs sixty-two gallons of F11. Going rate is 22,000 credits per gallon."

"Holy shit," Jim hissed. "Why so much?"

"It's bloody rare, son," the captain explained. "Very bloody rare. They've only ever found it near black holes, or in star systems that have had a supernova. A species finds a cache of F11, they've likely hit the big league."

"The Cavaliers have fought in two wars over F11 finds," Hargrave chimed in from across the bridge. He'd been engaged in a game of chess with the ship's computer. "Both were bloody affairs. The stakes are too high. No F11, no interstellar trade." The captain nodded.

"The Union is always concerned they'll run out," Winslow said.

"Has it, in the past?"

"Not that I know of. It's a queer twist of quantum physics – the bigger the ship, the less the F11 tends to be degraded from transition, and the less power to keep it in hyperspace. See that huge bulk-ore transport over there?" he asked and pointed. Jim looked and nodded. It was hard to miss a roughly spherical ship almost a half mile across, even in near space. "That great bloke likely gets more than 20,000 hours before needing a flush. And they come much bigger than that. I remember closer to the core worlds, I once saw a bulk transport more than a mile at the beam! They took a bloody hour to get it lined up with the stargate. But the biggest consumers are warships. Shields and beam weapons use frightening amounts of power, and that means F11 to keep the power plants running. War fleets usually have tankers with L-hyd and F11 with them."

Eventually the fueling was completed, and Captain Winslow wanted to know where to go next.

"If you wanted to see a black hole, there's one only two transitions away. The Union has a research station there, and we can refuel for not too much."

"I actually had another idea," Jim said. The captain waited patiently while Hargrave didn't look up from his game, but did stop making moves. "How about making course for Karma, please."

"Oh-ho!" the captain said with a knowing nod. "Curiosity? Or enterprise?" Hargrave had half-turned and was regarding the exchange.

"We'll figure that out when we get there," Jim said. Hargrave gave a little nod and went back to his game, though a half-smile played across his face.

The *Pale Rider* shot out of orbit and away from the trading center of Piquaw toward the stargate located at a stable Lagrange point a few light minutes out. Because the stargate operated on a schedule, they accelerated out at almost 3Gs for a day. Jim spent that time in a waterbed under mild sedation, to reduce the strain on his rather large body. After that, the captain reduced them to one gravity. Flipping at mid-point they slowed for three more days at one gravity as the ship approached the gate.

The ring of twenty-seven asteroids, each with a hyperspace shunt, was powered by mile after mile of solar arrays. Even from hundreds of thousands of miles away, it looked like a huge snowflake glittering in the sun. It took vast amounts of power to run the shunts, and operating them on fusion generators would take equally vast amounts of F11 and L-hyd, but solar power was all but free. It did, however, act like a flow restrictor, as only so many ships could enter at a time. Punching a hole into hyperspace was tricky.

As they approached to within a few hundred miles, the sheer size of the gate became apparent. Jim whistled from where he paused to take it all in. The gate in Piquaw was easily several times the size of the one at Earth's Lagrange point. There were already seven other ships waiting for their window to transit out of Piquaw. The gate was non-directional in the sense that it only provided a way to enter hyperspace, but didn't send a ship in any particular direction; the ships went wherever they wanted to from that point. Even with his pinplants, Jim found the calculations dizzying.

The captain guided them into formation with the other seven ships. On one of the Tri-V screens, a countdown marked the time until they would make transition. As it began to approach zero, all seven ships moved in perfect synchronization toward the array of asteroids. When they were less than a mile away, the space ahead...changed. Jim always thought it was like looking at a warped mirror in a funhouse. Only, no matter how hard you tried to focus on it, your eyes and brain couldn't put it into perspective. Staring into hyperspace was mind-bending.

"Stand by for transition," the captain said. The ship thrummed with power as the fusion drive spun up to maximum output and the ship's hyperspace nodes were powered up. Without both the fusion drive and the nodes, the ship couldn't remain in hyperspace for more than a few seconds. "Five...four...power steady...ready...one..." and they touched the event horizon.

For a split second Jim felt like he'd been obliterated. Every nerve in his body fired at once, then it was over. It wasn't pain, it wasn't pleasure. It was both being, and not being. Poets described it as a transcendent moment of un-creation creation. *Pale Rider* was in a dimension completely unlike our three-dimensional world. Scientists said the common hyperspace where ships moved was actually a fifth dimension. Looking out the window, it was not at all interesting. In fact, there was nothing at all. Computers recorded something, but not what that something was. Human eyes saw just pure white. Not a bright white, like from a light source, just a white as pure as the depths of space were black. Hyperspace was everything and nothing, all at the same time.

"Transition complete," Captain Winslow informed them. "Power nominal, we are tracking for Hydra Tau II, 169 hours, 57 minutes on the clock." The ship continued to thrum around them, and through the magic of a dimly understood alien science mastered thousands of years ago, the ship was pulled toward its destination.

Jim used the intervening seven days to do his homework. The *Pale Rider* had a very good Aethernet node with massive off-line storage. He'd made sure it had images of all the data types he needed before leaving, and he spent a good deal of the following days in null gravity pinned into the node, studying their destination and everything about it. Of course, there was still time to watch a few videos of his favorite cartoon and play a few games, too.

On the fourth day, Hargrave showed up at ship's dawn in Jim's room. The ship kept the same hours as Houston, out of tradition that ship's time matched its home port. He unhooked his arms from the netting that held him in place and looked at the older man. "Yes?"

"Time you get your ass out and moving, boss."

"I'll get moving; breakfast ready?"

"Something else first," he said, "get dressed." Jim looked at him for a long moment but Hargrave wouldn't leave, so he released the net, floated over to his clothes hamper, and found a clean pair of ship's shorts and a shirt. Like most people in space, he slept in the nude. Once they'd had clothes work themselves into truly amazing binds in null gravity once or twice, most people did. Jim was always self-conscious about how he looked naked, but shipboard it was hard to avoid dealing with it. There was only one null gravity bathroom all the staterooms shared. Even the captain had to come down and use it from his cabin by the bridge.

He used the handholds to work his way inexpertly into the clothing, stealing a glance or two at Hargrave while he did. He was better at it after weeks in space. The other man was feigning interest in several of the stuffed toys Jim had in a clear plastic display hooked to one wall. They floated around serenely in the null gravity of their enclosure. As Jim finished dressing, Hargrave spoke up.

"What's with the little horses?" he asked. "You don't have any kids, right?"

"No," Jim said too quickly. You'd have to have sex to have kids, he thought darkly. "I just like them."

"But they all look the same. Why so many?"

"They're not the same," Jim said. Finished dressing, he floated closer. "That one is Fluttershy, and this one is Applejack. I like her, but my favorite," he said, pointing to one with brightly colored mane and tail, "is Rainbow Dash." He looked over at Hargrave who was staring at him askance. "What?"

"Are you gay, boy?"

"What? No, damn it," he said and moved toward the door. "I'm just really into twentieth-century stuff. Besides, aren't we a little past that anyway, in the twenty-second century?"

"Oh, bugger anyone you want," Hargrave said and followed, pushing gently off the wall. "Shit, this one heavy weapons guy we had onboard about fifty years ago was built like Thor and could kick the shit outta just about anyone in a fair fight. Or an unfair fight for that matter. But he was as gay as a tramp freighter. That guy would suck –"

"Hargrave, seriously."

"What?"

"I'm NOT GAY!" he barked. "I like girls. I just haven't found one who likes me."

"Okay, fine," Hargrave said, and slid past him into the corridor leading forward. "Lots of guys like playing with little stuffed horsies named Flutterspark."

"Fluttershy," Jim mumbled as he floated after the man. He knew that trying to explain their appeal was a waste of time. Jim had a better chance of grasping hyper-spatial physics in the next hour. "Where are we going, anyway?"

"You'll see." The ship wasn't very big, and they traveled down the central shaft until they came to the rotating gravity deck. There were three hatches that moved around and around the corridor in time with the gravity deck's spinning. Situated amidships, the gravity deck reminded him of a hula-hoop spinning around a skinny dancer. When they were under acceleration, the gravity deck was locked in place.

One hatch led to the galley, another to the medical bay, but the third was a mystery he'd never gotten around to resolving. Hargrave headed for the third hatch. They climbed down the tunnel ladder to the mystery gravity deck, and Jim found out it was a gymnasium and therapy room. Jim started to leave.

"Whoa," Hargrave said. "Hear me out." Jim sighed and crossed his arms in an, "I'll listen, but I won't like it," sort of stance. "Your bio-monitor has shown a marked decrease in your basic metabolic health. We've been in space for three weeks, and a lot of that was in null gravity. During the acceleration out of Piquaw, your heart rate showed abnormal stress levels. So..." He spread his hands to take in the exercise equipment, "Unless you like the idea of living in space the rest of your life, or being confined to a hydraulic bed on Earth, you have a choice."

"You're just trying to make me lose weight," Jim said to the floor.

"That would be a good idea too." Jim looked up accusingly. "It would, and you know it. Your body wouldn't deteriorate as quickly if you didn't have an extra one hundred and fifty pounds."

"I've tried," Jim said, "believe me."

"I do," Hargrave said. He touched a slate built onto the wall and the display came alive with Jim's name and a list of exercises. "I used the ship's medical computer and designed the most basic exercise routine I could that would keep your gravity tolerance up, without making it seem like too much work."

"I could just chance it," Jim said defiantly.

"Yes, you could well do that," Hargrave agreed. "And Captain Winslow could then refuse to boost you in the *Pale Rider*."

"He wouldn't do that; he works for me."

"Bet me?" Hargrave asked. "You'd lose. He's responsible for his passengers. What would happen to his career if your fucking heart exploded during a boost into orbit or during an acceleration to a gate like we just did? That was only four gravities for twenty-five minutes four days ago, before the last jump." Jim tried not to let the surprise show on his face. Only four gravities for twenty-five minutes? "Yeah, that was all. Felt like a horse sitting on your chest, didn't it? So, what's it going to be? Go back to your quarters, rehydrated pizza, and horsey videos, or one hour of exercise per day when we're in null gravity?"

Jim stood for a long moment and considered his options, and reviewed how the acceleration had felt. After he'd gone over it, he overrode his own angry reaction to what Hargrave had said and walked over to the slate. "Treadmill," was the first exercise. "Five minute warm up, five percent incline at three mph." Without looking at Hargrave, he walked over to the treadmill, programmed it, and climbed on. When he was two minutes into the routine and already sweating, he glanced over to where Hargrave had been and found he was gone.

After the treadmill, it was fifteen minutes of upper body exercises, fifteen minutes of rowing, fifteen minutes of bicycle, and finally ten minutes in the countercurrent pool. By the end of it, he felt completely exhausted. The climb up the ladder back to null gravity left his arm and leg muscles quivering. It was only when he got to the top that he saw the gravity deck controls had the spin set to only two thirds of a G. He shook his head and headed for the next tunnel over and down to the galley.

Three days later, Jim was in the gym for his workout. It was the last day of the jump. He'd decided working out first thing in the morning was the best option. He felt rested and energized, and it actually seemed to make whatever he ate for breakfast taste better. He was huffing and puffing against the resistance of the rowing machine when Captain Winslow descended into the room wearing a tank top and shorts. He didn't notice Jim until he turned around.

"Oh," he said and nodded, "sorry, sir. I can come back later."

"Not at all," Jim said, huffing between pulls, "please go ahead."

"Very well, if you don't mind." Jim shook his head, and the captain jumped on the treadmill, quickly programmed it, and began to run. Jim wasn't too tired to notice how he'd set the machine. It was going at least six mph, and the incline was set to fifteen percent. Jim shook his head and kept rowing.

During the rest of his workout, he observed the captain on and off. He was in marvelous physical health – his body was whipcord thin and his muscles were clearly visible. He wasn't at all beefy like many mercs; his musculature didn't bulge and his neck wasn't as thick as his head, but he was obviously strong and fit. The man had spent most of his life in space, which meant the gym was a constant aspect of his life. He also ate sparingly, as Jim had seen at dinner, which was typically a meal everyone on board shared in the galley. When he finished his workout, the captain was still running and showed no signs of stopping. Jim was torn between envy of Captain Winslow and his body type, and hating himself. On the morning of their seventh day, when he got up for their transition back to real space, he weighed himself in on the gravity deck. To his surprise, he'd lost two pounds.

"Stand by for transition!" the ship's computer announced. The sensation of returning to normal space was quite different than that of entering hyperspace. There was an instant of falling, even in null gravity, and it was over.

The mechanisms of hyper-spatial interfaces dictated where in the vicinity of a star you would transition to normal space, and that varied greatly depending on the sequence and size of the star. In most habitable systems with O-, F-, or G-type stars, it was often pretty close to the Goldilocks Zone, also known as the life belt. A lot of speculation had resulted from that fact. In the nearly two centuries humans had owned hyperspace-capable starships, not one had ever transitioned into a planet or asteroid. Within the Union, there were, of course, legends.

"Transition complete," the computer announced.

"Conducting sweep," Captain Winslow said. He worked the ship's suite of sensors, and the Tri-V displayed their location. "Confirmed. We're in the Karma system." He manipulated the controls, and the ship spun and rotated on its axis revealing a mostly tan world with a few small lakes and strips of green around them. "Karma-VI in sight." The world of Karma had already been given an alien name when humans first happened upon it, but it didn't take those first human mercs long to give it a more fitting one. Many a merc had come here to find work and never returned. "Orbital transfer station?" the captain asked.

"No," Jim said, "take us down to Bartertown."

"Jim?"

"Yeah, Hargrave?"

"I'm going to advise against that." Jim floated around to look at the older man who'd been working on some sort of machine. He'd disassembled it and the parts all floated within reach. You could tell he was as at home in null gravity as a duck was in water. Jim could see the environment made all kinds of repair work easier, as much as it made them more difficult.

"Why?" Jim asked, more curious than annoyed.

"Son, you don't have to be a genius to see you're here to test the waters. I was kind of thinkin' that was your plan when we left Earth."

"Maybe," Jim said, to which Hargrave snorted. "Okay, that is my intention. What better way to attract attention than to show up unannounced in the *Pale Rider*? It's recognizable, and most of the aliens will realize who we are and come to us."

"That's the problem," Hargrave explained. "You're just a name now, son. The guild knows what happened. They had to because they control all the contracts, and those pending were canceled or bartered off to other companies when your mother burned it down."

"But you said the name was powerful," Jim complained.

"It is, son, it is. But that isn't enough to get the kind of contracts you need to rebuild. You don't have a single merc under your command right now. Not one. And hiring them back on Earth is going to be real touch and go, maybe worse than trying to negotiate a contract. If you come strutting in planet-side with this, flying over the city toward the starport, it's like skywriting an announcement. Half the bidders will come out to see if they can put a cheap and damned dangerous contract over on you. The rest will probably just waste your time." Jim considered for a moment. He'd never been to Karma, and he'd never sat in on a negotiation for a contract before, either.

"Have you ever been in on contract negotiations?" Jim asked.

"Aye, that I have," Hargrave admitted.

"So I best listen to you," Jim decided aloud.

"Quite right, you should," Captain Winslow chimed in. "A big part of being a merc company commander is listening to your subordinates, especially when they know more on a particular subject than you do. I remember when Hargrave came aboard, nigh on seventy years ago. Didn't do a lot of listening himself. Nearly ended up in a regeneration tank a couple times before he got it into his brain that maybe the old timers knew a thing or two." Hargrave was looking out the bridge's panoramic port at Karma. He wasn't avoiding the conversation. A bemused look on his face spoke volumes about his feelings. "How did I get back here?" Or perhaps, "I can't believe I'm back."

"Okay," Jim agreed, "the transfer station it is."

"Very good, sir," Captain Winslow nodded and began programing. "I'll see to refueling and maintenance while you are station-side. Prepare to maneuver," he announced, turning to project toward Hargrave. The older man came out of his reverie and quickly reassembled the machine. Jim did a double-take at the finished product. It was a compact battle rifle. He finished just as the ship came under acceleration.

"Come with me," Hargrave instructed Jim, "we need to talk." Now under light gravity from acceleration, the two moved aft via the now extended climbing rungs.

They ended up in Hargrave's stateroom. On the way, the ship bumped and changed acceleration from time to time. The older man never stumbled once. Each time he just shot out a hand or a foot to counter the random movement and maintain his "sea legs." It was instinctive for him. Jim nearly collided with the wall twice, and once fell flat on his ass. Hargrave helped him up without comment. Jim guessed he'd been just as clumsy once, many decades ago.

In Hargrave's room, the older man asked him to sit down while he opened a cabinet. From it he removed light combat armor in Jim's size, an equipment/tactical belt, and a brand new pistol. Jim was completely surprised.

"You've been planning this," he said, matter-of-factly.

"From the day I moved you into the tower, yes."

"And if we never came here?" Hargrave shrugged.

"Then I wasted a few hundred credits." He pointed at the armor. "Part of the reason I got you on that treadmill too. Another few pizzas and you'd never have fit into that rig." Jim looked embarrassed. "Don't worry about it," he said. "Now I meant to take you to the hold and do some weapons training long before this, but you didn't give me enough warning."

"We had seven days," Jim said as he began to put the armor on.

"Son, that isn't enough time. All it would do is give you a false sense of security."

"Then why give me the gun at all?"

"Because walking around Karma unarmed is asking for it in an epic way, that's why. You know Union laws?"

"Of course," Jim said, struggling with a buckle. Hargrave leaned over to help him. "We all study them in school. There are damned few of them, especially concerning personal behavior."

"Exactly," Hargrave agreed. "In the olden days they called it libertarianism, though this isn't really that. The truth of it is the Union won't protect you personally, only your species or your world. Lots of rules about war, just about none for individual people. You're free to sell a shitty product, and the customers you fucked over are equally free to hunt your ass down and kill you over it. There are more laws governing the adjudication of a killing than there are for the killing itself. You're expected to take care of yourself. The guild handles disputes involving mercs; they have the force of law."

"I've always wondered," Jim said, settling the thick armor trauma plate over his belly. It wasn't going to fit perfectly no matter what he did. "What about weak or helpless people?"

"Others tend to watch out for them," Hargrave said.

"Though surely not always." Hargrave shook his head.

"No, that's true. But no government, no matter how intrusive, ever did that worth a shit anyway. I'd rather count on the good graces of a stranger than the tender mercies of an all-powerful bureaucracy." Hargrave considered for a moment. "If you can't get justice yourself, that's what mercs are for. You can buy it."

"Sounds like anarchy," Jim noted.

"To someone who hasn't watched it work, yes," Hargrave said. "Some have said the Union is carefully controlled anarchy. There is some truth there. Okay, stand up and let's have a look at you." Jim did as he was asked. Hargrave made a few adjustments before pronouncing the results satisfactory. "Not bad," he said, and picked up the pistol Jim had put aside. "Okay, this is a C-Tech model GP-90 modular handgun. It's a moderately useful pistol I'm confident you can handle. It's modular because you can change caliber, magazine configuration, optics, you name it." He pulled the pistol from the holster and showed him. "I've put a holographic sight on it, medium 10mm barrel and caseless magazine. The GP-90 is selective fire, but I've locked out the automatic. Even at 10mm, it'll burn through a magazine on full auto in less than a second. You've shot some?"

"Sure, dad taught me when I was seven. I haven't shot much since."

"No, I suppose you haven't." He showed Jim the basics of operation – how to replace a magazine, where to find the button that made it load itself, how to activate the safety, and how to unload it. "The design is such that it only loads propellant when you pull the trigger, and it'll only fire if you have three positive contact points." He showed Jim three spots on the gun: the trigger, the spot where the web of his thumb would wrap around, and the place where his little finger would rest. "If you aren't in contact with all three of those, the gun won't fire."

"Why's that?"

Hargrave chuckled. "Alien safety."

Jim looked confused.

"There aren't any other species with these," Hargrave said and held out a hand. "Not exactly anyway. So there is no chance some alien bugger can grab this gun and use it against you."

"You think I'm going to need it?"

"I hope not," Hargrave admitted, "but I can't in all good conscience take you to Karma without it." He took the gun he'd finished assembling and pulled a magazine from a pocket, fit it in, and somehow made the gun disappear. An impressive feat for a weapon over two feet long. Jim had the impression *that* gun was far from moderately useful. "Here's the deal," he explained. "You follow my lead. If I say be quiet, do so. If I say run, do so." He patted the side of the light jacket he was wearing, it clunked against the concealed weapon. "And if I pull this out, you do the same."

"What then?" Jim asked, a little nervously.

"Shoot whatever I'm shooting." Jim didn't feel confident.

Hargrave helped him situate the holster on the belt then moved the magazine pouch holding the two spares to a slightly different location. After he had Jim feel where it was and showed him how he could remove a fresh magazine one-handed without even looking, he nodded in satisfaction. Lastly he clicked a little translator onto his belt and had Jim pin it into his implants.

"Wish I had implants sometimes," Hargrave admitted. "On a planet like this, I need to run translations through a full computer slate. Too many languages."

"They have their downside," Jim admitted, and Hargrave nodded. He understood that much.

"Okay," Hargrave said; "that'll have to do."

"Wait," Jim said, "should I get a coat to hide this, like you?"

"No," Hargrave said. There was a long moment of reverse thrust followed by a light clang as the ship docked.

"Why?"

"Because you are less of a threat by carrying openly."

"I don't follow," Jim complained.

"And I can't easily explain it to you. Come on, son, we've docked."

* * * * *

Chapter Nine

The captain was already busy with routine port duties as the pair bid him farewell. Despite the size of the ship, he seemed more than capable of handling the work alone. They floated over to the station and rode a glideway down to the gravity ring. It was basically a big pneumatic pressure tube that blew you along the path. Jim had seen his share of aliens in the past, but absolutely nothing compared to the variety of races here. Karma was the Mercenary Guild headquarters for this entire arm of the galaxy, called the Jesc Arm. Thousands of contracts were negotiated here every annocycle, and hundreds of races came here to do business. Just in the travel tube alone he saw three species he didn't recognize.

Once on the gravity ring, the pair took a small travel car to the area of the station Hargrave wanted to reach. From there they went on foot, and Jim followed Hargrave closely. A few aliens took note of them, though sometimes it was hard to tell where they were looking exactly. He saw a pair that looked like flies as big as dogs, and another that was a huge millipede with a dozen pairs of little pincers. Jim remembered it was known as a Jeha, and despite the resemblance to an insect, it wasn't one. It went by on all those legs at an alarming speed. But it was the spider the size of a small car that almost made him scream.

"Is that a Tortantula?" Jim gasped.

"Yep," Hargrave said and steered them around it. The thing was standing at the entrance to a shop too small for it to get into, apparently dealing with the merchant through the doorway. It had a ring of eyes on its cephalothorax (basically its head) that went all the way around. But unlike Earth spiders, these eyes all had irises and were looking all around. It had ten legs instead of eight, and its big abdomen was separated from the rest of the body by a petiole (similar to a wasp's "waist") that looked too weak to support itself. As it conversed with the merchant, its huge gleaming black pincers clicked together disturbingly.

"Gaspaatuu said the shipment would be ready," Jim heard in his head, the Tortantula's words automatically translated by his pinplants.

"I must beg your understanding," the shop keeper hissed and snapped; "the shipment is delayed–" They had already moved on before Jim could find out what the shipment in question was. Next, he heard a pair of badger-like Cochkala talking about trying to hire another squad of merc marines before they left. A moment later their long flowing tails whipped past, and that conversation was replaced by a big canid species mumbling to itself about the cost of Coppsusa on the station. Jim looked away. Its huge jaw full of teeth reminded him of a particularly frightening nightmare he had as a child about Little Red Riding Hood. He continued on in this way, hearing snippets of one conversation after another, until he almost lost track of Hargrave at one of the many intersections.

"Jim," Hargrave said, grabbing him by the arm. "Change the parameters on your translator to three feet before you run into something that takes your listening in on their conversation the wrong way."

"They can't know I'm listening," Jim complained.

"You want to bet your life on that? Besides, I need you focused and alert."

They walked for some time toward a destination Hargrave clearly knew well. They'd been on the station for almost an hour before they finally encountered other humans, a group of three in the typical human mottled green BDU, battle dress uniforms. They all had the big, muscled build typical of mercs. On the sleeve of their uniforms was a logo showing an oversized yellow bumblebee wearing a top hat riding a dropship. Bert's Bees was a well-known and successful merc company that specialized in shipboard marine jobs. He wondered if they were working for those Cochkala. They all nodded to Hargrave who returned the nod, while coolly and curiously regarding Jim. It was then that he noticed he wasn't the only being who was visibly armed, though almost all weren't.

"So how many of these beings are carrying guns?" Jim asked as they waited for a transport to cross the tunnel. Hargrave cocked his head and seemed to be considering his answer.

"All of them, probably." The transport passed, and Jim had to hurry to match the aging merc's long strides. He still didn't get the open- versus concealed-carry thing.

They turned a corner and Jim expected another long street teeming with aliens, but instead they entered an establishment. At first he thought it was a bar, but as he looked around he could see their specialty wasn't intoxicants. The room was lined with hundreds of flat displays, all showing scrolling data. Jim could recognize a dozen languages on sight, and sparingly read three. He didn't have to stretch his abilities because one of the screens was displaying English, the official language for Earth. He quickly read some of the data and realized it was displaying merc contracts.

"This is a merc pit," Jim said in amazement.

"Your old man never brought you to one of these?"

"He wanted to, but mom wouldn't have it."

"I like that woman less all the time," Hargrave growled.

"Whom do we have here?" Jim's translator spoke as a being approached. It was as tall as a human, but had a long body and rather short limbs. It looked for all the world like a short-nosed, white rat wearing huge sunglasses. Its nose was wide and flared as it approached. "I do not recognize these two humans in my pit." Jim had been so surprised at the huge dark sunglasses in the relatively dark space that he took a second to realize it was a Veetanho talking to them.

"We're looking for contracts," Hargrave said; "we're curious to know what's available."

"We have select clients here," the Veetanho said.

"We know, Peepo," Hargrave said. The alien cocked its head and leaned a little closer to regard him.

"You know me, human, am I mistaken and should know you?" Hargrave reached into his pocket and took out a coin, handing it to Peepo who reached out, took it, and held it close to one eye. It looked at the coin skeptically, then looked closer before slowly looking back up at Hargrave. "You are not jesting?"

"Does it look like I jest?" he asked.

"No, you do not." It handed the coin back. "I have not seen Thaddeus in here for several revolutions of our star."

"And you will not again. He passed away a while back." The alien looked down.

"Then I shall offer a toast…"

"No," Hargrave said. "I'm sure you have heard about our…recent setbacks." The alien gave a decidedly human nod of its head. Since it had little neck, it was almost a bow. "We wish to keep our company's presence here known to only a few."

"Are you negotiating?"

"Not yet. By the way, Hargrave's the name." It nodded again, then seemed to notice Jim for the first time. It looked from Jim to Hargrave.

"This here is Thaddeus's son, Jim," Hargrave said.

"I see," it said, and turned to Jim, put a hand on its chest, then reached out and put one on Jim's chest. "Our fates are shared," it said, "I mourn for your loss."

Not knowing what to say, Jim said, "Thank you, Peepo." It seemed to be enough.

"Peepo's Pit will always welcome you," it said to both of them, then gestured toward the bar. "Partake, and see what is available. If you honor us with your blood, we honor you with our treasure."

"We thank you for your treasure, and offer our honor openly and with conviction," Hargrave said. He touched his chest, then the alien's. Formalities completed, he walked in toward the bar that circled the center of the room.

"Why didn't it recognize you?"

"She," Hargrave said, "I don't think the male Veetanho are sentient. She didn't recognize me because I've changed since the last time I was in here." Jim regarded the older man with a critical eye. Hargrave ran deep, there was no doubt about that. He was only beginning to realize just how deep.

"She recognized the challenge coin, though."

"Son, there isn't a merc pit on Karma that wouldn't recognize a Cartwright's Cavaliers challenge coin." Jim just nodded. "I was never a contract negotiating type." They took a table near the bar and watched both the board and the visitors. As with anywhere else on Karma, they were all there for merc business of one kind or another. And in Peepo's, most were either mercs or working directly for them. There were hundreds of races who hired mercs, but only a handful of races who did that work. Of course there were other humans there, just not very many. Peepo's appeared to be an eclectic group. There were quite a few Jivool on the far side of the pit. They were huge furry mountains, and hard to miss. No Tortantula, but that didn't surprise Jim. Though excellent mercs, they liked fighting and killing far too much for anything other than contracts guaranteeing maximum carnage. There were also two groups of Zuul. Then he spotted one of those huge wolves he'd seen earlier. "What species is that?" he asked Hargrave.

"That's a Besquith," Hargrave said. "They're mercs, but also traders. Hard to figure out. Scheming and very unpredictable. I didn't know Peepo did business with them." The Besquith was in a heated discussion with a pair of Veetanho who were differently colored than their patron, Peepo. Judging from the rifles slung over their shoulders, unlike many of their species, these Veetanho actively worked as mercs. Most of their kind preferred to administer the lucrative merc contract bidding. Centuries of shrewd negotiations and careful deals had given them almost complete control of the guild. Even though not as imposing as many other species on the battlefield, they were incredibly adept field commanders and often found their way into command of other species' merc companies. To underestimate a

Veetanho commander, be it an entire company or even a squad, was to ask for a stinging defeat.

"How come I've never heard of the Besquith?"

"They don't do much business in our arm of the galaxy. They're not part of a trading consortium or anything like that. Not many species can play ball on the scale they do by themselves." Hargrave absently tapped the computer slate on the table, and the system automatically produced a glass and filled it with an amber fluid. "They're a type of buyer in the Union who can freelance around, I think they're called acquisitioners, or something like that. They have a special title and you can't shoot them on general principles without asking for a sanction. As I recall, the Besquith do that a lot. But they run strong-arm operations, too."

"Like the mob on Earth used to?" Jim asked. He'd been tapping away on the slate trying to find something to drink. There was no age limit in the Union, of course. If you could reach the bar, you could drink, snort, smoke, or inject anything you wanted. However, he wasn't really into that sort of stuff. There, at the bottom of the list, he found Coca-Cola from Earth! At one hundred and fifty credits a bottle, he almost blanched at the price but ordered it anyway. The table did not immediately respond.

"Yeah, like the mob. Only in the Union, the mob would look like pussies. A protection scheme here is perfectly legal."

"How can businesses survive getting shaken down like that?"

"Always a bigger fish in the pond," Hargrave said, the lines on his face shifting into a wicked grin. "Years ago when I was still active, we took down one on a small planet that was getting on the nasty side. They started honest enough, merc unit doing garrison. Then they upped the ante and started running what amounted to an extortion racket – looting and breaking shit unless they got "premiums" from some businesses. The company was big enough that none of the alien mercs wanted to deal with them."

"Bigger than the Cavaliers?" Jim asked. He eyed his order status on the slate. "Pending."

"Oh yeah, lots. Some of those alien merc companies are bigger than you can imagine."

"So how did we stop it?"

"Well, Thaddeus up and dropped a squad into that other merc company's headquarters and killed them all, and left nice and quiet-like. Never any clue who did it. Well, the assholes got all pissed and started threatening the locals. Set up a new, much more secure command base, and Thaddeus did it again. Only this time, he took the bodies. All they found were blood stains." Hargrave had a look on his face that made Jim shiver, even in the warm pit.

"What happened?" Jim asked in a hushed voice.

"What do you think? They packed up and left the next day. We cashed the check, and the locals hired more honest mercs next time."

"Wow," Jim said, shaking his head. He knew his dad had a reputation for taking contracts that were considered both impossible and lucrative, but he'd never heard a story like that. He guessed it wasn't the kind of dinner-table conversation you had with your twelve-year-old son on the rare occasion you had the chance to eat with him. Jim felt a bump on his leg and looked over to see a little tracked robot holding up a tray. On it was an old-fashioned glass Coca-Cola bottle, a light sheen of frost on the outside just beginning to melt in the room's warmth.

"Your beverage," the robot said. Jim took it and the robot deftly produced an arm with a bottle opener and flipped off the metal cap.

It hissed and a few bubbles came up. He caught the cap and set it down next to the bottle as the robot rolled away. Jim took a sip and his eyes bugged out. It was ice-cold, sweet to the point of eye-crossing, a little sharp to the pallet with carbonation, and the most incredible thing he'd ever put to his lips. It was nothing at all like the Coca-Cola he'd been drinking most of his life. He put down the bottle and picked up the cap again to examine it more closely. *Bottled under the authority of the Coca-Cola Company, Atlanta GA, 30327 – ©2010.*

"Holy crap," he said aloud.

"What?" Hargrave asked and looked over at him. "Jumpin' Tortantulas kid, you bought one of those?"

"Yeah," Jim said and took another sip. "This is real fucking sugar!"

"Bet your ass it is, at that price." Hargrave considered him for a moment. "You know your dad was one of the most badass, cold-blooded fuckin' mercs to ever draw a contract. He'd stand naked in front of a group of hopping mad Besquith armed with laser rifles and piss in their fur. And still, I never once saw him take more than a sip of wine or beer for a toast."

"Really?" Jim said, savoring the beverage.

"Yep. You know what he drank when he came here?" Jim shrugged. "You're drinking it. That's why Peepo and a few other pits here stock the stuff. I bet that bottle's been here for years. They haven't made it with the real thing since sugary drinks were made illegal on Earth." As Jim finished the bottle he made a note in his implants to investigate finding a stock. Wouldn't be easy to find almost 100-year-old soda pop. When he finished the soda, the table took the empty bottle away like any other. He held on to the cap.

"Hargrave?" asked a human voice. They both turned to see an older merc in civilian attire striding over. "That you, you old fucking shovelhead?"

"None other," Hargrave said and stood. The two embraced warmly, pounded each other on the back and laughed. "How the fuck are you, Treadwell?"

"Older and smarter. You?"

"Older, for sure. The jury's still out on the smarter, though."

"I ran into a guy from Bert's Bees a few hours ago who said he'd seen you in the district with some kid." Jim stood at Hargrave's beckoning.

"Treadwell, I want you to meet Jim Cartwright, Thaddeus's son." Treadwell looked taken aback for about half a second as he looked Jim up and down.

"Call me Jim," he said and held out a hand.

"Well, no shit," Treadwell said and took the hand. Jim gave it all he could and managed to come away without any broken fingers. "I knew Thaddeus had a boy, but I heard he was a weakling." Jim could tell the man had seen nothing to dissuade that rumor. He felt his cheeks getting hot.

"Jim here needs some work, but I can assure you he's Cartwright through and through. Jim, this is Eugene Treadwell, former First Sergeant of the Golden Horde."

"Pleased to meet you, sir." Treadwell just nodded and turned back to Hargrave.

"So what's an old burned-out grease monkey like you doing in a pit?"

"Just sightseeing," Hargrave said without missing a beat.

"Bullshit," Treadwell roared. Hargrave gestured him to a chair at their table and they all sat back down. He ordered drinks for himself and their guest, Jim bit his lip and thumbed for another Coca-Cola. The table filled the older men's drinks. They clinked glasses and talked about old times for a bit. Eventually, Treadwell circled back to where he started. "So, I'll ask you again, Hargrave. What the fuck you doing in a pit on Karma?" Hargrave looked at him for a second, then drew out a coin and put it on the table where Treadwell could clearly see.

"That answer your question?" The logo of the Cavaliers was clear, even though it was stamped on an old tarnished piece of armor.

"Well, no shit," Treadwell said again. "The Cavaliers are gutted, everyone knows that." He glanced at Jim as he spoke. "The government of Earth, lawyers, and every loan shark in the solar system feasted on the corpse like a Tortantula on a fat pig. All the juice was sucked out. What do you still got? That yacht up in orbit?"

"We're down, but not out," Jim said. Treadwell turned and looked at him again, then roared laughter.

"You gonna run the outfit, boy? Aside from an extra couple hundred pounds of lard, what do you have over your dad?"

"Nothing," Jim admitted, "but leave my dad out of it."

"Thaddeus would have been better off to leave you with that bitch he married," Treadwell spat. "The better part of you dripped down her ass and left a stain on the mattress." Jim's face wasn't hot anymore, his blood was. He clenched his jaw and snarled.

"Leave my fucking family out of this, you old asshole."

"Or what, boy, you gonna sit on me? Your dad—"

Jim's chair skidded across the floor as he shot to his feet in a white-hot rage, hands at his side bunched into fists. Treadwell stood up slowly and deliberately. The pit had gone completely silent.

"Jim," Hargrave said coolly.

"Shut up," Jim barked in the suddenly quiet bar. "This bastard doesn't close his mouth, he's going to be choking on his own teeth!"

"Jim, you need to—"

"I said shut the fuck up, Hargrave!" Treadwell regarded him, several inches shorter but puffed up like an adder. His eyes flicked down to Jim's waist and back up in a quick look. Jim figured he was looking at his belly and his vision began to turn red. He was unaware that people were moving in the bar, slowly moving out from a cone behind Jim and Treadwell both.

Jim changed the set of his shoulders slightly and the other man's demeanor changed. It was almost imperceptible, but it changed. Jim's right hand brushed the holster of the GP-90, and he was instantly aware that the other man hadn't been looking at his belly, he'd been looking at that holstered gun. The entire tone of the confrontation was changed. He was an adult, an armed adult, off planet, facing another adult in a merc pit. He was less than a second from dying.

"I told you he was Thaddeus's son," Hargrave said calmly. He hadn't gotten up like the other two men, but Jim noticed his hand was resting on the closure of his coat, almost too casually. Treadwell looked from Jim to Hargrave, and his eyes narrowed. Oh fuck, Jim thought, and wondered if he could pull the gun out without shooting his own ass off.

"Your beverage," said a little mechanical voice. Jim looked down and saw his ice cold Coca-Cola being held up on a tray by the robot. Dumbfounded, he took it, and the serving robot popped the top obediently. Treadwell looked gob-smacked. Hargrave gave Jim a little wink and lifted his drink to offer a toast.

"To Thaddeus Cartwright, and the Cavaliers." Treadwell shook his head, not in amazement but seemingly to clear the cobwebs, then picked up his own glass, slowly, never taking his eyes off Jim's.

"To the Cavaliers," he offered and raised his own glass.

"To the Cavaliers," Jim said, a little shaky. The three men clinked glasses, and the room went back to its previous noise level, albeit slowly at first. Jim savored the sweet burnt caramel flavor of the cola and hoped it was sweat he felt dripping down his pant leg.

"Your father drank that crap," Treadwell said, wiping foam off his upper lip with his shirtsleeve. Jim nodded. "Took balls to stand up like that. I could have shot you dead."

"Tch. Y-you could have tried," Jim replied, stammering a little. The older merc's eyes narrowed, and he nodded, then sat down. Jim retrieved his chair and sat as well.

"You're a Cartwright, all right. Not necessarily all that smart, but brave as hell." He and Hargrave laughed. Jim tried but knew it didn't sound very heartfelt. His chest hurt, and his sweat was cold on his back, the aftereffects of the adrenaline surge. Treadwell picked up the coin from the table and examined it for a moment, rolling it expertly on his knuckles as he thought. "I have a contract I've been trying to broker," he said. "It's only garrison duty, but the pay is pretty good." He looked from Jim to Hargrave. "Figure you can scrape together an entire company?"

"Sure," Jim said. Hargrave nodded as well.

"Okay," Treadwell said and drained the glass. "I'll make some calls." An hour later, Cartwright's Cavaliers, under Jim's leadership, had their first contract.

* * * * *

Chapter Ten

Once they got back to Earth, they started the nearly impossible task of assembling a working merc company in only thirty days with limited funds. Jim tried to keep to the gym schedule from the ship. Hargrave had hoped he would, and there was a treadmill, rowing machine, and weight simulator machine already installed in one of the unused bedrooms in his tower apartment. The second day after returning, he got another surprise. Captain Winslow showed up at his door at 8:00 a.m.

"Sir," he said in his upright, proper British manner.

"Captain, what can I do for you?"

"I understand you have a gym in your flat?" Jim nodded. "The treadmill in my flat at the hangar is broken. Could I join you in your morning workout?" Jim had planned to skip it that morning. He realized he was already becoming too happy to find an excuse not to work out. He looked down and nodded.

"Sure," he said, and headed for his private suite. "Let me get some shorts." After that, the captain was his regular morning guest. By the end of the third week, Jim had set a personal record. He'd lost over five pounds, though he couldn't tell to look in the mirror. He still thought he looked like an overfed manatee, but the scale was ruthlessly accurate, so he called it a victory.

His exercise regime was one thing. In addition, Hargrave had him studying daily. The course varied from basic aeronautics to how a ground transport worked, from merc law to the formation and regulation of the Galactic Union, from small arms to ship-to-ship particle accelerator cannon. A lot he already knew from school and his personal studies, though even more he didn't. Hargrave's files and saved searches on the Galnet were incredibly well-documented.

"I'm never going to absorb all this in just a few weeks," Jim had complained.

"With those pinplants?"

"They're not like something from Hollywood." Hargrave had just stared at him. "I can't *learn* anything with the pinplants, just store information, retrieve it, and access the Aethernet easier than you."

"Store it, and read through it later," Hargrave said, so he did. Jim began his personal transformation to becoming a merc. He had some weapons lessons, got fitted for uniforms, had his nano-therapy scheduled, and finally visited the storage hangars where teams of techs were going over equipment. Hargrave hadn't been kidding about collecting all kinds of equipment. What he hadn't said was why.

"This isn't random," Jim said, "or for historic purposes." On the floor were 100 Binnig Mk 7 CASPers in various states of disassembly. In the next hangar, four of the *Phoenix* dropships were being checked out, along with four M-336 Powell APCs. "These were retained as contingencies against just this sort of turn of events." Hargrave shrugged, but a hint of a smile was on his face. "When did you start this collection?"

"We've always maintained this level of backfill," Hargrave said. "Your dad called it the "Rainy Day Fund. There were minor setbacks in the past. No one ever thought the Cavaliers would be so wrecked they'd need it. Turns out we were wrong." Jim finished his review of the equipment and shook his head.

"It's not much."

"A lot more than you could afford to buy," Hargrave said. "It may not be state-of-the-art, but it's paid for." Jim looked dubious. "Think of it this way: it's a lot more than Jim Cartwright, Sr., started out with." It was hard to argue with that statement. The Four Horsemen generally completed their contracts without the benefit of much advanced tech or the use of CASPers. The contract they'd drawn in this case was garrison duty. It was unlikely they'd even fire a shot.

The next morning, three weeks into preparation, he exited the door of his building and found his small car from the trust motor pool missing. It took him a few seconds to recall it had been brought in for routine maintenance. He could go back into the building and down to the basement tunnels, but that was a lot of stairs. He needed to get to the main building for the first senior command staff meeting. He just couldn't be late for this and walking across the tarmac was against regulations.

"It's only a half a mile to the captain's hangar," he said aloud. He could see the working hangar open. The *Pale Rider* was sitting outside, gleaming in the Houston morning sun. The captain had moved it outside while he worked on another project. Despite the heat, the self-cooling clothing he wore would keep him comfortable in temps well past 110 degrees Fahrenheit. He knew the captain would have a car. He went around the back of the old control tower building, through the gate, and started walking toward the captain's hangar.

He had his pinlink in and was reviewing some documents as he walked. Hargrave had hired a whole score of office and logistics staff, temporarily, to get the Cavaliers back up and running. They'd put the word out, and much to his surprise, had hundreds of people vying for the forty-four open combat positions. At this point, he'd only gotten a glimpse of a couple of them since so much was going on. He did know that starting tomorrow he was to begin undergoing his leadership orientation. He was both looking forward to it and dreading it. He just knew the mercs would take one look at him and laugh. So he had personnel files running through his implants, memorizing names and duty assignments and was completely unaware of where he was.

"Hey fat boy, where you going?" Jim was jerked out of his reverie by the strange voice. He almost tripped into a big pothole in the old maintenance road. There were three men, all in their twenties, all wearing dark clothes, all looking like serious predators.

"Oh fuck," he hissed under his breath. He'd walked out the back gate and hadn't even realized he was now off the airport grounds. "I'm just going to a meeting," he said stupidly. One of the guys laughed and walked out of the shadows. He held a very long knife in one hand and had morphagenic tattoos all down his arms. Jim couldn't tell what they were, and he was too scared to care.

"Oh, you got a meeting," the man laughed and came closer. Jim backed in the direction he'd been heading, glancing over his shoulder. It was at least another 500 feet to the security gate by the captain's hangar. When he looked back the other two were moving, in opposite directions. Pincer, his mind told him, they're trying to get behind you.

"I have some money," he told them, "a few hundred credits." The lead one stopped, surprised by that.

"Yeah?" he asked.

"Sure," Jim stammered, and reached into his pocket. The man licked his lips and stepped toward him as Jim drew out the C-Tech

GP-90. The man stopped dead in his tracks. Jim didn't raise or point it. He did just what Hargrave had instructed, he kept it flush against his side, trigger finger extended along the trigger guard. He was sweating, despite the cooling clothes, and visibly shaking, but also strangely calm in his mind.

"You put that gun down before you get hurt, fat boy."

"J-just w-walk away," Jim said, then again, calmer this time. "Just walk away."

"Fuck that," one of the others said, beginning to move again. "I bet that's one of those plastic guns punks is usin' to scare off people."

"You'd be wrong," Jim said. He flicked his thumb and released the safety.

"Your fat ass is worth a lot more than a few credits to the organ exchange," the leader said. "Get him!" He pointed and Jim sensed the other two begin to move.

Over a month ago he'd been handed the GP-90 by Hargrave. He had carried the gun without knowing a thing about it, and almost got in a duel with an old, deadly, and very experienced ex-merc. He had barely been able to load the thing without dropping it. But that was weeks ago. Jim raised the gun smoothly, mentally triggering his pin-link with the gun, allowing its holographic multi-spectrum sight to feed the data directly into his brain. The gun locked squarely on the target's center of mass and Jim stroked the trigger. It was set for burst fire. All three rounds punched through the man's body, from just below his breast bone, center of chest, and neck. The hyper-velocity 7mm light armor-piercing round penetrated clean through the man with three cracking sounds, blowing holes through his back five times the size of the entrance wounds. He was dead before the sound of the first shot.

Immediately after returning to *Pale Rider* from Karma, Hargrave had taken Jim to an empty cargo hold and started instructing him in the use of the weapon. In the four weeks since receiving it, Jim had fired the little gun a thousand times. He felt very confident with it. Shooting the man was like shooting a paper target.

The two others staggered in their surprise. Jim did as Hargrave had taught him, cutting sideways and letting his pinplants draw the target. With the live feed he didn't have to see what he was shooting at, the sight from the gun was like an extra eye. It didn't hurt that he'd played a thousand video games just like this. But a bit of his brain was screaming at him, there were no extra lives or respawn here. The second man came on target in his brain. Jim fired another burst. This one wasn't as accurate. Only one round hit, on that man's shoulder. It was enough to stagger him.

Jim turned his head toward the last attacker. The man was close. Damned close. Lacking the time to turn properly, he just cocked his elbow and moved the gun cross body. The man screamed something and lunged. Jim stroked the trigger once, twice, again. The man took most of the rounds in the gut and pelvis, and was nearly cut in two. He crumpled to the ground at Jim's feet, screaming in agony. Jim looked down at him in shock. The games weren't like this. A single booming shot rang out, and Jim staggered forward, an intense pain in the small of his back.

He tried to turn, got tangled in his own feet, and went down. He'd slipped and gotten wrapped up in the dying man's spilled intestines. Jim tried not to puke his breakfast as he struggled to hold on to the gun while rolling over in the piteously screaming man's guts. His back didn't hurt badly, and that scared him.

"Fucker!" the last bandit screamed. He was working to reload a single shot pistol – the kind of POS you could buy from a 3D print shop anywhere in Startown. Jim tried to finish rolling over, but his own bulk and the gore he was lying in were working against him. The gun the punk had was indeed crap, but he had clearly practiced with it. He was going to beat Jim to the shot. Jim realized he was going to die.

"You killed Spade and Rollo," the man said. He finished reloading, and aimed at Jim's head. "Now you gonna–" He never finished what he was going to say because his face exploded in a fountain of gore, and he fell like a sack of meat. Jim shook his head as blood and brain rained down on him, his own gun still not up all the way. Somewhere in the back of his perceptions, he recalled hearing another gunshot.

"You okay kid?" Jim looked past the newly dead man to see a huge guy striding toward him, a massive ultra-short carbine held expertly in one hand like it was a toy as he surveyed the alley for more threats. Jim started to raise his gun. "Hey," the man said and carefully pointed his weapon toward the ground and raised the other hand, palm out. "Don't go all PTSD on me, kid, I'm a good guy."

"They were going to sell my organs," Jim gasped, starting to feel faint. The new arrival might have been wearing Cavaliers sweats, or not. He was struggling to focus.

"Yep," the man said. After he finished surveying the area and making sure the guy with his guts all over the place was too busy trying to put them back in to be any threat, he looked down at Jim. He was not only imposing but older than Jim had realized at first.

His face, neck, and what he could see of his chest showed lots of old scarring. His brow furrowed as he looked at Jim. "You sure you're okay?"

"I think they shot me," Jim said. The last thing he remembered was falling back and his head going splat into a puddle of blood and guts.

"Come on, kid," he heard, and someone was slapping him. "Come on, wake up." Jim jerked his head and opened his eyes. Hargrave's face was just inches away from his, concern clear on the wrinkled face. "There you are."

"I'm shot," Jim moaned. "They shot me."

"Aye," he said, then winked, "but you wore your armor. Smart boy." Jim looked up at the hazy blue sky for a moment, trying to reconstruct the morning. After his workout, he'd been about to leave, then remembered the light armor vest Hargrave had given him with the admonition to wear it out and about on the property, because security wasn't as good as it should be. "And you decided to go for a stroll behind the airport? What were you thinkin', boy?"

"I wasn't," Jim admitted. "The thieves?"

"Two dead, one wishin' he was. You killed the shit out of one of them." Jim looked moribund. "Hey, none of that now! They'd be chopping you up into convenient, marketable pieces right now if you hadn't done the right thing."

A pair of Startown constables came over when they realized Jim was conscious and conversational. He looked around and saw there were multiple law enforcement flyers, a couple of ambulances, and a hearse.

"You ready to talk, kid?"

"This ain't no kid," Hargrave said. "This here is Jim Cartwright, commander of Cartwright's Cavaliers." They both looked at Jim, over 300 pounds of soft city boy dressed in shorts and a faded vintage *Half Life* tee shirt all covered in blood and gore and shook their heads.

"I'm sure you can prove that," the older of the two said. "And explain what you were doing wandering around out here with a 'kill me and sell my liver' sign on your back?"

"He got turned around," Hargrave said. "He's only lived here a few months." Jim handed the officers his UACC. The younger one took it and made a face at the sticky blood on the card as he used his slate to check it.

"I was walking to the captain's hangar," Jim added, pointing toward the building in question. He then explained how his car was out for repairs and the rules against just walking around on the tarmac.

"And what about the one who blew that man's head half off?" the younger cop asked, pointing with a stylus at a sheet covered body.

"That was my work," another voice said. It was the old guy who'd saved Jim. "Murdock, First Sergeant of the Cavaliers." Jim glanced at the man, remembering the name on the personnel report for his hiring.

"Bodyguard?" the constable asked. Murdock shook his head.

"Out for a stroll."

"Well, that I believe," the older cop said. "What fuckin' idiot would mess with you? Especially with that street sweeper on your belt?" Jim noted that Murdock had the carbine on a custom holster hooked to his right leg, carrying the damned thing like a pistol. "I wouldn't try to go out into town with that thing."

"No shit," Murdock growled, and the officer looked at him through narrowed eyes. Another constable came over, this one in a suit with a badge-holder clipped to the suit's breast pocket.

"Looks like a clean shoot," he said after listening to his men for a moment. "You," he said pointing at Jim, "better either open-carry, or stay inside the perimeter." He glanced at the bodies being bagged. "All said, I consider you did us a community service today. If this becomes a habit, though, we'll have to wonder if you're playing vigilante."

"And what if he is," Murdock chuckled, "looks like you need the help."

"I've heard plenty about you," the inspector said to Murdock. "You've spent as much time in our lockup as you have in the companies." Murdock fished a stick of gum from his pants, popped it in his mouth and chewed as the inspector continued. "You have a real attitude problem, you know that?"

"Blow me," Murdock retorted. The inspector took a step toward Murdock, and Hargrave stepped between them.

"Gentlemen," he said, "this is all just a misunderstanding." While Hargrave tried to cool things off between the constable and Murdock, one of the medtechs came back over to Jim.

"You okay now?" the young man asked.

"Better," Jim said. "My back hurts, still."

"Bruising," the medtech said. "The bullet was simple lead and the armor did a perfect job. Guy would have gotten you in the kidney. Not good."

"The second one going to live?"

"The one with his face blown off? He was dead when we got here."

"No," Jim said, and looked down at all the gore on his clothes. "The one I shot in the stomach."

"Yeah," the medtech said and shook his head. "He's alive. I doubt he can afford the replacement parts though. They'll plug him into life support and see if he lives. If he does, we'll go from there."

"I didn't think the gun would do that much damage," Jim said, still having mixed feelings.

"You know what they wanted to do to you?" Jim nodded. The medtech looked around to be sure none of the constables were listening. "Then, good job. We've picked up dozens of people just this week, all missing parts. Serves that son of a bitch right, what you did to him." Jim frowned and mumbled something indifferent, still not convinced. The medtech handed him a printout and a little plastic packet of pills. "Take one of these every two hours if you have pain. Monitor your urine for any blood. Take it easy for a day or two." He looked down unconsciously at Jim's gut. Jim blushed. "I know you're not happy with your weight."

"Yeah," Jim said sheepishly, "I've been working on that."

"What I was going to say was that the padding saved you a ruptured kidney this time. Sometimes, things happen for a reason." He patted Jim on the arm. "Now get your not-dead self off my gurney! We have another call."

After a trip back to his tower to shower and change, escorted by Hargrave, a car was waiting outside to take him to the meeting he was late for. It was the first time he got to meet the command staff of the Cavaliers all in one place. It was also the first time he'd put on a legitimate Cartwright's Cavaliers BDU. When he looked at himself in the mirror he thought he looked like a clown. The BDUs weren't intended to be worn by fat people.

Hargrave had taken care of everything with his contacts. From the hiring of office staff to logistics and maintenance. As he approached the conference room that had once been an elite flyers' club at the Hobby Airport overlooking the concourse, Jim could hear Hargrave discussing the new Cavaliers.

"I know you've all heard rumors that the Cavaliers had been bought by a consortium." There were some grunts. "Another one says that one of the other Four Horsemen own us now." More mumbles. "Even one that Thaddeus is really still alive, and he's about to walk in through that door." A few people chuckled this time. "Yeah, you should laugh at that. Thaddeus Cartwright is gone. But his only son, is right here." It was Jim's cue, so he walked through the double doors into the conference room.

He looked around at those seated at the table. He found mostly unfamiliar faces, with a few exceptions. Hargrave sat next to the head of the table where Jim's empty seat waited. He looked at Jim and gave him a wink and nod of encouragement. Along one side of the table were his trooper commanders, led by Lieutenant Bran Parker. Next was First Sergeant Murdock, whom he now knew. The next one was platoon Sergeant Paul Rodriguez who would command Second Platoon of twenty CASPer troopers. They were still looking for a Sergeant to ramrod First Platoon.

The other side of the table was support and flight. Two APC commanders, Corporal Okoda, and Corporal Glazer. Next to them the four dropship pilots, Prescott, Miller, and Chin, with their command pilot Lieutenant Stackhouse. A pair of engineers sat next to Hargrave, under his command.

The reactions of those around the room varied from recognition by Murdock, to disbelief by the troopers, and maybe confusion by a few. One took it worse than others.

"This is a pretty fucked up joke, Hargrave." The man looked infuriated.

"Not a joke, Stackhouse," Hargrave replied evenly. "This is Jim Cartwright, Thaddeus's son."

"I met Thaddeus once years ago," Stackhouse said; "his kid was with him on a mission." He looked at Jim like he was looking at a bug on his dinner. "I see he's just as much a slug now as he was then."

"That's enough," Hargrave said.

"Well look at him." Stackhouse laughed and pointed a knife-edge hand at Jim. "He's what, eighteen or nineteen? He looks like a quarter ton of chewed bubblegum."

"You can stow that shit," Murdock growled from across the table.

"You on his side?" Stackhouse said incredulously. "Murdock, man, you want that commanding you? What was his VOWS, 700 at most?" All eyes turned from Stackhouse to Jim who sighed and spoke for the first time.

"My combined score was 664," he said. The trooper sergeants looked at each other, while others shook their heads. Hargrave's mouth tightened into a line. "I'm never going to be a trooper." He gestured down at himself. "Yeah, I'm a fat kid. Well, so fucking what? I've studied how to run a company most of my life, from financial to operations. And what I don't know, that's what I have you here for. But I know what it means to be a merc. It's in my family's blood."

"Looks like it skipped a generation," Stackhouse snorted.

"I said that's enough of that shit," Murdock said menacingly.

"Why are you taking up for that tub of lard?" Stackhouse demanded. "First shot hits the command ship or the APC he's huddling in, he'll piss himself and crawl into an equipment box." Murdock slowly got to his feet, and all eyes turned to him.

"You gonna shut your miserable cake-hole for a minute, or do I have to close it for you?" The muscles in Stackhouse's jaw bunched, but Murdock was twice his size, and three times his age. "You're a fucking pilot."

"So what?"

"Last warning, flyboy." He leaned forward, and the big conference table groaned. "One more peep out of you before I have my say, and I'll take you outside and rub your ass in the dirt until you can't stand." Stackhouse leaned back and threw his hands out in a 'go ahead' gesture. "We're troopers," he said to the men on his side of the table. "We get in the shit. Face to face, we slug it out until we're dead, give up, or the other side calls it quits. We don't drop bombs or fly into LZs. We're the ones you fly there. Your ass is in the shit too, I know that. But if you get your ticket punched, it happens in an instant. I've talked to plenty of pilots." He pointed a beefy finger at Stackhouse. "You guys don't really think about it," he moved the gaze to the other three pilots, "do you?" The other three shrugged; Stackhouse just stared.

"Any of you been in a hand-to-hand fight? I don't mean in a bar or with some chick, I mean fight or fucking die?" None of them said anything. "I didn't think so. Different, ain't it? That's what we troopers do. Kick their asses, face to face. A little bit of armor between us." He paused for a moment. "This kid here; this man, actually," he pointed at Jim. "Yeah, he's a round boy that got shit for his VOWS. Not a fucking merc company on the planet would hire him for anything except office work. Maybe not even then. But they don't know anything about him. I do. A couple hours ago, he went for a little walk behind the wire here. By himself. In the starport." They all looked at Jim curiously. "You can guess what happened."

"Got his fat ass kicked?" Stackhouse asked, casting a baleful glance at Jim.

"He got jumped all right. Three body jackers cornered him behind a hangar and figured he'd make an easy mark." Murdock turned and looked Stackhouse square in the eye. "Well, he killed one of them, nearly cut the other in half, shot the third once in the shoulder. Only mistake he made, not finishing the job. All he had was a little GP-90. This one." Murdock pulled out a rag from a pocket, opened it and dropped the bloody gun on the table with a metallic thud. Jim grunted. He'd wondered where his gun went after the shooting. He'd assumed the cops took it. "I finished the job for him after one of the jackers shot him in the back." He pointed at Jim, but never took his eyes off Stackhouse. "He was knocked on his ass, rolling around in one of those punk's fucking guts, trying to get his gun back up and finish the fight. He didn't stop, he didn't cry, he didn't beg for mercy. *He fucking fought like a Cartwright!*" Murdock nearly yelled the last, making several in the room jump.

"So, Stackhouse, I'll tell you what. You want to judge this kid because he's fat and looks like a lazy fucking pizza eater, you go right ahead. I might have done the same a few hours ago." Murdock looked at Jim. "But I've seen his heart. He's his father's son. He doesn't have any quit in him, and I bet he has the instincts to be a first rate merc commander, too. So I'll follow him, sure. And if you don't like it, you can take a long deep suck on my balls." He nodded to Jim and sat down.

The room was completely silent for a minute. Jim had never got to the point of sitting down, everything had happened too fast. He looked around the table, a little nervously. He was confused by Murdock's speech. He hadn't done anything special, he just reacted as best he could. He knew the punk jackers wouldn't have given him any slack no matter what he did, so giving up was a waste of time. What else could you do in that situation but fight? Murdock looked at him and Jim saw the tiniest hint of a nod there. Okay then, Jim thought.

He stepped up to the table and scooped up his gun. He verified it was on safety, popped the magazine and saw it was still loaded, returned it and holstered the weapon. It was all done smoothly after weeks of practice with Hargrave. The gun holstered, he moved to the head of the table and took a seat. The seat of the commander of Cartwright's Cavaliers.

"Don't mean shit," Stackhouse said, looking around for support. He didn't find any.

"You have a problem with me?" Jim asked. The chair felt comfortable. It felt right. He began to radiate confidence as he settled into it.

"Yeah, I do," Stackhouse said, trying to sound as confident as Murdock had sounded, and failing.

"Okay, fine," Jim said. "You're fired."

"What?"

"The *commander* said you're fired," Murdock growled. "What, you fucking deaf, too?"

"You can't fire me," Stackhouse said.

"Bet me," Jim said and gave a little laugh. It wasn't a nervous laugh; it was a confident one. The laugh of someone who wasn't impressed with the person he was dealing with. He gestured at the conference room door. "Stop at payroll, draw your cache, and get the fuck out, or I'll throw you the fuck out."

"You…" Stackhouse started to say, then he noticed the look on Murdock's face. The old merc gave Stackhouse a wink, then looked down at the bloody rag on the table. Stackhouse grunted and stood. Jim tensed slightly. "Fine," Stackhouse said and headed for the door. "To hell with all of you. If you want to get killed with this fat kid in charge, I'll enjoy reading about it."

"Just get out," Hargrave said. A moment later the doors closed behind the man. "Well, I guess we need a new head pilot."

"Anyone else?" Jim asked. Everyone stayed in their seats. "Good, thanks for coming. You all have a special place in history. Cartwright's Cavaliers has been at a low point, but now we're on the way back up. You all stand to make a hell of a lot of money from this." Now there were some smiles and a couple murmurs of appreciation. "Two full platoons are hired and our equipment, while not new, is undergoing checkout as we speak. Hargrave assures me it's all in top condition, and we have plenty of spares. I've filed the paperwork with the Mercenary Guild on Karma, and we already have our first post-reconstruction contract. I've made Hargrave my Executive Officer, so I'll let the XO lay out the mission." The other man stood up and gestured at the windows that overlooked the concourse. They changed to translucent and maps of the galaxy appeared.

"Thanks, boss," he said and pointed at a section of the galaxy that then began to expand. "Here we are, Tolo arm of our galaxy, Cresht region. Home."

"How sweet it is," Murdock grumbled, several nodded in agreement, and some chuckled. Hargrave waited for them to die down then continued.

"Trailward of our arm is the Jesc arm, the Centaur region. It's a very populous region. The Galnet lists just over 500 occupied worlds controlled by 400 species." Someone whistled. "A very diverse number of species, on mostly native worlds. It doesn't have a high density of wealth though, so when it's found, it's pretty hotly contested. And as usual, as long as the locals play by the rules, the Union lets them deal with it." The view moved to the Jesc arm, Centaur region. For a moment all the inhabited systems flashed green, then only one remained lit and the view zoomed in.

"This is Kash-Kah, home of the race called Duplato." He pronounced it "Dew-play-toe." "They're not one of the big players, not signatories of the Mercenary Guild, and don't belong to any of the cartels." The screen displayed a species which most thought looked like a bipedal tree sloth. One was displayed next to a human for reference, and was almost as tall. Their arms were long enough for the six long fingers to brush the ground, even when standing erect. They wore extensive thick furs. "The planet, as you can guess, is cold. They farm mostly fungus underground. The planet's surface growing season is extremely short."

"Why do they need mercs?" Jim asked.

"I was getting there," Hargrave said. "They are adept miners, thanks to the underground farming techniques they developed over thousands of years. They've made modest amounts of credits for their planetary economy through the rare earths they've found. Even some precious metals." He gestured, and a small ore processing plant near a cave complex was displayed. Arrayed out from the caves were avenues and dwellings of all types. "But they've come upon a sizeable quantity of radioactive ore, mostly Uranium-238. It might not be F11, but it's valuable." The display changed once more to show overhead maps of the Duplato's settlement.

"Over the last few months they have been the victims of numerous raids against their stores of U-238, as well as some of the rare earths they were stockpiling for trade. Like most species in the Union, they are non-combatants. They tried automated defenses and repelled one raid. The next one came in overland and bypassed the defenses. Their application to the Mercenary Guild for a garrison contract was granted." The contract came up on the screen.

"It's for six months. At that point they will have completed extraction and processing of the ores. We will escort their transport to the stargate, at which point our contract will be complete." He gestured at the screen. "Retainer is for ten million credits. Combat bonus of five percent per engagement, maximum of fifty percent total. Safe delivery of goods to the stargate pays a twenty-five percent bonus. Even if we don't catch any action, we're looking at twelve point five million credits. For a garrison duty, and only two platoons, that's pretty juicy."

Jim noted people nodding around the table. It sounded pretty good to him as well. The balance of the available trust funds he'd taken over started at just under five million. He'd spent half of it getting the company up and running, mostly in contracts for troopers, office staff, and consumables. Of course everyone he hired and took off-world needed a hazard waiver through the guild. It wasn't a fortune, but it was still money. They needed this to go well.

"We're paying standard rates. We could have paid less, but we risked getting nothing but leftovers and troublemakers." Hargrave glanced at Murdock who flipped him the bird. "So that's fifty percent to the company. The rest is for the contractors. One half share for Earth-side staff. One share for troopers, maintenance, and logistics. Two shares for sergeants, APC drivers, and drop ship pilots. Three shares for 1SG there and four to the LT, drop ship commander (when we find a new one), and Captain Winslow who will be taking command of *EMS Traveler*. Bonuses paid at the same level." Hargrave spread his hands. "That's about it, any questions?" Sergeant Rodriguez raised his hand. "Go ahead."

"Do we get back-up with this contract?" Hargrave glanced down and shook his head.

"The Duplato couldn't afford it, and neither could we." There were some mumbles. "I know, that could put us in a tight place. However, we have two full platoons, and two drop ships. With *EMS Traveler* in orbit, we have high watch as well. We don't have any armor yet beyond the APCs, but that's still a lot of firepower. I have full briefings for you on what the raiders have been using, and I can assure you it isn't anything compared to what we're packing." Hargrave looked around the room. "If you want out, you can resign right now, and we'll hold you harmless. Just keep in mind you'll be walking away from a contract with Cartwright's Cavaliers. We won't be calling you back." No one said anything, so Hargrave turned and nodded to Jim.

"So that's the contract," Jim said, repositioning himself a little in the chair. The middle of his lower back was throbbing. "We're going to deploy on Kash-Kah in two elements. One will be garrison, the other on alert. The plan is to repel the raiders when they come, then track and ambush with the second group. The Duplato have given us full leave to deal with the raiders however we want. So we find them, and then we waste 'em." There were grunts of agreement around the table. "We want a good review after this contract. Let them all know the Cavaliers are back. Okay, we have one week left before we head up to the *Traveler* – let's make it count."

"You did great, son," Hargrave said after everyone had left, and he patted Jim on the shoulder with genuine warmth.

"Yeah?" Jim asked. "I was nervous as shit when Stackhouse started to go off."

"You were?" Hargrave laughed. "I was afraid Murdock was going to rip his head off and shit down his neck. You made quite the impression on him."

"Hargrave, I barely know what I'm doing." Jim sighed. "I've read all the books, and I've played plenty of tactical simulations, but in a few weeks, more than a hundred men's lives will depend on me. I'm not ready."

"No, you aren't," Hargrave agreed.

"Well, that's filling me with confidence."

"You want me to blow F11 up your ass? I won't do it. I'll tell you this, though. No commander is ever ready the first time he leads men into combat. No matter what they might say or think, there's a damned good reason they strap you into that thing in a diaper. And it's not because you'll be in the suit for hours." Jim gaped at him. "Get some rest, take those pills. Tomorrow we take you to the next step." Jim nodded and blew air out between his teeth, then paused before speaking.

"The nano treatments?" Hargrave nodded. "I wish I'd gotten them earlier."

"They don't stop bullets, son. Anyway, get some rest."

* * * * *

Chapter Eleven

Jim sat on the table answering thousands of questions from the nurses who appeared to be wiring him up like a prop in a bad Sci-fi film. The hookups went from bio-monitors to IV drips, and of course the two dozen shunts painfully inserted into many of his arteries that would deliver the therapy.

"Now Mr. Cartwright," the doctor, an attractive woman who was looking at her slate and not at him, said, "you fully understand this procedure is likely to involve significant physical discomfort, yes?" He nodded absently, and she looked up at him curiously.

"Yes," he said impatiently, "I know it will hurt."

"Most people who undergo this treatment are in ideal physical condition. You...are not."

"Oh, so you noticed?"

"Mr. Cartwright, these nanotherapies draw from your body's metabolism to affect changes to your skeletal system, musculature, and ligaments. That puts quite a strain on your body. As a general rule, those who are given the green light to undergo this therapy are both young and very fit."

"Can I survive it?" Jim demanded.

"Of course, or I wouldn't have allowed you to get this far along in the process. You may not be in tip-top shape, but you are young, and that works in your favor."

"Fine," he said, "then do it already." She looked at him and sighed.

"Your family is well-to-do; why didn't you just get nano-therapy to..."

"Get rid of the fat?" he snapped. "Because my father wanted me to manage it by myself. When he died, my mother said I could do it when I turned eighteen. Unfortunately, once I actually did turn eighteen, the money to pay for this sort of thing was gone."

"So have it done now," she said.

"Takes too long. We deploy in a few days. Doctor, please, just go ahead." She shrugged and picked up the machine's control slate.

"Energizing base charge," she said, and he felt a tingle from head to toe. "The nanites cannot function without a specific electrical field. It's a safety feature." He nodded, his eyes wide with apprehension. She tapped on the slate once more. "And introducing nanites in three...two...one..."

Several hours later, Jim opened his eyes and groaned. Everything hurt. Absolutely everything. He was in a recovery room – he knew that much – but couldn't remember why.

"How are you feeling, Mr. Cartwright?" He turned his head and groaned again – just moving his neck muscles that little bit was agony. A nurse was sitting next to the bed with a slate. The monitor screen over his head beeped in unison with her tapping.

"Terrible," he croaked. She smiled and leaned over to him, a cup with a straw in her hand.

"Please take a drink." He did, suddenly realizing how incredibly thirsty he was. Another couple of sips, and she took it away. "Not too much at once," she said. He took a deep breath, and – oh God! – even his ribs hurt! He repositioned his body and doing that hurt. He rolled his eyes and that hurt. But...he also felt different in a way he couldn't really understand. The door opened, and the familiar aged figure of Hargrave came in.

"How you doing, boss?" Hargrave asked.

"I hurt," Jim said simply. Hargrave made an understanding face. "Did it work?"

"The therapy was worse in my day," Hargrave replied; "they've perfected it a bit since. If you're still here, it worked."

"Like being beaten all over with rubber hoses." Hargrave nodded his head in understanding.

"I'm administering a slight analgesic," the nurse said. A minute later the same doctor who gave him the therapy came in.

"How's my patient?" Jim was beginning to feel progressively better.

"Getting better," he said. She nodded and took the slate from the nurse to examine his condition.

"Your procedure went as planned. The nanites have been deactivated and will be passed from your body naturally over the next few weeks. Nothing unusual was detected by the scans as the procedure proceeded."

"What do you mean 'passed from my body?'"

"You'll piss them out," Hargrave said with a wink.

"What's that like?" Jim asked.

"They're microscopic," the doctor said, "so your penis won't notice, regardless of how big or small it might be." Jim could feel his cheeks getting hot. "You ready to get up?"

"I don't know," Jim said. The doctor nodded to her nurses who came over and took Jim's hands to gently pull him upright. He grunted a bit, but felt only mild discomfort. Once his legs were over the side of the bed, one of the nurses removed the IV in his arm and held onto him as he put his feet on the ground. He was amazed at how quickly he was feeling better. He could stand just fine.

"Great," the doctor said and consulted her slate one more time. "No side effects."

"You say that like it's a common thing," Jim said as he moved around a bit.

"The nanites are made with tech we don't understand, by aliens halfway across the galaxy. One thing we can say is the little robots always work. The only thing we can't guarantee is your body will accept it. That's why all the tests. We know a lot of indicators that could cause problems. There's a good reason you have to undergo the procedure in a Startown, Mr. Cartwright. Most of the world's governments consider them highly illegal. However, they tend to do their job just fine." She checked her slate one more time. "You are ready to be released." She gestured to his clothes on the dresser. "Once you're dressed, you can take this form down the hall and check out." They all exited at once, and he was quickly alone.

He wasn't hurting as much anymore but found his joints stiff and slow to respond. It was easy enough to get the overly revealing hospital gown off, but it took a few minutes more than planned to get dressed in his new Cartwright's uniform. To his surprise, it fit better.

"Doctor," he asked outside, "did the nanites make me thinner?"

"Not in the truest sense," she said, "but some of your surpluses were used by them to fuel the modifications to your body. In the case of more fit patients, we inject metabolic fuels for the nanites. We didn't have to do that in your case, it just used what it found."

"Is that how they can make me...more normal?"

"That therapy is a little more complicated and lengthy. Due to the extensive modifications, you'd be put into a medically-induced coma."

"Because it hurts so badly," he said, not really a question.

"Yes," she agreed. "It takes about a week for the procedure to complete. Multiple injections of nanites are used as they are expended in the operation. Then another two weeks of therapy afterwards."

"What kind of therapy?"

"Well, you'll be a lot lighter, for one thing, and unused to moving around at that weight. It's physical therapy designed to get you used to your new body." He nodded in understanding and considered. "Are you thinking about it after all?"

"Not now," Jim said, looking over to see Hargrave waiting by the elevator. "Maybe after this first contract. I need to get the Cavaliers back on their feet. Now's not the time to take a three-week vacation."

"More like six weeks," she suggested, "we don't recommend you engage in any strenuous activity for three more weeks after your treatment and physical therapy are complete."

"I understand. Maybe I'll see you in a year or so then." He shook her hand and met the two men at the elevator.

The next day he woke up feeling fine. More than fine, actually. He thought about the billions of little dead robots riding his piss like a waterpark as he relieved himself and went down to meet the captain for his workout. Afterwards, for the first time, his joints didn't hurt. They'd always hurt when he worked out. The therapy had toughened everything up.

Breakfast complete, he dressed and met his XO downstairs.

"Ready?" Hargrave asked.

"Yep," Jim replied.

"Good," Hargrave said, "it's time to introduce you to a new friend."

The hangar was buzzing with activity. Vehicle operators were moving crates, unloading trucks, and storing goods. Elsewhere, technicians pushed tool racks about or analysis equipment or worked on machinery and weaponry of every variety, much of it older technology that hadn't been used for years. One wall of the massive hangar was lined with dozens and dozens of CASPers.

A few troopers were undergoing checkout on the old Binnig MK 7 combat systems. They were some of the last to be qualified, and some of the last suits to be brought back online and checked out.

Everyone watched as a suited trooper fired his jumpjets with a hissing snap, launching himself in a low parabolic arc across the work area. Almost a half-ton of advanced alloy hurtled toward the concrete floor. A scant few feet before impact the jets fired again, and the operator slowed it just enough so it came down with a resounding bang and flex of the powerful mechanical knees. It was a nearly perfect jump in a confined space.

The suit turned to face the group, its slightly bulbous operator canopy split and opened with a hum of motors. First Sergeant Murdock grinned at them from inside. The haptic feedback helmet left more than enough of his features visible for his scarred visage to be recognizable.

"Man, I love these suits!" he crowed. Jim stood in his combat uniform, a haptic suit with helmet in one hand, haptic links all in place, and coiled interface cables hanging loose. His eyes were wide in admiration of how the First Sergeant handled the war machine.

"Those Mark 8s are lighter and faster but not as well-armored or roomy as these old Mark 7 suits!"

"You are amazing," Jim said, his voice full of admiration. Murdock made the huge powered armor suit look like a second skin – like he was some kind of superhero from the comic books. Anyone *should* be capable of doing what he did, but Murdock made it look easy.

"Jim," Hargrave said, "First Sergeant Murdock is our most experienced veteran with the Mk 7 suits, so he's going to go through your intro. Look over here," he said and pointed. Jim turned and saw a lifter moving over with a MK 7 CASPer, its canopy open and empty. Hargrave was holding the lifter control and maneuvering it closer. "This is yours, boss."

"Yeah," Jim said and eyed it dubiously. He knew this moment had been coming from the moment he decided to go to Karma and see if a contract could be had. To say he was intimidated would have been a severe understatement. He gathered all the cables to be sure they didn't get caught on anything and walked to the lifter. A tech rolled a gangway into place, and he climbed it.

Stopping at the top, he looked inside. Even though the suit had been cleaned and every system gone over in great detail, it still looked heavily used. Torn padding had been patched and sealed in places, the paint flaked away here and there, and a few of the indicators had been replaced with new ones. It was most definitely used. The Cartwright's Cavaliers logo was shiny new paint, as was the name plate "Jim Cartwright – CO." Jim touched the name plate, took a breath, and began to climb in.

He'd submitted to the indignity of a detailed laser scan days ago, and the suit interior was adjusted via moveable padding and straps to be a nearly perfect fit. He got onto his knees and backed into it, pointing his feet as he'd been instructed and wiggling. It was like trying to put on a particularly tight pair of pants that happened to be made of rigid plastic and didn't bend at all. It seemed to take an embarrassingly long time before his feet found bottom and he felt the leg splits nudge up against his crotch. He flexed his arms backwards, found the arm holes, and worked them in next as he pushed his torso back into the suit. The arms weren't as snug, by design, and he slid back fully into the suit.

"Great," Hargrave said, taking up the haptic relays and beginning to plug them in. Normally the operator would do that as the plugs were inside and invisible to the ground crew, but Hargrave did it easily by touch alone. The relay input indicators turned green one after another. "How's it feel?"

"Snug," Jim said, "but not unpleasant."

"Good," Hargrave said and patted him on the breastbone. "Here goes the head connections." Since Jim had pinplants, he didn't need the same helmet. The one he wore was solely for protection. Hargrave took the two head connections and felt along Jim's hairline, searching for the touchpoint.

"Higher," Jim said. "A little farther back."

"Sorry, boss," Hargrave said.

"Don't worry about it," Jim said as the first one clicked magnetically into place, and Jim felt the suit's computer link with him.

"I had a guy in a unit years ago who had pinplants. He was a scout and could do amazing things with these suits."

"Don't get your hopes up," Jim said.

"Don't worry kid," Murdock said a few feet away. "You'll do great, and you only have two days to get ready."

"Thanks. That helps," Jim moaned. Hargrave shot the old merc a dirty look as he found the haptic connection on the other side of Jim's head and clicked on the lead.

"Okay, you're hooked up and ready to go." Hargrave patted him again and went down the gantry as it was rolled away. "Standby for startup," he said, and a moment later the power indicator on the interior went from blue for standby to yellow for startup. He felt the suit start to vibrate as the hydrogen-powered generator spun up, and the suit came alive.

"Good power-up," a technician to the side said. "Clean board."

"You are live," Hargrave said. "Now, like we did in the simulator."

"Okay," Jim said. You can do this, he thought to himself. With his right hand he pinched his index finger and thumb together, while doing the same with his little finger and thumb on the other hand. The suit's indicator went from yellow to green.

The suit wasn't designed to be run from inside his pinplants – and Aetherware had never been customized for that purpose. Instead, his pinplants established an interface with the suit and fed it biometric data, which was accomplished in a normal suit via haptic skin sensors built into the helmet. With the suit fully powered up, Jim simply spoke. "Close canopy," he said, and the clamshell canopy quickly descended, came together, and closed with a thump. He felt a tiny bit of pressure in his ear as the full atmospheric system sealed, and then the inside of the canopy came alive. It was like he was looking through glass to the outside, only there was thick hardened steel between him and those looking up at him. He used a finger gesture to activate the suit's exterior loud speakers.

"I'm powered up, all good," Jim told them. As he looked around a series of reticles followed his gaze, his weapons systems indicators. There were also a number of bar-graph indicators letting him know vital stats for his suit. Remaining fuel, current power output of the generator, backup battery status, life support endurance, and many other statistics were there.

"Good," Hargrave said, taking a slate from a tech. "Let's go over functionality." While he hung suspended from the lifter, Hargrave had him do a long list of seemingly mundane motions. They felt incredibly clumsy at first, but after each series of motions, changes were made to the suit's internal calibrations and eventually the movements felt natural. When they were done, Jim could control the arms and legs perfectly, and the suit no longer felt like it was fighting his actions. He had to consciously think about how it felt to move, to maintain constant awareness that he was surrounded by hundreds of pounds of movement-amplifying battle armor. "I think we're ready," Hargrave said to the side.

"Let's give it a try," Murdoch said, Jim turned his head and saw the other man button up his canopy and step closer while all the unarmored humans backed away. "Ready to release?"

"Ready," said the techs. And a second later Jim's suit dropped to the ground with an echoing clang. He tried to stand, promptly over-compensated and fell backwards against the lifter with a sickening CLANG!

"Shit," Jim barked and leaned forward. It turned into a stutter-step, and he would have face-planted if not for Murdock who expertly caught him with his own suit. The two metal behemoths slammed against each other with a screech of metal on metal that sent some of that new paint flying into the air.

"Easy son," Murdock said and got him back onto his feet. "Want me to control your suit?"

"No," Jim said. "I need to figure this out myself."

"Okay," Murdock agreed and stepped back. Jim slowly turned his suit, weaving slightly until he was aligned along the practice area, and took his first step. It was more of a stuttering stumble. Murdock caught him once more, this time from behind by a set of handles installed for just that purpose.

"Take your time," Murdock advised. He hung on as Jim experimentally took tiny baby steps, letting him get used to how the haptic feedback system interacted with his body's actions. After a few stumbles, Jim slowly began to perceive that tiny, almost immeasurable delay between his moving his foot forward in the suit, and the suit responding. It made him second guess his own moves.

"What's going on?" Hargrave asked.

"There's a delay between my movements and the suit's response," Jim explained.

"Safe the suit," Hargrave ordered. Instantly Jim felt the suit freeze and come to attention like a soldier on a parade ground. His movements had no effect, and a yellow telltale announced "Suit in Safe Mode" on his HUD, heads up display. "Jim, this is Adayn. She's our chief armorer and is a specialist in CASPers." A woman who looked to be in her late twenties came around so he could see her and Jim blinked. Most of the men and women who worked on the suits and weapons were grease-monkey types. They tended toward short hair, well-worn jumpsuits, and calloused hands. Adayn did not fit that description in the least. She was short, had a beautiful face, and her outfit was spotless. She also had nearly waist length raven-black hair braided in an elaborate ponytail that currently fell over her left shoulder and down her back. She looked up at him and smiled, her sky-blue eyes twinkling in an almost mischievous grin. Woah, Jim thought and grinned back without realizing she couldn't see him.

"Commander Cartwright," she said, "I'm going to access the engineering controls on your suit." He just stared at her in rapt amazement. He didn't think he'd ever seen a more beautiful girl in his life. It was creating a short circuit between his brain and his mouth. "Sir?" she asked.

"Jim," Murdock said and rapped on the back of his suit, which was like being inside a ringing bell.

"Ouch," Jim said, and tried to cover his ears. Of course, with his suit locked, he'd have more luck trying to lift a pickup truck with his bare hands.

"Pay attention, kid."

"Yeah, sorry," Jim apologized. "Go ahead." Adayn nodded and came forward, taking out a special slate with a cable she attached to Jim's suit.

"Accessing haptic controls," she said. Jim's indicators showed she was modifying the system. "Can you tell me what it feels like?" Jim described the phenomenon. She made some entries, then disconnected. "Okay, try that."

"Take it off Safe," Hargrave said, and the suit's status light returned to green. Jim took a step, and then another, and another.

"Hey, I can walk!" he laughed.

"Take it slow, kid," Murdock said behind him.

"Don't let go," Jim ordered.

"I did two steps ago." Murdock laughed.

Jim spent a few minutes walking, turning and just generally practicing movement. It took shockingly little effort to move. He understood now how a trooper could fight for hours in one of the suits. His fuel indicated ninety-nine percent after his practice maneuvers.

"Okay Jim," Hargrave said, "let's move on to some more advanced stuff." They ran him through a series of basic actions, starting with getting back on his feet after falling down. That one took almost an hour to master. Next was climbing steps. Less time for that one. Then came manipulating small objects without destroying them. Adayn had to do some more haptic adjustments after he accidentally crushed a steel ammo crate like it was a pop can.

"The CASPer will never play a piano," Murdock said, "but with some practice you'll be able to pick up an unarmored human without injuring them."

Not anytime soon, Jim thought as he picked up another ammo crate, and this time only slightly dented it. "I think I'm getting the hang of it," Jim said as he caught a steel pallet Murdock tossed him on the first try.

"Good," Murdock said; "let's take it up a notch."

They moved to advanced control of the CASPer. First jogging, then running. After Jim demonstrated a basic mastery of that skill, he proceeded to jumping with suit legs, and his first attempted use of the jumpjets. That resulted in his first serious crash-and-burn. He lifted off badly, tried to compensate mid-jump, did it poorly, and tumbled. Murdock shot in and managed to check the fall, preventing Jim from coming down cockpit first. The impact resulted in a crushing rebound that sent Jim crashing to the deck, first on his shoulder, then rolling into one of the reinforced nets strung around the maneuver zone.

"Ouch," Jim moaned as he rolled himself and the suit into a sitting position.

"Believe it or not, kid, that wasn't the worst first jump I've ever seen."

"What was the worst?"

"Guy killed himself and trashed his suit," Murdock said simply.

"Yeah, that's worse." Jim flexed his neck and flinched. The impact had strained a few muscles. Then he realized that yesterday, the impact might well have killed him. The treatment. "I'm okay," he said and, following the training Murdock had given him earlier, rolled over, and got the suit back to its feet without help. "Status board indicates damage to some arm actuators," he reported.

"Checking," Adayn said. "Nominal function, you should be okay."

"Tough suit," Jim said.

"Saved my bacon more than once," Murdock replied. "You want to go on?"

"Yeah," Jim said as he worked the new kink in his neck. "I'm ready."

"Good man!" Murdock said, the approval in his voice evident. "Let's go."

It was three more hours before Jim went through the shutdown routine with his CASPer, backing it into the maintenance harness and setting all the safeties. The suit status said ninety-five percent of his hydrogen fuel remained, after almost five hours of continuous use. Their endurance amazed him, and as the canopy split and opened, he said as much. Adayn was standing on the gantry as it was rolled into place, a smile on her pretty face.

"They're designed that way," she said. "Granted, you were just playing around."

"Playing," he scoffed.

She chuckled. "Yes, playing. What you were doing is nothing compared to what the suits are capable of."

Murdock's suit was docked next to him. Unlike Jim's, there was no gantry. He just extracted himself, swung around, and without looking climbed down the outside of the ten-foot-tall machine to land smoothly on his booted feet. He was drinking from a water bottle chatting with another armorer while Jim was still struggling with all the haptic connections. Adayn laughed and leaned into the cockpit.

"Here," she said, "let me help you with that." She began unhooking the connections. As she leaned over him to release the last of the restraints, Jim was distinctly aware of her breasts pushing into his chest. "There you are," she said and backed out, "how was that?"

"Wonderful!" he said, grinning ear to ear. She gave him a demure grin and walked down the gantry. Jim tried not to watch her bottom sway as she went down the stairs, but failed.

"You gonna stare or get outta that thing?" Murdock asked.

"Sorry," he mumbled and began to squirm his way out. While Murdock's extraction looked like an old Earth fighter pilot climbing down in a 2-D movie, Jim's probably resembled a rhinoceros giving birth.

"Need help?" Hargrave asked from nearby while he examined the suit's diagnostics.

"No," Jim mumbled. It took an embarrassing amount of time to finally crawl free and get to his feet. He was sweaty and tired, but he'd managed to not kill himself getting familiar with the CASPer. "I did it!" he said and smiled. "I actually operated a CASPer." Adayn looked up from the diagnostic she and Hargrave were doing on his suit. She grinned and gave him a thumbs up. Jim felt his heart flip-flop inside his chest. He wanted to climb back in and learn to do back flips on the off chance she might smile at him like that just one more time. "When can we practice again?"

"Tomorrow," Murdock said, tossing the empty water bottle into a nearby garbage can and heading for his own suit. "For now, I have another checkout to run." He gestured to where a different suit was being rolled up, and a trooper was coming out of the changing room holding haptic connections just like Jim had. It was obvious Murdock had more work to do. With his training done, Jim decided it was time for dinner and headed for a car to his tower. At the door he glanced back to look at Adayn one more time. When he saw she was looking at him, he felt his face burn and quickly left.

Jim finished the afternoon in his office, approving and reviewing reports. The final hiring dossier had come in from the personnel office in Houston. They had a new chief pilot, Jane Wheeler, who was the daughter of the Wheeler's Dealers' owner. They'd parked her in recruiting and she got bored, so she'd started looking for an adventure. Probably couldn't pass up the chance of working for one of the Horsemen, either. Murdock had recommended her for the vacant position; he knew her from when she'd recruited him into the Dealers before he'd come over to the Cavaliers. Jim nodded when he saw she had experience in the *Phoenix*. Good call.

Also listed in the report was a reply to his inquiry about hiring one Rick Culper. A formal request had been sent to the guild, but the response was that Rick Culper already held a contract with the Winged Hussars as a private and was currently off-world. Jim was disappointed he couldn't hire his friend, but also pleased to know Rick was on board with one of the Four Horsemen. Maybe someday they'd cross paths, if they both lived long enough for that to happen.

So he now had more than 100 employees, most of them either direct combat personnel or combat support. That was impressive in a way and sad in others. He knew from the company's records that, just before his father died, the Cavaliers had more than 2,000 employees. Of course, they'd been worth almost a billion credits in liquid assets at the time and several times that in equipment. He was taking almost everything they could muster off-world, and it was a force that would have constituted the smallest unit they would have sent off-world only a year ago.

He hadn't decorated the little office in the old airport administrative building very much. He had better things to do. The one thing he had done was put up a picture of his father, Thaddeus Cartwright. The man stared at him from years gone by, a slight smile on his lips and a hint of optimism shining in his eyes. When had that been, five years ago? Ten? He couldn't be sure.

"Am I doing this right, dad?" he asked the picture. Of course, it didn't have anything to say. He sighed and went back to work.

* * * * *

Chapter Twelve

The ship skimmed in low over the horizon, approaching the site with as much stealth as was possible. The captain piloted the ship himself as no one knew exactly what they were heading into. A courier had passed through the system over a month ago and had received no response when it attempted to contact the base. As a result, they had decided on this reconnaissance, and it was the project head himself who came to investigate.

"How long until we reach the site?" Ashattoo asked.

"Just a few minutes," the captain replied. The Bakulu turned one of its eye stalks to regard the passenger. Ashattoo tried to ignore the smell of the gastropod. They were incredible pilots and versatile in space, but the briny fish smell...

When they'd emerged from hyperspace, they had tried to communicate with the processing and storage center but got no response. Ashattoo then decided it was best that they approach from the far side of the world. It would take more time, but increased their chances of coming in undetected. A Wathayat combat unit was available, but with 170 hours each way, any help they might need was a long, long way off. He kept wondering what could have happened? The briefing on the base's defenses indicated they were formidable – considerable air defense and an entire company of Zuul mercenaries.

"The installation should be coming into sensor range," the Bakulu said. On the tiny bridge screen, the sensors showed the planet's mundane terrain sweeping by below. A moment later, the outlying buildings of the facility came into view.

"There it is," Ashattoo said and gestured at the screen. "It must just have been a communications failure."

"Unlikely," the pilot said and overlaid additional data. There were no energy emissions from the installation at all. A moment later, the orderly lines of buildings gave way to complete devastation.

"Entropy," Ashattoo spluttered as they flew over the remnants of Wathayat's Slost depot. Weeks ago it was a massive gas transfer, purification, and storage facility. Now it looked like a giant had rampaged through it with a rake the size of a mountain, tearing the base from the surface of the planet and leaving miles-long flaming rents behind.

They flew along, following the surreal path of destruction. It moved back and forth around the base, leaving nothing untouched. Eventually they arrived at the center of the installation and came upon a single crater where once the main starport and receiving terminal had been. It was easily a mile wide and spoke of a massive high order explosion, possibly nuclear in origin. The sensors found no life anywhere.

"What are your instructions, administrator?" the captain asked.

"This is all recorded?" Ashattoo asked. The pilot indicated it was. "Then get us out of here. We must report before whoever did this comes back."

The scout ship angled upwards and rocketed into space, leaving the dead system behind.

The new contract luncheon was a tradition in most merc companies, and Jim had no intention of discouraging it. The restaurant was also traditional. In the case of the Cavaliers, they frequented a place called Little Joe's, about a mile from the airport and museum. Jim had visited it once, when he was a pre-teen, to celebrate a particularly successful contract. As he pulled up in a cab with Hargrave, he noticed it wasn't what it used to be. When he'd contacted them for a reservation, they'd told him any time was fine.

"I was here quite a bit back in my day," Hargrave said as they got out, and the cab rolled away. The façade of the restaurant was faded, and the canopy torn in a few places. No one manned the valet parking station. "Looks like they haven't done well lately."

Jim and Hargrave climbed the few steps to the entrance and went inside. A bored looking woman stood at the maître-d's station, watching a show on an older model slate. Jim stood waiting for her to notice, but when she didn't seem to, or was purposely ignoring him, he went over and cleared his throat.

"What?" she asked without looking up. "No public bathrooms."

"We have a reservation." She looked up and then at him. She took in his company uniform as well as Hargrave's.

"This some kind of a joke?" she asked. "There ain't no Cavaliers no more."

"We disagree," Hargrave said and swept his hands down his own uniform. "Where's Little Joe?"

"In the kitchen. There's a big group coming in this afternoon." She looked down at her slate and tapped at it. "You Jim?" she asked.

"That would be me." As if on cue, the door opened again; and First Sergeant Murdock came in with a tall woman, both laughing at some joke. Behind them were a dozen more. She looked at the growing crowd in surprise, then turned and yelled.

"Joe, Cartwright's is back!"

Shortly, every member of the Cartwright's Cavaliers was gathered in one of Little Joe's seldom-used banquet rooms. A couple of poorly maintained service robots were bustling about setting plates, silverware, and glasses full of ice water. When the places were set, the robots went around taking orders. Shortly thereafter, drinks and appetizers began to appear in abundance. The party was well underway.

The food showed up, plentiful and well-cooked, with a variety of real beef dishes, fresh fish, and all kinds of sides. The Cavaliers dug in with enthusiastic abandon. Finally, after a good hour of eating, the voracious mercs began to slow down. Deciding it was the right time, Jim stood up and clinked his wine glass with his fork. Slowly the conversation fell off.

"Cartwright's Cavaliers," he said loudly, "tonight we toast to rebirth. This company has been around since the dawn of our current era. Of all the companies who fought in the Alpha Wars, only four of us came back. And through all the intervening years, we've led the way to success after success." He looked down and thought about his next words. "It is ironic that it took deceit to bring us down, and it was even more ironic this deceit came from within. From one of us."

"She was *not* one of us," an older merc, who was one of the few who'd been part of the unit before, said. There was a chorus of agreements making Jim hold up both hands.

"No, she was one of us. My mother. What she did was wrong, but it's done. It's in the past," he said and thumped the table with both hands, making a serving robot jerk in surprise. "It's not a part of the future. You," he said looking around the room, catching everyone's eyes, "*you* are part of the future. Together, we'll make Cartwright's Cavaliers even greater than it was before. And I'll do my best to make that come true." Jim lifted his glass in toast.

A second later everyone in the room cheered and lifted their glass to salute back. Jim smiled and took a drink. Hargrave nodded to him, and Jim knew he'd said what needed to be said. A little bit later, Hargrave came over and sat next to him.

"Good job," he said and patted Jim on the arm.

"Thanks," Jim said. "I think we're ready to go."

Hargrave agreed. "The transports started taking off an hour ago." Jim liked the sound of that. "Captain Winslow elected to take command of the *Traveler* for this mission."

"That's good news too!"

"I agree," Hargrave said; "he's the perfect choice, and he has experience with the *Enterprise* class that the *Traveler* is based on." He took a drink of wine and grinned. "And one more thing. You know that squad sergeant position we didn't fill?"

"Yes, we were talking about whether we could promote a trooper to fill it."

"We don't have to do that now."

"You found someone?" Hargrave smiled again. "Is the person experienced?"

"You could say that." Hargrave looked at his personal communicator. "He's here now, just came down from his ship." Jim looked up as the banquet room opened, and a huge figure strode in, a giant duffel bag over his shoulder that looked like it weighed a ton.

"Lemmas, iki kaikua'ana!"

"Buddha!" Jim cried and leaped to his feet. The big man dropped his heavy bag with a thump and crossed the room to sweep Jim into a massive, bone-crushing hug.

"You have lost weight!" he said, swinging Jim back and forth.

"A little," Jim moaned as Buddha put him back on the floor. "I thought you were signed with the Band of the Grand?"

"I was. The CO let me out of my contract when I explained you needed me. If you do not, I can go back."

"No!" Jim laughed, "I'm glad you are here! Will you take First Squad, First Platoon?"

"By your side? I would have it no other way." He looked around and sniffed. "Is there more food?"

Hours later, the party had broken up, and many of the Cavaliers were already on their way back to the barracks to rest before heading up to orbit in the morning. Eventually it was only Hargrave, Buddha, and Jim. They all left together after Jim had paid the…rather startlingly large bill. He'd had more than his share of alcohol, something he'd seldom done. Despite this, he was no lightweight. Being a large man, Jim had the advantage of a lot of poundage to soak up alcohol. Even Murdock had given the kid his due when it came to drinking.

"Jim Cartwright?" someone called out as the group waited for their cab. Jim turned on somewhat unsteady legs, still laughing from an outrageously inappropriate joke Hargrave had just told. A woman was standing a few feet away holding something in her hand. Jim was still trying to figure out what it was when Hargrave and Buddha both stepped between him and the new arrival. Guns had appeared in both men's hands almost like magic. The woman, who was rather attractive, almost had a heart attack.

"Stop!" she yelled and slowly held out the thing in her hand so they could better see the compact recorder, the same type reporters commonly used. "I just want a word with the company commander of the Cartwright's Cavaliers." Even though she was shaken, she recovered her composure quickly.

"Sure," Hargrave said, and the gun disappeared. "How about 'Go. Away.'"

"That's two words," she said. "How about it, Mr. Cartwright?" She moved sideways, trying to get a clear view of Jim.

"It's okay," Jim said, "but no camera."

"Great," she said and put the device in her shoulder bag. Hargrave and Buddha looked at each other, then moved aside. Buddha looked even less thrilled than Hargrave. With a triumphant smile, she stepped forward.

"First, what's your name?" he asked her.

"Melanie O'Donnell, Aetherwave Live."

"Aethernet report, huh?" He gave her an appraising look. Young, not much older than him. Unlike a lot of Aethernet reporters, Aetherwave didn't employ just anyone. A reporter needed to have real chops to get on their feed. "You get three questions," Jim said, and glanced at the street, "or until our cab gets here." She looked slightly deflated as she checked the street. No cabs were in sight at that moment. "Better ask quickly."

"What's the hurry, Mr. Cartwright?"

"We have plans tomorrow," he said. She screwed up her face. "And that's one question." A hint of annoyance crossed her face.

"How did you manage to bring the Cavaliers back? You were broke! The bankruptcy took it all."

"A foundation endowed the company with some starter funds. Not much, but enough. Last question."

"Where's the Cavaliers' contract?"

"Off-world," Jim said and winked just as an oversized cab pulled up. "Good afternoon, Ms. O'Donnell." His men made sure he was the first on board and began piling in behind him. As the cab pulled away, Jim glanced back to see the reporter standing there, empty-handed and open-mouthed.

* * * * *

Chapter Thirteen

Four *Phoenix* dropships squatted on the airport tarmac, baking in the Texas heat. Unfortunately for the hundred-odd people standing around, nothing was getting done. Hargrave and Jim had spent the last few hours finalizing arrangements to keep the museum and its trust operating while they were all off-world. Of all the things they expected to find when they arrived at the hangars, four dropships sitting idle was not one of them.

"What the fuck is going on?" Hargrave asked as he jumped out of the vehicle. The chief pilot, Jane Wheeler, stood next to a support truck with her other three pilots drinking sodas and looking annoyed.

"You tell me," Jane replied. "We're still waiting on transports to take the deployment supplies up to the *Traveler*." She gestured to hundreds of pallets stacked outside the main operations hangar, loaders waiting next to them with their operators lounging as well.

"This was scheduled more than a week ago," Jim said, accessing the plans through his pinplants and confirming what he already knew. He and the senior staff had set up the schedules and turned everything over to logistics to plan and execute. "Where is Lieutenant Sommerkorn?" he asked. The chief logistics officer, Captain Zeamon, came over at a run.

"Commander, he's at the main starport terminal."

"What's he doing there, when he should be here?" Captain Zeamon looked both upset and somehow amused.

"He's trying to get us a heavy lifter." Jim and Hargrave exchanged looks.

"Maybe you should explain in more detail?" Hargrave asked. Jim had to smile – Hargrave looked more than a little uncomfortable in his new uniform, a silver oak leaf for second-in-command on his shoulder. Jim felt more than a little conspicuous with a silver eagle on his.

"Well, Mr. Sommerkorn created a logistics plan that was incredibly complex and well laid out. It had every aspect and detail accounted for down to the last man-hour of loading and lift to orbit."

"Then why do we have a few hundred tons of supplies sitting here cooking in the heat?" Hargrave asked.

"Because he was up late last night making a lot of revisions. He was sure if he kept working on it, he could cut the man-hours down and save some money. He fell asleep and never transmitted the lift orders to the contractor." Jim and Hargrave exchanged a look again. The logistics chief looked like he wanted to crawl under a dropship and bury himself. Jim considered the situation. While amusing on the surface, they were going to quickly lose their launch window, and that could cost them their position at the stargate. Since Earth was such a small system, the stargate matched its importance. It only cycled once every twelve hours. You could order an expedited jump, but that was expensive with a capital E. In the end, he decided fuel was cheaper than time.

"Hargrave, get a platoon of men in the CASPers, we need to get this giant moveable feast in the air."

"Yes, sir," Hargrave said. "First Sergeant?" Murdock was standing a respectful distance away pretending not to listen.

"Sir?"

"Get a platoon armored up, loading detail. Combat deployment speed. Five minutes!"

"Yes, sir," he said and saluted. "Sergeant Buddha!" The big man came ambling over. His uniform was slightly nonstandard; as in it was cutoffs and short sleeves. He liked the sun on his skin.

"Yes, First Sergeant?" he said, coming to casual attention and winking at Jim who grinned.

"Get your platoon armored up, loading detail. Combat deployment speed. Five minutes!"

"Yes, sir!" Buddha said, saluted, turned, and ran. Jim had never seen him run before. He was amazingly quick. "First Platoon, get in your armor! Move it, shovelheads!"

Jim had never watched the men do a combat deployment, and that was basically how they were treating it. The suits were hanging from their loading racks, no weapons or field gear. In a way, they were just super-heavy versions of the loaders used in starports. Smaller and weaker, but much tougher and faster. In less than five minutes, all twenty men and their platoon sergeant were in armor, including Murdock. The *Phoenix* dropships were manned, and their cargo doors open, noses popped and angled upwards allowing access from front, rear, and both sides all at once.

With incredible quickness and order, fifteen of the suited men began to grab crates and, using their jumpjets, bounded back and forth between the hangar and the ships. They would set the crates down and bound back, jumping higher than they had carrying the crates, thus passing over others coming toward the ships. The other seven formed a loading brigade with five passing crates between them up and into the ship, where the last two stowed them. It took just under ten minutes from the initial order to when the first *Phoenix* was fully loaded.

"Loaded and stowed," Jane Wheeler called out from the open cockpit. Jim shielded his eyes as he looked up at her. She had her flight helmet on, and her copilot was in the seat above and behind her busily flipping switches.

"Boost for orbit," Hargrave ordered. "Return ASAP after offload. The *Traveler*'s crew is waiting."

"Aye, sir!" she said, and a second later the ship's four hydrogen-powered lift fans spun to life. In a second, the drone became a yowl, then a scream. A moment later, it lifted off and angled down the tarmac in a storm of dust. Everyone on the ground either turned away or shielded their eyes. The dropship picked up speed down the runway until its forward momentum was enough to provide lift, then the fan's power was ducted entirely out the rear. Full power was applied and Jane pulled back on her stick. With a thunderous roar the *Phoenix* turned its nose spaceward and shot into the blue. It was out of sight in seconds.

Back on the tarmac, the platoon was well into loading the second dropship. Jim marveled at how well they worked together, both smoothly and without wasted effort. Thinking back to the couple of times he'd donned the CASPers, he was coming to realize just how little he knew about the suits.

The second dropship was loaded much faster, the first one requiring some time to organize the effort. The third about the same as the second, and the last was quicker still, only holding their medical team, their equipment, and other non-combat personnel. As *Phoenix* 4 shot into the sky, multiple sonic shockwaves announced the return of *Phoenix 1*. Jim checked his time schedule. They were only a few minutes behind their planned launch time.

"As soon as number one touches down, get Second Platoon First Squad's racks and personnel aboard." Hargrave nodded. "We're going to have to use ground loaders on the last squad," he said and made a face. But Hargrave shook his head.

"Won't work," he said, "no way to fit them and troopers out of their suits." Jim scrunched up his face as he used his pinplants to compare spaces. Hargrave was right, of course.

"Shit. We can't leave any troopers behind; we'll be under strength. I guess that means we'll need another dropship to make a third run."

"Just leave behind one of the CASPer racks," Hargrave suggested. The racks were designed to hold the suits for quick donning by their wearers. Essential for quick deployment and easy maintenance. "We can maybe improvise something aboard the *Traveler* in route."

"Okay," Jim said, "I'll go with that." He gave the order, and as *Phoenix 2* came in, *Phoenix 1* was taking off with its cargo bay completely taken up by suits and racks. The next two were the same, as *Phoenix 4* returned. "Everyone aboard, last squad stay in suits. Lock in deployment harness in the dropship, the rest of us will squeeze in."

Hargrave went around to make sure each of the suited CASPers were locked into the frame built into the dropship bulkheads. With a couple dozen unarmored humans in the central area of the ship, if any of them came unstuck from the wall, people would die. The *Phoenix* had the room to carry an entire platoon of CASPers – the manual said as much. It also said the manufacturer strongly advised against it, just as it advised against carrying unprotected human cargo. Finally, everyone was aboard. Well, almost everyone.

"Sir," Hargrave said, "what about Mr. Sommerkorn?" Jim looked surprised, in all the confusion and rush to load he'd completely forgotten about the overly-detailed logistics man.

"Can we operate on mission without him?" Hargrave laughed. "Right, okay. I guess he stays."

"Terminate him?" Hargrave asked after giving the order to lift off. He had to yell, it was almost as loud inside the dropship as it had been outside when the craft took off. Jim reviewed the man's record. He seemed a capable man. His fitness reports were accurate, though unbelievably wordy. His commanders' only negative notes were things to the extent of "a little too detail-oriented." Jim now thought he understood what that meant.

"Yes, please close his contract. Inform Personnel to put a letter of recommendation from me in his file and discharge him." Jim shrugged. He figured the man would find a job in another company and maybe learn from his experience. Reviewing the deployment spreadsheet, this had only cost them a few hundred credits over the fees a heavy lifter would have run. Maybe it had been a useful exercise as well. He hoped the man would do well in his future endeavors.

Two hours later a cab pulled up to the hangar that had once been full of pre-deployment men, equipment, and combat gear. Lieutenant Chris Sommerkorn got out and looked at the hangar and lack of dropships in confusion. A few of Cartwright's personnel were finishing stowing ground servicing equipment and doing other duties associated with putting the facility to bed until it was needed again. He walked over to one of them who looked curious to see one of the combat arm of the company show up, in uniform, when all the others were long gone.

"Excuse me," Sommerkorn said, "uh...where did the company go?"

* * * * *

Chapter Fourteen

As they were already behind schedule, the *Traveler* powered up her main drive and, as soon as the last drop-ship was locked in its cradle in the cruiser's cavernous main bay, began thrusting out of orbit.

"Are we going to make it?" Jim asked Captain Winslow over the cargo hold's squawk box. He and everyone else in view was holding onto whatever they could find as the huge ship quickly went from null gravity to over one gravity of acceleration.

"We'll make her, Sah," the man replied in his crisp British accent. "I'll need to push her up to 3G once everything is secure aboard."

Jim turned to Hargrave and Zeamon. "Can we offload safely in hyperspace?"

"No problem," Hargrave said. Zeamon nodded in agreement.

"Captain, give us five minutes to get this gear secured and for us to get to our stations, then go to full thrust. We'll finish unloading the equipment once we're in hyperspace."

"Understood," the captain replied. A second later a claxon sounded, and a woman's voice came over the PA.

"Attention all hands, acceleration in five minutes. Repeat, prepare for high gravity acceleration in *five minutes*."

The hold came alive with men moving quickly. Those less familiar with orbital operations moved toward their assigned acceleration stations, others helped the logistics staff and the *Traveler*'s load master make sure all the hundreds of crates and CASPers were secured.

At three gravities, even a single hundred-pound crate coming loose could do serious damage to personnel and cargo inside a ship. Jim, feeling like a fifth wheel, headed for the bridge, which was his combat station as commander.

He'd only been up to the *Traveler* once, a few days earlier, to do a last-minute inspection and declare the ship operational. Even after his father commissioned *Bucephalus*, *Traveler* was still licensed with the Traders' Guild. She'd been mothballed in orbit because that was the best place to keep her safe and secure, owned and maintained by the family trust, and well out of his mother's grasp.

The ship was thirteen hundred feet long – shaped like a truncated barbell with cylindrical hulls extending out from both ends. One narrowed to a dull point; the other flared a bit into a fan shape, where the ship's propulsion sat. The bulges of the barbell were the ship's two gravity decks. As a warship, it had held a massive armament, multiple drone decks, and a crew complement in excess of a thousand. As the Cavaliers' mercenary cruiser, most of the armament was gone along with all the drones. It was designed now to service a complement of up to four platoons, or two company-sized ground assault units. It operated with a crew of only fifty-two; not having to wrangle dozens of weapons systems and space combat drones helped.

The bridge was at the center of the ship, as with all warships, surrounded by the heaviest bulk of the vessel; decks upon decks of super tough alloys stood between the bridge and any enemy's weapons. Many aliens ignored gravity in their warship designs, but humans preferred to operate within a fixed frame of reference. The bridge was designed such that thrust-created gravity provided the crew with a point of orientation. Whenever the ship was under thrust, they knew their feet were always toward the rear of the ship.

Captain Winslow sat in the command chair, an array of Tri-V displays circling him at eye level. On the screens, he could see everything about the ship's operation as well as the course and nearby battlespace. The bridge crew were spread out in equally ergonomic workstations, mostly virtual like the captain's. Hard screens were folded into recesses, should damage or other problems require their use. The bridge crew was the only part of the ship's complement which was larger now, instead of smaller.

"Attention all hands, thrust begins in one minute. One minute."

"How's *Traveler*, Captain?" Jim asked as he took one of the open seats to the side of the captain's.

"All systems nominal, sir," Winslow replied. "Fuel reserves are sufficient for this increased delta-v."

"Very good," Jim said and set his safety harness. A moment later Hargrave came in and hurried to take the seat next to him.

"We're secured in the landing bay," Hargrave said. "All troopers and support are reporting in," he added as a screen came up showing crew status.

"Attention all hands, thrust begins in ten seconds." The computer pivoted their seats back to nearly perpendicular with the deck. "Thrust begins," the computer said, and it did.

The trip took three jumps total to reach the Kash-Kah system. *Traveler* had good legs, as Captain Winslow described it. They made two completed jumps before needing to stop at a station and refuel.

176 | MARK WANDREY

"We have thousands of hours' worth of F11," Winslow explained. "The reactor was flushed right before she was put to bed."

"More planning?" Jim asked Hargrave, who just smiled.

The captain took a little more time in the intervening system, preferring to accelerate at zero point eight from the arrival spot to the stargate. It allowed the crew to enjoy gravity and keep in top readiness for their arrival. When they stopped just before the final jump to refuel, no shore leave was granted.

"Keep them fresh," Hargrave advised. "That jump is 170 hours, but it'll go fast as we begin to prepare for deployment. We've had an update from the Duplato, and we know they haven't been hit in a while. We don't know what to expect." Jim considered Hargrave's advice well worth taking. There were no complaints from the men.

Once they were refueled and back in hyperspace, the ship and crew began preparation for combat in earnest. All the CASPers were gone over in detail, their operators doing final checkouts. Jim got another chance to watch Adayn Christopher working on the suits. She had a team of ten but seemed to always be in the middle of everything – standing at a testing station, running for a part, or hip deep in a suit checking some function or another.

Jim had a few minutes in his own suit, being extremely careful with his movements as he walked it into *Phoenix 1* in preparation for deployment. Once they were all safely in their mounts inside dropships, the ordinance teams went to work arming the suits. Each suit was equipped with their designated weaponry – lasers, rockets, area denial explosives, or magnetic accelerator cannons. Some carried multiple weapons. Murdock's CASPer fairly bristled with firepower, as did Buddha's and Sergeant Rodriguez's. As the *Traveler* approached Kash-Kah, all work came to a stop.

"All crew to combat stations," the computer announced as the lighting took on a red tinge and a claxon sounded three times. "All crew to combat stations. Hyperspace emergence in five minutes." Jim buckled into his seat on the bridge, his pulse pounding in his ear and sweat breaking out on his forehead.

"Everyone ready?" Captain Winslow asked as he constantly scanned status screens. "Report."

"Shields ready."

"Weapons ready."

"Tactical ready."

"Navigation ready."

"Engineering ready."

"Troopers ready," Jim called out last.

"Very good," the captain said. "Emergence in five...four...ready...steady..." There was an instant of distortion and the stars popped back into view on the wrap-around displays.

"Clean emergence," Navigation announced, "position is nominal." They'd arrived where they were supposed to be.

"Very good," Captain Winslow said. "Helm, set course for Kash-Kah Four, one gravity constant."

"We have a bogey in our threat bubble!" Tactical called out. A large Tri-V display oriented in front of the captain came alive with a 3-D representation of space around *Traveler*. Kash-Kah Three was on one extreme edge while a few larger asteroids were in the intermediate range, still within L2, which was that system's emergence point. There was a flashing red point near the closest asteroid.

"What do we have?" Captain Winslow asked.

"Working it," Tactical announced. Jim could see the team of three bridge crew members manipulating sensor data trying to identify the bogey.

"It's moving," Jim noted to Hargrave sitting next to him. The older man nodded and tightened his restraints. "Maybe it's a local asteroid miner?" Hargrave shook his head no.

"The locals don't possess any type of spacecraft," Hargrave said.

"The bogey is accelerating," Tactical confirmed. "Approximately nine gravities."

"Oh, shit," Jim hissed.

"Prepare for combat," Captain Winslow said. "Helm, reverse our course, match their approach. Engineering, full power to the reactor. Shields, forward shields at maximum. Weapons, load the tubes for anti-missile fire." All the bridge stations burst into action.

"The contact is splitting," Tactical said. "Designating Bogeys 1, 2, 3, and 4. They are at 1.4 light seconds and accelerating toward intercept."

"Acknowledged," Captain Winslow said. "We have four bogies on the board. Transmit in the clear, please." He waited a moment for the radio to be engaged. "This is *EMS Traveler*, in the Kash-Kah system on a sanctioned contract. Unidentified craft, kindly identify." Seconds passed as the distance closed faster and faster. "*EMS Traveler* here, if you do not state your non-hostile intentions, we will deploy defensive tactics."

"Is this smart?" Jim asked. "They're closing fast!"

"It's standard procedure," Hargrave replied. "You can't just light someone up if they fly at you."

"Earth vessel," a translated voice rang out on the bridge, "you will deactivate your defensive systems and prepare to surrender your craft."

"Identify yourself or be declared hostile," Captain Winslow insisted. "This is your last warning."

"Distance 1 light second," Tactical said. "Bogeys 3 and 4 are maneuvering radically."

"I'm declaring these as valid combat targets," Captain Winslow said. "Enter it in the log, please."

"Logged," the computer automatically responded.

"Very well," he said. "Tactical, prepare a firing solution. Charge main particle cannon. Helm, prepare for combat maneuvers. Get the ship ready for incoming."

"Attention," the speakers boomed. "All stations set Condition ZEBRA!" Throughout the ship, all the air-tight doors slid closed, minimizing potential damage if the hull was pierced. "All hands, prepare for possible radical acceleration." Jim's seat angled back slightly, and he felt pads raise along his arms, legs, and chest.

"Hang on, son," Hargrave said.

"What can a ship this size do against ships that small and fast?" he asked.

"Watch," Hargrave said.

"Tactical has a solution." Up on the board, the four enemies approaching grew flashing blue cones ahead of them, and yellow dotted lines within the cones.

"Blue is their possible maneuvers based on data we have," Hargrave explained. "Yellow is the predicted course." The two bogeys that had split off showed blue cones that enveloped *Traveler*, but yellow dots that passed by. The two still coming straight at them had huge blue cones covering half the sky, and yellow dots that also passed close by.

"We believe they're going for a maximum-closing-speed pass to use velocity bombs," Tactical advised.

"Thank you," the captain said. "Weapons, firing range?"

"Ten seconds," the Chief Weapons Officer said. "Charged and standing by."

"How long can they handle that kind of acceleration?" Jim wondered. Nine gravities? That was insane.

"Humans, not long. Some aliens, no problem all day." As the seconds ticked by, the blue cones and yellow dots made minor adjustments. When it was one second from the main battery range, the two targets coming straight at them suddenly exploded into a hundred targets.

"They're jamming," Tactical announced.

"Confirmation yet on the bogey classification?"

"Still working," Tactical replied. A moment later. "Missile launch detected!" A pair of tiny flashing red points lanced away from the interference around the two coming at them.

"Launch anti-missiles," the captain ordered. Tiny bumps reverberated through the hull as anti-missile missiles were launched. On the board, four green dots reached out from the *Traveler* toward the incoming red dots. Jim watched with wide eyes as the two marks came abreast, and each of their missiles flashed. It only took a moment, and all the enemy missiles were gone.

"We have laser impacts on the forward shields," Shields announced. "Estimated twenty-megawatt yield."

"Update on aggressors," Tactical announced immediately. "They are Zuul Type Two corvettes. Estimate has high confidence." A Tri-

V showed the probable ships: cylindrical pods with stubby wings and missile bays. Fast and deadly looking. A list to the side showed capabilities including ECM, electronic countermeasures jamming, maximum ten gravities acceleration, missile bays with five ship-killers each, and a single dorsal-mounted twenty-megawatt laser.

"Thank you," the captain said. "Reload tubes two and four with ship-killers. Let's drop their numbers, shall we? Helm, skew turn to bring main batteries to bear on Bogey 4. Weapons, fire as we come to bear."

A klaxon sounded a warning and suddenly Jim squeaked in surprise as more than five gravities slammed him down and sideways. *Traveler* danced sideways in a maneuver far in excess of its initial design parameters. The engineers with Cartwright's Cavaliers, upon taking possession of the ship, had stripped off all offensive weaponry. The much lighter ship was then able to be fitted with structural reinforcements and engine improvements.

"Firing!" The lights dimmed as ten gigawatts of energy poured from one of the ship's two main particle accelerator turrets. "Slam dunk," Weapons called. Bogey four flashed out into a cone of expanding debris.

"Good kill. Fire missiles on Bogey 3."

"Birds away," Weapons announced. Again, green dots flashed away from *Traveler* toward Bogey 3 which began to spin and evade at the maximum ten Gs. *Traveler*'s forward shields recognized hit after hit from the two other corvettes that were all but invisible at the moment. The hits were insignificant; the ship could absorb hundreds of such shots.

"Alter orientation to Bogeys 1 and 2," the captain ordered and Jim gritted his teeth as *Traveler* once again spun and thrust at full

182 | MARK WANDREY

power, coming around almost 180 degrees end-over-end. The missile flashed, and another bogey disappeared.

"Grand slam with birds," Weapons said.

"Very good," Captain Winslow said, "Get a seeker in the black so we can get a weapons lock on Bogeys 1 and 2."

"Seeker away," Tactical said.

"Sensor drone," Hargrave told Jim. As the little dot of the seeker raced toward the uncertainty of the jamming, false readings began to disappear one after another until good data was left.

"Missiles inbound," Tactical announced. "Tracking 8 inbound missiles."

"Bollocks," the captain cursed. "Fire what anti-missiles we have, and prepare for impact."

"We've resolved Bogeys 1 and 2," Tactical announced. "Main batteries are almost to bearing."

"Abort shot," the captain said, "maneuver to evade incoming missile tracks."

Once more, the warning klaxon sounded, and the *Traveler* danced on her tail in a change of delta-*v* only a ship one quarter her size should have been able to accomplish. Jim gritted his teeth as nearly six gravities crushed his body into the acceleration couch. Around them, the ship moaned like the bones of an ancient dragon awakening to find its treasure had been pillaged.

"Two, no three incoming missiles intercepted!" Tactical gasped between gulps of air. Jim tried to look around, but his head had sunk half a foot into the liquid padding of the chair. All he could see was the main situation board that showed five nuclear missiles still streaking toward them. "Point defenses are engaging!" Small one-megawatt lasers mounted all around the hull pulsed like machineguns in a last-ditch defense to destroy or disable the missiles before they could detonate. "Three have stopped tracking, two are still live."

"Brace for impact!" Captain Winslow said. The ship gave one more sudden roll and thrust. An instant later one of the missiles splashed against the shields without detonating. The eighth (and final) missile, however, turned into a miniature sun as it passed close aboard the cruiser. Although it didn't hit the ship, the cruiser was close enough to be within the blast radius of the missile, and Jim could have sworn he saw the flash through the hull as several pounds of radioactive material went supercritical and released a megaton of pure explosive force. In a microsecond, the radiation washed over the shields, turning them pure white, with the shockwave right behind.

The blast struck the ship at the port bow, a tidal wave of force creating sudden reverse acceleration that slammed crewmen against their restraints, broke tie downs, sent cargo flying, and stressed the hull's internal structure to its limits. All the bridge screens flashed white and then returned to normal function. Thrust immediately fell off to less than one gravity, and everyone shook their heads to clear the cobwebs.

"Bogey 1 and 2 have evaded," Tactical announced. "They should be out of missiles as well."

"Very well," Captain Winslow said. "Damage report?"

"We have minor structural damage in the forward sections," Engineering announced. "We have minor pressure loss ahead of frame twelve. Shield generators four, five, and nine are overloaded. No damage indicators, but it will probably take an hour to reset them properly."

"Dispatch damage-control parties to assess the structural damage and see to the pressure loss."

"What about the other two bogeys?" Jim asked, still shaking with adrenaline. The captain looked at him.

"We're maneuverable, sir, but they have the advantage." On the board, the very ships they were talking about were reacquired by the seeker missile, well on their way back toward the asteroid they'd come from.

"We can catch them," Jim said, "and obviously, the raiders have a base."

"Jim," Hargrave cautioned.

"No," Jim said and held up a hand. "I want to know why we don't finish them."

"It's simple," the captain explained. "This is a cruiser, but it isn't armed and equipped as a cruiser. We don't have any fighters, and we don't have the firepower we once did. We're lighter, faster, and better shielded. If we didn't have the shields we do, that ship-killer would have done us in. As it is, we're hurt and down three main shield generators. Another missile like that and we're a radioactive cloud. Those two corvettes," he pointed at the screen where the last two bogeys were retreating, though not too quickly, "are baiting us. They either have more corvettes, fighters, or maybe their own capital ship skulking behind that rock. If we pursued..."

"They'd ambush us," Jim finished. The captain nodded.

"You handle smashing things on the ground," Winslow said sternly, then gave him a little wink. "I'll get you there. Deal?"

"Deal," Jim agreed.

* * * * *

Chapter Fifteen

Kash-Kah was a glittering ball of white with swirls of cotton candy clouds orbiting in the abyss of space. Tiny spots of green showed where volcanic vents created zones with sufficient heat to allow plants to grow on the surface. The Duplato had evolved under the ice and snow, in caverns where they learned fungiculture and raised subterranean animal flocks. Slowly they'd gained some level of science. The Galnet didn't tell how the Duplato had first been contacted. Considering how they lived, Jim didn't think the Duplato were capable of mounting a flight to orbit, and surely not one outside their solar system.

Traveler took up a geosynchronous orbit over the chief industrial complex of the Duplato's largest settlement and established communications with the ground.

"Cartwright's Cavaliers, we welcome you," replied the Duplato representative. "Your arrival is as arranged, and we are glad. A large amount of ore is nearly refined and ready for delivery. This is when the raiders typically strike."

"This is Jim Cartwright, commanding the Cavaliers. Please acknowledge for the record your recognition of our arrival, meeting the primary line of the contract."

"We gratefully acknowledge," they responded right away. "When will you be landing?" Jim glanced at Hargrave. They were in the company planning room, directly adjacent to the main hold. Numerous Tri-V displays were showing approaches to the planet's surface, combat resources, and noncombat resources. Hargrave held up two fingers.

"We'll be ready to land in about two hours."

"Thank you again, Cavaliers. We are honored to have such a storied mercenary company as yours coming to our aid." The connection was severed.

"We're not nearly as storied as we used to be," Jim mumbled as he typed in the data informing the logistics team they would be landing in two hours and instructing them to prepare the dropships. "Are you sure this plan of leaving Second Platoon in orbit is the best one?"

"I think it's wise," Hargrave said. "They can deploy to the surface in under twenty minutes. More importantly, from up here, more than half the planet's surface is only a few minutes further away. We'll have First Platoon and both APCs. If and when the raiders attack, we'll push them back, and then Second Platoon can drop behind their position. We'll have them in a nice, tidy box." Jim chewed his lip and nodded. For some reason, he didn't like the idea, but the books on modern tactics he'd read and Hargrave's decades of experience agreed.

"Okay," Jim affirmed with a sigh. "We have a plan."

"Good," Hargrave said. "Better go get suited up."

"Are you sure we have to deploy in CASPers? Seems a bit excessive."

"Wouldn't do for the Cavaliers to come in on foot, now would it? These beings paid for a merc unit, not tourists." Jim nodded again and floated into the changing room. He emerged in a few minutes in his haptic uniform. Hargrave was already waiting for him wearing his own. Jim nervously looked around, all too aware of how the special uniform was basically form fitted to his body. "Don't worry kid, just remember Murdock's lessons, and you'll do fine. You don't have to fight, just walk down the ramp."

"I'll do my best." The deployment bell chimed three times.

"Time to go."

The platoon troopers, in their suits, clomped up the ramps into the dropships. Jim, the commander, and his 1SGT were the last aboard. It was surprisingly easy to maneuver the suits in micro gravity – as long as you moved slowly to avoid sending your suit into a spin, the internal gyros would compensate. Jim fumbled a bit as he pushed back into the bulkhead lock, but finally heard it click and felt his suit pulled into the wall niche. The displays projected on the front of his protective cockpit showed a good connection, and data was fed to him from the dropship's command network.

"Cavalier Actual," he called over the radio link. "We're aboard and secured."

"Roger, Commander," was Jane Wheeler's reply. "*Phoenix 1* and *2* are ready to deploy." He felt the ship jostle as the hold's crane moved it toward the deployment cradle.

"First Platoon, call out!" Murdock's voice rang over the platoon channel. Second Squad from the other dropship was first to call off finishing with the senior corporal. Next came his own dropship ending with Buddha and himself. "All troopers present and accounted for, Commander." There was a jarring shudder as *Phoenix 1* locked into its cradle in the drop position.

"Very well," Jim said, managing to keep a quaver out of his voice, though only just. "This is Cavalier Actual...drop, drop, drop."

The drop cradles were locks built into the hull in the cargo holds of the *Traveler*. Clamshell doors were fixed with magnetic bolts that could be triggered by the drop leader. At the press of a button, the bolts released with explosive force, the atmospheric pressure of the hold blew the doors open, and the dropships were shot from the cradles into space, the air pressure acting like a gun. Inside the dropship, there was instant acceleration of nearly 3Gs and an almost incredibly loud roar as the ships were fired into space, followed by the sudden and all-encompassing silence of the void.

Expelled from the hold, the acceleration from the initial shove of exploding atmosphere went away as they plummeted toward the planet. Jim's command feed provided him with images from the cockpit. The planet was rushing toward them at a startling rate.

"Was a combat drop really necessary?" Jim asked Hargrave over the command circuit. The entire squad chuckled in reply. Jim shook his head. "You bastards," he said laughing along with them.

"Commander's first combat drop," someone said.

"Yee-haw!" someone else screamed, and others whooped and hollered. The dropship lurched violently as it hit the upper atmosphere of Kash-Kah.

"Now the fun begins," Murdock said.

Hooked into mounts on the side of the dropship's hold and standing upright, the troopers experienced the sudden and frightening deceleration of the dropship as sideways force. It went from a barely perceptible force to three Gs in a matter of seconds.

"Glide path is nominal," Jane Wheeler said over the squad network. Jim had access to the flight data from the cockpit. He could see their flightpath as a curve that leveled out and reversed after several minutes, but the height of the curve, indicating G forces, was still ahead of them.

"How many G's can the *Phoenix* take?" he asked her.

"Oh, the book says twelve," she replied, "but I've pulled fourteen a few times during hot drops. Bent the wings on one about thirty years ago. My uncle was pissed." She laughed, and sounded genuinely amused. Jim shuddered.

As the glide path predicted, the ride got more jarring, and the G forces worsened until they topped out at just under six. Jim clenched his jaws and shut off his radio so no one could hear him whining in fear. The forces had him crushed against the left side of his suit. It was padded, but not like the gel seat on *Traveler*'s bridge. It was just a half inch of dense foam. There were going to be bruises. He understood the nano-therapy even better now.

He'd made one small modification to his suit's interior. Through extreme effort, he was able to turn his head just enough that he could see it. Fixed to the instrument readouts on the far right was a miniature stuffed animal with a rainbow tail. It stood out sideways from the string connecting it to the emergency canopy release.

"Hang in there, Dash," he said through gritted teeth. And just like that, the gravity began to finally decrease.

It wasn't a real combat drop. If it was, Jane would have flown almost straight down and then pulled up low to the ground, opened the side-drop doors, and the CASPers would have spilled out fast. Instead, Jane brought them in low and slow, using the dropship's lift fans to showcase the *Phoenix's* short takeoff and landing ability. She landed on the industrial complex's runway and taxied toward a series of low hangars. Compared to the drop from orbit, it was a piece of cake. Jim toggled his radio back on.

"You did fine," Hargrave said and patted his suit on the shoulder with a clunk.

"Asshole," Jim said, only half-jokingly.

"Clear and locked," Jane announced from the cockpit, and they could hear the engines spinning down even inside their suits.

"Prepare to disembark," Jim ordered.

"You heard the CO," Murdock said, releasing his clamps and dropping a foot to the reinforced deck with a resounding clang. He tramped to the rear gate that was already rotating open. "Let's move it, shovelheads."

All the way in the back, Jim activated his CASPer's full power and released the clamps. He didn't stick the landing like his First Sergeant, but he managed not to fall on his face before turning and following the older man. At the bottom of the ramp, Murdock stood to the side just short of the world's soil. He came to attention and waited. It had been tradition that a Cartwright was always the first to set foot on a world in a contract, and the last to leave.

"Ready, sir," Murdock said. Jim threw a quick salute with his suit's arm and stepped onto the concrete tarmac, which was dusted with snow. The Cavaliers were aground.

"Disembark them into the garrison building," Jim said and pointed with the suit arm. The building was just as specified in the contract. Standard Union design, built by robots in hours. It would have the internal facilities necessary to maintain the entire company, even though only half were on the ground. A small ground-effect car of a common design was buzzing down the runway. *Phoenix 2* was parking a short distance away. The car came to a stop, and four Duplato climbed out and approached in their strange short-legged gait.

"We welcome the Cavaliers," one spoke, "I am known as Klent, industrial leader of the Duplato. These are my assistants." They were all thickly furred, yet still wore heavy cloaks. Jim wasn't surprised they needed the protection, his environmental sensors said the temperature was hovering around -11 degrees Fahrenheit. "There have been no signs of the raiders. We were expecting...Thaddeus Cartwright?" Klent said with some confusion.

"This is Thaddeus' son, Jim," Hargrave said, coming up from behind. "I'm his XO." The alien observed them both with tiny black eyes as both dropships finished unloading troopers who then started moving ordinance.

"And the other platoon? The contract was for two."

"They are in our cruiser," Jim explained. "We were attacked immediately after transitioning to your system."

"Is this true?" Klent asked, as his aides jabbered excitedly. "The raiders have never harassed space traffic before."

"Because the transports had escort," Hargrave explained. "We were a single ship, and they attacked with a squadron of corvettes. They thought they could get the upper hand."

"But you won?" Klent asked.

"Call it a draw," Jim said. "We believe they have a larger ship or a base in one of the asteroids near L2. They knew we were coming."

"Mercenary contracts are public record," Hargrave noted for them, though Jim already knew that. "Whoever is raiding your shipments isn't happy that you've hired us."

"Perhaps," Klent said, "now that you have deployed, they will consider it too risky?"

"Unlikely," Murdock grumbled.

"Klent, this is my First Sergeant, Murdock," Jim introduced him.

"They lost some of their corvettes, and those aren't cheap," Murdock postulated. "They'll want to recoup their costs."

"If you would join us in the garrison headquarters," Jim indicated the structure, "we can get out of this winter cold to discuss defenses, and you can share more details on previous attacks."

"Winter?" Klent wondered. "Commander, this is a lovely spring day." As they tramped toward the buildings, Jim shivered despite the heat provided by his suit's environmental system. What must their winter be like?

Inside the facilities, living conditions were tolerable, if not warm. Jim guessed the temperature to be around 60 degrees Fahrenheit, give or take a bit. The Duplato immediately removed their cloaks and slung them around their waists while Jim, Hargrave, and Murdock parked their CASPers in a long garage that would eventually hold all the planet-side suits. The two men extracted themselves and easily slid-jumped down to the floor. Jim, on the other hand, never quite mastered that technique. Adayn had installed a rope ladder accessible just inside the hatchway. Klent and his assistants waited patiently as Jim did his best not to look like a fool climbing down. He largely succeeded.

Even with his extra body padding, Jim immediately felt chilled. Though their haptic uniforms were made of advanced wicking fabric, the combat drop had left him somewhat sweaty. The cool air hit him like a winter gale, and he instantly began shivering. By the looks on Hargrave and Murdock's face, they weren't very comfortable either. He caught Hargrave's eye.

"We need to add cold weather gear to the CASPers," he said, and Hargrave nodded. The suits were large enough to have several external storage compartments. They held various survival aids as well as some limited repair equipment.

"That's a good idea," Hargrave said and made a note. "It's possible we could become disabled outside. A trooper would freeze to death in hours." Part of the survival equipment was a sleeping bag and heater, but it wasn't designed for this extreme an environment. More troopers were clomping into the far end of the garage, opening the doors and sending an even colder wind blasting through. "Let's go see what info they have."

The briefing only took an hour. The Duplato had some images taken from the last raid, months ago, as well as the first attack long before that. The first attack involved the corvettes, which Jim remarked would have been nice to know about in hindsight. The second attack was led by a number of medium tanks of several different designs.

"This isn't what I expected," Hargrave said, shaking his head.

"What do you mean?" Jim asked. Hargrave pointed to one image that showed a pair of tanks rolling across the snowy plain just outside the Duplato's tank farm. One was a multi-wheeled affair similar to the old American Stryker design, the other a ground-effect hover-tank that was a newer design. Both had numerous men riding them in standard combat armor. Hargrave enhanced the image to show one of the group of riders. Just like the tanks, their armor varied in design.

"The theory about them being a rogue merc unit doesn't add up, does it?" Jim asked. Both Murdock and Hargrave shook their heads no. "So what are they – some group of criminals? Pirates?"

"Pirates tend to stay mobile," Hargrave said, "attacking shipping or doing lightning raids on remote locations. This," he said and indicated the Tri-V screens, "is neither. Despite the age and haphazardness of the equipment, it's all good enough to do the job."

"Then what?" Jim asked again. Neither of them had an answer to that. "Well, the transport for the next delivery of radioactives is in two weeks, yes?" Hargrave nodded. "We can probably expect something by then. Let's get moved in and prepare. Have *Traveler* send down the anti-aircraft and APC when *Phoenix 1* and *2* get back up. We should be hot ASAP, just in case." He looked at the tanks again. "Shifts are twelve-on, twelve-off. We can't afford to have less than a full squad on alert at any time. That means they're in the ready room outside the garage, not playing cards or watching Tri-V."

"Agreed," Murdock said.

"After the next transport comes and leaves, if these raiders haven't attacked, we'll rotate the platoons," Jim ordered. Everyone agreed on the plan. "Maybe they'll decide we're too much for them." Even though he'd been the one to say it, he wasn't at all convinced that was how it would go.

The platoon was moved in and ready in under twenty-four hours. The planetary day on Kash-Kah was just over twenty-nine hours, which made for a difficult period of adjustment. Within three days, most of the men were showing signs of fatigue.

Since many of the troopers were inexperienced, the command staff put the extra time to good use by developing a series of training exercises. The locals used geo-thermal power, so there was no reason to ration power for their suits, and it freed the unit from bringing down a portable fusion plant, which would have been a tactical liability. Training began in earnest.

Jim split his time between operations and training in his suit. As the first week drew to a close, he was overjoyed to be able to execute a short jump without face-planting in the snow outside the garrison.

He had a brief but interesting tour of the Duplato city near the industrial facility as well. They preferred it cool and dark. As a result, the Cavaliers on the tour had to wear LI goggles – Light Intensifying vision wear. These were standard equipment on deployments and were kept in the equipment bays of the CASPers as well. The Duplato city was mostly invisible – dug into cavern walls or out of live stone – but there were places that provided beautiful vistas over larger caverns, some with vast fields of stalactites and stalagmites and long underground rivers or lakes. Some had fields of carefully cultivated fungal growth, some bioluminescent. It was alien but beautiful.

The humans preferred their own food, though they sampled some of the local fare. The fungal staples were okay – at least those they could eat. The meats tended to be strong in taste, but a sort of meatball with fungus proved edible and popular. One of the Cartwright's chefs incorporated them into a pasta dish that became an overnight favorite. The Duplato were good hosts, and appeared honestly grateful to have the Cavaliers on station, though, like most species, they didn't really understand the mindset required to make warfare a lifestyle.

By the end of the first week, everyone had adjusted to the new day/night cycle as best they could. Nights were now a uniform ten-hour sleep cycle, and that meant a nineteen-hour awake cycle. Often troopers looked like zombies as the nineteenth hour approached, and on Hargrave's suggestion they were all issued stimulant packs should an alert happen in the hours before a shift change, which was con-

196 | MARK WANDREY

sidered the highest risk of activity. As the second week wore on, Jim decided to rotate First Platoon back to orbit so that Second could get adjusted to the new environment. Of course, that was when the raiders arrived.

* * * * *

Chapter Sixteen

J im checked the spreadsheet floating over his desk for the sixth time before he realized he'd read the same page of data yet again without absorbing a single bit of it. He looked at the clock display floating in the corner. It read 23:00 hours. Still two hours before his rack time. He yawned hugely and picked up the small, tawny-colored plush pony sitting next to the lamp and looked at it.

"Applejack, I'm crashing, dude." The toy had no response. Hargrave had pushed him to grab a small nap on afternoons when he was in the middle of his shift, to avoid this late crash, and at lunch time, 15:00, he'd been doing fine. Now eight hours later, he admitted to himself he'd made a mistake. Worse, he hated coffee, and they were already out of the generic cola he'd brought along. At least all that had made it. Buried in the logistics report was a note that Mr. Sommerkorn had failed to order the ten cases as instructed, but instead ordered only one. Thus, Jim had been hitting it hard, not realizing there wasn't anymore. A cup of tea sat next to his Tri-V display, cold and untouched. He yawned again. "Fuck."

The office had a desk, two chairs for guests, a set of Tri-V displays for planning meetings, a tiny bathroom with a shower, a dressing cabinet where he kept uniforms, and a couch where he slept most nights. Hargrave bunked in the next barracks with Second Squad, minimizing the possibility that both the CO and XO might be taken out in a single attack. Jim hardly ever seemed to make it into his bunk. He'd spent more than a few nights passed out on the couch in his little office. Luckily his age helped him there, and it was good enough. Most days.

He got out for an hour or so of exercise every day after lunch with the squad, and that helped, but he'd been too busy with the unit's organizational roster. It was twelve days in, and the rotation was coming up, so he'd begun planning for when the transport arrived in three days. Worse, as commander, he'd have to stay down on the planet. It was beginning to look like the next six months were going to be the longest of his life.

There was a shrill buzz from his company computer, and a Tri-V screen lit up showing a topographical map of the valley. At the end of the valley, channeled to a narrow point of a scant mile between a pair of mountains, was the Duplato settlement and the industrial complex. It was surprisingly defensible since anything coming in from the south would have to skim the mountains and present themselves as handy targets at over ten miles in altitude so according to Union law, they couldn't fire back. However, to the north, the valley spread out to more than eight miles wide until it ended at the shore of a frozen inland sea. It was the obvious approach. On the map, the zone was now flashing red.

Jim sat up, put the pony down, and gestured at the map, blowing up the area. He was examining the lay of the land when his office door burst open. Hargrave angled for the couch, realized Jim was at his desk, and altered course. Jim could see the older man looked pleased to find him at his desk.

"You get the alert?" Hargrave asked.

"Yeah, was just checking it out." When they'd arrived they'd seeded the area with hundreds of little sensor robots. No bigger than grasshoppers, the robots were solar powered and moved every few hours at random times and directions. You could find them if you looked carefully, but it was almost impossible to find them all. One of those sensor bots had made contact with a vehicle coming through the frozen waste of an ancient forest nine miles northeast of the facility. "I'm moving some of the other sensors to get a better look."

"Shouldn't we maybe launch a few more?" Jim shook his head and grabbed a pair of connectors, snapping them directly to the pins behind his ear. Hargrave always gritted his teeth when Jim did that. It just looked painful.

"If I can get another nearby I'll have enough. That one robot saw a vehicle doing about fifty mph. It can be in weapons range in only five minutes. It would take that long to get more out there, and by then it would be too late." Hargrave nodded, deciding to trust this young man who actually had computers implanted in his brain – he probably better understood what they could do.

Tapping directly into the company Aethernet, he took full control of the hundreds of robots in the field. He balanced half in and half out of the virtual world the computer created, able to feel input from all the robots at once and interpret the data in more detail than the simple program they'd been using. Of course, now the vehicle was way past the robot that had initially detected it. However, the sensor had still been able to provide him with a direction and rate of travel, and that was enough for Jim to build a theoretical cone, just like aboard *Traveler* weeks ago.

Using his pinplants, he woke up every robot within a mile of that theoretical area and set them to active mode. The little machines couldn't operate long when using IR sensors like that, but it didn't matter as he had his results in only a few seconds.

"Got 'em," Jim said and the map updated with six new red targets. "I have six tanks, coming in on the indicated plot." Quickly the display resolved the six tanks and then began to fill in more detail as additional robots flew in to examine them. "Looks like about five troopers riding each tank."

"Sounds a lot like that last raid," Hargrave nodded. "I'll sound the alarm. Get First Squad up and out the door."

"Yes," Jim agreed. He sent a flash message to orbit as well to warm up Second Platoon. They'd been maintaining overwatch in space, so another full squad would be racing to get in their suits already locked in *Phoenix 3*, the pilot sitting in his bird ready to go. The order given, he detached his connection and stood. "Let's go," he said, with more determination than he felt.

In the hall, the ten men in his squad were already running by. Murdock was bellowing for them to run faster. Jim threw his jacket at his locker as he left the office and crossed the hall at a fast jog. In the garage, all ten suits were already swinging open, heat shimmers rising from the interiors. The maintenance teams under Adayn were running from suit to suit, detaching power and data cables.

"How do we look?" Jim asked Adayn as he huffed across the bay. He was stronger than he'd been and had better endurance, but he still couldn't run to save his life.

"First Squad is powered up and ready," she said with a big smile and a thumbs up. "You're good to go, Commander!"

"Thanks," Jim said and flashed her a thumbs up in reply.

"Need help, sir?"

"No," he barked. "Get Second Squad powered up. They'll be out in a few minutes after they wake up. We might need them if the raiders have air support."

"Roger that," she said and gave a shrill whistle. "You heard the boss, let's go!" The dozen techs under her finished the last power-up of Jim's squad and ran as a group to the next garage.

Jim climbed the metal gantry and spun around, fairly jamming his leg into the suit. He reached back and found the haptic cables and connected them in order by feel. He'd done it dozens of times now and it went quickly. Grab the cable, snap it in place, and slide a leg in. Grab the next one, snap it in place, and slide the other leg down. PUSH until you felt your feet seated. Next, adjust and seal the torso, etc., until completely connected and enclosed.

It always seemed to take forever, but as he grabbed the helmet off the hook and slid it on, snapping the specially made cables into place on his implants, he heard Buddha's voice shout out.

"Squad all online. You there, Jim?"

"You bet," Jim said as he snapped the last connection in place. A field of green relays showed on his status board under the rainbow tailed pony. "Good to go," he said.

"Button up!" Murdock barked. Jim slid both arms into the suit and felt the control studs under his fingers. He pushed them in the preset sequences, and the protective cockpit cover began to pivot down. A second later, it latched into place with a THUNK, THUNK, HISSSsss of the suit pressurizing around him. The air blowing on his face was warm and slightly metallic smelling.

Unlike all the other suits in his squad, his CASPer fed data directly into his brain. Jim felt the suit come alive as he took control of it. Just like before, he could see the status reports on his weapons, only this time they were loaded with live ammo. Oh boy, he thought. Oh boy.

"Opening doors," Hargrave said from the next garage where he was buttoning into his own CASPer. The XO would be with Second Squad, just in case something went wrong. He'd wanted to stay with First Squad, to keep an eye on Jim, but Jim wouldn't hear of it.

"We stick to the normal command structure," Jim insisted. "I have the First Sergeant and Buddha with me. If I fuck something up, they'll be there."

The doors swung open to show the system's yellow star low on the horizon and about half the size of the one he grew up with. The suit said it was about 12 degrees Fahrenheit outside. A fine Kash-Kah spring evening, in other words.

"Take them out, First Sergeant!" he ordered.

"Yes, sir!" Murdock replied. "Let's move, shovelheads." In formation, all ten CASPers pushed their gantries away to the side and stepped out into the garage, turned, and walked toward the now fully-open doors. The Sergeant held back and Jim fell in with him. The ten-foot-tall suit he controlled with his arms, legs, and mind walked smoothly down the concrete floor. The twelve of them clomping forward at once made the walls reverberate until they'd cleared the entrance to where the huge, squat APC was waiting, its cavernous doors open for their arrival. Most of the squad was already aboard and settling in as Jim and Murdock joined them. With twelve CASPers crowded in, the transport was packed.

"Buttoning up," Razor, the driver, announced as the doors slid closed quickly and the interior glowed with reddish illumination.

"Check the fresh coordinates," Jim told Razor. Inside his suit, he'd once again started getting fresh feeds from the sensor robots.

The tanks were now only four miles out and were slowing. The enemy had just destroyed a sensor bot. "They know we've made them." Jim updated the enemy location once again and fed it to Buddha and Murdock. "Where do you suggest we deploy?"

The APC roared to life. An older model that rode on eight huge, solid, synthetic rubber tires, it didn't have great ground clearance. It did have dual hydrogen fuel cell-powered engines that could operate in a vacuum if necessary, and it managed almost 120 mph on roads, or 50 mph over broken terrain. The tanks were faster, but the APC was more maneuverable and had excellent forward armor. A spot on the terrain map just to the west of the line of approach lit up. It was a point almost fifteen hundred feet above the dry riverbed the tanks were moving along.

"Here, sir," Murdock said. "Unless they stop and climb here," another spot flashed, "they'll be fully exposed there. It's not the best ambush spot, but it's a damned good one with our CASPers' superior jump ability. Plus, Second Squad will be coming up in another ten minutes." He flashed a spot a mile further along the river bed closer to the installation. "Have them leapfrog on jets in this direction to provide a cutoff in case any of the tanks get past us." Another spot along the enemy's route that they'd already passed appeared. "Have *Phoenix 3* prepare to deploy Second Platoon First Squad there, and keep *Phoenix 4* with Second Platoon Second Squad in the other APC on standby. If we can route them toward their drop off, and hopefully put guns on the enemy's own dropship, we may be able to clean up the whole nest."

"Sound plan," Buddha sounded off.

"I agree," Jim said, nodding in his suit. "Razor, go for the indicated coordinates. Once we deploy, go hot and prepare to provide fire support."

"Will do, boss," the APC driver replied.

The APC raced down the tarmac and off the end onto a barely improved road, racing along at over eighty mph. Jim watched the data on the enemy positions, keeping them in sight even though he lost two more robots because another six now had them in sight. The little machines weren't cheap at almost two hundred credits each, but the intel was far more valuable. Besides, unless the raiders turned tail, he was about to get one of those five percent combat bonuses in the contract, and that was a cool five-hundred thousand credits. As long as they didn't have any casualties...

"Deployment site in one minute," Razor barked. A second later, the roof in the rear of the APC over their heads split and opened like the doors of a toolbox, revealing the clear sky overhead. Shortly thereafter, the APC's wheels ground to a stop. "Go, go, go!" Razor barked.

"Jump now!" Murdock ordered. In almost perfect unison, all twelve CASPers fired their jumpjets and roared out of the compartment of the APC. Now empty, the doors began to fold in on themselves, while the floor split open and the vehicle's main gun, a five-barrel Gatling accelerator gun, popped out and locked into place with two missile pods joining it on either side, former roof now serving as armored sides. The APC had transformed into a formidable gun and missile platform. Razor steered the APC off the road and up the ridge opposite the direction the troopers were taking.

Jim managed a halfway decent jump to clear the troop compartment, though his aim was less than perfect. He came down in the center of a copse of old trees, firing his jumpjets moments before impact. The brittle, frozen trees exploded with a resounding crash as he fell through their canopy. He almost managed to stay on his feet, grabbing the half-shattered trunk of a medium-sized sapling to catch himself. Of course, the suit was unhurt; it took more than a few trees to damage a half ton of alloy and woven ceramics.

"You okay?" Buddha asked over the command channel that only he, Hargrave, and the sergeants shared.

"Yeah," Jim growled, using his pinplants to push the suit's muscle boost and break free without wasting more jump juice and looking even more foolish. "Still getting the hang of jumping."

"Two more jumps up the hill," Murdock said. "We gotta move." Already he could see the troopers lifting off with hissing puffs of rocket power. The powerful armor soared with remarkable grace when driven by a skilled operator who could manage the interwoven gyros and stabilizer thrusters. Jim was mad at himself as he'd mastered games in Aethernet far more complicated than these suits. Why would physical skill be so much more complicated than mental?

He finished clearing the trees, looked up the hill, and picked a spot. Flexing his knees, he jumped while triggering his jumpjets. He held the thrust this time and bullied the suit into behaving. It was one-third dance, one-third martial art, and one-third mental gymnastics to make the fucking thing do what he wanted. Mostly it was like his worst day in gym class back in fifth grade, when all the kids were learning to do vaults, and he almost broke his neck. Twice.

He stuck the first landing pretty well, actually. Since it wasn't a horizontal jump, he didn't need the jets to break his landing – he just set down nice and easy on the shelf halfway up the ridge. He waited until his pinplants told him the jets had cooled down to green, found his target, and hit them again. He had a small amount of confidence after the last jump, but that turned to shit as he realized he'd overshot.

Jim tried to break his forward momentum and failed utterly. He plowed face-first into the ridge almost twenty feet above the rest of the squad. Luckily, the CASPer was designed to take a beating, just like his ego. When he realized he'd screwed the pooch, he spread his arms and grasped as he hit.

"Oof!" Jim grunted and dug his fingers into the rock. Surprisingly, he held on!

"Jim, don't move!" Buddha called from below, "I'll come up for you."

"Belay that," Jim barked.

"It will only take a minute."

"I said no, those tanks will be in ambush position in two minutes. Proceed, I'll catch up."

"Murdock can take the squad," Buddha persisted.

"No," Murdock agreed with Jim, "he's right. Can you handle this?"

"Yes," Jim lied.

"Good," Murdock said and addressed the squadnet. "Everyone jump." And with a whoosh, eleven suits rocketed by him toward the ridgeline above.

He used his pinplant sensors to evaluate his situation. It could be worse. The rock face was somewhat crumbly, which provided possible handholds, but it also meant it could give way. If it did, he still had his jumpjets. And as long as he didn't fall the whole 150 feet and land on his head, the suit would keep him alive.

"All right," he said inside the suit, radio off, "get your shit together..." Dash swung a foot away. She seemed to be shaking her head. "I didn't ask you." Jim pushed power into the legs and swung first one, then the other in a hard kick, digging the toes into the rock. They stuck, allowing him to free a hand. The rock face was about twelve degrees off vertical. Still too much to easily jump. His jets would wash off the face and fling him backwards, and then he'd be fucked. "I guess I do this the old-fashioned way," he said and reached up to grab rock. Once he had a grip, he pulled a foot out and moved it up.

His entire body pushed away from the wall a bit as the knee ground off dirt and rock. Jim swallowed his heart and dug the foot in, unhooked the other foot and opposite hand and went...up.

"A hundred thousand credit combat suit," he mumbled as he climbed, "and I'm going up a rock wall like a fucking kid on a jungle gym." Still, it was working, if too slowly. The angle decreased to about twenty degrees off vertical and he increased his pace. One hundred feet above him, the squad had reached the ambush point.

"We're in position," Murdock reported.

"Roger that," Jim grunted as he climbed. "Deploy two-on-two for cover, and watch for potential flankers." He stopped climbing for a minute so he could give the sensor robot data his full attention. "They may have left a tank behind or sent it on a different route. I only count five tanks now."

"Got it," Murdock confirmed.

"Second Squad is moving out," Hargrave said from his position with Corporal Akido and Second Squad. "ETA ten minutes."

"You want to send the APC back?" Murdock asked Jim.

"No," Jim ordered, climbing again. "I'm really wondering where that other tank is, and I'm concerned about air assets." He redirected more of the robots to begin transmitting active detection to try and find anything else. "*Phoenix 1* and *2*, report!"

"*Phoenix 1*, standing by," Jane Wheeler reported.

"*Phoenix 2*, standing by," Prescott reported a second later.

"Power up, but stay groundside. Be ready to provide CAS at a moment's notice." CAS, or close air support, would be vital if the enemy had heavy firepower.

"Understood," both pilots reported immediately. Jim climbed as fast as he could.

"Contact," one of his troopers on the ridge above called out. "Marking five dozers," he stated, using the slang for tanks, "call it one thousand feet, speed four-five mph."

"Confirmed," another trooper agreed. "Five dozers, all mediums." Jim sighed; he wasn't going to make it.

"Hargrave, be sure Second Squad is ready to cover First. Move it as fast as you can, but be conscious of leakers."

"We got it."

"Good. First Sergeant?"

"Yes, sir?"

"Clear to engage as planned."

"Roger," was the immediate reply.

Jim slowed just enough to free a little of his brain to watch the battlespace, a 3-D representation of the ambush site built from the images of all eleven troopers on the ridge. The tanks were hauling ass in rough, rocky terrain. The ground-effect tanks were in the lead, picking out a route, with the wheeled ones following close behind.

He could clearly see the soldiers in armor on the tanks now; it looked like Jivool and Zuul troopers.

"Preparing to engage," the First Sergeant said. In his mental battlespace, Jim saw the tanks reach the optimal position. At exactly that moment, all eleven troopers fired.

Six of them carried rockets designed to engage medium-armored targets. The others didn't have heavy weapons of that caliber, so they opened up with their shoulder-mounted rail guns. The first tank took two missiles and instantly turned into a metallic fireball, along with all of the troops hanging onto it. One of the missiles must have found its magazine or its fuel tank. The fifth and last tank took the last two missiles. One was a little ahead of the tank, and the concussion lifted it off the ground like it had driven over a ramp. Several of the troops flew clear from the sudden jump. The second missile struck it between the squat turret and the chassis, separating the two parts and filling both with fire and death. Another couple of troops were obliterated by the blast.

"Lead and trailing down," Murdock confirmed as railgun rounds slammed into the middle three tanks, some just damaging armor, others chewing up troops hanging there. "We're moving!" All eleven CASPers stepped forwards, and plummeted off the ridge as fire began to flash up at them. It was all aimed at where the humans had been moments before, and hit nothing.

While he climbed like an idiot, his troops were in their first fight. He felt a combination of frustration and embarrassment and began to think about heading back for the base. As the battlespace showed a third tank go up from a perfectly placed missile, he didn't think this was going to last long. That was when the gunship showed up.

"ECAS!" someone yelled. Jim's battlespace updated to show an enemy airborne target flashing down the approach used by the tanks. Enemy Close Air Support, or ECAS. A dozen possibilities for the asset were listed, from a space fighter to a multi-rotary winged craft. It was moving at about 150 mph and coming in fast.

"Murdock!" Jim barked.

"On it," the older 1SG replied. "Decoys!" he ordered. All eleven CASPers landed and fired one of a pair of decoy pods they carried. The pods flew up a dozen yards and popped, releasing strings of sensor tape, flares, and smoke. The ECAS dove on the Cavaliers' CASPers only to find nothing to aim at. The ground was covered in hundreds of overlapping targets. The frustrated pilot, having no clear targets to aim at, unleashed a long strafing run with the craft's under-slung railguns. Hypersonic slugs tore up the wintery landscape, exploding frozen trees and shattering rocks and ice. No rounds got within a foot of a Cavalier.

"Simpson," Buddha called out, "splash it."

As the craft passed over, a multi-ducted fan gunship identified as a Piqui 104, one of the squad's two anti-air equipped troopers fired on it. The two-megawatt, chemically-fired laser pulsed faster than the eye could follow, punching a series of holes in the craft's starboard wing that compromised a primary drive fan. The blades, spinning at more than 30,000 rpm, exploded spectacularly. It yawed hard to the right, then corkscrewed down. The pilot fought the controls all the way down as the craft spun faster and faster, until it slammed into the ridgeline with a thunderous flaming crash. There was no ejection; the pilot fought it to the end. Jim hoped there weren't many more of those, his squad only had one more pod each.

"*Phoenix 1* and *2*," he called, "lift off and provide CAS. We have ECAS."

"Affirmative," Jane's voice came in, the sound of her engine's scream already audible over the radio, indicating she'd begun taking off as soon as the enemy Piqui had attacked. Jim had stopped climbing as the air attack took place. His arms were starting to ache. Despite the suit's enhancements, he was becoming exhausted.

On the other side of the ridge, his squad had spread out as the troops on the tanks unassed and began engaging them. As the platoon commander, Jim had detailed readouts on all the men under him, so when the first one took a hit, he saw it. And the second. Jim sucked in his breath as the trooper's suits handled the damage. No injury to the operators noted. He heaved a palpable sigh of relief.

The last two operational tanks were trapped on their chosen path. Faced with destroyed vehicles front and back, they cut sideways to the edge of the dry river bed they'd been moving along and found several large boulders to maneuver around that allowed them to present a hull-down defensive position. Their troopers rallied on that position. It was starting to look like they'd dig in when *Phoenix 1* screamed over and strafed them with dual streams of railgun rounds. A split second later, *Phoenix 2* followed on a parallel path. Jim was just cheering the air attack when he saw it. The sixth damned tank, and it was a heavy.

"I got that last tank," Jim said over the command net.

"Observe and stand by," Murdock said.

"We'll have these in hand shortly," Buddha agreed, his transmission interspersed with the thudding of his CASPer firing its magnet accelerator. "We can be there in a few minutes."

Jim examined his battlespace. The tank was massive. It had to be one of the fusion-powered beasts he'd read about. Which meant shields and energy weapons. It was heading down the same gap the APC had taken, so it was heading toward Second Squad, and fast.

"Shit," he said.

"Jim," Hargrave said, "we're in position. What are you doing?"

"Leading the charge," Jim said, and jumped outward from the rock wall.

* * * * *

Chapter Seventeen

The CASPer dropped like a rock. Since it was big hunk of steel, that only made sense. Jim did his best to carefully tweak the jumpjets to guide his descent, and almost flipped head over heels.

"Shit, shit, SHIT!" he yelled as he desperately tried to control his fall. He'd timed it to land behind the racing tank, with the intention of firing a rocket right up its ass. As his suit began to yaw out of control, that plan turned to crap in an instant, and it was all he could do to keep from landing head first. He managed that at least.

He got his legs back in proper landing position just twenty-five feet above the ground. He squealed in panic and crushed the jumpjets control for all he was worth. Although he managed to kill most of his downward momentum, the bad news was he'd also considerably altered his final landing point. In the instant before hitting, he realized that, though he'd managed to keep from hitting the ground and cratering like Wile E. Coyote, the tank he was after was directly under his feet.

"Fu-" *Wham!*

His CASPer collided with the tank's turret, which he found to be rather like…hitting a tank. He folded like cheap lawn furniture over the tank's turret with a "Whumph!" The suit's servos cried out in protest, and his face smacked painfully against the cockpit shield. He understood the chin shield in the helmet much better now. Dash bounced off his face, her tail tickling his cheek. He didn't find it amusing. The suits really were tough as hell, though, and aside from a few bruises, he was unhurt. The only problem was, he was bent over the turret of a very, very big enemy tank.

It was a beast – at around forty feet long and twelve feet wide, it was the size of a large dump truck back on Earth. There was a massive-but-sleek turret mounting a single energy weapon – probably a particle accelerator cannon. Numerous lasers were mounted for light duty as well as what had to be five or six retractable missile launchers. A fusion power plant drove the weapons system and the four independently-stabilized treads which moved the ninety tons at startling speeds. He knew without having to check it would have shields too. It was a high-tech mobile killing machine, and it was heading right for Second Squad.

The inside of the suit's cockpit functioned almost like a window, the images projected there by miniature Tri-Vs. He shook off the stunning impact and looked up at the turret to see an armored camera turn to look right back at him.

"No free pictures," he said as he reached up and smashed the lens.

Jakutah was pleased. As the most experienced tank crewman in the gang, he and his nine fellow Zuul had been given command of the heavy tank, which happened to be of Zuul design. His long muzzle skinned back over sharp teeth as he imagined the profit they would make from this raid. The Duplato were easy targets. Even with a few mercs here now, it shouldn't be a huge challenge, not with the kind of firepower they had. Naturally he was as surprised as the rest of his crew when the heavy combat-armored trooper crashed onto the turret like an unexploded bomb. Much better than the exploding kind, of course. But now he had a damn trooper on top of his tank, and it had just crushed a camera!

"Anti-personnel gunner!" he commanded.

"Sir!"

"Get that cursed thing off my tank."

"Right away, sir!"

The threat buzzer went off on Jim's display. His head spun around as a laser slid out of a recess on the turret's side and spun around toward him.

"Oh crap!" he barked and raised his right arm. It was an instinctive move, and the right one, completely by accident. The motion was preprogrammed into the suit to trigger a defensive system. As the arm came up, the brace on the forearm sprang open into a shield just as the laser fired. The shield was highly reflective and hardened armor. The laser's pulses ricocheted in every direction as the weapon tried to strafe him. "Forgot about that," Jim said when he realized he hadn't been perforated. Several of the reflected beams struck the tank. One blew off the primary communication antenna. The other...

Jelltoh, the chief anti-personnel gunner of the tank, had been forced to flip up a visor to see the armored attacker who'd destroyed the only camera with a clear view. Luckily the visor had a built-in display interface so he'd put the cross hairs on the center of the huge armored figure's 'chest' and hit the activate button.

216 | MARK WANDREY

The laser popped out and spun on target. The enemy trooper brought an arm up with incredible speed and timing, deploying a laser treated shield that sent the beams bouncing like crazy.

"Communications are down!" Jistoop the radio operator yelled.

"Damage to targeting system," Jinpaka the main gunner cried out.

"Jelltoh!" Jakutah barked, "I said kill that!"

"I'm trying, sir," Jelltoh said, and he slewed the lasers' aim. As the gun moved along the shield, it found a very specific angle. The next beam pulse melted a little of the shield. Unfortunately for Jelltoh, it also bounced most of the beam right into the barely five-inch-tall visor aperture. An incredible shot, actually. The heavy-duty optics reflected the nearly 1 megawatt of attenuated light before melting. The beam flashed into the crew compartment, melted Jelltoh's face, and exploded his brains all over the inside of the turret.

The laser stopped, and Jim glanced around his shield. It was just sitting there, still pointing at him. Several important-looking pieces of equipment on top of the tank were smoking, but the laser was still there. He swung his left arm around, activated his sights, and fired a burst of light accelerator rounds that tore the laser apart. Lowering his right, the shield immediately retracted onto the arm. Well that worked! Encouraged, he clamped onto the broken remains of an antenna and pulled into more of a crouch before looking around to see what other kinds of damage he could do.

"**G**ah!" the other two crew members in the turret yelped as Jelltoh's brains and blood were spread around the compartment.

"What was that explosion?" Jakutah demanded below.

"The anti-personnel gunner," replied Jinpaka.

"Is that armored trooper gone?" Jakutah asked.

"I cannot tell," Jinpaka said, "the observation port is burned out." He leaned over his former crewmate's body and triggered the laser again. It flashed a red telltale, meaning it was not responding to commands or firing. "The gun is out of action, too."

Jakutah snarled and spat on the floor of his command position. He could run the entire tank from there if necessary, so he knew about the gun being out. The tank's shield would have kept anyone from getting on it, but he'd been running without it to decrease the chance of being spotted. Besides, he'd always thought it made the ride bumpier.

From the sound on the chassis, it appeared the nuisance was moving around to the rear of the tank. At least it could do less damage there.

"Reactor Thermal Vent Number One has been sealed," Joshpa, the engineer reported. Jakutah felt his hackles rising in fear and anger. "Vent Number Two is sealed too! Reactor overheat and shut down in one minute."

"Entropy!" Jakutah roared. "Driver!"

"Yes, sir," Juslogo, the driver replied instantly. He was less than a foot away from his commander, with his back to him, so he was already quite afraid.

"Get that damned *thing* off my tank, I don't care *how* you do it! Do you understand?"

"Yes, sir!"

The Zuul were known in the merc world as being quite literal. This translated into following orders both precisely and with very little imagination. That was until they were told to do it however they could. In moments like that, a Zuul could do the most unpredictable and nonsensical things. Often described as anarchy under orders, those who employed the Zuul were always careful not to leave any of their orders open to improvisation or interpretation. Juslogo interpreted his order as just that, an order to improvise.

An enemy trooper was on top of their tank perpetrating mischief, and he had to get it off. He looked through his screen displaying the layout of the ground ahead of them, the tank's treads chewing quickly toward their destination. Off to the left was a dense copse of ice-encrusted trees and the ground slowly climbed upwards. The trees had numerous low branches.

"It will be done, sir," he said, then both accelerated and slewed them off the mostly clear path and began crashing into the trees. He accelerated, jerking the tank from side to side.

"Son of a...ahhh!" Jim caught a foot-thick tree branch right in the middle of his suit, about where his chest was on the inside. The tank was still going over fifty mph as it left the clear area of the trail and careened into the thick growth of trees. The deep-frozen branch met hardened armor and exploded, nearly sending Jim flying off the back of the tank. He'd been partially bent over, jamming another vent on the tank's fusion reactor closed. They'd been easy to spot: the air was super cold and the vents were like white hot lasers to his IR sensors.

He'd sealed the second one by just bending the cover closed and was standing up again when the branch nailed him.

Jim did a wonderful CASPer version of a windmill with both arms before flipping over on his back with a crash and sliding half off the tank. At that moment, the tank hopped over a low hummock, launching him into the air and over the back.

"Hah!" Juslogo barked and yipped. "That got him!"

"Excellent job, driver," Jakutah complemented. "Now get us back on track! We can expect more resistance. Joshpa, update on the reactor?"

"I've managed to partially open one of the vents. If we keep the reactor at twenty-five percent like it is now, we're fine. Anything higher and the temperature will spike. I'll have to go outside to fix it."

"Any signs of that fur-scratching combat suit?" the commander asked. All of his crew indicated negative. "Fine, we can take a minute. I'm sure the rest of the force is mopping up the enemy defenses. Driver, halt while repairs are made."

Jim didn't know what he was holding onto, but it was attached to the tank, and he was being dragged through the snow, ice, and rocks. He was afraid to let go, because who knew what would happen? He was afraid to hang on, because who knew what would happen? And he was terrified of trying to use his jumpjets, because— fuck! So indecision, more than anything else, kept him hanging on as his suit's systems racked up an impressive list of damage from the impromptu road-hauling.

"Jim…status?" he heard from his radio once, but he was too busy keeping his brains from being beaten out on the side of his own cockpit and didn't answer. The call started again, but cut off mid-transmission.

The insane ride continued for another minute, then the tank came to a quick and sudden stop. Jim ended up laying on his suit's back, looking up at the sky and breathing hard.

Well, that was fun, he thought, and opened his hand. Some kind of cable had become wrapped around his whole lower left arm. Using the technique he'd learned from Murdock, he sat up and rolled onto his feet. Speaking of Murdock…

"Cavalier Actual. Anyone out there?" No response. He repeated his call and got nothing again. He started to get worried, then realized the radio status indicator was red. The suit was chiming a trio of master alarms. He went down the list quickly. None of them put the suit out of commission, so he dismissed them for now. A clanking from the tank reminded him he was still in a combat zone. He turned to see a Zuul climbing out of a hatch, a toolkit in hand.

The alien walked calmly toward the back of the tank, looking left and right down at his feet, examining the tank, unconcerned with what was around him. He's out to repair, Jim realized as the alien knelt on the rear deck next to one of the vents he'd vandalized and started unlocking it. Jim checked his options, found an operational weapons system, and raised his right arm. The Zuul finished fixing the vent, nodded in satisfaction, and reached for his toolkit.

Joshpa growled and mumbled as he unjammed the vent. It was difficult because the super-hot exhaust had made it too hot to touch, forcing him to use heavy gloves. The damned enemy merc had done a hell of a job on the vent, but he finally managed to pop it open. It wouldn't close again without a lot of maintenance, but it was open, and that was better than closed. He stood and grabbed the toolkit, and there was the enemy merc, just a few feet behind the tank.

Joshpa hadn't known it was that big. It had to be one of those human suits he'd heard about. Entropy, they were huge! And it was pointing an arm at him. He moved his head a fraction, looking back at the hatch he'd come up from. It was six feet away. Too cursed far by a long shot. The suited merc took a step toward him. Joshpa sighed and raised his hands to surrender. He never felt the explosion.

Jim held his arm on target, fingers ready on the triggers. The alien stood and saw him, freezing instantly. It was obviously surprised to see Jim standing there pointing a weapon at him and didn't know what to do. Jim was waiting and weighing his options when the Zuul suddenly moved. The alien never finished the gesture because Jim triggered the railgun.

The gun cracked once, firing a hypersonic round that hit the Zuul center of mass and blew him apart. By the time he realized he'd shot the alien, all that was left was flying arms and legs.

"Damn," he said. It almost looked like the mechanic was trying to surrender. "Oops."

"What now?" Jakutah demanded after the thump above them. "Joshpa, report? Joshpa? Someone tell me what is happening."

"The engineer is dead!" one of his surviving crew barked. "The armored trooper is back, and it killed Joshpa!"

"Button up!" the commander ordered, and the hatches automatically slammed shut. A moment later the hull resounded with a bang as the enemy trooper once again landed on the tank's deck. "I have had enough of this!" he roared in frustration at continually being thwarted by this mecha-monstrosity. "Driver, move! You shook it off once before; do it again – permanently!"

"Understood," Juslogo said and threw the tank into gear, this time pushing the throttle all the way forward.

"Fire anything you have up there to get him off!" the commander ordered. Weapons popped out and spun, firing in random directions as the tank careened madly through the frozen landscape, jumping over hillocks, tracks throwing rooster tails of dirt and snow behind as it lurched forward. With the engineer, Joshpa, splattered all over the top of the tank, no one was manning his station. Thus no one took notice of the rapidly climbing temperature reading from the fusion reactor.

On top, Jim had a secure handhold on the tank's main gun, the reinforced barrel of a particle-accelerator cannon, and he held on for all he was worth as the tank's driver went absolutely apeshit. Several more lasers popped out and started randomly firing, none coming anywhere close to hitting him. A good part of Jim was thrilled that he was causing so much alarm. Another part of him figured that, sooner or later, they were going to succeed in scoring a good hit.

"Might as well see how much I can screw this thing up in the meantime," he said. The barrel of the particle cannon looked expensive. It was too big for him to bend, even using the enhanced strength provided by his suit. As luck would have it, he didn't have to bend it. The focusing channel was crystalline, running down the center of the barrel and protected by a spun steel shroud with gaps for cooling. He made a knife edge of his right hand and pushed it through the gap.

"Alarm from the main gun!" Jinpaka barked and swiveled the turret without waiting for orders. "The cursed trooper is trying to take out the main gun!" He swung the gun back and forth as fast he could, but the alarm continued to sound. Worse, the beam-focusing crystal was sending an alarm, too. Any more flexing and...

"Not my gun," Jinpaka moaned and swung the turret around as hard and fast as he could. It spun a full 360, the tip of the barrel probably going 120 mph. It was tracking slower than spec; something had to be pulling against it. He added up and down motion to the barrel. With a resounding crash, the turret stopped spinning and its motors exploded.

Jim pushed as hard as he could. The hand of the suit was a good eighteen inches from his actual fingertips which were roughly around the suit elbows. The sound of tortured metal on metal was relayed up the suit's arm as his suit hand screeched its way into the armored barrel shroud until he just scraped the crystal core. Just a little...bit...further...in...FUCK!

The barrel and turret swung right toward him, slamming him in the suit's midriff and bending him over like he'd been hit in the gut by a telephone pole. Worse, it swung him right out over the side of the tank and stopped, almost flipping him off completely. Jim grabbed the barrel with his left hand and then wrapped that arm completely around it. Overriding the maximum strength control, he hung on for dear life as the turret swung back and forth with increasing desperation, all the while Jim digging his hand in deeper. If he could just take out the particle cannon, the tank's effectiveness would be considerably reduced. If he could just reach a mechanical finger around the focusing crystal...

The turret suddenly reversed rotation, hard. In an instant, he was flipped end over end, still holding on to the barrel, and slammed against the tank's chassis. It felt like he'd just been smashed in the back with a sledgehammer.

"Ouch," he said, feeling the suit's back articulations bend in ways they weren't meant to bend. More red status lights on his board. When the barrel crushed him into the chassis, Jim finally felt the crunch of the weapon's crystal. "Well, there's that!" he said as he pushed back and slowly got the turret to rotate enough to get free. The tank continued to drive crazily, but was now on a relatively flat section of ground. He was intensely aware they should arrive at the point where Second Squad was deployed at any time. Even with the particle cannon disabled, the tank was still dangerous. He needed to take it out of commission completely.

The remaining crew in the turret cried out in alarm as the main drive motors overloaded and exploded. At the same time, the gunner growled in consternation as the status alarm on the cannon went off. The trooper had destroyed the main gun!

"Entropy!" Jinpaka growled. "Main gun is out!"

"Gunner, get your assistant out there and shoot that robotic dung off the tank!"

"But we are driving!" Jinpaka complained.

"I will shoot you myself if you do not! We have a mission to complete – or die trying." Jinpaka looked at his assistant, both staring wide-eyed in fear. They were tankers, not troopers, and that powered armor was virtually unstoppable, its operator skilled beyond reason. Look at what it had done all by itself – and there were many more of them out there. The logical thing to do was flee. On the other paw, he knew with certainty that if they disobeyed, Jakutah would, indeed, kill them. It was the way of a pack leader among their people. They agreed without speaking and both reached for weapons. Jinpaka stopped in mid-reach for a gun when the hull rang from an explosion. Everyone looked around in surprise as another one made the chassis ring like a bell.

"The trooper is using grenades!" another crew member said. The assistant gunner, who was already armed, leaned over his controls and cursed.

"The left missile launcher has been damaged."

"Get up there while we still have a tank," the commander spat.

His suit was not in good shape. The right hand wouldn't properly grasp anymore after he'd used it to tear apart the tank's main gun barrel and break the focusing crystal. Being flung around by that hand also damaged the shoulder and elbow. The back articulations were bent, and a number of the sensors were either destroyed or clogged with dirt and snow. The crashing around and being dragged had also knocked out several weapons. As he climbed back up and managed to grab on with the mostly wrecked right hand, he realized he still had a number of grenades at his disposal.

"Better than nothing," he said and snatched one of them from the belt holder. It armed immediately, and he stuffed it into an important-looking hatch. He crawled quickly away, and the grenade exploded, tearing apart the target. "Well, that worked," he said as he snatched another grenade and stuffed it into a piece of machinery. Boom! He gave a little laugh and armed a third grenade just as something hit him in the back of his suit.

Jim turned to see a pair of Zuul halfway out of the turret hatch. One had a huge laser rifle which he'd just used to shoot Jim in the back; the other had some kind of rocket launcher he was aiming.

"Damn it," Jim cursed and snapped his left arm up, moving the grenade to his right hand. The Zuul with the laser was trying to load another chemical charge, while the other was struggling with the rocket launcher. Jim tried to get the right hand of his suit to cooperate. He finally got it to grasp the grenade and quickly brought the left up and triggered the magnetic accelerator. The suit sensors weren't working worth a damn, so he aimed based on where the rounds threw sparks off the tank turret as they gouged the metal. The Zuul ducked as the rounds flew past them.

Jim turned back around. He was near the front of the tank now, and he thought he spotted what looked like an opening – an important one. He moved as quickly as he could to stuff the grenade into it.

Jinpaka almost soiled himself as the suited trooper unleashed a deadly hail of fire at him. He and the assistant yipped in panic and dove out of the way as the human's rounds ricocheted off the turret and hatch. His assistant was shaking so hard he couldn't reload his laser rifle. Jinpaka had to stop the trooper himself!

It took a phenomenal effort of will to push himself back out of the hatch. The rocket launcher was so big he had to lift it out first. The trooper had his back turned and was moving toward the driver's compartment, another of those grenades in one hand.

"You have done enough damage to my tank!" Jinpaka yelled and leveled the rocket launcher. Not remembering or caring about the firing guidelines, he triggered the weapon just as his assistant, who'd finally reloaded his weapon, popped up right behind him. The back blast of the rocket firing nearly decapitated the hapless assistant.

The rocket lanced out and hit the trooper square in the back. The suit jerked and both arms shot up as if it were surrendering. Fire flared and exploded from the back of the suit, even though the rocket hadn't detonated. Jinpaka had forgotten the rocket needed at least fifty feet to arm and the armored trooper was only ten feet away. Just as well, as the rocket explosion would have killed Jinpaka too.

The trooper staggered, obviously badly damaged. Jinpaka was trying to remember where the spare rockets were stowed when the suited trooper did a half pirouette and plummeted off the front of the tank, which bumped upwards as it ran over him.

"Yes! I did it!" Jinpaka cheered, turning to share the moment with his assistant. He was too stunned at the sight of the burned corpse of his former assistant to see the grenade, released from Jim's damaged hand when he fell, as it rolled past Jinpaka and fell into the tank's interior. The grenade rattled around for a second, lodged next to the extra missiles which Jinpaka had just been wondering about, and exploded.

* * * * *

Chapter Eighteen

Jim wondered why he'd set the alarm so damned early. He felt like he'd only just gone to sleep, and it was beeping, beeping, beeping, and beeping. He shook his head in annoyance and instantly regretted it. It did, however, drive home the realization that he was not, in fact, at home in his comfortable bed. He was inside a CASPer, lying on his face on an alien planet, and he hurt. Everywhere.

"Oh...shit," he moaned and opened his eyes. The projection system that showed an exterior display on the inside of his cockpit was no longer functioning. The feeds into his pinplants had become disconnected. The status board to his right, where Dash used to hang, had broken free from the strut it had been welded to and was no longer working. The parts that were still powered and at least partly functional showed red on their status indicators. The air was still moving inside his suit, so at least there was that. It was quite possible to suffocate inside a CASPer, even on a world with breathable air, if its life-support system failed. He'd learned that in his brief training session. He decided to take stock of his situation by reconstructing, in his mind, the last few moments of the fight.

Jim remembered firing at the two Zuul in the turret, then turning to use his grenade. Then something stabbed him in the back. He spun and fell off the tank. I fell, he thought, some more of the cobwebs clearing. Oh, right, I fell in front. And then the tank ran me over. Yeah, that had hurt. As the tread hit his leg, effectively dragging him under, he'd been slapped to the ground and had smashed his head against the cockpit side. He glanced at the controls that had broken free. Right. So that's how *that* happened.

He wanted to feel his head and back, but his large arms were wedged so tightly inside the suit there was simply no way he could pull them out by himself. Since he was lying on his face, he also knew there wasn't much chance he was getting out the normal way either. Boy, Adayn was going to be pissed at him, and that was too bad. That girl was cute!

"You've got bigger worries than a pretty gal who doesn't even know you're alive," he berated himself. "Let's see if this thing still works at all." Jim tried moving his arms and found to his amazement they worked. Then his legs. Nothing. "Well, not walking out of here." The standard radio had been out since the beginning of his little tussle with the tank. He'd resisted using the emergency beacon, for obvious reasons. However, under the current circumstances – specifically that he was lying in the dirt in a mostly dead CASPer – it seemed like a good time to call for help. Using a specific combination of finger presses in his gloves he activated the flashing blue strobe of his emergency radio beacon. It occurred to him that, if he made it back alive, the engineers who designed that feature deserved a nice bonus.

An alarm started warbling. Jim looked around for it. Fixed to the left side of the cockpit, opposite the redundant controls, were a number of instruments. Atmosphere, temperature, pressure, and radiation. The radiation alarm was screaming. A neutron source nearby was emitting dangerous levels, and it was rising.

"That's not good," Jim said. "That's *really* not good."

He considered crawling, but with zero outside visibility he was just as liable to crawl toward the dangerous source of rads as he was to climb away from it. No, he needed to get out of this thing and away from here.

"Eject, eject, eject," he said. Nothing. He hadn't expected the voice system to work, but it was worth a try. He gave the sequence of finger pushes designed to initiate an ejection, basically counting to ten with all his fingers, then again in reverse order. Nothing again. "*So* not good." It was an incredibly fool proof system, so the damage was either severe, or some safety was keeping it from functioning because if it did work, he would be in worse shape than where he was. The radiation alarm tone grew steadily louder. "I'm not going to lie here and die," he decided.

Since crawling away wasn't an option, and the ejection system through the back was also out, that left the main cockpit exit, but lying on his belly, or basically the cockpit, kind of made that a no-go as well. Then he remembered his arms still worked! Jim tried pushing with his right arm. The motors whined a little and he heard a popping sound quickly followed by ozone wafting down the arm opening.

"Okay, that didn't work." Of course, he knew the right arm was already pretty screwed from his tank-turret whirligig routine. So that meant the left one. He pushed, and the suit shifted, maybe a couple of inches. "Come on," he grunted and pushed harder. It felt like the feedback was set at about half of maximum, and that was a problem. Lying on his stomach he was basically trying to do a one-handed pushup. "Damn it," he cursed, "damn, damn, damn!"

Still, it should be possible, he thought, and pulled in on the arm as hard as he could. It moved about a third of the way to a pushup position. Not nearly enough to get the leverage he needed, especially at half power. The slowly growing tone of the radiation alarm was a ceaseless and increasing threat. As he'd flexed his back, he could feel wetness spreading. He wasn't hot, so it couldn't meant sweat, and that meant blood. For the first time, he realized his right hand was feeling cold.

The only other way to override the strength enhancement was by removing the haptic uniform. Inside that uniform was the feedback system which made operating the suit possible. But to remove it, he had to get his right arm out. He'd seen thinner troopers do it, so he knew it was possible. He started twisting and pulling.

At first he thought there was no way. No matter what he did, it was as if his right arm was caught in a giant, mechanized Chinese finger puzzle – he simply could not get it out without more room inside the suit. He didn't give up, though. He kept twisting, and pulling, and twisting, and pulling. His face was jammed up against the left side of the cockpit so hard it hurt. He pushed even harder against the side and pulled with all his might.

"Arrrrrrrggghhh!" he screamed, and his arm moved! He was so surprised he almost lost the little bit of progress he'd made. He held his position, though, and pulled again. His arm moved another couple of inches. "Damn," he said and pulled more. He rotated his body to the left while pulling and his arm suddenly jerked free. He cried in pain – the angle and the swiftness of the motion almost dislocated his shoulder. He clutched his right arm tight against his chest and fell back into the center of the cockpit with a sigh. "Ouch," he said to his throbbing shoulder. "Let's never do that again!"

With his arm finally free, he wiggled it around behind him and felt his back. There was still a lot of wetness, and then pain! "Hssss," he gasped as he delicately probed the contours of his wounds. There were a half a dozen punctures of some kind. He felt the rear of his cockpit where his back had rested against the padding and found it torn and wet with his blood. Shrapnel? The missile couldn't have exploded; he was still alive. The CASPer was tough. Damned tough, but not against an anti-armor missile. If it had exploded he wouldn't have shrapnel damage to his back, he simply wouldn't have a back.

The radiation alarm was getting shrill, and that brought him back to the moment. He got his hand back around his front and slid it around to his left side, finding the haptic cable for his left arm and, tracing it down to the plug, yanked it free.

"Yes," he said, pulling his left arm in. The suit servos grated in protest, and he could hear and feel dirt dragged up under the suit. He made his hand flat against the ground and tried yet again for the one-handed pushup. Free of the limiting haptic system, he was at last able to maneuver the suit into a weird, one-sided pushup. His right arm was locked out to the side so it wasn't perfect, but he was up a foot or two, and that was enough. He had room under the cockpit now.

Jim entered a sequence with his left hand in the suit glove, and prayed. An instant later he was rewarded with a wailing alarm. He gritted his teeth and entered the sequence again triggering the miniature explosive bolts on the cockpit. Only it didn't fall off.

"Uhm…" Jim said, and reached out his right to push against the line which split the cockpit, and jumped when it screeched and fell away with a bang. "Fuck!" he gasped. He gasped again as bitterly cold air and swirling smoke rushed in. The frigid bite of the planet's cold air hit him in his thin haptic uniform like a two-by-four to the face. "Oh…" he breathed and coughed, "oh my." He got the harness' quick releases and pulled, dropping him less than a foot to land on

234 | MARK WANDREY

the inside of the cockpit hatch, which was now lying on the ground. As he fell, his other arm came loose.

Jim caught himself rather un-gracefully and began sliding forward, pulling his legs free, the haptic plugs pulling out as he moved. His hands landed in snow and dirt, making him hiss at the pain the extreme cold caused. It felt like needles in his fingertips.

"I need to get the survival gear," he said to the wind outside. He'd never set foot outside on the planet since they'd arrived without having his CASPer around him. He didn't realize it was this windy. Or so goddamned cold! He was about to crawl toward the lower part of his now crippled suit when he remembered something. He turned around and lay on his back, slipping an arm back inside. It was still a little warmer in there. "Maybe I'd be better off staying in the suit?" he wondered as he searched. The wailing of the radiation alarm told him that was a bad idea.

As he felt around, his knees got steadily colder, even though there were two inches of metallic spun carbon fiber between them and the ground. The wind blew on his feet, covered only in the thin boots with haptic sensors, it made him shudder from head to toe almost uncontrollably. He felt something furry. "There you are," he said, and pulled out Dash. She looked a bit worse for wear.

The cold bit at his flabby chest as he unbuttoned the top of his uniform and slipped the toy inside, then he turned around and crawled off the fallen cockpit hatch and onto the snow-covered ground.

"Oh this is just great," he cried as he moved. In seconds his hands were numb from the cold. He reached his destination, the thigh of the dead suit and reached for the release. His fingers wouldn't respond. "Come on," he implored the shaking digits to no avail. He cursed and rolled onto his back, and the cold ground hit the blood soaked into his uniform back and bottom. It was many times worse than the air.

Jim curled up as best he could in the space available, tucking his hands under his armpits and shivering almost uncontrollably. As he curled up, he could feel the uniform tear at the wounds on his back. The blood was freezing his uniform to his skin.

He sat as long as he could, rocking and moaning from the pain in his back, his feet, his face, the wind whipping across the desolate terrain that surrounded him.

What time was it? Late afternoon? No, early afternoon. Where was the rest of his company? Did they stop the attack? Were they looking for him?

His fingers were working again. He reached up to the latching assembly and worked the release quickly. For the first time since the battle began, something worked perfectly. The hatch popped and the contents fell onto his chest in a cascade.

Jim almost cried with happiness as he pulled the pack open hastily and yanked out the cold weather survival suit. Working quickly in the cramped space, his movements jerky with near panic, Jim slid into the clothes. He had to fight for a bit to get them over his belly and his arms into the sleeves. It was custom fit to him, but he wasn't custom fit to wear these kinds of clothes. Finally, gratefully, he zipped the front up, shoved a hand into the pocket and found the control. His fingers were stiff again, and he was thankful the control was simple. Within a second of turning it on he felt the warmth flood over his body as the power system energized heating coils woven into the suit.

From another pocket, he donned the gloves, being sure to click them into the power grid on the survival suit's sleeve. They got warm quickly as well. He stripped off his helmet and dropped it in the snow, then reached up and pulled the hood over his head and snugged it around his face, completely wrapping himself in its almost smothering warmth. It was so intense, so much of a relief, that he lay there for several long moments and just sighed, until a noise tugged at his consciousness.

"Jesus," he hissed, "the radiation alarm!" Jim grabbed the survival pack and reached into the storage space inside the suit's thigh. He unsnapped the rifle there and unceremoniously rolled/dug his way out from under the suit and into the planetary afternoon. The wind was still blowing, and now it was starting to snow.

As he pulled out the clear face shield for the suit from its storage place in the collar and attached it, he saw the tank that he'd had such an intense battle with. The last snap in place, his eyes went wide with terror when he realized where the radiation was coming from. The tank had only gone another hundred yards or so before hitting a big boulder and grinding to a stop. It was in ruins, and flames were licking out of the turret as well as another hatch he could see to the side. That one had a body dangling out as well. The body was burning, and even through the arctic bite of the planet's wind, he thought he could feel a touch of the heat coming off the tank.

It wasn't the cold that sent shivers of fear up his spine. It was the twin plumes of superheated air blasting from the rear deck. The vents for the fusion drive. The air was nearly on fire coming out of those vents. And was the fucking hull starting to glow?

Jim didn't think; he turned and ran. The tank's fusion plant was obviously in melt down. The crazy fucking Zuul had either overridden the safeties, or the explosion that had crippled it had jacked the system up. It was burning all its fuel as fast as it could and, based on the radiation his dying suit had picked up, the F11 in its core had reached saturation and was no longer dampening the reaction. Inside the tank, a tiny sun was struggling to be set free.

He ran like he'd never run before, his feet taking any path he could find as he crashed through the frozen underbrush, nearly tripping a dozen times over limbs or hollows in the ravine. He wished his suit had survived so he could have just bounded away, but he was also grateful he hadn't decided to stick with the stricken CASPer. It could have protected him from the radiation, for a while, but not from what was about to happen.

It seemed like hours, though it was likely only a few minutes of running before he began to slow. His chest rose and fell as he gasped for breath and searched for a place to hide. He stopped for a second to fit the pack over his back and set the rifle on its sling. He ran onward, now turning upwards as the hill rose. He saw a little gap in the hill to his left and made for it.

"It...will...have...to...do..." he choked between breaths. God, it had to do! Behind him he could hear a rushing scream, like Hell's own kettle boiling away for Satan's morning tea. It couldn't be much longer, he knew. The gap was getting closer. Either he'd make it, or...

He made the last few steps and lunged more than climbed through the gap. He lay there on the rocks just over the ridge, trying to catch his breath and not puke at the same time. He knew if he threw up, he'd pass out. And he needed to keep going. After a minute, he looked over the top. The tank was down there, glowing like some crazy Christmas ornament. The heat plumes made the air shimmer like Texas asphalt in July.

He got to his feet and started going down the other side. Every foot farther away he got increased the probability he'd survive. Jim reached a level spot and stopped again, leaning against the gnarled stump of a tree and breathing as hard as he could. Little lights floated before his eyes. Wait, he was casting a second shadow? *Boooooooom!* The ground rolled, and he flew through the air. Someone was screaming, then the world seemed to go dark.

* * * * *

Chapter Nineteen

"Cavalier Actual, report!" Murdock yelled into the radio. It was over half an hour since they lost contact with Jim, and fifteen minutes since they got the suit's distress signal. It only lasted a second, but it was unmistakable. They'd mopped up the raiders when the last two tanks surrendered and then moved as quickly as possible to Jim's last known location. "Jim, respond!" He cursed and switched channels. "Simmons," he called to the squad's scout, "you got anything?" The man's CASPer had more advanced sensors.

"I've got his suit transponder," Simmons replied. "Power seems low. It must be really jacked up."

"Hurry," Murdock told his squad, "switch to bound." They'd used a fair amount of jump juice during the fight; this would use up the rest. Murdock took five troopers plus himself to look for Jim. They had two suits damaged, though the troopers were unhurt. He'd left the other three under Buddha to guard the captured raiders. Hargrave had his squad split between security back at the facility and running down the raiders' landing spot. Second Platoon had remained on board *Traveler*.

The squad began using their jumpjets to bound forward in huge leaps – hundreds of yards at a time, eating up the distance to their commander much faster.

"I am picking up more data on his suit," Simmons said. Murdock grounded and jumped before replying.

"Go ahead."

"His suit is disabled, main radio is out." Simmons examined the readouts. "He tried to eject, but the system was too badly damaged. The cockpit is compromised." Murdock gritted his teeth and pushed even harder. Just before they'd landed, he'd promised Captain Winslow and Hargrave to protect the kid. Leaving him dangling on that wall appeared to fit that bill during the beginning of the attack. Who knew the boy would come across a heavy tank and try to attack it single-handedly? They'd been tracking the tank. It was obvious by the bits and pieces they kept finding that the kid had caused them a great deal of grief. Fuck, the crazy path through the frozen woods was proof enough of that. "Wait!" Simmons suddenly yelled. "Everyone stop!"

"What?" Murdock demanded. "They can't be more than two miles ahead of us."

"I'm getting a radiation warning." The squad landed next to the scout who took a moment while they were stationary to deploy his suit's sensor mast. It rose from the back of his pack like a long whip antenna. "Neutron radiation, and it's climbing."

"Where?" Murdock asked, landing next to the scout with a precise gust from his jumpjets, creating a swirl of snow around his knees. The scout, Simmons, looked at his sensor data and pointed in the direction the tank tracks led. "Neutron radiation? What do you think?"

"Either a neutron cannon, which is unlikely or we would have seen a starship come down, or it's an overloading reactor."

"If it's a reactor, how long?"

"Hard to say right—" All their radiation alarms blared at once. It meant a powerful burst of radiation was upon them.

"Blast protocol!" Murdock yelled. As a unit they spun around so their backs were to the radiation source and dropped down on one knee with their suit's hands dug into the ground. A second later, the explosion lit up the ravine and the blast wave rolled over them.

"Murdock!" Jane Wheeler cried out over the command channel. She rocked the dropship around into the blast wave as it hit. She'd been flying a few miles away when the reactor blew. Even though the mushroom cloud wasn't very big, it was well-developed and climbing into the sky. "*Phoenix 1* to *Traveler*, we have a nuclear detonation on the planet's surface!"

"*Traveler*, Winslow here," the captain came back. "We're scanning the detonation. It is not, I repeat, it is not a high-order nuclear explosion. We estimate it was a reactor overload."

"Acknowledged, *Traveler*," Jane said as she tried to calm herself. The blast wave was past and the mushroom cloud already dissipating. She set the dropship into a long, low glide path.

"*Phoenix 1*, are you okay?" Prescott in *Phoenix 2* called from his support of the group searching for the raider's landing spot.

"No problem," Jane replied. She tapped the radiation monitor and saw she'd taken a few rads, but not much. "Stay on mission." Prescott acknowledged the order. "Topovich," she called to her gunner sitting above and behind her. "Sweep for anything moving below. I'm hoping we didn't just lose six men in a nuclear explosion."

"Too much interference at ground level right now," he said from his seat. "I think I'm getting suit transponders, but it keeps fading in and out. That was quite an explosion." They knew from their commander's last report that he'd spotted a heavy tank, so that meant a fusion reactor. Small reactors like that could get out of hand fast, but they rarely blew up!

"*Phoenix 1*, this is First Sergeant." The transmission was somewhat garbled, but clear enough to understand.

Jane managed to not cry out in relief.

"There you are," she said. "Report."

"We think the explosion was from the tank Jim was messing with."

"Winslow concurs with that theory," Jane replied.

"Radiation is dropping down here, but we still took a real hit. Our suit shielding handled it. I'd rather not hop us into that cloud at the present moment, however. You're sealed — can you do a flyby?"

"Roger that," she said. "Topovich?"

"Verifying seal," he said, and a second later confirmed they were trimmed for space, which meant the external air chargers were closed. "We're good."

"*Phoenix 1*, going down for a look."

"Secure from blast," Murdock ordered and his team all stood. "Report?" Everyone called out. No damage. "Give me your radiation levels." He checked his own, and found they'd taken very little. There was a low hill between them and the explosion, and that had probably shielded them from the worst of it. The dropship screamed by a few miles overhead.

Jane leveled off and began a low and slow bank around the site of the blast. The winds had already dispersed most of the mushroom cloud. The forest for half a mile in all directions was aflame, and the snow and ice within the blast radius was completely melted.

"You have anything?" she asked her gunner, who, having nothing that needed shooting at present, could spend his time concentrating on instruments.

"There's a shitload of debris down there," he said. "Here's something." On her HUD a picture came up. It was a tank turret, mostly melted yet still recognizable. "That's about a mile from the blast. It was the tank's reactor all right."

"Any sign of the boss' CASPer?"

"No signals," Topovich said, "and the interference has cleared."

"Hargrave here," her radio called, "you find him?" Another image appeared on her HUD, sent by the gunner.

"Yes," Jane said as she looked at the melted remains of a CASPer crushed into the side of a rock outcropping, "the commander appears to be KIA."

* * * * *

Chapter Twenty

Jim didn't think he ever actually lost consciousness. The blast threw him at least a hundred yards into a massive snowdrift. He climbed out in a twilight fog of half wakefulness; the survival suit's plastic face mask kept him from being instantly smothered by the snow. It was still a close thing by the time he reached clear air; his vision was narrowing, and he saw spots floating in his vision.

He half-crawled, half-swam out of the drift until he could put his feet down again, at which point he began to move on hands and knees. He had to get away from the blast! The suit provided no protection from radiation to speak of, so as soon as he could get to his feet, he did. As he walked, he got the respirator mask out of the survival pack and pulled it over his face shield. They were designed to integrate. His feet were cold, despite the heater, and sore from all the walking. Now that the blood on his back had thawed, being thrown in the explosion had reopened the wounds on his back. The blood flowed down his back and into his ass crack. It was both painful and distinctly unpleasant, but at least it gave him something else to think about.

He put one foot in front of the other, stumbling every so often, but he managed to keep moving. After a while he realized his shoulder hurt badly. The strap from the rifle he'd taken was digging in to his skin. Surprisingly he hadn't lost it when the explosion threw him. He stopped to switch it to the other shoulder then continued.

Jim's head hurt, and he felt disorientated. He didn't know how long he walked, only that he didn't stop, even to drink. There was a bladder in the survival pack. He found the hose and slid it over his shoulder. He got one sip filled with ice chips, then nothing. He sucked hard, and got a tiny amount of water. He clipped it back to his suit front and continued onward.

Eventually he realized he was stumbling in circles. How far had he gone? He stopped and half fell to his knees as he pulled off his pack. Inside was a small relay navigation device. It would receive the passive coded signal from the ship above. And he felt like an idiot; it had a radio too.

"You're a moron," he said into the breathing mask as he opened the radio. It fell apart in his hands; apparently he'd crushed it when the tank exploded. "Great." He dropped the shattered device in the snow and moved on into the deepening dusk.

Jim wondered how he ended up sitting down. One minute he'd been walking slowly, trudging one exhausted step at a time, the next, he was sitting against the bole of a tree. He shook his head. Had he fallen asleep? The sun was down, and it was dark. He had apparently skinned the sleeve of his survival suit at some point, because the cold was biting the exposed skin in that spot like a rabid animal. Hissing, he looked at the time. Yes, it was four hours after dark. He'd been asleep for about six hours. He didn't feel like he'd slept for six minutes.

He struggled to his feet. As he did, he recovered his arm, pulled out the survival suit's control, and looked at it. The sun was down, and the air was now -14 degrees Fahrenheit; the suit was using power at a frightening rate. However, at least the radiation meter showed he wasn't going to glow in the dark. Jim chuckled at his own gallows humor.

Walking onwards was going to be tough. The little flashlight built into the survival suit's arms barely cast enough light to see a few feet in front of him. He used the light and moved slowly through the woods. It had been surreal before, like an old cartoon or something. Now, in the dark, it was just plain frightening. He found himself thinking of old stories from his childhood. Of Mirkwood or The Forbidden Forest from Harry Potter. If he didn't know from the briefings given by the Duplato that there were no predators bigger than a house cat, he would have been sure he was being followed. The feeling was almost overwhelming.

Because of the uneasy feeling, he made very little progress. He kept looking over his shoulder and scanning around with the dim flashlight.

"Stop being paranoid," he said aloud, his voice vibrating against the plastic face shield. Then a branch broke under his foot, and he almost jumped out of his skin. He spun around, the flashlight giving off a little circle of crazily dancing illumination. The shadows played against each other, and his mind created all kinds of creatures stalking him. Jim stopped and stood still, pointing the light at his feet, controlling his breathing.

After a long minute, he was calmer. All he could hear was the wind howling through the rocks and trees, and the sound of branches moving and snow falling. He took the pack off his back and rummaged inside it. Finding what he sought, he removed the pistol (a version of the C-Tech GP-90 he knew so well) and checked the action. It was loaded, chamber empty. He slid it into the holster built into the survival suit. It wasn't very heavy, but he felt more reassured with the weapon, even though it was much less powerful than the rifle. He was familiar with the GP-90. Intimately familiar. He only wished it had the linking module so he could interface it with his pinplants.

Chastising himself for waiting to do this until now, Jim checked the pack for anything else immediately useful. There was a camp light, but it didn't throw a directional beam. He wasn't interested in something that would draw attention to him from miles away, so he left it there. There was more water, all frozen like that in the bladder built into the pack. A little energy stove, if he could find shelter, a solar charger, a slate with survival manuals, and other survival gear.

"Thirsty," he said and slung the pack. There was an icicle hanging from a branch nearby, so he broke it off and chomped the end. It tasted a little strange, something to do with the planet's atmosphere. Traces of ammonia? But not dangerous. Didn't taste very good. He let the crunched-up ice melt, swallowed, then took another bite. The water was brutally cold as it went down and once the skin on his lips froze to the icicle, making him accidentally tear his lip. That reminded him of the back wound. He hadn't thought about that in a while. It didn't hurt much, because his feet hurt worse.

The few bites of ice helped. He tossed the rest of the icicle away and started walking again. One foot in front of the other. He didn't know where he was going, but at least he was going somewhere. It was sometime later when the swaying flashlight caught a break in the low rock ridge to his left. He stopped and played his light around. It wasn't much of a break. Maybe it led to a cave? A sheltered overhang? He wasn't much of a climber. Still, what choice did he have?

The climb quickly got steep and treacherous. He was immediately grateful for the heavy gloves built into the survival suit, and regretted the boots weren't nearly as tough and did not provide nearly as much gripping ability. Plus, bending over to find handholds made his back hurt. A lot.

"Fuck," he mumbled as he stopped for a break, "this was a bad idea." The cleft was narrow, barely wide enough for him, and exhaustion was overtaking him. He knew the battery in the survival suit probably wouldn't make it through the night. He leaned against the rock wall and worked at catching his breath, looking to the side and down to the gloomy woods now many feet below. The snow was letting up and the stars peeking through provided a little light. And he couldn't feel the cold though his hands on the rock wall. What?

"Shit," he said and fished out the control, immediately afraid the power was failing and his hands were becoming numb. His fingers worked and the control showed almost thirty percent power remained. In fact, his hand got colder when he took his hand away from the rock wall. That didn't make any sense.

Jim replaced the controller in his pocket and slowly pulled the glove off. The cold bit at his bare skin like a piranha. Shaking, he reached out and gingerly touched the rocks. They were warm.

"A geothermal vent?" he wondered aloud as he slid the glove back on. He used the flashlight to look up. Yes, the cleft above him had steam coming out! With fresh energy driven by hope, he renewed his climb.

Jim reached a ledge of sorts. It was small, maybe smaller than him. He was desperate, so he tried climbing in. Yes, it was too small. He had to back out and kneel on the ledge while he tried to figure out how to get inside. He tried a second time before he realized why it wasn't working. The rifle and pack were catching on the lip of the entrance. Grumbling about his stupidity and realizing just how much real world experience he lacked, Jim stripped them both off, pushed them into the cave and followed them in. He'd crawled about twenty feet or so when he felt the shaft start to go downward. Before he could investigate, he rammed his head into a rock, and the lights went out.

J im was having the strangest dream. He was lying in a sauna, in darkness, and butterflies kept flapping along his cheeks and face. He laughed and tried to brush them away. When he did they turned into miniature Zuul, their jaws snapping and teeth red with his blood.

"Stop!" he cried and woke up. "Oh," he moaned and reached up to his head. His mask was gone and the hood shoved away. He felt a moment of panic, had he frozen half his face off? No, the air on his cheeks was warm, and he was sweating in the survival suit. The flashlight on his right arm waved around to show him the inside of a cave. He touched his head and held the hand under the flashlight. It was bright red with blood. "I'm a mess," he said. He wiped his hand and started looking around with the light.

Eventually Jim found the cave entrance he'd come through; it was more than ten feet above. Judging by the bang on his head and the additional bruises, he'd cracked his noggin in the tunnel up there and fallen into the cave. He reached in and shut off the power on the survival suit, and unzipped it. It was quite warm in the cave.

He found a flat place and made himself comfortable. Based on his watch, he'd been out for an hour. The water bladder in his pack was now thawed, thank goodness, so he drank almost half of it. As he drank, he examined the rifle which had landed nearby. It seemed unharmed. No surprise, a laser rifle of that type was meant to take a beating. Next, he began cataloging in more detail the contents of the pack itself. As he laid out the items, he occasionally felt a chill draft from above. With the suit's heating element off, it was just warm enough that he didn't feel very cold, only chilly.

Jim knew that merc troopers had all kinds of survival training when they first began working. Of course, he'd gotten none of that. He'd scanned and stored the manuals, but that wasn't practical knowledge. He realized he should have memorized the contents of the pack, at least. Inside he found a flare gun with an integral five-shot magazine. His people were looking for him, and that would have helped a lot. He made a note to go over the manuals later. What the damned pack didn't have was any rope. Now that would have been useful. There was a little polycord, though.

In one of the outer pockets he found the medical kit. Time for some first aid. The back wounds were as he thought, shrapnel damage from the missile hit. After he gave himself a pain killer from the medkit he could feel the fragments with his fingers. He spent a fun hour with tweezers and a scalpel digging them out. The contortions necessary while lying on his considerable belly were far less than fun, and he had no clue if he'd gotten them all when he was finished. At least it felt like he did. They'd all been shallow, less than a quarter of an inch deep in his skin. He concluded he'd been extremely lucky.

Jim used the mirror to look at his head. There was a nasty bump and a nice little cut that had stopped bleeding while he worked on his back. All in all, the repairs were as good as they were going to get. With blood still dripping down his back, he dug out the little nano-treatment unit and read the instructions. Unlike the therapy he'd gotten, these nanites didn't require an external power source. They were short-lived and worked very quickly. He dialed the selector on the cylinder for "skin closure." It was designed for direct application, so he set the other selector to "Small," covered his eyes with his left hand, and sprayed his forehead. It hurt like crawling fire.

"Fuck!" he cursed as the little robots did their thing. "No one said this shit would *hurt*!" After a minute, the pain faded, and he looked in the mirror again. There was an angry pink line where the skin had been torn, and that was all that remained of the wound. The status on the applicator read "10." "And now the fun one," he said adjusting the sprayer. He selected it for "Moderate" this time. The two controls varied the tasking of the nanites and the amount dispensed. The indicator on the applicator went from "10" to "7."

"Maybe I can get by without it," he thought aloud. But his back was hurting much worse after his first improvised surgery. The survival manual made it clear that in any exposed environment, closing wounds was a major priority. The nanites would also clean the wound of any foreign organisms. He had to do this. His hands shook nervously as he leaned forward and took the applicator. Even though it was supposed to be sprayed directly on the wound, the manual said you could use a hand to apply it, if you were quick. He sprayed the dosage into his right hand and quickly reached around behind and smeared it up and down over the wound.

If the face wound had hurt, this was pure agony. Where his scalp had felt like crawling fire, this felt like something inside his skin eating the flesh! "Oh," he cried, "oh, ow, ow, ow, it hurts!" Tears rolled down his cheek, and he bit his lip hard enough to taste blood. It seemed like an hour before the pain began to fade. His hands were shaking uncontrollably as he reached behind him and felt the skin, now only bumpy in places where the shrapnel had been. It was all still tender. "That was horrible," he whimpered. He tried not to imagine what it would be like for an internal injury. He was glad he'd been unconscious for his treatment back on Earth.

With the wounds taken care of, he washed his hands with a little water, as recommended in the manual, and settled back. He took a blanket from his survival pack and wadded it up as a pillow, and another as a cover, and curled up on the rock floor. In minutes, he was asleep.

* * * * *

Chapter Twenty-One

Murdock watched from almost a mile away via remote link as a pair of specially-fitted CASPers examined the blast crater and the area around it. The tank had gone up with the force of almost a kiloton. The biggest part of the war machine they'd found was a track assembly and the turret. Unfortunately, Jim's suit was in similar condition.

"Any sign of a body?" he asked his troopers on the ground. He was in his own suit, as was Hargrave, standing next to him in the circling dropship, *Phoenix 1.*

"No sir," the trooper reported. "The suit is fucking torn into at least a dozen parts. The cockpit looks like a bomb went off inside it."

"Acknowledged," Hargrave said. "Get the pieces into containment and back to the hangar so we can go over them."

Adayn Christopher, who'd been in the dropship on the off chance they'd find Jim, and her armorer expertise would be needed, did her best to mask her shock and concern for Jim's well-being with efficient professionalism, but it wasn't a very convincing act. Murdock was beginning to think the hot little girl had a thing for his pizza-eating commander. There was no accounting for taste.

"I tried to tell the kid to just hang on there and wait," Murdock said. "Stupid move, taking on that tank."

"As you were, 1SG," Hargrave said. "That kid probably saved my squad." He pointed at the blast crater, almost 100 feet across, then at the blasted forest. "Took some serious balls to jump that beast, and he took it out."

"We don't know if it was just luck," Murdock grumbled. "I never doubted the kid had guts – just no skill."

"He needed time," Hargrave said; "now he'll never get it."

Murdock knew the old guy blamed him for getting the kid killed. He wondered if there was some truth there. Sure, it was his job to take care of the kid, but it was also his job to carry out the mission and protect his subordinates. There were a lot of green troopers in the command. It was a miracle no one had died in that engagement. Well, almost no one.

Below, one of the troopers who'd been going through the wreckage jumped to the top of a ridge and deposited a mangled CASPer leg. Murdock had seen such sights a hundred times on as many worlds. He shook his head. The kid should never have gone out on deployment with them; it was that simple. "What about the Cavaliers?" he asked Hargrave.

"The trust is clear. Without a Cartwright in direct command, the assets revert."

"And what about his mother?" Hargrave's suit turned toward him and Murdock could almost feel the stare through the armor. "Fine, forget I said it."

"No, don't worry about it." Hargrave was silent for a few minutes while more pieces of shattered combat suit were delivered. "We might need to face the fact that, with Jim Cartwright dead, the Cavaliers may be dead too." Still, Hargrave thought about one more option, out there in the galaxy somewhere was a last-ditch contingency. It was the last thing he'd hoped he would ever have to do.

Jim woke up feeling better, even though he was as sore as he ever remembered being. He had bruises on almost every area of his body. Only his back and forehead, where the nanite therapy had been used, felt unharmed. When he felt his back after stretching he was annoyed to find a single sore spot, with a lump under the skin.

"Must have missed a piece of shrapnel," he said in the nearly dark cave. His voice rebounded around the cavern. Feeling better, he decided food was in order. As soon as he made that decision, his stomach threatened to consume his entire being. How long had it been since he'd eaten? It had been nearly the end of their shift when the alarm had sounded, hours after dinner. According to his watch it was just over a day, or thirty-two hours ago.

He dug out his energy stove and set it up, removing the power cell from his survival suit pocket and connecting it as well. The cell powered many of the tools in his survival pack. And if he could get outside in the daylight, he could recharge it. For now, it still had a third of its original charge, enough to cook a couple dozen meals.

The food was compressed, dehydrated concentrates of various flavors. There was a total of twenty-one meals in the pack: six breakfasts and fifteen dinners. He opened one of the breakfasts, crushed the cube with his hand and sifted it into the stove's pan then added a few ounces of his water. With power turned on, the water was boiling in just under a minute. He used the spoon to stir it until the water was absorbed, leaving him with a pan full of egg-like substance mixed with sausage-like substance and bits of cheese-like substance. He tasted it with a spoon and found it uninteresting.

After it had cooled, he added some of the salt and pepper in the rations accessory pack and that made it a little more palatable. He removed the flashlight from the suit and connected it to the power cell. There was enough energy to run that item for years. He used the light to explore his surroundings as he ate. The entrance he'd fallen in through was way too far up to jump to, and it overhung the opening slightly. No way could he climb up to it. He'd have to find another way out.

As he was wiping the bottom of the pan with a finger, licking off what remained, he realized the breeze he was feeling was moving through the cavern, not just into it. The food was gone and despite how badly he wanted to open another packet, he didn't. He put everything away, shouldered the pack and the rifle, and got up to look around.

Jim felt considerably invigorated after the meal, regardless of how small and tasteless it was. He explored the cave while whistling a tune he'd heard from somewhere. He'd been looking for several minutes with the pathetic flashlight when he remembered something in his pack. He took it off and dug down in the bottom and found the lantern he'd completely forgotten about and swapped the battery into it. Instantly the cave was lit with brilliant light.

He blinked and gasped, the light was so bright after many hours in near total darkness that it almost hurt. He found the control and turned it down a notch. Now every crevasse in the cave was visible, including where the wind was going. An exit that angled downward off to one side. It was a lot bigger than the one he'd accidentally fallen through. He considered whether going onward was a good idea, then decided he'd at least explore it a bit and crawled in.

He was smart enough this time to keep his rifle off and slide it along his side. The weapon was quite resilient to damage, and that was a good thing. He was still careful how he pulled it to avoid getting anything in the aperture. He carried the lantern in his teeth like a dog, although he felt stupid doing it that way.

The tunnel angled downward, just like the one in which he'd hit his head. Jim guessed the cave complex had been formed by volcanic activity. It wasn't smooth like water formed it, and it surely wasn't artificial. As he crawled, he was a little worried that he'd fall into a lava pit or something. He'd seen a lot of movies and anime similar to this situation, and it always seemed to end up with the good guys in a lava-lake-filled underground chamber full of monsters.

"Quit being an idiot," he mumbled as he slowly worked his way through the rough, rocky tunnel. His voice echoed once and was swallowed by the darkness. The lantern light only seemed to go a few feet. The blackness was all-consuming.

Jim wasn't sure how long he crawled, only that his knees and elbows were raw, and his damned gut hung down enough that it was too. At least the survival suit was tough, and that kept his skin from getting torn up. It hurt, though, and he had to keep telling himself it couldn't go on forever. Could it?

He eventually had to stop and rest. The tunnel was still twice as wide as he needed to keep going, though not nearly high enough to stand, or even crouch. He rolled onto his side and got ahold of his pack, pulling one of the plastic water packs up and biting the tip off to drink. He was just swallowing the last bit when he thought about his bladder, and how much he'd drunk in the last day. He had a vague memory of pissing during his stumbling trip through the woods. The cold bit into his penis so he'd pissed as fast as he could. It was one of the few times he'd been glad the fat around his dick made it harder to get it outside his pants. Now in the tunnel with the zone of light created by the lantern, he was suddenly acutely aware of his bladder.

"Son of a bitch," he said, and his voice gave a resonate echo ahead of him. Much deeper than it had before. Then the echo came back again, even further. "Whoa," he said and tried to aim the lantern down the tunnel. Was the darkness a little deeper ahead? He rolled back over and crawled a little, and the light stopped showing the tunnel walls, because there weren't any. It opened into an abyss. "Wow," he said and crawled closer. The darkness continued to swallow the light whole.

The floor was lost in a few feet as well, and he carefully moved the lantern around to see the end of the tunnel better. It didn't end immediately; instead, it angled downward more and then tapered to a cavernous opening. There was no way to get any clue as to how steep the drop was beyond the meager light of the lamp, never mind how far down it went.

"Oh," he said when he remembered something in his pack. He pulled it up to his head and dug into a side pouch and pulled out a package. He tore it open with his teeth, pulled out the cylindrical item inside, folded it until it cracked, and then shook it. The space was quickly flooded with intense green light. He had five more of the glow sticks in the pack.

The glow stick came with a ten-foot length of twine. He removed that from the package, crumpled the wrapper into his pocket and tied one end of the twine to the hole in the glow stick. Jim lowered it over the edge. It went down a few feet to show the tunnel floor continuing at a steep angle. It was pretty bumpy, offering a lot of possible hand and foot holds. The glow stick caught on a rock and stopped. He jiggled the twine but couldn't make it go any further, so he reeled it in and this time tossed it.

The stick sailed down to the end of the line, and snatched it right out of his hand.

"Shit," he said, making an ineffectual grasp at it long after it was gone. He saw the green light fall, bouncing occasionally as it went downwards until it finally came to a stop. It was at least 100 feet away, and it was lying flat in the open. He squinted to try and see walls. There appeared to be a stalagmite near it. There hadn't been any in the tunnel until now. That suggested the tunnel had ended. He held up the lantern and looked above him. No sign of a roof. "Why is everything so damn hard all the time?" he asked, his voice echoing out in all directions. "Hard...hard...hard...ard."

"Hello!" he said louder, and it really reverberated this time. "Helloooo...helloooo...hellooo...loooo...oooo." Making up his mind, he started down the tunnel.

The climb down was easier than he thought it would be. As he'd seen above, there were lots of handholds, so the going was quick. He still took it slowly regardless of what he thought, and the gloves on the survival suit helped considerably. After almost half an hour of descent, the grade began to level out. He reached the glow stick, tied it to his pack, and crawled a little further.

Jim took the lamp from where he'd clipped it on his back to provide some lighting, and he held it up to see if there was a visible tunnel above him. There was nothing. He dug a loose rock out of the floor and tossed it up and toward the direction he'd been going. He heard it hit about where he'd thought it would land, not impact a ceiling. He got another and this time really heaved it upwards toward the distant ceiling. No sound came from hitting a roof, only a clatter as it hit the ground somewhere a couple of dozen yards away.

"Okay," Jim said and climbed to his feet. Still leery, he stood slowly with a hand above him lest he brain himself. He felt nothing and soon was standing again. His back spasmed a little from all the climbing. It felt good to be vertical once more. He stretched, and the muscle spasms stopped. With the illumination of the glow stick and the lantern, he began to explore.

An hour later he was examining one of the stalagmites when a thought occurred to him. He hadn't been keeping track of where he was wandering. He looked about for anything that seemed familiar. After a bit, he was forced to admit he was lost. He looked for anything familiar for another hour before he gave up. He was just wandering around making it worse. The situation reminded him of an episode of Star Trek, where Kirk was in a featureless place where everything looked the same and there was no sense of distance. That had only been a soundstage; this was reality.

Eventually Jim found a comfortable-looking bowl in the stone flow and set his gear down. He sat on the rolled-up survival suit and blanket to cushion the hard stone and sighed. First, he got his CAS-Per shot to shit, then caused a fusion explosion on a client's planet, and finally ended up lost in a cave. "Some commander I am," he said quietly, his voice still echoing. The light from the little lamp gave him some solace, but not much.

After he'd rested for a time he got up to look around. He set the lamp on a high spot, took the glow stick, and moved outwards until it was only a little spot of light. He guessed it was at least 200 yards. "Wow," he said as he began circling. He walked twice that far until his foot went "Splash!"

Jim stepped back in surprise and almost tripped over a rock. He recovered and took the glow stick, bending over to examine the water. It was a tiny stream, and it was moving to his right, away from the little camp he'd created. "Nothing is ever easy," he said, standing up and taking his bearings on the distant point of the lantern. He slowly followed the tiny stream. After a few minutes, he could no longer see the lantern.

His anxiety level rose considerably. This space was huge. Beyond huge. It had to be at least a half a mile on a side. He was about to turn back when he saw that the stream ended in a larger body of water. He held the glow stick high and water reflected the green light for many feet. A pond, a lake, or a subterranean ocean? It was so warm down here, he was amazed it didn't teem with life.

Something splashed in the water, and he almost screamed. He did jump, just a little. A second later another splash. It sounded somehow familiar. "Wait," he said and took a couple steps out into the water. The boots were knee high, so his feet stayed dry. With the water lapping up around his ankles he knelt, holding the glow stick just above the surface. Splash! He had a glimpse of something sleek and silvery. "A fish!" he laughed. So, there was life down here after all. That was good, because if he couldn't figure out how to get out, he was screwed without some source of food!

Jim found the stream again and backtracked it. There was the tiny glow of the lantern, which he followed back to camp. It was an incredible relief to find everything where he left it. After examining the area, he decided it was as good a place as any to make camp. He sat back down and set about making himself as comfortable as possible. At least this would make a good base while he searched for another way out. He planned on exploring the rest of the visible perimeter his lantern created first, and then maybe the shore of the lake. For the moment, though, he was hungry again. He accessed his pinplants and decided to amuse himself with one of the simple games he kept stored there while he prepared the food.

* * * * *

Chapter Twenty-Two

"We have the results," Hargrave said as Murdock came into the mess hall. The senior staff sat around the table that served as the officers' mess looking excited.

"And?" Murdock asked, nodding to Jane, who winked back.

"No biological data," the company doctor reported.

"I went over every piece of the suit," Adayn Christopher said, "and other than a little skin on the inside of the right arm, there wasn't anyone in the suit when the explosion hit it."

"Damn," Murdock shook his head as he sat down and took the tray of food a cook brought him, "that kid was tougher than I thought."

"Told you," Hargrave said. "He's Thaddeus's kid."

"I'll give you that, but it didn't help in the end."

"Why do you say that?" Hargrave asked.

"It's been five days, boss," Buddha said behind a pile of emptied food trays.

"Did you find the survival pack?" Hargrave asked Adayn. She shook her head no.

"But we didn't find most of that leg. It was high and toward the blast."

"So, what are the options?" Murdock asked.

"Well," Hargrave said, "there are only a couple. One," he ticked off fingers, "the commander was standing next to his suit when the blast went off. In which case there wasn't enough left of him to find. Adayn confirmed he got out of the suit."

"Yes," she agreed, "the cockpit was opened, though only a little."

"Next, he was still in the suit and so thoroughly vaporized you can't find pieces."

"Not possible," Adayn said, "the suit was seriously trashed, but some of the synthetic rubber padding survived in the intact leg and arm. If he was in the suit..."

"Right," Hargrave said. "Last, he got out and got away before the blast. With or without the survival suit."

"It was well below freezing during the battle," Murdock reminded them, "if the crazy kid didn't have the suit he froze to death in an hour. Two, tops."

"And we didn't find any bodies," Jane reminded them. "*Phoenix 1* and *2* ran a sweep."

"But only for a mile," Hargrave said. "We were sure he was in his CASPer, and now we're sure he wasn't."

"So, what are you saying?" Murdock grumbled, stuffing half a breakfast burrito in his mouth and chewing.

"I'm saying we need to start looking for him. A detailed sweep with at least a platoon."

"That's a lot of our manpower," Buddha reminded him.

"I understand that, but we're going to do it. If we find any evidence he was blown up, or we find his body, we're done. But I have a feeling he's alive."

"It's been five days, Hargrave," Murdock said. "The survival suit power pack would be good for a day, tops. Even if he survived he's a corpsicle somewhere."

"I'm not writing him off that quickly," Hargrave said. "You have your orders. Start searching."

Jim's regular explorations took on a desperate edge the sixth morning. After day five he'd cut back to two meals a day, which in his book was about as much fun as slowly sawing off his own foot. But he'd already eaten fifteen of the twenty-one meals. At two per day instead of three, he'd extended his time to another three days instead of only two. As the day progressed past lunch he began to regret that decision. Even more than he regretted not trying to fish. It had just seemed too much work. Then, there was the place twenty or so feet away that he carefully avoided except when...necessary. Of course, he wished he'd picked a spot further away as the smell was atrocious, but the ground was mostly rock, and there was nowhere to dig.

He'd just gotten back from his third scouting trip along the edge of the lake and was looking at his watch. At least four more hours until he could justify dinner. He opened his pack and looked at it. Beef stroganoff, one of his favorites of the varieties available. Then he realized he was having trouble reading the label.

"What the hell?" he asked and looked sharply at the lantern, which was growing slowly dimmer. "Oh, no, no, NO, NO!" he yelled and snatched it up. He flipped it over and checked the readout on the power pack which once ran his survival suit. It read zero. He cursed himself for not monitoring the rate of power consumption. His pulse racing, he watched as the lantern grew dimmer and dimmer, until it went out entirely. He let out a steady stream of curses that echoed in the cave's gloom. The darkness was all-encompassing.

Jim sat in complete darkness for several endless minutes berating himself. How could he have been so stupid? He'd let the lamp run nonstop since coming down inside. If he had turned it off each night, it would have at least outlasted his food. Between the stove and the lantern, he'd depleted it in only five days. Another stupid decision. Bonus, now he had no way to cook the remaining meals. Not only were they not intended to be eaten without cooking, they were only barely edible if not heated and rehydrated.

He hadn't been in complete darkness before. The glow sticks lasted for almost a day, but he'd used the last one yesterday searching the edge of the lake. He'd had one going each day when he'd cooked meals on the energy stove. Even without it, the thermal unit on the stove threw a surprising amount of light. Now the darkness began to eat into his soul.

In his last scouting of the lake, he'd spotted the edge of the cavern. It had something to do with how the light from his glow stick had reflected from the water. It looked different somehow. He'd at least learned how to get around out there with minimal light, even in camp. The lantern had never thrown a huge amount of light, and whenever he got between it and what he was doing, the dark it made was intense. So he'd laid out things where they were easy to find, and made sure to put them back after use in the same location.

With the light gone, he decided he couldn't wait in the dark for something to happen. He began packing everything back into his backpack. He'd used all the sealed water and had been drinking from the stream after adding purification tablets to it; there were enough of those to last him the rest of his life. Without the water and most of the food, the pack was considerably lighter. He considered and discarded the idea of leaving the stove. If he found an exit he could leave out the solar cells and charge the survival battery in just hours. So, it all went back in.

It took longer than he thought it would. Despite remembering where everything was, some items didn't seem to be where he thought they would be. In only moments, he had an intense respect for blind people, especially ones who lost their vision as adults. He felt like he was lost in space.

When everything was finally in the pack, and it was on his back, he picked up the laser rifle and shouldered it as well. The most useless part of his equipment thus far, he still refused to leave it. This was still an alien world, and there were raiders on it. The last thing he needed was to run into some of them with nothing but the little pistol in his pocket and a pack full of mostly useless survival tools. He went around half-crouched in camp feeling the rocks until he found the one he knew led toward the lake and set out.

This was the route he'd used the most during the five days of his stay. He knew how it went, the lay of the rough cave floor, even where a few of the bigger rocks and stalactites lay. He found the pair he'd dubbed The Sisters in a few minutes, two tall pointy stalactites. Shortly beyond that there was a little depression. In the bottom was the stream. He turned and followed it to the water. By then he was starting to feel some confidence. At the water's edge, he turned right and began to follow it.

It didn't take much longer to reach the point where his familiarity ended. He tripped on a rock and almost went face first into the water. He ended up on his knees, hands barking hard against the rock floor. He felt skin scrape, even through the reinforced gloves and knees on the survival suit. At least he hadn't hurt himself badly. After that he moved much more slowly.

Time's passage was lost to him unless he checked his watch. He was amazed to see it had only been two hours since the lantern died. That didn't seem possible, it felt like half a day. The mildly radiant hands on the programmable watch had barely been visible in the daylight. Down in the caves, they were so bright he was amazed he couldn't use the watch to light his path.

As he'd thought, Jim found the edge of the cavern. The trouble was that, with no light, he was like the blind guys trying to understand an elephant by touch. He slowed to a crawl as he felt along the wall. One direction led out into the water. He slid inch-by-inch deeper and deeper into the water. He knew from past exploring that it wasn't ice cold, but still not warm. Before it could get over his boots he went back to shore and considered.

He had no way to get warm again if he got soaked. The power was gone on the survival suit; even though it was naturally water-wicking and insulating, he'd be chilled coming out of the water. The boots were sockless, but they were already starting to acquire 'locker funk.' The last thing he wanted was to get soaked if he could avoid it. He decided to start in the other direction. He stopped long enough to fill the water bladder in his pack and add a purification tablet.

He was able to move a little faster in his chosen direction because he could just slide along the wall. He still had to watch his footing, but at least he didn't expect to run into a crazy overhang. He reached up from time to time just to be sure, though. He slid along like that for the better part of an hour. It was long enough for him to be relatively certain he was angling to the left, and that there were no exits. Shit. He was beginning to realize just how truly massive this little underground lake was.

When he got back to the water he stopped and sat there for a time. He considered getting out the survival gear and going fishing, then discarded the idea. With no light, he was risking losing some irreplaceable gear, and even though there were items that could be configured for fishing, he didn't know what he could use as bait. Besides, he'd never been a fan of sushi. Instead he drank some water and tried to ignore the rumblings from his stomach.

He resigned himself to going into the water. With the decision made, he took off his boots and stuffed them into the pack, which had a zip closure he hadn't used since he found the caverns. The only thing he couldn't keep from getting wet was the laser rifle, which was sealed (for the most part). With the pack back on, and the rifle over his shoulder, Jim slowly walked into the water.

Yeah, it was cold. Colder than he had anticipated. Why were things always colder on your feet than on your hands, he wondered as he slid along the wall and went deeper into the lake. Soon the water was up to his waist – oh, that was all kinds of fun. Yay, cold! He had to pause a second while certain things retracted and shrunk. He pulled his arms in tight and shivered almost uncontrollably.

Eventually he got control of himself and proceeded with his exploration. He began to float, and still the wall kept going. The water gently lapped against the wall as he moved along. He stepped as gingerly as he could, concerned he might slice open one of his feet on some unseen sharp object beneath the black depths. The floor of the lake was extremely smooth and only had occasional bits of water-rounded gravel. It had the feel of an ancient seabed. Next thing he knew, his feet were floating off the bottom with the extra lift from his backpack. The wall was still very much before him.

Since he was already floating and completely wet, Jim decided to keep going. He was in no danger of sinking with the backpack acting as a life vest, so he paddled and pulled himself along. Eventually glancing at his watch, he saw he'd been floating for almost an hour and the wall was doggedly still there. It appeared as though the lake was just a low point at the far side of the cavern, and nothing more.

In the utter darkness of the lake he floated and tried to decide what to do next. He hadn't found the initial place he came in, he hadn't found a way out, and he had no way of calling for help. The cave had been the refuge he needed in the initial aftermath of the battle. He should never have left the first place he landed where he was still able to see the cold Kash-Kah sky above. It was yet another mistake in a long line of mistakes in his life that looked like would culminate in his death. As he floated there, he contemplated the end. Take the backpack off and sink? Go back to shore and eat the muzzle on the laser rifle? Starve? Well, that one would happen by itself if he did nothing, though Jim doubted his ability to just sit on a rock and starve. He decided to push on.

It was almost another hour later when he realized his feet were going numb from the cold. By now he was almost two hours away from the spot where he'd begun. He'd never found the wall in his exploring the lake. What if it went on for a mile or more? He had probably only gone for a few hundred yards in the water, and he had no idea how far there was left to go. His lower legs and hands were going numb, while his thighs tingled from the cold as the water began to reduce his core temperature. He started to think his decision on how to end it all had been effectively taken from him.

Jim noticed he was being ever so gently pulled. There was a current here. He followed the direction of flow, especially since it was the way he'd been going anyway. Every minute that passed, he felt colder. Worse, he was starting to feel drowsy. He shook his head, whistled, yelled, and even slapped himself to stay awake.

The intervening time became blurry as he kept his legs pumping and followed the current wherever it was going. By the time he realized he'd floated away from the wall and there was nothing under his feet, he was too far gone to care.

* * * * *

Chapter Twenty-Three

"Oueeert...<*cheek!*>"

I'm dead, Jim thought.

"Ceeeesheee...<*klee!*>"

If I'm dead, what the fuck is that noise?

"Chiii, chiii, queeeeet....<*creet!*>"

Jim opened his eyes and coughed. He was lying on his back, and he rolled over onto his side, feeling water splash under him. Amazingly, he could see! He was in another cavern, bigger than the first one, much smaller than the second. Unlike the last one, this was about as brightly lit as Earth on a clear, moonlit night. A few feet away was a strangely shaped fungus, the underside casting a light bright enough to read by. There were hundreds of them around. Elsewhere patches of mold on the walls glowed. From the ceiling, about one hundred feet above, another type of fungus that reminded Jim of a chandelier crossed with a jellyfish writhed back and forth – twenty-foot-long tentacles dangling delicately and swaying side to side. They glowed dimly from the bulbous body, but shone brightly from the tips of tentacles that were like gracefully waving fiber-optic cables. Something flew toward one of those tentacles and it was snatched from the air and carried up to the hanging body above.

"Sheeek, sheeek...<*coooo!*>" Jim rolled onto his other side to see a creature sitting there. It looked a little like a monkey with huge light-gathering eyes. It was small – maybe the size of a large cat – with long arms tipped with proportionately long, dexterous fingers.

275

Were those opposable thumbs? The rear legs were short, and it was bent over, much like an arboreal species on Earth...which was puzzling, considering there were no trees down in these caverns. It didn't have a nose like a terrestrial monkey, just a pair of slits. Its ears were almost elfish and nearly half a foot long at the points. Its tail was enormous – at least twice as long as its body – and it was covered in dark fur. It was cute!

"Hi," Jim said. It cocked its head, listening. "Are you friendly?"

"Seeetootoo, pieeeee...<*skeee!*>" Jim saw a mouth of short, sharp teeth as it spoke with its musical tones. It's not just animalistic vocalizations, he decided. Another sentient species on Kash-Kah? Why hadn't the Duplato mentioned them? He took note that this water was warm, compared to the other cavern, and so was the air. He crawled the rest of the way out of the water and checked himself over.

The warmer water had erased all signs of the cold. He guessed he'd passed out and the little thing pulled him ashore, though he didn't know how. It was a fraction of his size and didn't look wet. How long had he lay there in the shallows?

There was no sign of his laser rifle. The pond here appeared to be about two hundred feet across. A waterfall poured into the far side from halfway up the wall, likely where he'd come in. He felt his head and found a bump.

"Did you pull me out of the water?"

"Qweek, sheee...<*skeee!*>" Jim narrowed his eyes, and opened a file in his free memory using his pinplants. He could record some things and make text files. He started one on this creature's sounds. If they were intelligent, he'd be able to isolate a pattern sooner or later. He looked at the creature and figured it was far too small to have pulled him from the water. He glanced around where he lay. The ground was partly rocky, and partly muddy in places. There were quite a few of the creature's little footprints. More than one could have made? Maybe the creature had help rescuing Jim; it was hard to tell.

He felt good enough to get up. The creature didn't respond when he did; it just watched him. Jim marveled at the calmness around him. Most animals instinctively feared anything bigger than they were. Of course, those pointed teeth suggested it was a carnivore. Was he in danger?

"Chee, chee...<*clee!*>" Jim nodded, he had a feeling it had just said he was in no danger.

"Well, you need a name," he said to the little being. It gave a disturbingly human nod of its little head. The overly long ears gave him a thought. "Okay, how about Yoda?"

"Creen, shoo...<*clee!*>"

"Right, stupid idea." He looked around the cavern and grinned. "How about Splunk?" The creature cocked its head. "You want to be known as Splunk?"

"Keetoo, Sheeti...<*skee!*>" and gave a little hop.

"Okay, Splunk! I'm Jim."

"Shooku, chee...<*creet!*>...Jim." Jim's eyes almost bugged out of his head. "*Splunk!*" it said and touched its head. "Splunk, Splunk, Splunk!" And Splunk proceeded to run around jumping from rock to rock singing its name.

"Okay, I guess you like that then."

"<*skee!*>"

Jim was sure now that meant yes. He just wasn't sure why those little ending words sounded so funny in his head. Almost like Splunk was somehow talking in more than one tonality at the same time. He'd have to use a good recorder when he got home. He found a rock to sit on and sighed. Home. Fat chance of that happening. What he really needed was some heat so he could cook some food.

"Shiska, choo…<*cheek!*>" Splunk said. Jim cocked his head and wondered if the little creature had understood him.

"Can you get me heat to cook? Fire maybe?"

"Qweek, fire…<*skee!*>" and it ran off like a shot.

"I can't keep calling it an it," he said as he watched the feisty little creature race away. Somehow he knew she would be coming back. Just like he knew Splunk was a girl. He just knew it. Jim pulled his pack away from the water a bit and set it against a rock. Opening the waterproof top, he found it had done the job and the interior was bone dry. Before he'd even thought about it, he had the stove taken apart and the heating elements removed. It doubled as a cooking stand if you had wood or other combustible materials. He'd been sure the fungus wouldn't burn, though. Regardless, just as he finished setting it up he heard scurrying sounds nearby and Splunk raced into sight.

She ran up on her rear legs. Not nearly as quickly as she'd left, when she'd been using all four to run. She carried something in both arms against her furry body as she approached, using her long tail held out behind her to help with balance.

"What do you have?" he asked her.

"Shooo, fire…<*skaa!*>" She held a bundle of moss, or so it seemed to Jim.

"How is that fire?" She looked at him with, he could have sworn, a frustrated expression. "Okay, can you make the fire here?" he asked and pointed at the stove's skeleton, ready to receive a heat source. Splunk put the bundle down and went to examine the stove. She picked up the lightweight metal and turned it over and over with her delicate fingers. Jim noticed she had three fingers with those dexterous thumbs. Each finger seemed to have a retractable claw, just like a cat. He looked at the moss and resisted the urge to see what it was. When he looked back she was eyeing him suspiciously. He could swear she'd read his mind when he thought about looking at the bundle.

Splunk put the stove back, exactly as she'd found it, and went to the bundle. Taking it over to the stove, she squatted on her haunches and carefully unwrapped it. Inside were a pair of clay lumps. She tipped them both into the stove and put the moss aside, then drew a tiny knife from somewhere. Jim almost jumped to see it. Not only a tool user, but a tool builder? The knife seemed perfectly designed for her hand, and the metal looked like steel.

She used the tip of the knife to carefully chip at one of the two balls of clay. The blade appeared to be made of good steel and showed no damage. After a moment, a tiny piece of clay chipped off and the ball began to emit a reddish light and smoke. She went after the next ball the same way, and in a second it was chipped open as well. This one had bluish light and smoke. She daintily moved the two together with the knife blade. As soon as they touched there was a pop and a flash. Purple colored flames sparkled in the stove. Intense flames too, Jim could feel the heat from several feet away.

"Wow," Jim said, coming closer. It was clean too, the smoke was more like steam, dissipating about a foot above the stove.

"Shoo, fire...<*skaa!*>"

"So it is," he said and put the pot onto the fire and filled it from his backpack bladder. It started to steam in just seconds. "Wow," he said again as he started crumbling beef stew cube into the bubbling water.

Later he sat spooning the food into his mouth and wondering why it tasted so much better than before. The fire had burned for almost a half an hour. Once his food was done, Splunk had investigated it. She sniffed once and shook her head, leaving for a few minutes she returned with a small dead lizard which she stuck on the tip of her knife and roasted over the flames.

"Lizard kabob," Jim chuckled.

"Fee, kabob...<*cheek!*>"

"Kabob," he nodded and said around a mouthful of stew. "Lizard on a stick." Splunk shrugged and Jim almost choked on his food. After she'd toasted the animal, she ate it, bones and all, cleaned the knife and made it disappear. The fire went out a short time later. Jim had to know more about that fire! It was fascinating!

After he'd eaten, he felt incredibly better...and incredibly tired shortly thereafter. He made a sleeping space on the ground and stripped off most of his clothes, then wrapped up in both blankets. When he looked over he saw Splunk had made a bed for herself out of his pack. Smiling, he closed his eyes and was asleep in less than a minute.

Jim woke up and looked around the alien environment lit by glowing fungus and yawned. It was very different from the world of the other cave, up the waterfall. This was tolerable, being able to see beyond the few feet around him. He felt almost reborn and somehow infused with a sense of well-being he hadn't felt in some time. And he had no idea why he felt that good.

"Chooey, chaka...<*cheek!*>" Splunk said from on top of his pack.

"Good morning to you too, Splunk," Jim said and yawned. This little creature had emptied his pack and laid out everything. His first instinct was to be worried, some of that survival gear might be essential later. Then he saw that none of it appeared to be missing or damaged in any way, so he relaxed. Splunk appeared to have been studying each item in turn. "Anything interesting?" he asked, gesturing to the equipment.

"Opoo, Ceek...<*coo!*>" Splunk held up the nano-treatment unit. It was huge in her tiny hands.

"Nanites," Jim said and took the offered unit. "They fix injuries." Splunk cocked her head and regarded him. Jim smiled and reached out. She took his hand and felt it while he examined hers. She was quite warm to the touch.

"Shepa, Leek...<*cheek!*>" Jim shook his head and chuckled.

"I wish I understood you," he said. Again, Splunk looked like she was studying him. "Can you bring more of the hot rocks so I can cook?" She gave a quick chirp and raced off, returning in minutes with more clay lumps, and another dead lizard. Jim already had the stove set up, and soon the water was boiling, and the reptile roasting.

After he'd eaten, he dressed in his mostly dry clothes and explored the cave. This one, unlike the other, was teaming with life. The lizards were numerous, and of several different species. There were insects too, both flying and crawling. And, of course, a multitude of lichen and fungus. The lizards and insects all appeared mostly sightless, or with low-light adaptations. Splunk, not so much. Her eyes were big and sensitive, more like a nocturnal creature than a subterranean.

There were others of her kind too. He had glimpsed them, but always at a distance. When he tried to approach them, they would quickly disappear into the fungal wilderness. When he returned from his explorations, Splunk running along with him, Jim was faced with the fact that he only had one meal left. And he wasn't looking forward to finding out what lizard kabob tasted like.

"Splunk," Jim said, "I wish I could get out of here."

"Geeka, out...<*cheek!*>"

"Yeah, out." Splunk turned and pointed as if she was indicating where the bathroom was. Jim laughed out loud. She turned to look at him.

"Out...<*cheek!*>" she said, and pointed again. Jim stood for another moment then began frantically packing his gear back up. When he was done, he gestured.

"Lead on," he said, and Splunk took off at a run. Jim fell in behind. He knew he couldn't keep up, so he just moved as best he could while avoiding falling or turning an ankle. Every time he lost sight of Splunk, the little creature stopped and waited for him to catch up before continuing onward.

Others of Splunk's kind began to eye them as they moved through the cavern. Just like before, they observed the pair, but did not approach. He wanted desperately to get a better look at them, but Splunk chirped annoyingly at him whenever he stopped, so he continued following her instead. They arrived at an almost invisible fracture in the cavern wall. Splunk stood at the crack and pointed inside.

"I hate this job," Jim said and shook his head. Splunk pointed again, and he nodded assent. Once more into the darkness.

After going a few yards inside he saw that they weren't in total darkness. Splunk held a strange frilly mushroom bunch with her tail, and it was glowing brilliantly. He recognized it as one of the kinds that hung from the roof of the cavern. When had she found time to go and get it? Did one of the others of her kind bring it to her? That not only implied intelligent language, but also the ability to do so silently. What, telepaths? He chuckled at that mental image. Out of the thousands of races, none of the carbon-based "main" races possessed verifiable telepathy. A couple had a sort of natural psychic link, but of a type that could be channeled using instrumentation.

Jim almost lost track of his guide, he'd been too busy trying to figure out the bioluminescent fungus and forgot to follow her. The tunnel turned and ahead there was a glow. He sped up and, as he cleared the bend, there was Splunk, squatting in the space, glowing fungus held up in her tail and looking at him impatiently.

"Sorry," he said.

"Cheep, akeeto…<pree!>" Jim guessed the last was not a positive comment.

He continued to follow his guide for more than an hour through the glowing spaces, and he spent a lot of that time climbing. When he felt the first chill wind he got excited. Then it got a lot colder, and his excitement was tempered by a shiver.

"Splunk," he said, "I have to put on my cold weather clothing." He opened the pack and pulled out the survival suit he hadn't worn in days. Splunk sat down and watched him with interest as he got the suit on and enjoyed the basic warmth. But without power, it was just a fancy set of long johns. "Okay," he said at last, "continue."

They resumed their climb upwards once more. A few minutes later, sunlight was illuminating the tunnel ahead of them. The cold was also much more intense. Jim was surprised by how the light hurt his eyes. Splunk had it much worse. She was holding a hand over her eyes and looking away from the light. She was in pain from it, and he knew it.

"I'll be right back," he said, while slipping the suit's gloves on. Jim climbed up to where the light was shining and opened his pack. A minute later he slid back down next to Splunk, and then further around the corner where the sunlight didn't reach. Splunk took her hand away and winced back in the direction of the sunlight unhappily. Jim made sure the line he'd trailed down from the solar cells was sound and checked the battery. It already had a one percent charge. "And what do I do when it's charged?" he wondered aloud. For once, Splunk had nothing to add.

Jim found a comfortable position and relaxed. After a while, he slept. He didn't know how long, but when he woke up Splunk was gone, and the battery showed it was twenty-eight percent charged. He pulled his glove down far enough to reveal his watch. He'd been asleep for four hours. He needed another sixteen for the charge to be complete, but the meter showed no more power coming in. It was night above.

"Splunk?" Jim called, his voice echoing down the long tunnel he'd climbed up hours ago. No answering chirps or other strange sounds followed. He sighed and dug his last ration cube from the pack along with the heater, which, thanks to the solar cells, was now working again. He'd gotten used to the heating stones Splunk provided and was amazed to realize they were faster than the energy stove's normal source. "I wonder if there is a market for alien heating stones?"

The last of the food tasted good, and that annoyed him because he remembered just how bad it had tasted the first time he'd tried it almost a week ago. Still, it was better to have a full stomach than an empty one. After he'd cleaned up and stowed his cooking gear, he accessed his pinplants and went over the files he'd made while underground, including estimates of travel distance and direction. He hoped it would help him find his way back to his company's camp. Either way, he was tired again so he set an alarm in his implants and allowed sleep to take him. He drifted off hoping Splunk would be okay, and grateful for the little being's help.

* * * * *

Chapter Twenty-Four

Murdock watched the data feeds from the dropship's cockpit as it flew over the frozen landscape only a thousand feet below them. They'd been searching for a week now, and despite Hargrave's unwillingness to give up on the kid, it had just about reached that point. There were a pair of Duplato aboard to provide local area knowledge. They'd pointed out a few caves in the area. Nothing that could have kept someone alive without extensive skills or tools, though, and Jim Cartwright possessed neither of those.

"We're bingo fuel," Jane Wheeler called to Murdock over the internal link. "I guess that's it."

"It's been a week," he replied. "I know you all love the fat little dude, but he should never have come out here. He could have run this op from orbit."

"That tank was a piece of work," she said.

"I'm still not convinced it wasn't just luck." Crazy-assed good luck, he thought, just not enough of it.

"Coming around to head for base," Jane said, and the dropship banked.

A while later, Murdock was going over some of the reports he needed to sign off on as First Sergeant. The dropship flew toward base and was approaching the site of the battle where Jim was lost. He accessed the dropship's cameras inside his CASPer and could see the huge, black scorched section of ground less than a mile away as they flew past. And then he saw a spark of color flash into the sky.

"We have a flare," Jane called out a heartbeat later, and the *Phoenix* banked hard in that direction.

"Careful," Murdock cautioned, "it could be a trap."

"No sightings in days," she said, "besides, it matches the thermal signature of our emergency flares."

"No fucking way," Murdock said as he detached from the lockpoint holding his CASPer in place and moved aft using the intermittent handholds. The three other troopers with him watched as he held on while the dropship descended and flared to land, the dropship door lowering just as it settled in a swirl of snow and ice. A shape came walking forward in the storm of debris kicked up by the dropship's landing, holding up an arm to shield his face from the flying snow and ice. There was no mistaking the portly shape of Jim Cartwright.

"Yes, fucking way," Jane said from the cockpit, a laugh in her voice.

Murdock clomped his suit down to the bottom of the ramp as Jim leaned against the wind of the idling dropship engines. Murdock could just make out the young man's broad grin through the environmental mask. Jim tossed aside the flare launcher as he approached and spoke.

"Thanks for picking me up. I only had about twenty percent power left in the survival suit." Murdock laughed and shook his head. Then he brought the CASPer to attention and affected an awkward, overly long-armed salute.

"Welcome back, Commander."

"Good to be back," he said.

"Glad you made it, sir," Jane Wheeler said over the cabin's PA, "but we're bingo fuel and not 100% sure there aren't any unfriendlies around, so if you can get aboard?"

"Of course," he said and climbed the ramp. Jim managed to not convey just how terrified he'd been only moments ago as Murdock followed him inside, and the ramp began to retract. The other men had the canopies open on their suits and were looking at him in amazement as he stripped off the mask and gloves, revealing that he looked no different than when he'd been lost. His cheeks were a little furry, but he'd only needed to shave once a week anyway. He held onto a strut as the engines spun up to their normal scream, and the *Phoenix* climbed back into the air.

Murdock locked his suit into position and popped his own cockpit so he could see his commander with his own two eyes. Jim took one of the unsuited rumble seats as the two Duplato came back to regard him with curiosity.

"What's everyone looking at?" Jim asked.

"A ghost," one of the troopers said without hesitation.

"You've been gone for over six days," Murdock told him. "This was the last search flight, actually. We were about to declare you lost in action." Jim shook his head. One moment of luck after another. He hoped he had a lot more for the future.

Jim unzipped the top of his suit, and Splunk stuck her head out.

"Capoo, skee!" she chirped at all the strangers. Her eyes were covered with a pair of sunglasses Jim had improvised from some plastic in the survival kit and a little paracord. Her eyes lit on the CASPers, and she got excited. "<*Cool*>"

"I know," Jim said; "impressive, aren't they?"

"What the fuck is that thing?" Murdock asked as he looked at the creature. In a flash Splunk extracted herself from inside Jim's survival suit where she'd been wedged against the cold, and she leapt a dozen feet to land on Murdock's CASPer. Before he could do a thing, she was inside the cockpit with him examining all the instruments and controls, all the while chirping, hiccupping, and babbling happily. "Is it dangerous?" Murdock asked, trying not to touch it.

"No," Jim laughed, "she saved my life. Well, others of her kind probably helped. But she's smart, and I'm certain her species is sentient." The little being figured out one of the maintenance releases and a hatch popped open on the suit, much to Murdock's chagrin. "She really likes mechanical stuff. A lot."

"You found a Fae," one of the two Duplato said, and pointed a long claw at Splunk. She stopped for a second to look out of an access hatch on Murdock's suit and examine the speaker. After a moment, she was back at it.

"You know of them?" Jim asked.

"Of course, they share our world. Every winter they move underground to the many hot spring caverns to live and wait for spring."

"I wondered if there was ever a spring here," Jim said. "I mean, we saw the trees and were confused."

"Yes," the other Duplato said, "it takes many thousands of years between seasons. We are close to spring again. Fall was more than 20,000 years ago. We live underground all the time, so we do not notice the changing of the seasons nearly as much. To the Fae, it is normal." The other Duplato made a slight bow and spoke.

"We are sorry, we did not know there were any underground habitats near here, or we would have searched them for you."

"Yes," Jim said; "there are some just a couple miles north of where you found me. Two caverns." He described them as the dropship flew, including how Splunk had come to him. Even how she'd appeared just as he was ready to emerge and refused to be left behind, despite the bright sunlight hurting her eyes. The two Duplato spoke to each other for a few moments then to Jim.

"That Fae has bonded with you," it said. "This is rare and wonderful for you. It has not happened in my lifetime."

"Wow," Jim said and smiled. He couldn't help but think it was like having his own My Little Pony character. "Are they intelligent?"

"You mean like us?" the Duplato asked. "They have an order of intelligence, including their own language." Jim already knew that. His recordings were beginning to put Splunk's speech into context. "However they are not independent tool makers, despite the ability they demonstrate to repair technology. It is what you would call a savant ability."

"Shouldn't we put it back where it came from?" Murdock wondered as Splunk examined the haptic feedback system hooked to his head.

"That would kill it," the senior Duplato explained. "They are bonded now. That bond will only be broken by one of their deaths. And if Commander Cartwright dies, the Fae will not live out the rest of that day."

"I guess we're friends then," Jim said. Splunk emerged from her examination and jumped back to Jim, apparently content. Murdock went through the diagnostics on his suit and found nothing amiss. In fact, one of the haptic sensors on his left leg had been giving him trouble, and now it appeared fine. Interesting creature.

"We'll be landing in a minute," Jane's voice called out. "The entire company has turned out to welcome you back, Commander."

An hour later Jim felt like he'd won the big football game. As Jane Wheeler had said, the entire company was on the field to welcome their commander back. Murdock gave him a quick debrief. The attacking raiders had been soundly defeated in the battle he'd been in and then twice more in cleanup raids. Only a few days ago, *Traveler* had ambushed the raider's light cruiser trying to sneak through the stargate and had destroyed it with precision weapons fire.

When the *Phoenix* set down and taxied over to the hangar, the door opened to a crowd of applauding Cavaliers. Hargrave was at the front of the group applauding with the rest. When he caught Jim's eye he gave a parade ground-perfect salute. A moment later a silence fell over the crowd and, as one, they all came to attention and saluted Commander Jim Cartwright. He stood up straight and returned the salute, tears glistening in his eyes.

Hargrave dropped the salute and strode forward to seize Jim in a bear hug, to which Splunk chirped indignantly because she'd been caught in the middle of it. Hargrave pulled back in surprise.

"What the heck is that?" he asked. Splunk stuck her head out of the survival jacket where she'd been enjoying Jim's body heat as well as a nice nap. She looked at Hargrave, then up at Jim, and made a trilling sound before disappearing back into the folds of the coat.

"That," Jim said, smiling, "is my friend." An assault company like the Cavaliers didn't tend to have a lot of women, CASPers just took too much upper body strength. The women who were there let out an audible "Oooh!" at the sight of Splunk. A few minutes later Jim was surrounded by the entire company, all asking questions about what happened and how he survived. The women seemed much more interested in Splunk.

After a short time, the little Fae became less shy and was willing to let a girl tickle her nose. Splunk let out an incredibly musical "Shooooo, teeek...<*Cooo!*>"

"Is that its language?" Hargrave asked.

"Her," Jim corrected, "Splunk is a girl."

"How do you know?" Jim thought about that for a second, then grunted.

"I don't rightly know, I just do. Anyway, yes, it is her language. I've been storing some phrases in my pinplants, but most of the sounds are combined in a dizzying variety of ways. I'm sure that last sound was an 'I like that' sound."

"What does she eat?" Jim looked up and saw Adayn looking at Splunk who was still mostly inside Jim's survival suit.

"I haven't seen a lot of her eating," he admitted. Adayn pulled a standard issue protein bar from one of the dozens of pockets on her work coveralls, tore off the end of the wrapper and held it close to Splunk. The Fae leaned out a little and sniffed.

"Foo, Ptoo...<*Pree!*>" she spat.

"That's a no," Jim said as she retracted a little into the suit. Adayn popped the bar into her mouth, and fished out a package from another pocket. This one had a zipper closure. She opened it and pulled out a piece of beef jerky. Immediately Splunk popped out, sniffing the air.

"Sak, Shoo...<*cheek!*>" she said and leaned a little further out.

"Oh, you like meat?" Adayn asked.

"Who doesn't," Murdock asked. He had his CASPer off, and it was being taken away by some of the techs.

Splunk reached out one of her delicate hands and took the offered jerky. She didn't snatch it, like a wild animal would, she took it almost gingerly then nibbled on the edge. Her long feathery ears rose, and her eyes narrowed as she chewed.

"I think that's a yes," Adayn said. She reached over and scratched Splunk behind her extra-long ears. The Fae practically purred. "You've made yourself quite a friend," she told Jim.

"Yeah, I get that impression." He was practically surrounded by every woman in the company, all cooing and trying to offer Splunk treats. It was the first time he'd ever been surrounded by girls who weren't making fun of him.

"Splunk," he said quietly, "you're the gift that just keeps on giving."

"Faa, Scoos... <*Skaa!*>"

J im watched from the hangar entrance as the last heavy transport clawed up into the morning sky toward orbit. The veins of radioactive elements were played out, and the Duplato's profits would be secured as soon as the transport made transition. *Traveler* awaited it in orbit to escort it to the stargate. The remaining months of the contract had passed without incident, and he felt quite satisfied with their performance. Even with losing his own suit, there were no other significant losses and the worst injury had been from skiing – a broken collarbone.

"*Traveler* will be back in about eight hours," Hargrave said behind him. Jim glanced back and saw his Executive Officer standing with a steaming cup of coffee. The hangar doors were only open a few feet and the air outside was only slightly below zero, a fine warm summer day. Almost two degrees warmer than last year, according to the Duplato. Summer was returning to their world.

"I'm cold...<*Pree!*>" Splunk said inside his jacket. Jim was not quite used to her being as fluent as she'd become in the intervening weeks. It was almost freaky how fast she'd learned.

"Just a few more minutes," Jim implored, then turned to Hargrave. "So, the contract is fulfilled?"

"Yes," Hargrave agreed, "and they're very happy. They included an extra two percent bonus." Jim smiled, that was good news. "Shall I begin preparation for mobilization?"

"Yes," Jim said. "Plan for the first dropships to lift off in twelve hours."

"You got it, boss." Hargrave turned away from the cold air to begin organizing their departure.

"And you aren't staying?" Jim asked Splunk.

"No, go...<*Skaa!*>" Jim smiled again. He knew, of course, that the Fae would go. The Duplato said if they bonded with someone, and it didn't happen very often, it was for life. They also said the Fae were extremely intelligent, with a simple society and affinity for machinery, even though they had never developed any technology of their own.

"Okay," he said and reached in to scratch her ears. "We're going to the stars soon."

"Like, stars...<*Coo!*>"

"Me too," Jim agreed. The transport was now a tiny point of brilliant light as its fusion-powered engines worked to thrust it into orbit. Soon it was lost to him. He turned and went inside.

* * * * *

Chapter Twenty-Five

"Combat configuration, Miss Paka!"

"Aye-aye, Ma'am!" Paka activated the inter-ship public address system. "General quarters, set Condition One, I repeat, set Condition One. Transition to the Morphut system in twenty-nine seconds." Paka, the Executive Officer of *EMS Pegasus*, watched her boss closely for signs of what other orders might be coming. Being a high-ranking officer aboard the most powerful warship in the human merc companies was challenge enough, but being an alien made it even more so. Still, she considered herself both lucky and among the elite. Her ship's Situation Controller, or SitCon, waggled its tentacles at her, confirming the order complete. "Condition set," she told the Commander.

"Very good," Alexis Cromwell said and settled back slightly in her chair as the clock reached fifteen and continued counting down.

"Any reason for the extra concern?" Paka asked. She adjusted the goggles over her emerald green eyes. The light was too bright, but it almost always was for a Veetanho.

"Nothing really," Cromwell said, her eyes narrow with concentration on the ship's status board as the count passed five, "and everything."

"Transition in three," the engineer spoke over the 1MC, or ship wide intercom, "two...one..." There was a jolt, and *Pegasus* was again in regular space.

"We have potential bogeys," the sensor tech yelled almost immediately.

"Launch ready-alert drones," Paka ordered, "shields up!"

"Bring us about and away from the transition point," Cromwell ordered as the alert claxon began to chime repeatedly. "Azimuth 125 relative, attitude 0! Make our acceleration five gravities."

The alarm for combat maneuver and high G acceleration sounded as *Pegasus* spun and began to burn her engines, hard. A squadron of four interceptor drones and their controller flashed from one of her three landing bays and immediately took up protective covering positions around their mothership. Despite the size and power of *Pegasus*, she was vulnerable to enemy drones, especially at the relatively slow delta-*v* the ship retained when making most transitions.

"Give me situational scans," Cromwell ordered. "What's going on?"

"Multiple contacts," sensors replied, "none of them are under power. I have sporadic energy signatures. If I had to, I'd say we're looking at the remains of a fight."

As *Pegasus* accelerated to get maneuvering room, her shields intermittently flashed as the ship collided with debris. Most were small, the size of a bolt or a coffee cup, but others closer to that of an entire drone. The shields would flash crimson, and a tiny shudder pass through the ship's hull at those impacts.

"Do we have any active threats?" Paka demanded.

"I'm not getting any attempted target locks," the sensor tech finally relented.

"Whatever happened here, we missed it," Paka told her commander. Cromwell looked around the bridge at the eyes of various races regarding her. They all had the same unspoken question in them. How the hell had she known?

"What about planetside?" the commander asked. "Is the Wathayat installation on Crig answering hails?"

"Nothing," Commo confirmed.

"Keep up the attempt. Navigation, set a high G course to Crig. I want a solution that lets us bypass and run for the stargate."

"High gravity course to Crig, aye; solution to include option to bypass and run, aye."

"Send the alert drones ahead to the planet to scout. Orders are to only fire if fired upon." Paka acknowledged the orders. "I'll be in my wardroom," she said as the acceleration fell off, the ship changing orientation to follow the new course. "Let me know the minute there is any response from Crig – or any information at all about the situation down there."

Three hours later Paka knocked once and entered, as was the standing order for any senior staff. Alexis Cromwell was strapped into the chair behind her ornate and very out-of-place-looking desk, hands on the greenish wood, staring vacantly off into space. Anyone who saw the commander for the first time in one of these states would have thought she was having a seizure. She shook occasionally, her eyes open and staring, and her mouth moved but no sounds came out.

The door behind Paka slid closed with a "snikt" sound, and she stood waiting. She hoped it wouldn't be long; there were only five minutes before they needed to resume acceleration or begin braking, but after a couple of moments Cromwell shook hard once and pulled her hands away from her desk. She smoothed her hair and blinked several times.

"What do you have, Miss Paka?" she asked.

"The drones reached Crig, ma'am."

"No base?"

"Correct," she said. "There are numerous bombed-out locations; Tactical believes based on the residual radiation that the weapons yields are likely nuclear in origin. No radio communications established. We can only assume no survivors."

"Understood. Orders are to continue the run for the stargate. The contract is terminated. Send message drones ahead. One to the Mercenary Guild informing them of the status here, and one to the nearest Wathayat-held system with the same information."

"Yes, ma'am," Paka said and turned to go. Then curiosity got the better of her, and she looked back. "Ma'am, may I ask what you think is happening?"

"A sign, I fear," she said, shaking her head. "A sign of what is ahead."

* * * *

Chapter Twenty-Six

The ice-cold Coca Cola was just as good as the first time he'd tasted it, over half a year ago. They were sitting at the same table where he and Hargrave had sat then, meeting with Eugene Treadwell for the contract they'd just completed. His second-in-command raised his glass of wine in salute. Jim smiled at Hargrave and returned the salute with his cola.

Karma was on the route back to Earth, so Jim decided they would stop along the way. Besides being a center of merc activity, home to a dozen notorious pits, it was also a great place to purchase munitions and supplies. *Traveler* had suffered minor damage in her battles, so Captain Winslow was taking the opportunity to perform repairs and refill his missile magazines.

"I am pleased to see you return, Jim Cartwright."

"I am glad to return, Peepo," Jim said as the owner of the merc pit approached.

"News of your success, and the return of Cartwright's Cavaliers has spread all over Bartertown. Likely throughout the Union. Those raiders were well known. You have done their many victims a great service."

"And we were well paid for it," Hargrave joked.

"As you should have been," Peepo agreed. Jim grinned. The job had put 11.5 million into the Cavaliers' coffers. Already, back on Earth, the logistics teams were busy activating another company of troopers, preparing two more dropships for operation, and more

APCs. He hadn't taken a single credit for himself; it all went to paying shares to the company members and activating new forces.

Hargrave left to use the bathroom, leaving Peepo and Jim alone. A moment later they got another visitor.

"Tasteful, meat...<*Skaa!*>" Splunk chirped, jumping up to the table. She had a choice-looking piece of steak. Jim had no idea where she'd gotten it, but he suspected that, somewhere in Peepo's Pit, a patron was looking at his empty dinner plate in confusion. The little Fae used her razor-sharp teeth to excise a chunk and chewed happily. As he watched his friend eat, Jim became aware Peepo was staring at her.

Peepo slowly reached up and lifted her goggles, revealing the Veetanho's reddish eyes. She examined the Fae, leaning even closer.

"Jim Cartwright," she said. "What is it you have here?"

"Her name is Splunk." Peepo gave the Fae a serious examination.

"Splunk, is it?" she asked.

"Splunk, yes...<*Skee!*>" Splunk confirmed.

"It is intelligent?"

"Sure is," Jim confirmed.

Once they made orbit around Karma, Jim had accessed the Galnet and did a search on Splunk and the Fae. In all the thousands of species and races listed, the Fae weren't shown.

"It is an interesting creature. Will you sell it?"

"No," he said without even thinking about it. Splunk glanced up at him as she continued to tear pieces out of the steak.

"I have a friend who studies new sentient species. They will take excellent care of her, and will give you a million credits." Jim blinked in amazement.

"She's my friend," he said with finality.

"I understand," Peepo said. "Well, good luck on your next contract," she added, and just like that, she was gone.

"What the fuck was that all about?" Jim wondered as he took a sip of his Coke.

"She, knows...<*Creet!*>"

"Knows what?" Jim asked. Splunk finished her steak and began licking her dexterous fingers clean. She apparently didn't have anything more to say.

"Where'd Peepo go?" Hargrave asked as he walked up. He'd gotten a sandwich from one of the autocookers on his way back from the bathroom. Splunk immediately took notice. "You keep your thieving hands off my dinner," he told the Fae.

Jim opened his mouth to tell Hargrave about the exchange, then closed his mouth when he thought better of it.

"She had other things to do," he said. "So, let's look for another contract." In the end, Splunk got the better part of Hargrave's sandwich.

* * * * *

Chapter Twenty-Seven

A year had passed, as well as three contracts. Jim had managed to lose one CASPer per contract, despite his best efforts and nearly constant training. The first was on a recon contract supporting a heavy assault. His suit was hit by an EMP that knocked out all its electronics. The second contract, he was disabled by multiple hits of medium-powered lasers. None of them penetrated to injure him, but the damage eventually rendered the suit combat-ineffective. The last contract was on the world of Topsol, their first assault mission. They were tasked by the Otoo to retake a petrochemical refining installation from an elite Jivool merc unit.

The attack was Jim's first HALD, high-altitude, low-deploy, jump in a CASPer. He drilled in the simulators all the way to Topsol to be ready for it. Despite all the training, he ended up nearly having to order Hargrave to allow him to lead the assault.

"You only land successfully about half the time," his mentor reminded him.

"It's a hot drop; we'll need every suit on the ground. With only two full companies in the drop, it's sketchy at best." Jim argued his point strenuously.

"Exactly, I don't have the manpower to babysit you."

"Then don't," Jim finally snapped. "Damn it, am I the company commander or a mascot?" Hargrave had jerked in response to that as the accusation hit home. Jim regretted it right away, and Splunk had looked up from where she'd been trying to subvert the lockout on the meat locker in the Commander's Mess aboard *Traveler*. The Fae looked between them curiously.

"Okay Jim," Hargrave finally agreed. "But damn it, be careful."

The HALD was the second most frightening event in his life, right behind the protracted tank battle on Kash-Kah. He and the rest of his First Platoon were dropped from *Phoenix 1* at just under one hundred miles above the surface as the dropship executed a steep, powered climb, effectively firing them at the planet below. Topsol was rated Human Nominal with a thicker-than-normal atmosphere, so his CASPer was fitted with a faring to shed heat. The ten CASPers burned in, accompanied by twenty decoys – nothing more than thin ceramic alloy weighted shells that provided extra targets for ground defense.

He rode down in the preprogrammed part of the drop in a constant state of terror. Just like all the previous regular deployments, Splunk was nestled in the suit with him. When they'd first buckled him into a suit for a contract after Kash-Kah, Splunk had snuck into the suit. After that, he stopped trying to keep her out. On the drop to Topsol, Splunk climbed up from the more spacious thigh area shortly after they were ejected from the dropship. She seemed to sense his fear, and nestled against his chest. He felt her there, nuzzling his flabby belly and trilling. In moments, he'd calmed down. He was still terrified, but the fear wasn't threatening to overwhelm him.

At the preprogrammed altitude, the faring was blown away by explosive bolts and he had control of the suit for the last ten miles. It was done at that altitude to ensure the troopers didn't deploy weapons too soon in violation of Union law. The night sky was alive with lasers crisscrossing the sky trying to take out the attacking Cavaliers.

With the discarded four sections of each trooper's faring added to the dozens of decoys, the entire platoon came through without a scratch.

The ground rushed up, and Jim used the jumpjets as judiciously as he could. To his joy, he set the suit down with the perfect amount of remaining velocity, the knees bending to absorb the impact.

"I did it!" he crowed in the cockpit.

"We, land...<*Cheek!*>" Splunk asked.

"Yep," Jim said as he activated the suit's normal ground operations programming, and they began to regroup.

As the mission progressed, he started to hope he'd make it through the attack without a scratch. His platoon assaulted their assigned avenue of attack, breaching the Jivool defense perimeter. The ursoid race used exoskeleton suits with strategic armored plates in combat and preferred to close to point-blank range and brawl. Unfortunately for them, that tactic didn't work with the well-armed human CASPers. They were absorbing horrendous casualties as they charged the Cavaliers repeatedly. Jim was about to try and reach their command circuit and ask the defenders to surrender when one dropped onto his suit from an overhead gantry.

He spun, trying to dislodge the bear as it clawed at his suit. He got ahold of its arm and yanked, sending it crashing into a building in a shower of masonry. Unfortunately, it had managed to grab the suit's control pack, and it shredded the armor with its steel-reinforced claws, tearing loose the module and taking it with the Jivool as it went airborne. His controls shorted out in a shower of sparks, and he crashed down on his face.

"Oh no," he moaned and desperately tried to regain power, "not again!" The suit's nominal AI wasn't responding through manual input or through his pinplants. The damned Jivool had ripped out the suit's main computer, and likely damaged the backup as well.

"No, fight...? <*Pree!*>" Splunk asked, squirming out from under Jim.

"I know, I'm upset," Jim said and tried using hand sequences to activate the emergency backup power. Nothing. "We're dead in the water." Splunk wasn't just trying to get out from under Jim, she was working around behind him. Then he heard and felt the interior access panel to the electronics pack open. "What are you doing?" he asked her. Only a chirping trill of contented Fae came back. "Splunk, this isn't the time to mess around!"

There was a snap and he smelled ozone. He was about to yell when the lights came on again, and amazingly, he had control! The AI wasn't there, but haptic feedback systems were working. He put a left arm under him and leveraged upwards. The cameras were alive too, enabling him to see that the Jivool was still alive – and pointing a weapon at him. Jim squeezed his left thumb and pinky together and prayed. The back mounted laser snapped up and fired, nearly cutting the enemy in half. Surprised he was still alive, Jim got the suit to its feet.

"Better, Jim...<*Skaa!*>"

"It sure is," he agreed. "How did you know what to do?" But Splunk wasn't interested in talking anymore; she was back in the roomier thigh area and nestled in.

After the assault was over and Jim was out of his suit, he met with his platoon leaders to discuss the mission debrief, then returned to the landing zone where Adayn was tending to his suit. She looked both annoyed and confused.

"Sorry about the suit," he said as he approached. Splunk was with her, perched on the suit's shoulder and eating, as usual.

"What did you do to it?" Adayn asked.

"Jivool ripped the brains out."

"Yeah," she said, "I noticed that. I mean how'd you do this?"

"What?" he asked and climbed the gantry. Behind the suit he could see that not only was the suit's computer control module damaged, it was completely gone. There were a few computer memory and program chips that were mounted in a secondary box, usually used to control the software on the HALD. They'd been removed and patched together where the computers used to be. "Huh?"

"Yeah, exactly," Adayn said and looked at him through slitted eyes. "You cobbled this together in the middle of an assault?"

"No," Jim admitted. "I didn't. She did." He hooked a thumb toward Splunk who was happily enjoying the meal she'd recently purloined.

Word quickly spread of the incident with Splunk even while Jim met with the Otoo to settle the contract. Hargrave was already there, and Jim didn't like the way things looked. His friend and mentor looked pissed.

"What's the score?" Jim asked.

"Cracked Crab there can't pay us."

"What?"

"Yeah, they admitted they didn't expect us to be quite this successful." The contract was for twenty-three million credits, contingent on 100% successful taking of the installation. There were extensive lists of damages that could be caused by the assault and deductions from the contract payment based on those damages. It was the reason they'd elected for a HALD assault, effectively drop-

310 | MARK WANDREY

ping right into the Jivool's midst. The plan had worked so well that none of the listed facilities were damaged, leaving the Otoo owing the entire fee.

"So maybe we should blow up a few buildings to bring the price down?" Jim growled. The crustaceans looked alarmed, if a crab with extra arms could look alarmed.

"We apologize," they said through the translators several times.

"Apologies are nice, but how do you plan to settle the debt?" Hargrave persisted. "We will turn this over to the mercenary guild, if we must. They may even allow us to keep this facility." Jim lifted an eyebrow at Hargrave but the other man gave him a wink. What the hell would they do with a petrochemical processing facility anyway?

"We can offer you some Raknar!"

"Some what?" Hargrave asked. A short time later they were being shown to the administrative complex of the operation. It was a common Union design tower a few dozen stories tall, only in front of it were a pair of huge, vaguely humanoid robots. "I've seen those before," Hargrave said, "some kind of ancient mecha."

"Yes," the Otoo said, "Raknar! Valuable and rare."

"Not that rare," he told Jim *sotto voce*. "I've seen them on a dozen worlds, usually in pieces and in worse shape.

"They're *awesome!*" Jim said, looking at the machines that were easily a hundred feet tall. "Do they work?"

"No," the Otoo admitted. "Well, they can be made to walk. They are very ancient, used in the war against the Kahraman a long time ago."

Splunk was riding on Jim's shoulder and, for a change, had nothing to say. She merely observed the Raknar with quiet intensity.

"We offer these two Raknar to you in lieu of payment."

"No way," Hargrave said. "They're lawn decorations."

"They'd look pretty cool in front of the headquarters on Earth," Jim admitted. Hargrave looked chagrined. "These two Raknar and twenty million." The Otoo clacked claws in consternation and made a counter offer. An hour later negotiations were completed.

"There is no way those two hunks of junk were worth three million apiece," Hargrave said, shaking his head.

"I haven't taken a dime in four contracts," Jim said. "If they're worthless, then I'll take them for my share."

"Jim, that's crazy. It's your company. You get some of the profits and spend them however you want."

"Then stop complaining," Jim said as the heavy transport began to lift the first one onto a truck bed. He was grinning ear to ear. Who else on Earth had their very own giant robots? "I wonder if I can get three more and combine them together?" Hargrave just shook his head and put his face in his palm.

* * * * *

Chapter Twenty-Eight

Business was good – almost too good. Jim hadn't yet returned to Earth as there were simply too many contracts available and all at increasing payouts. Something was up, and no one seemed to know what. *Traveler* was docked at the orbital station of Karma where he'd rented facilities that the Cavaliers could use as their off-Earth base. Many of the contracts coming up were in this region, so it was just an expedient. *Traveler* consumed too much F11 to have it flitting back and forth to Earth between contracts. Instead, he sent personnel and equipment via commercial transport at a fraction of the cost.

Jim signed the Cavalier's first contract in which he would not personally join in the deployment. He sent a single platoon on a scout mission to assist the Spinward Rangers all the way over on the far side of the Praf region, coreward in the Jesc Arm. They were due back in a couple of months. He'd tapped Buddha for that op and sent him and his team along with the Golden Horde because they were heading the same way. The Horsemen often hitched rides for free – a perk of being in the club.

Minus the one platoon, he had his entire strength on hand and was faced with a hard choice of contracts at the moment. Many of them were tough, direct-heavy, or medium-assault ops. His entire outfit was composed of veterans now, even himself, though he admitted, in his own case for his own sake, a bit less so. At least he had a HALD drop under his belt. And four mostly trashed suits in the

313

depot. He'd spent a lot of time with Adayn as she led her team keeping the older suits up and running. It was also an opportunity to let Splunk mess around in the shop, though always under close supervision.

One day, shortly after they'd moved onto the big spinning station, Splunk went missing. Jim found her hours later in an equipment room of another merc company. She'd been in the process of building a CASPer from spare parts, and was well underway. Luckily Adayn knew their armorer and she made up some cock-and-bull story to distract and appease him while Jim snuck her out inside his uniform jacket. Splunk had fought and complained the whole time. Adayn had nicknamed her Watchmaker. It took Jim a full hour of research to find that reference. When he did, he was glad it wasn't entirely accurate. Jim had Splunk and Adayn spend at least an hour a day working together. Adayn had been helping Jim plumb the depths of Splunk's abilities, and they seemed formidable. Especially if you consider that her race lived in underground caves and had no obvious tech.

A chime from his office door made him look up. The camera was on and showed Hargrave outside.

"Come in," he said, and the door slid aside. "What's up?"

"Wondering if you've gone over that list of contracts Peepo sent up?"

"Yeah," Jim said and held up the slate showing them. "Looks like a large collection of shit sandwiches."

"And most without mayo," Hargrave agreed and came across the office. It had been a little disconcerting at first watching people walk in the station. The personnel offices and barracks were all outside the outermost wall of Ring A on the station, their feet facing out toward space. Composed of four large, concentric rings spinning in orbit, each ring had a higher gravity. Ring A, furthest out, had the highest gravity (nearly one G nominal). Ring D, just off the hub, only one-tenth of a gravity. It held mostly workshops and warehouses. The hub was docking bays, all in microgravity. *Traveler* was docked there along with a dozen or more other ships at various times. It was a huge station; the circumference was more than a mile. Even so, when people walked around you could tell the floor was curved.

"I'm leaning toward these three," Jim said and handed him the slate. Hargrave took it and grunted.

"Yep, good choices. Same ones I'd earmarked myself." Jim smiled, glad his instincts were good.

The first was a medium-assault – a vendetta mission between two neighboring star systems. Ironically, the combatants were of the same race. Jim figured it was some kind of religious dispute. Didn't really matter, their potential employers wanted their adversary's ability to strike at them neutralized before the other guys could start it. Smash and run. It was the easiest of the three, but provided the least profit, and the highest possibility of civilian casualties. However, there was little possibility of major opposition.

The second mission was to provide one of four elements in a heavy assault. It was a hot conflict that had been going on between two merchant consortiums over a series of deep bore mines on a barren world in the middle of nowhere. The mines were of questionable output, but that wasn't deterring the fighting in the least. It had the highest payout, and the highest risk. The enemy of the contractor had a history of hiring Tortantula merc units, and they weren't pushovers.

The last was the wildcard. The Wathayat trading consortium wanted a garrison unit rated for medium-to-heavy assault on a remote gas processing facility. And that spoke of F11. Fighting over the rare gas was common and often contentious. Wathayat had a reputation of shrewd deals for rare elements, and rumor was they'd recently added a new race to their number that brought, you guessed it, F11 to the table. Its payout was a little above average, and would take all their available forces. The employer had already tried to hire The Golden Horde, the member of the Four Horsemen that specialized in defensive work, but that company was unavailable.

"So, which is it going to be?" Hargrave asked. Jim scratched his chin and thought. Splunk was over on a bookshelf taking apart an antique alien-manufactured timepiece Jim had purchased the other day. He rolled his eyes and chuckled. He also made up his mind.

A shattoo watched from his office as the tanker settled into the docking cradle. Being put in charge of the F11 operation had been a great honor he wasn't sure he really wanted. From mining chief to F11 production manager was further than he ever thought he'd go, especially when his brood mates had first proposed the operation. But ever since the Athal joined with the Wathayat, the operation was hounded by disaster. Epic disaster, and death.

Three processing and storage facilities had been destroyed, one after another, and each not long after the decision to use that facility was made and assets began to move. It was out of desperation that the operation was finally moved to the world of Chimsa. It wasn't a far-flung and remote processing operation of the Wathayat. Chimsa was a heavily-populated planet of the elSha. A technology center that supplied goods all over the Union. Attacking Chimsa would be an act of borderline insanity. Ashattoo was counting on that defense, but he was also savvy enough to know he needed more than that. He needed insurance.

Hours before the tanker arrived, he'd gotten confirmation from the mercenary guild. Cartwright's Cavaliers had accepted the contract and were on their way. One of the human's legendary Four Horsemen, the Cavaliers were a merc company of unbelievable prowess. They were feared and respected throughout the Union.

"Come attack us here," Ashattoo said, looking up at space and rubbing his wings together. "None can stand against these human powerhouses!"

G alrath put the slate down and considered the news carefully. The moves over the last year had been carefully orchestrated to get the bothersome Wathayat to do just what they'd done. They were going to concentrate all their F11 processing and storage at one location they considered unassailable. Who would attack a world like Chimsa? A world so populous, so valuable as to be well-defended.

Galrath licked his lips unconsciously at the thought of the fight to come. The previous tests of Project K had all been successful, if a bit disappointing on some levels. Still...successful enough to take it to the next level. In a few months, there would be millions of liters of F11, all processed and ready for the taking. It would be both a master stroke of opportunism and a statement that the Acquirers were now the preeminent force in the galaxy. As an added bonus, the guilds would soon be on their way out.

He tapped a claw on the slate and brought up a map of all the galaxy's F11 production facilities. To date there were thirty-nine of them. Far too many and far too spread out to easily deploy his new force. He sorted them by size. Five of them accounted for almost seventy-five percent of all the galaxy's production of F11, and Chimsa was ten percent of that, the smallest of the five. He plotted the other four on his slate and his lips pulled back in an unconscious snarl. Maybe he was being too conservative? If the Chimsa operation was successful, and he knew it would be, the next move was obvious. If the entire galaxy had to come to the Acquirers for F11, they would control the galaxy. The inefficient and ineffectual Union could finally be done away with.

Still, he was getting ahead of himself. Victory was not assured. On the slate was still the latest news from his contacts at the Mercenary Guild. Cartwright's Cavaliers had accepted a contract on Chimsa, as an assault company. The Wathayat knew the game after all, or at least some of it. So be it. Galrath typed an order. He'd studied the entropy-cursed humans and knew some of their history. Even the Four Horsemen had their Achilles heels, only it had a lot more than two sets of heels. He licked his lips and wondered if he'd just made a joke.

* * * * *

Chapter Twenty-Nine

The last thing Jim wanted to be doing in the hours before *Traveler* would depart with most of the Cavaliers aboard was to be searching Karma station for his mischievous friend. Hargrave said the little bugger was better at disappearing than your last credit.

Most of the long-term residents of the station knew the Fae by sight; she was a common feature of his own comings and goings, but she was just as likely to turn up with Adayn or by herself in a late-night prowl. The lights of the station were somewhat subdued by human standards, which made them almost ideal for her. Still, she'd taken to wearing a simple belt around her middle in which she kept a few possessions, a couple of simple tools, and a pair of tinted goggles she'd fashioned herself. Neither Jim nor Adayn had made the belt for her – further proof of her abilities.

Any new or different piece of technology drew her like a moth to a flame. Jim had won more than a few bets in the station's bars when he was presented with an obscure piece of alien technology that no one else could figure out. Splunk always made sense of it eventually, the only question was how long. The records so far were five seconds for a strange solar-powered light a trader had given her, and two hours for a life-signs detector that may well have been made by the Kahraman. Jim had won one hundred credits on the life signs detector, then lost 500 when Splunk refused to give it back and ran away with it. Jim never found the device, nor any number of other random pieces of equipment. He suspected she had a stash some-where on the station. He only hoped she wasn't building some kind of death ray, or something worse.

Adayn kept in touch with him as they searched separately, the station was far too big for one person. It wasn't like they could actually search all possible locations, just that they doubled their chances of coming across someone who'd seen his companion.

"Just finished my tour of the shops in the hub," she said over the radio linked with his pinplants, "moving out to ring D."

"Thanks again," he said.

"Anything for you," she replied. Jim blinked and blushed in the dim lighting. They spent a lot of time together, and he liked that. She didn't see the awkward fat kid who'd inherited a storied merc company, she just saw him. Sure, Splunk had a lot to do with it, but that didn't enter his mind.

They continued searching, he from A ring down toward her. Like several times before, they met up in C Ring without any luck.

"I wish I knew where Splunk's secret hiding place was," Jim said when Adayn hopped up. C Ring was only at one-quarter gravity. It was a little like walking on Mars. "And what she's up to."

"Maybe she *found* something interesting in Trader's Alley and is engrossed it in?" Found, Jim thought, funny. When it came to finders-keepers, Splunk was essentially amoral. She never hurt anyone and demonstrated compassion for the sick and injured, but to her, possession was nine-tenths of the law. Should they ever be offered it, her race would be fine candidates for the Union. But, her habits were a little worrisome and often expensive.

"Possibly," he agreed and checked his watch. It was twelve hours before *Traveler* was scheduled to leave, and the last transport from

Earth was arriving only a few hours before that. Cross-loading would be a major logistical challenge. The ship would contain troopers, techs, armament, and some backup suits. "I need to finish a couple of reports and get some downtime. Can you keep an eye out?"

"Sure," she said and touched his arm. It made him shiver. "You get some rest, she'll turn up." He nodded his thanks and left so he didn't have to stammer when he spoke. Besides, the uniform made erections too visible, even the way he was built.

Jim caught a lift back to A Ring and Cartwright's compartments. He spent two hours in his office signing off on orders, paying bills, and making sure everything looked right. Thanks to the pinplants, that went a lot faster than someone who would have had to read everything! When finally done, he went through the adjoining door and into his personal quarters. It was ten feet by ten feet with its own fresher, quite a luxury on a space station. He was the only one in the company with a private bathroom, but Hargrave had insisted, so Jim relented. Able to get a quick shower, he once again was glad he'd done so. With six hours until the transport arrived, Jim set his implants to wake him in five hours and crawled into bed. As he drifted off he was thinking of how nice it felt for Adayn to touch him.

Something made Jim stir from his slumber. He rolled over and tried to concentrate. Was someone in the room with him?

"Splunk?" he asked dreamily.

"No," a feminine voice answered, "it's me." In dim ambient light, he saw the lithe form of Adayn by the door to his tiny quarters.

"Wha?" he said, still not quite awake. He could see the lines of her face, a slight smile as she moved toward him. Her uniform fell away and he looked at her body. Thin waist, graceful hips, tiny breasts. "Adayn, why?"

"Shhhh," she hissed and slid under the sheets with him. It was a small bed made all the smaller by his size, yet somehow she fit with him. He was so hard it hurt. She found him with a hand and felt his hardness. "Isn't this what you want?" she purred in his ear.

"Y-yes," he answered, shivering with anticipation, "more than anything!"

"But you've never done it, and you're afraid?" He nodded. "Don't worry, I'll take care of you." And she was on top of him, straddling his bulk with her small frame, lean legs on either side. She took him in her hand and rubbed him against her wetness. He shuddered in fearful anticipation as she began to push down onto him, and he exploded.

Jim sat up, the buzz of his pinplant alarm jarring him awake like a lightning bolt through his brain. He felt like he'd been ripped from one world into another, rudely and without warning. He felt a hand and looked to the side. Splunk was sitting there looking at him, her huge eyes staring, long delicate ears almost straight up like antenna, head cocked, and just pulling her hand back. That hand had been touching one of the external points of his pinplants.

"I see you finally came back?" he said. She nodded. He reached up and touched the metal point embedded in his skull. "Are you curious about those?" She'd never given them any attention before. She didn't say anything, just trilled and jumped onto a shelf nearby. It held an old equipment box that she'd adopted as a kind of cubby, lined with one of Jim's old worn sweaters. "That was weird," he said and sat up, feeling dampness under the sheets. The smell left little doubt what the incredibly vivid dream had resulted in.

"Fucking great," he said, lifting the sheets and looking at the mess. Plus, he was still hard as a titanium strut. He tried to recall the dream, but already it was fading into that etherealness where all dreams go upon waking. He considered doing something private, but looked up and saw in the near darkness two slightly glowing ovals examining him. That put paid to the idea. Instead, he bundled up the dirtied linen and his sleeping clothes and stuffed them into the auto cleaner. He jumped in the shower and set it for extra cold.

A few minutes later, he zipped up his uniform light duty jacket and headed for the door. Splunk hopped onto his shoulder automatically, and Jim pulled the door open. He almost collided with Adayn.

"Oh!" she gasped. "You scared me."

"S-sorry," he said, and instantly the image of her naked and willing came unbidden to his mind. The shower hadn't been quite cold enough.

"I see our little Watchmaker has returned at last."

"Hello, funwork...<*Otoo!*>" The last was relatively new to her vocabulary. Jim had assigned it as a greeting.

"Hello yourself, Splunk," she said and scratched behind the Fae's ears. She chirped and trilled appreciably. Adayn noticed the way Jim was blushing. "What's up with you?"

"Just nervous," he lied. The way she felt as they pushed together. Oh, fuck. "Look, I have to hurry to meet the transport." He pushed past her and fairly ran down the corridor. Splunk looked back and watched her as Jim rushed away. Adayn looked totally confused.

The transport had already docked and begun disgorging cargo when Jim arrived. The center of the station was a series of massive open bays in microgravity. Ships were held in place via delicate mooring arms, cables and hoses attached to transfer fuel, remove wastes, and provide station power if necessary. Like most space-going bulk transports, it looked like a child's version of a toy dirigible. Huge sections of the hull were now open and loaders (zero-gravity tugs, really) were moving goods in and out. There were several viewing verandas where customers or inspectors could observe the work. Jim met his command team there.

"You're late," Hargrave said, without looking up. Jim maneuvered into the room carefully, using handholds until he reached a place where he could wrap a loop of the ubiquitous Velcro on zero-gravity decks around one arm so he didn't float away. Murdock was nearby in conversation with A Company Commander, Lieutenant Parker, and the relatively new B Company Commander, Lieutenant Kipp Duggin. All three men nodded at his arrival.

"I was detained," Jim said. As soon as he'd secured himself, Splunk leaped from his shoulder and caught a handhold next to the viewing window where she watched the activity outside. Clearly, she wished she was out there examining the machinery. Jim was glad she wasn't. "Everything okay?"

"You wish," Hargrave said. He consulted his slate, then pointed outside. "You're just in time for the show," he said. Jim looked and then gawked. Crews were maneuvering two Raknar, strapped together via a carefully constructed framework, clear of the hold where they were left temporarily floating.

"What the fuck?" Jim asked. "Those look just like my two mechs."

"That's because they are," Hargrave sighed and handed Jim the manifest. Yes, they were there. They'd never been unloaded at Earth.

"What happened?"

"I can't be sure, but my guess is groundside logistics screwed the Zuul."

"I thought I ordered Sommerkorn cashiered!"

"He was," Hargrave confirmed. "The problem is he was actually pretty competent overall; he just got a bit tied up when he was excited. The new logistics guy is a full-blown clusterfuck. The Raknar isn't the worst of it. Look at items thirty-six, thirty-seven, and thirty-eight." Jim scanned down and his eyes got even wider.

"You have got to be kidding me!" Jim shook his head. "Why would they—"

"No clue," Hargrave said, cutting him off. Outside crews were clearing the aforementioned line items from the transport's cargo hold. Several movers had stopped flying about to look at the huge steel things in rapt amazement.

"Tell me we at least got what we actually called for?"

"Yes," Hargrave said with an obviously relieved expression on his face, "this stuff just cost us a shitload to move here. And, to put the cherry on the tart, we don't have anywhere to put it."

"Right," Jim said, "I signed to release most of our warehouse space because we're deploying in a few hours." Hargrave just nodded.

"Decided you wanted your big toys along?" Murdock laughed from a few feet away. Jim stared daggers at him, to which he roared with laughter. The two company commanders looked on with mild amusement. The operations of the merc company didn't interest them, as long as they had what they needed to kill aliens and break shit when they got there.

Jim accessed his slate via his pinplants and began looking at figures. Hargrave recognized the spaced out look on Jim's face and let him work. There wasn't any storage to be had on Karma station; a lot of shit was moving through just then. He considered just selling it all, then discarded the notion. He wouldn't get one percent of their value here on such short notice. Besides, the mechs were his, damn it! Then he found some space. It was going to be close, but enough.

"Okay," he said, turning to Hargrave, "stow it all on *Traveler*."

"Oh, Captain Winslow is just going to love this."

"Offer my apologies, but explain it's the CO's prerogative. Get the loadmaster to start modifying cargo hold Number Two. Put it all in there and get it secured. We depart for Chimsa on schedule." Jim turned to other details, then stopped. "Oh, and fire the asshole who did this and get us another logistics head. Jumping shit, there has to be someone competent left on Earth, right?"

"Raknar, kaboom...<*Cooo!*>" Splunk said with appreciation as she watched the giant robots and the three wayward items begin moving toward the *Traveler*'s docking bay. Jim shook his head. At least he wasn't fixating on Adayn's naked body anymore. Nothing like a good old fashioned Zuul screw to get your mind off your other troubles.

* * * * *

Chapter Thirty

Chimsa was all the way over in the Peco arm of the galaxy, in the populous Cimaron region. Halfway across the galaxy from Karma in the Jesc arm, or nearly sixty thousand light years. They'd make it in four transitions, or about a month total travel time. Long hauls like that were one of the reasons *Traveler* was fitted with a gravity deck. Humans lost muscle tone and bone mass readily during extensive exposures to zero gravity. The day spent between each transition cruising from arrival point to stargate only provided a brief respite from the nullness of hyperspace.

The crew kept busy, running tests on equipment, performing routine maintenance on their suits, training in simulators, and exercising. Jim was amazed that career soldiers could so easily handle the long, tedious hours spent traveling to and from contracts. It was hard to underestimate how important patience, and the ability to avoid being bored might be as qualifications to serve as a mercenary in the twenty-second century.

Splunk loved zero gravity, of course. As an arboreal species, she was as happy flying down corridors or bouncing around open spaces as she would have been climbing oversized, glowing, subterranean fungi. Her unusually long tail functioned as a perfect counterbalance to help her in those endeavors as well. Watching her soaring down the main dorsal companionway of *Traveler* reminded Jim of another creature from a childhood movie – Falkor from *The Neverending Story*.

She could use it to change angles and direction almost as if her species were born in zero gravity.

Jim continued his daily workouts. They'd finally become a part of his routine. He never enjoyed them, but it had increased his ability in the CASPers, so he stuck with it. The scale said he'd lost a total of seventeen pounds since he'd first started exercising shortly after reactivating the Cavaliers. At this rate, he'd reach normal weight for his height just before he turned thirty-two. He celebrated his nineteenth birthday in hyperspace crossing the five-thousand-light-year void between the Tolo and Peco arms of the galaxy.

There was a surprise party, much to Jim's chagrin. It was the strangest setting for a birthday he could have imagined: thousands of light years from the nearest star, hurtling through the vast expanse of interstellar space at inconceivable speeds. All the officers and NCOs were there in the main dining hall of the gravity ring. He'd just come from his workout, listening to music on his pinplants, and they yelled, "Surprise," catching him completely off-guard.

There was cake, of course, and the ship's autochefs produced the food: Jim's perennial favorite, pepperoni pizza. He also received a few gifts. Many of the NCOs had joined in to get him a silver-tipped swagger stick, which was a bit of a gag gift, but he appreciated it nonetheless. Hargrave gave him a computer chip holding all the episodes of *Lost in Space*, an old Earth TV series. But it was Adayn who got him the most interesting thing.

"Here," she said and handed him a small gift-wrapped box.

"Thanks," he said and opened the package. Inside was a watch. He looked at it curiously.

"It's an antique," she said as he tried it on. Once it was fastened on his wrist, she leaned over his shoulder. He was far too conscious of her breasts pressing into his back as she reached to adjust the watch. Most modern watches didn't have winders anymore. This one did. "I thought you would appreciate something with some class – something more befitting a merc commander."

"This is awesome," he said. "Thanks!" Nearby Splunk was sitting on a table busily munching a small pile of purloined pepperoni. She looked up at him, chewing contentedly.

"Pepperoni, tasty...<*Skaa!*>"

"Yes, they are," Jim said and looked back at Adayn, still leaning over him. He was starting to sweat. She was just inches away. He could smell her perfume and see what a startling shade of brown her eyes were. How carefully she'd tied her long ponytail. He swore he could feel her body heat. "Adayn?"

"Yeah?" she asked. Jim felt lightheaded. He knew what he wanted to say, but couldn't make himself say it. The dream all those weeks ago flashed through his mind like a zephyr wind. "What is it?"

"Nothing," he said and shook his head. "Thanks for the watch."

"Sure," she said and touched his arm. A moment later she went to get a piece of cake, leaving him feeling like he'd just made a huge mistake.

"I have something for you too, Commander." It was Hargrave. Jim turned to face him. He took out a little silver case and held it up. It looked a lot like a typical ring box. He popped it open to reveal a pin. The Cartwright's Cavalier done in silver suspended ridiculously from a parachute. "You should have received this right after the mission."

"Aten...shun!" Murdock barked in his command voice. Jim obeyed without considering he was actually the one everyone else was standing at attention for. Everyone gathered around as Hargrave spoke.

"Commander Jim Cartwright, having executed a HALD drop in your CASPer, and survived..."

"Barely," someone mumbled, and everyone chuckled, even Jim.

"Still, survived," Hargrave said, "and as such you have earned the right to be a drop-pinned CASPer trooper." And he fixed it on Jim's uniform board to a round of applause from the others. Jim smiled hugely. He felt closer to these people than he ever had to any of his family, except maybe his father. Someone handed him another Coke, he'd had two cases put aboard. He took it and popped the top, eager for the adventure ahead.

* * * * *

Chapter Thirty-One

"Set Condition One throughout the ship," the 1MC barked throughout *Traveler*. The gravity deck spun down to a stop and the air-tight doors closed automatically. "Battle stations. Battle stations!"

Captain Winslow decided their arrival in the Chimsa system would be, in his words, with teeth bared and claws out. Arriving at their last stop, they'd received notice from Wathayat that there had already been scouts encountered on Chimsa, and that meant significant forces were already in the system. Allied space forces were supposed to be holding it.

"But you can never trust other mercs to cover your ass," the captain told him. When it came to ship operations and tactics, Jim deferred to Winslow, just as his father had. He said to always listen to experience, and Winslow was that experience.

"Transition in one minute...one minute."

"Troopers report," Winslow called over the command channel.

"Cavalier A and B are all reporting as ready," Jim replied, "we're locked and ready." Splunk purred against his right thigh. This was becoming old hat to her.

"Dropships report."

"*Phoenix 1* through *8* report ready," Jane Wheeler replied. "Launch systems are armed and standing by." The clock ticked down to the last seconds.

"Transition in 5...4...3...2..." One moment of discontinuity and they were in the Chimsa system, and in the thick of hell.

"Jim...Jim, come in!"

He shook his head and tried clawing up through a sea of cobwebs. What the hell? He forced his eyes to open as the sounds of his suit's systems, and the data feeds to his pinplants slowly came back to his consciousness. He was spinning on all three axes, and falling.

"Yeah," he moaned, his head hurting. "Yeah, I'm here."

"Thank God." He finally recognized Hargrave's voice. "I thought we lost you when your *Phoenix* was hit."

"*Phoenix* hit," he said, trying to force his brain back into activity. He used his pinplants to stabilize the CASPer's attitude. As he did so, his memory returned. He also felt Splunk stir against his thigh. "You okay down there?"

"Dizzy, sore...<*Clee!*>" she chirped.

"Yeah, me too."

As soon as *Traveler* came out of hyperspace, they'd dropped into the middle of a massive space battle. The mercenary cruiser's electronics warfare specialists identified ship after ship, and they struggled mightily to find out who was on whose side. Unlike conventional warfare where governments faced off, merc battles involved units with no set allegiance. It was quickly obvious that many of the ships so engaged were just as confused as they were!

"I'm getting us clear!" Captain Winslow announced. There were at least two Dreadnought-class ships in the melee. *Traveler* was based on an Enterprise class cruiser hull, but her armaments were far less than that of an actual ship of her class. Plus, she was almost thirty years out of date. What she did have was legs far beyond her obvious capacity, benefits of shaving armament and armor.

With the ship already at battle stations, there was no warning as the cruiser pivoted on her central axis and piled on the Gs, well beyond what she should have been capable of. The troopers, snug in their CASPers were rocked against their padded interiors, silently offering earnest prayers to whatever god or gods might be listening.

Traveler's shields team focused on energizing her aft shields to maximum as the captain desperately tried to pry them out of the threat box where behemoths many times their size were slugging it out with energy beams and missiles. It almost worked, too.

Less than five minutes in, they felt the first missiles being launched from *Traveler*'s defensive batteries. Her maneuvers became increasingly radical, too. Everyone locked in the ship's belly knew they were fighting for their lives – even Jim, who'd never experienced such a battle before. The ship shuddered as impacts hit her shields, then bucked mightily as the first beam weapon penetrated them.

"I need to shed weight!" Captain Winslow said. "There's debris everywhere. You guys will be safer out there than in here, and losing eight dropships just might give me the edge I need. Permission to deploy, Commander?" Jim's eyes were wide as the meaning of his request came home. He wanted to launch all the dropships amidst the maelstrom. It was a desperate move. It also meant that *Traveler* was likely doomed, and Winslow was hoping to give Jim and his troopers a chance, even if it was an insanely small one.

"Permission granted," he said, managing to keep the shake out of his voice. "Good luck, Captain."

"And to you," Winslow replied. "Godspeed. Your father would be proud." Jim felt his eyes tear up as the captain gave the order. "All ships, drop, drop, DROP!" And with a shuddering blast of compressed air, they were propelled away from *Traveler* and into space.

The captain had brought his ship into an attitude to help aim his departing craft at the distant target planet. It also put *Traveler* between them and the swirling mass of fighting and dying starships. Jim could only see it as an abstract representation on his CASPer's command channel. He could see *Traveler*'s sleek form with bulbous gravity deck yawing upwards as it released the dropships. He also saw an energy beam carve a huge chunk out of her side.

"Oh god," he moaned as the ship seemed to shudder, and then come apart into pieces. All those people. And Adayn! Oh, no, not Adayn. Tears filled his eyes. He shook his head to clear it, there were more depending on him, those that were still alive.

"Scatter!" he called over the command channel. "All *Phoenix*, scatter and make for the planet!"

"Cover *Phoenix 1*," Hargrave ordered.

"Belay that," Jim snapped immediately. "Do not put additional units at risk just to protect me!" He was shivering with fear when he gave the order, but he knew it was the right thing to do. "The planet is under heavy assault, and with *Traveler* gone, our only hope of surviving this is to get as many of us on the planet as possible. Now, proceed as ordered!" A second later, he watched on the display as the eight dropships split formation.

The pilots did the only thing they could – they took advantage of the debris of their own starship for cover. The cruiser destroyed, the enemy ships who'd destroyed it didn't waste any more shots on the relatively tiny dropships. Instead they sent drones after them. They were generally robotic, sometimes remotely controlled, had hugely powerful engines with weapons systems and little else, and were notoriously deadly and efficient.

"Hang on down there," Jane told her troopers secured in the hold, Jim among them. "We've got drones incoming."

The *Phoenix* ships were capable of many more gravities of thrust than *Traveler* had been, and Jane didn't take it easy, either. She pushed the old dropship for everything it was worth. Jim gasped under nine Gs of acceleration. Because of their orientation in the ship's bay, it was being slammed into his right side. In seconds, he began to see floaters behind his eyelids and he was fighting for every breath. Splunk let out a single incomprehensible squeak of protest.

"Hang...in...there...kid," he heard Murdock gasp between his own labored breaths. Jim couldn't respond. He just fought for consciousness. Down in the right thigh of his suit, Splunk struggled against Jim's flabby leg which was being deformed by the ship's thrust. He tried to shift off her and was unable to budge his own bulk. Would this ever end?

The Gs fell off, and the ship maneuvered. Jim had a second to think they were out of it when he felt the unmistakable jolt of missiles leaving the dropship's tubes. They were engaging the drones, and that was bad news. Up in the cockpit, Jane had abandoned any concern she had for injuring her troopers through radical maneuvers. Two of the nimble alien drones were homing in on her. She'd already watched *Phoenix 7* die in a ball of expanding gas and debris, just as she'd seen several of the drones go down from her fellows' missiles. Now it was her turn.

She unleashed ECM pods, filling the space around her with tiny robots that thrust and produced electromagnetic signatures like a dropship. At the same time, she unleashed half of her interceptor missiles, aimed at the attackers to their aft. She spun and slammed the thrust lever forward, telling her gunner to do what he could. They had worked together as a team now for almost a year. It had been a good partnership. He used the turrets mounted on the dropship's roof and belly to fill the space before them with bursts of laser fire.

One of the drones exploded. She didn't know if it was from her missiles or her gunner's lasers. It didn't matter. A second later a tight-focus particle beam punched through the cockpit and blew her gunner all over the inside. Systems shorted from the energy discharge, and the cockpit decompressed instantly like a cannon, sucking out bits of her friend and anything not tied down. Her flight suit sealed instantly, and she flew on.

She told the computer to fire the turrets automatically as she ranged for the last drone. Her own ECM was making it hard to find. She knew it was close, since the particle weapon didn't have a lot of range. She took a best guess and let the rest of her missiles fly. A second later, another explosion.

"Eat it, muthafucka!" she screamed in triumph. Then, the drone's missile, which it had launched a second before being destroyed, hit the *Phoenix* right behind the cockpit, cutting the dropship in half.

The cable runs cut, the dropship's engines ran wild, as did its attitude thrusters. Twenty gravities of thrust pushed, twisted, and spun the crippled dropship for three seconds before the forces tore it apart and spilled the troopers into space. It was that insane thrust that had finally knocked Jim out and scattered his squad.

"What's your status," Hargrave asked, his signal slightly broken by static.

"Suit's intact," Jim said and went down the status list. "Oh fuck, jumpjets are out." He turned off the radio. "Splunk, can you fix that?"

"Sure, fix...<*Skaa!*>" his friend replied, and he felt her moving up the suit leg to the rear internal system access.

"Can you get it fixed?" Hargrave asked anxiously.

"I'm on it. What about the rest of my squad?"

"You're the only one I've gotten in contact with."

"They're all dead?"

"I don't think so, or you would be, too. Use your command channel and sweep for them."

Jim did. Using the suit's functions he located eight CASPer ident markers varying in range from one to ten miles away.

"I have eight markers," he reported, "I'm down one."

"Considering you had your dropship shot out from under you, that's not bad. Look, none of them are responding, so I think they're out. Your...extra weight helped you a bit in that situation. You need to take remote control of them, rally to your position before reentry."

"Reentry? I thought we were a couple hundred thousand miles out."

"We were, son, but you've been out for hours and the pilots were hauling ass toward the planet. If you don't manage their attitude, you're all going to be a very pretty lightshow planetside in about an hour."

Jim checked his radar. Sure enough, the planet was only a few thousand miles away, and coming up fast. He had the computer run the reentry and didn't like what he saw.

"Splunk, hurry!" An annoyed chirp came from behind the small of his back followed by the sound of electrical snaps and pops. He swallowed and trusted her as he accessed the command link and began gathering the flock. Hargrave must have been right, because none of the troopers overrode his remote orders to their suits. The furthest away took a few minutes to reach him, but inside of five minutes they were all in formation within a hundred yards of each other. He had a minute to check their idents. Murdock was the only one missing. "Fuck," Jim muttered, feeling sick and angry all at once. His position in the dropship was forward, just behind the cockpit.

The jumpjet controls went from red to yellow, and then to green. He thanked Splunk. She chittered and continued to mess around in the access panel. He hoped she hadn't decided to fiddle, not at a time like this anyway. He linked all the CASPers to his flight computer, and initiated the reentry program.

"Come on, Splunk," he said, "finish up, we need to land."

"Land, good...<*Skee!*>" she replied.

"Yes, it is good, but I don't want to smash you with my butt, so get out of there now." Without further orders, she closed the panel, and he felt her retreat into the thigh area. Outside, superheated plasma began to streak along the heatshield faring.

"Going to lose you soon," Hargrave said. "I'm transmitting rally coordinates near the base where we were supposed to land. I don't know...<crackle> or not, so better to be...<hiss> than sorry. <Snap> luck, son."

"You too," he said as he watched the reentry program run.

Because of their original speed and angle, they had to burn a lot of their jumpjuice to create a viable reentry angle. Even so, their reentry farings were burning like meteors as they blasted into Chimsa's upper atmosphere. The suits began to initiate another controlled jumpjet burn, when the alarm light went off on Private Buckley. Jim checked the readout. His suit was out of jump juice. It must have been damaged when the dropship was destroyed.

Jim watched helplessly as the CASPer fell out of formation at far too steep an angle. The reentry faring burned up and flashed away, the suit began to melt from the intense plasma soon after. Buckley's life sign alarm went off as the suit was breached, and he was cooked alive in less than a second. The suit was consumed shortly thereafter.

"Damn it," Jim yelled. He wanted to kick, punch, or throw something. "God damn it to hell!" Instead, he was wedged into his suit like a statue, waiting to see if he would be the next to burn alive. The gravities grew quickly as the suit slammed into the planet's ever-thickening atmosphere. He was entering feet first, and the suit was designed for this sort of stress. The internal harness and structure held his body, and he tolerated it much better than the radical maneuvers of the *Traveler*.

The G forces topped out and began to decrease as he heard atmosphere screaming over the reentry faring. Another minute passed, and the computer controlling reentry blew the faring, the individual sections arcing away as they were designed, creating extra sensor echoes to confuse ground forces. The computer told him they were five minutes from landing. He was just beginning to get worried when the first of his squad came around.

His radio was filled with frantic calls for updates in seconds. He quickly took control.

"Quiet, everyone!" he barked. They instantly shut up. "The *Phoenix* was hit, we've lost two men from the squad, including 1SG. I've made contact with other units and have initiated landing. Call out to verify your condition." One by one, in proper order, they all confirmed their suits were mostly in good shape. Some minor damage, a few dislodged weapons, but good enough. "Okay men, two minutes! Let's stick this landing."

After all that had happened in the short time since their arrival in the Chimsa system, from the destruction of *Traveler* to having a dropship destroyed around him, Jim found himself surprisingly cool as the ground rushed up at over 200 mph. Splunk chittered a reassuring sound against his leg and he concentrated on the task. At 500 feet above ground he pointed his toes, firing the jumpjets. They roared and burned steadily as the altitude ticked off, fast at first, then slowing. The HALD computer had been programmed with the planet's gravity and atmospheric density during drop preparation. All he had to do was exert manual control based on the profile.

The ground came up at the precise moment he'd planned. At less than five feet up, Jim cut his jumpjets and fell. He spread his suit's legs and bent the knees slightly as the suit thumped to the ground in a perfect landing. He'd expected nothing less from himself, and he wore the pin as proof. Jane had lifted a toast to that landing. As he turned his suit around and checked for the rest of his squad, he remembered that she wouldn't ever hear of his second successful HALD drop. There was little chance she survived her dropship's destruction.

"Jim," Hargrave called over the command net, "status update?"

"Eight of us made it down," he reported to his second in command. "Private Buckley and Murdock didn't make it."

"Damn," he said; "understood." Jim started getting data on his command. They'd only lost one squad in its entirety when *Phoenix 6* was hit. Unlike his own dropship, it caught a direct anti-ship missile hit and was vaporized, troopers and all. Two other troopers had been lost from other squads, so he had a total of sixty-six soldiers, himself included. There was no word from the dropships that had carried the APCs, so he took them off the table. With the loss of those APCs, and no resupply from orbit, they were in deep shit.

"What are the conditions of your dropships?"

"We're all fine," Hargrave told him. "You're the only squad forced into a hot drop. The ships are all mostly out of ammo though."

"Okay, make entry on my coordinates," Jim ordered, "I'm going to try and contact our client and get an update. That battle in orbit makes me wonder if we just dropped from the frying pan into the fire."

"Roger that," Hargrave said and began gathering the flock.

"Chimsa defensive command," Jim called on the frequency he'd been provided by the client, "Chimsa defensive command, this is Cavalier Actual reporting."

"This is Chimsa defensive command," a hissing reply was translated for him, "we are glad you are here. The main facility is under heavy attack. I am sending you coordinates for you to land."

"Chimsa, we were caught in the space battle. Our ship was destroyed. I've lost ten percent of my force as well as my ground support, and we have no air cover."

"Oh," the reply came a second later. Clearly the operator had been hoping for more than Jim had to give. "Are you in position to assist, in condition with your contract?"

"We are not defaulting," Jim assured him, "I am just informing you that we are at reduced capacity. Transmit the details of the attacking force so we can plan your relief."

"Details coming to you now," the controller said. Jim watched as his maps began to update with the information. It didn't look good. Clearly, the space battle was lost. There wouldn't be any more assistance coming. Jim examined the area they'd landed in. A low scrub forest of orange-tinted trees was a short distance away, as well as a harvesting station with dozens of unusual trucks laden with cut trees.

"Hargrave, let's talk when you've landed."

* * * * *

Chapter Thirty-Two

"How long to complete setup on the cannon?" the force commander demanded. The technician looked up from her controls. In the near distance, dozens of robots labored to finish construction of a battery of particle-beam cannons. Huge blast deflection shields of energy-reinforced metallic plates acted as cover, while hundreds of troopers waited next to transports. The city center where the industrial complex was located was only a mile away and in clear view of the cannon's sights once they were operational. The city's shields would be no defense for them.

"Another hour," the technician said and went back to work. The force commander reviewed the work with her multifaceted eyes and clicked in satisfaction. She needed to see about getting her armor ready. The assault would come soon. She was pleased that her mercenary company, Grik-fo-no, was chosen for the mission. The race of MinSha stood to profit in both status and credits from this operation, although working with the Acquirers was not the best way to make a profit. They were far too good at turning situations to their own advantage, often at a major loss to any non-Besquith mercs crazy enough to work for them.

A flight of missiles left the target city and flew toward the MinSha lines. Laser clusters engaged them, shooting down several, and the defensive buttresses absorbed the massive explosions of the rest. No damage was caused to the systems being set up.

"Fools," the commander said as more missiles flew, "spending their weapons so soon." She activated her command channel. "Be vigilant, the enemy may be preparing an attack." All the shiny, multi-faceted eyes watched the city for signs of the attack from the front of the city; none watched behind.

Finally, a laborer returning to a landing craft for parts noticed something unusual. Just a mile away, a line of ground transports was moving. She used a pair of vision-enhancing goggles to examine them. There were about ten tracked civilian vehicles. They were moving quickly past the weapons battery construction site and appeared to be carrying loads of equipment. Civilians running from the battle? She considered for another moment, then her supervisor called for the needed parts, and she went back to work.

She arrived with the container of parts to replace those that had been damaged during installation. The supervisor took them and demanded to know why she was so tardy.

"There were civilian vehicles nearby, and I was observing them." The supervisor looked up from her examining of the parts.

"What civilians? Scouts said that all civilians fled five planetary days ago when the combat began." The laborer would have blinked in confusion, had she possessed eyelids, instead their species clicked their antennae together. She turned her head to look at the dust billowing into the afternoon sky. She looked back to the supervisor who was already taking the parts to the assembly teams. She stood for a moment, then looked back at the vehicles. They were still almost a half mile away, but they weren't on the road anymore. They were heading straight toward the construction site. Really fast, too.

The laborer turned toward the construction team, searching for the supervisor. Something was seriously wrong. The transports were only a hundred yards away when dozens of jumpjets fired and the Cavaliers flew into the sky on high-arching trajectories.

"Oh, that's not good," the laborer said. She ran, all six legs working furiously. The supervisor saw her flash by out of the corner of her eye. As she watched the laborer rush by, the sound of racing motors caught her attention. She looked toward the noises just as the first transport slammed into a dropship a few yards away. Thousands of gallons of liquid hydrogen, fuel for the fire base's fusion generator, detonated in a titanic fireball, killing the supervisor instantly, along with most of her construction crew.

The laborer knew the combat suits were coming for her. Terrified, she jumped aboard the first vehicle she came to and raced away from the coming catastrophe.

The force commander turned in the direction of the thunderous explosion as the shockwave rolled over her position two hundred yards away. An entire platoon of elite assault troopers was blown into the air, sending them cart-wheeling into other troopers, injuring them all and wrecking much of their equipment.

"What in entropy just happened?" she demanded of her assistants.

"I'm checking, Commander," her second said as she called for an update over their command network for details. The construction crew didn't answer; they and their supervisor had been blown into little, chitinous bits.

Another signal came in, and she looked up in surprise. She listened intently as more explosions punctuated the roar of the burning equipment. "Commander!" she finally yelled. "We're under attack!"

"Where?" the commander demanded.

"Behind us!"

"The explosion wasn't an accident!" the commander swore. She turned, starting to reorient her defense, just as a squad of CASPers soared into view.

U sing the locals' logging trucks to get in close had worked brilliantly, Jim saw, especially since the elSha had kept the MinSha soldiers' attention with their constant missile barrage. They hadn't wanted to spend the missiles as a diversion, but Jim had convinced them the missiles weren't really good for much else and could be better used to create a diversion.

"Cavaliers!" Jim yelled over the radio, "Jump! Hit 'em hard!" All sixty-six surviving Cavaliers leaped into the air on their jumpjets and rained high explosive K bombs down on the MinSha unit. The little bombs were standard for all CASPer troopers. They weren't de-signed for hard targets, but they worked *really* well against troops in the open.

Each CASPer carried a dozen of the K bombs, and the troopers dropped half their loads with the bombs set to detonate on contact. Over 400 explosive charges, each with almost a pound of K2, rained down on the mercs of Chaka-Cha.

Each bomb had the explosive power of an entire block of the old C-4, and the rolling wave of detonations crashed through the ranks of workers and partially set-up weapons batteries. Equipment and aliens were blown apart in spectacular sprays of blood and parts, while the munitions cooked off and secondary explosions spread the carnage.

Sailing over the carnage, Jim fired his jumpjets and came in for a not-quite-perfect landing on top of an alien-designed APC. The top turret was open and the MinSha gunner looked at him with an expression of surprise that would have been recognizable in any species. Jim shot the gunner through the head at point blank range with his left high-velocity machine gun, while his right hand snatched his seventh K bomb and dropped it in the hatch. He heard the animated chatter of confusion from inside the APC as he did a non-assisted jump off the side of the vehicle. The explosive went off, slaughtering everyone inside. The hardened armored vehicle held in the detonation, only blowing out the top hatch in a gout of flame and debris.

On the ground, Jim found himself in the midst of an entire platoon of MinSha, all as confused and surprised as the gunner. They wore what was, for them, standard light body armor – color-shifting and form-fitting. Most weapons were still slung, and none had helmets on. Jim activated the high-velocity machine guns on both arms, gritted his teeth, and started spraying.

Surprise turned to horror as Jim dispensed with the MinSha mercs. His entire squad had the same task, to completely disrupt the enemy merc company and keep them from forming a coherent defense. Hargrave had command of the rest of the company and a substantially different mission. Jim could hear the thunderous crashing of their heavy shoulder-mounted cannons in the distance.

The bulk of the enemy troopers fled toward the nearest APC. The door on its side opened, and a MinSha gunner leaned out, bringing her weapon to bear with two arms and gesturing for those nearest to jump inside with the other two. Her weapon fired, and a pulse laser slashed out.

Jim whipped his left arm out and up, triggering the laser shield. Laser beams flashed, bouncing wildly off the shield, some scoring

348 | MARK WANDREY

hits on his shoulders and waist. Yellow warning lights came alive on his status displays, and Splunk came alert in her little safe place.

"We're okay for now," Jim said, and he leaned the suit forward into a loping run. The MinSha gunner chittered in alarm, but didn't try to shift her aim to less-defended areas of Jim's suit. A dozen more laser bolts were deflected by the shield as he raced toward her.

A handful of alien troopers were trying to scuttle into the APC past the gunner. Jim turned his approach slightly and rammed into the backs of the rearmost MinSha troopers. He was nearly three times their size in his suit, and five times their mass. Servo-driven legs made him into a pile driver. The gunner stopped firing for fear of hitting her own compatriots, and Jim collected three of the troopers before slamming the entire assemblage into the side of the APC like a raging bull.

Jim gave a guttural roar as the suit collided with a thunderous crash. The craft used ducted fans to move, and it balanced on re-tractable landing gear when grounded. As Jim slammed into it, he crushed the troopers, and the force of the impact tipped the APC sideways.

As it came back down to level, Jim jumped through the door. The interior of the APC was a whirling dervish of blood and flailing MinSha limbs. The suit was a hulking behemoth, leaving little space for movement. As he entered, several of the soldiers tried to fire their weapons at him. Bullets and laser beams flashed and ricocheted around the inside, doing little to his heavily armored suit, but far more to the lightly armored troopers. Seeing no more movement, Jim dropped a K bomb, stepped out, and triggered his jumpjets. He rocketed up out of the APC, watching it detonate below him a second later.

"This is kind of fun," he said.

"Smash, fight...<*cheek!*>" Splunk asked.

"Oh yeah!" Jim said, checking for signs of organized resistance. Below, at least a platoon of enemy troopers was wrestling a heavy laser into position to fire at Hargrave's wrecking crew. He angled to the right, set his legs, and closed his eyes. The half-ton combat suit came down feet-first on top of the heavy laser like a sledgehammer.

Like most portable lasers in the Union, including the ones in the CASPers, the laser was chemically powered. A mixture of halogens and hydrogen halides was introduced into the lasing chamber, hit with a relatively low electrical charge, and the result was a powerful beam of coherent light. The resultant inert residue was flushed from the chamber, and the process repeated. It did not have a high cycle rate, but the power was considerably more than one of the same size that ran on direct power. The downside was the chemicals, if mixed in an uncontrolled fashion, were rather...excitable.

Jim's suit and his own bulk crashed into the laser and its associated hardware. The chemical tanks for the laser, even though they were made of a high-tech monocarbon filament, weren't made to be smashed by more than 1,000 pounds of hurtling steel. Several burst open, and the bulk halogen and hydrogen halides mixed with the predictable results.

An impressive explosion was produced, vaporizing the gun, crew, and blasting Jim into the sky. He had a moment to think, "Oh fuck, not again," as a dozen system alarms went off. He cartwheeled through the air, struggling to control the flight.

"Not, good...<*skaa!*>" Splunk cried. Jim was too busy to reply as he focused on stabilizing their crazy flight and neutralizing the spin. He looked up just before he hit the ground.

* * * * *

Chapter Thirty-Three

The Cavaliers marched in through the gates of the city/industrial complex to a cheering crowd of elSha defenders. Their buildings tended toward tall and spindly with many handholds and exterior doors. As an arboreal race, they just climbed up the buildings and through entrances. Multi-race structures were more recognizable to the humans.

The city had weathered the battle well. Just because the elSha wasn't a merc race didn't mean the citizens wouldn't fight if their lives were threatened. In fact, their defenses had been designed by The Golden Horde, and they had held up quite well. The defenses depended on having an offensive-capable garrison to work, though, and the attack had begun before the Cavaliers could get there. They had clearly arrived just in the nick of time.

Jim walked on foot along with two other troopers, their suits disabled during the fight. The jubilant cheering of the reptilian elSha wasn't quite enough to overcome Jim's frustration at having destroyed his fifth CASPer in as many engagements.

"Don't worry about it, son," Hargrave said. "Your plan with those logging trucks worked to a T. The MinSha never knew what hit them." Splunk glanced at Hargrave without interest. She rode on Jim's shoulder, untouched by the battle, as usual.

He'd managed to control their spin and slow the descent. When they'd hit, it was on top of a MinSha transport. It cushioned the impact, saving Jim and Splunk at the cost of his suit, and the transport.

Unable to bring the suit back to life, Splunk had spent the rest of the battle noisily devouring the beef jerky she found digging around in his equipment pack.

The remainder of the battle hadn't been close. The MinSha tried to rally twice, and both times were met with withering fire from the heavily-armed and disciplined Cavaliers. Knowing they had no back-up or retreat provided Jim's mercs with considerable motivation as well.

The orderly procession of Cavaliers reached the town center where the elSha leaders waited. They all bowed to Jim as Hargrave stopped his CASPer, popped open the cockpit and scrambled down to join them. The party of roughly two-foot-tall lizards in vests would have looked strange in any other situation.

"Jim Cartwright, commander of Cartwright's Cavaliers," Jim said as he returned the bow, "and this is my Executive Officer."

"Asa-Took-Pashka-Grato," the elSha leader chittered with a flourish of arms, "my title would roughly translate as Prime Minister of Chimsa. You may call me Grato, if you wish. This is my Defensive Commander, and this is the Installation Executive," he said indicating two others. "We thank you for your timely arrival and mourn your losses, particularly that of your starship."

"Thank you, Prime Minister Grato," Jim said, biting his lip as he thought about those who'd died getting them here.

"Unfortunately, it happens," Hargrave said. "The Cavaliers have lost ships twice before, though we've been lucky and haven't for many years. We understand you have a stockpile of standard ammunition suitable for our weapons?"

"Yes, of course!" the Defensive Commander exclaimed, snapping his short jaws for emphasis. "The warehouse is over here. Anything you need is yours, per the terms of our contract."

"Great," Jim said. "Hargrave, get the dropships in here and rearmed." He turned back to Grato. "Can we access your communications system? We're hoping to regain contact with any other friendly merc units."

"Of course," the Installation Executive said, "I can take you to our communications center."

"Hargrave, have a comms expert get on that. See if any of our missing sheep are still out there." Hargrave nodded and gave orders that sent a pair of now unsuited troopers after the executive. Nearby, the three disabled CASPers were positioned next to each other after being carried in by a squad of functioning suits. Jim's looked by far the worst, blackened and twisted. It looked like it had been blown up and dropped from a high altitude, which was almost exactly what had happened. The other two were in better shape; one had its power and control systems wrecked, the other one had both legs seriously damaged.

"Get our best tech on those," Jim said, gesturing to the ruined suits. "See if we can put together even one functional suit out of them. At least strip them for weapons and ammo; we might be here for a long time." He looked at his perpetually hungry companion. "Are you done eating yet?" Her extra-long ears stood up at the word eat, and he sighed. "I need you to help with those," he said and indicated the three wrecked suits. "And I don't mean just take them apart, see if you can get them working. All, if possible."

"Yes, fix...<*Skee!*>" she chirped and jumped off onto the nearest suit. In moments, access panels were opened and protective skirting removed as she began to work. He should have known better than to suggest she not take them apart. Her thought process seemed to start at disassembly, before progressing to repair. A pair of troopers arrived at Hargrave's orders holding tool kits. They'd both been around Splunk, so they were used to the little Fae's affinity for hardware. Jim was actually kind of glad she had the suits to work on. Turning her loose on an alien world full of new technology was not an optimal scenario.

A flash caught his eye, and he looked up into the bright sky. More flashes, hard to see in the light, and tiny stars moved and flared.

"The battle continues," Grato said, noticing it as well. "That is bad."

"Not necessarily," Jim said, "if it were over it could be because our side lost. Given that as an option, I'd just as soon they fight on." As if that had been a cue, a pair of surface-to-air missiles lifted off nearby with a loud "WHOOOSH!" and raced into the sky. The Defensive Commander tapped an implant on his head and spoke for a moment.

"Several heavy transports are landing about 100 miles to the east," he said and indicated the direction. "We shot down one, but the others made it through." He listened some more. "The sensor technicians also say some units or vehicles with friendly transponder codes landed a dozen miles to the west. They say the codes were yours, Jim Cartwright."

Jim thought about racing out and investigating them, then flushed with embarrassment when he remembered he was on foot. Thinking about the weapons stores, he addressed the elSha commander.

"Are there any craft in the defensive stores? APCs or drones?"

"There are no combat vehicles, no," he said. "However, there are a few scout craft. Toboo-class ground-effect skimmers."

"That'll work," Jim said. "Please, lead the way."

The Toboo reminded Jim of a cross between a hydroplane racing boat and a pickup truck. They were meant to cross open terrain and water at relatively high speed with modest cargo. This one had a pintle mount on top sporting a medium laser and room for a dozen unarmored troopers. Jim liked it just fine.

"Jim," Hargrave said before he could climb in, "there are others who can do this." He eyed the craft with a dubious gaze. "And that thing is hardly something you want to rely on so close to a combat zone."

"It'll be harder to detect than a dropship. It flies low, and there may be enemy scouts about with anti-air. As for anyone else to do it, they all have jobs and armor. Let Splunk and the techs work; I can be spared at the moment." He could see the distress on his second-in-command, so he added, "Send two troopers with me, for security." That seemed to placate him, so Jim and the troopers quickly loaded the vehicle. The driver started it, and the craft floated up a dozen feet, its electric-powered fans screaming as they taxied from the warehouse and raced off down the hard-packed dirt road.

The two troopers stood in the open cargo area, the magnetic clamps in their boots anchoring them securely to the bed. They looked in opposite directions, their suit's sensors scanning for danger. Jim rode shotgun next to an elSha driver, a specialist with an unpronounceable name whom he'd nicknamed Bob. The little reptilian drove the Toboo with a reckless abandon that any Baja racer would have found enjoyable back on Earth. For Jim, it meant he tightened the harness straps as tight as they would go – thankfully, they were more than long enough – and hung on with white knuckles as they shot out the west entrance of the city at more than 100 mph.

Unlike the east, where their battle had taken place, the grassy and tree-scattered landscape here was all but untouched. There were occasional burnt patches here and there, or a smoldering pile of wreckage to mark where a stray missile had landed or a downed enemy drone had perished. The city had accounted for itself quite well. From what Jim had heard about the Horde, that didn't surprise him one bit. The problem was, he knew the enemy would eventually be back and would try to set up more heavy weapons to assault the defenses. Worse, it looked increasingly like Cartwright's Cavaliers were the only merc company of the eleven contracted to defend Chimsa to actually make it to the ground.

Given the lightning speed of the skimmer, the trip only took a few minutes. As they approached, the troopers in the back alerted him.

"We have the signal," one of them announced. "Looks like three separate signals, and they match our codes."

"Keep your sensors open for any sign of attack or sabotage," he told them. He instructed the driver, "First hint of a trap, get us the hell out of there."

"As you order," Bob said. A moment later, they passed through a line of trees into a wide-open area of fallow farmland. Jim's jaw dropped, and he gawked. There sat part of the *EMS Traveler!* Not only had it landed, but it had landed completely intact. Rocket nozzles were still emitting gas after breaking the descent, and dozens of parachutes were collapsed on the ground and blowing in the breeze.

Clearly the section had been designed to survive reentry. And that meant the other two signals were more parts of the ship!

"Is that our ship?" asked one of the troopers.

"Sure looks like it," Jim said.

"I didn't know it could do that," the other said, echoing Jim's thoughts.

The skimmer zoomed close and slowed, the section of hull looming tall over them. The hull was scorched and ablated in places. The reentry hadn't been an easy thing, but still, here it was. Now that they were next to it, Jim recognized the section as one of *Traveler*'s massive cargo holds; Cargo Hold Number Two, to be precise.

"Stop!" Jim ordered Bob, who quickly complied. The skimmer came to a stop and lowered to the ground, and Jim popped open the passenger compartment and got out. He half-jogged over to the side where the access controls were located, but before he could use them, the wall split open, and the massive doors yawned wide. Light spilled from the interior revealing eight APCs with various crew and drivers standing near them. A man came forward and saluted.

"Glad you made it, sir."

"Damned glad you made it too, Corporal Glazer," Jim said and returned the salute. "How many in there?"

"All the APC drivers and our mechanics. About two thirds of the ship's crew. Everyone who wasn't on the bridge, basically. And all the non-combat trooper staff."

"What about..." He'd been about to ask about Adayn when she pushed past the APC crew and gawked.

"Jim?!" she said, shock on her face. He smiled and was about to say something flippant when she flew down the ramp and into his arms. He was too shocked to do anything but grab back and be the recipient of the most tearful, heartfelt kiss of his life. Fireworks exploded somewhere in his stomach and his brain. He didn't even hear the hoots and cheers from the other men.

Adayn finally broke away, pushing back a bit to look at him. Her customary ponytail was loose and mussed, and her face was tear-streaked. "We didn't have a powerful enough transmitter to call," she explained, still crying, "but we could listen. We heard your orders to the dropships after the captain broke up the ship. Then," she shook with a sob, "we heard your ship get hit...and I thought you were dead!"

He had a few bandages from the thrashing he'd gotten when his suit exploded. Most were just there to let the nanite therapy finish its work, but she still gingerly touched them, then his cheek. Never had another's touch felt so good to him.

"I want to talk," he said and gently detached himself from her, "but give me a minute to do my commander thing?" She looked nonplused and backed up. "Corporal Glazer?" he called.

"Sir?"

"Start unloading the APCs and personnel for movement to the city." The corporal saluted and Jim accessed the radio through his pinplants to call Hargrave. "You're never going to guess what I found," he said and quickly explained the situation.

"That Captain Winslow was a resourceful bastard," Hargrave said after Jim was done. "I knew it was possible, but didn't dare hope. I was in my suit just like you and didn't have a good view when *Traveler* was hit."

"I have the APCs unloading, and we've got just enough room for everyone, including crew, to fit in seven. I'm taking the eighth APC and my bodyguard, and we're going to check out the other two hull sections."

"Roger that," Hargrave replied. "We'll get ready to receive the survivors. We're still trying to contact any friendly forces in space. No joy yet, but we'll keep trying. Keep me apprised, please."

"Will do," Jim said and signed off.

As soon as the first APC was unloaded and fired up, Jim took it and his guards to head for the next signal, sending Bob back in the skimmer. No need to keep him now that Jim had proper transport. Adayn joined him in the commander's compartment where they had some privacy at last. She hadn't let him out of her sight since the cargo doors opened.

"I still can't believe you are alive," she said as soon as they were alone.

"You were worried about me?" he asked. She nodded and started to cry again. Was she ever going to stop?

"I was afraid you were gone, and before I could...I mean before we even had a chance to..."

"What?" he persisted.

"Jim, you are so clueless!" she moaned. "I kept trying to hint that I like you, and you just kept ignoring me."

"I didn't—"

"Clearly," she pouted, finally getting her crying under control.

"No, dammit," he barked. "I was going to say I didn't have the guts to tell you I like you, too!" She blinked for a second.

"Y-you do?"

"Yes!" he said. "I was trying to tell you at my birthday party when you gave me the watch." He held up his wrist to show her he was wearing it. "It just all...oh, hell! Why would you think I didn't?"

"Because of how you acted at the party; like you didn't want to talk to me. Besides, you're a merc commander, rich and powerful. I'm a nobody, and I'm older than you."

"I don't care how old you are," he said, then thought she had no idea how little money he had. Especially since his ship just blew up. He took a deep breath, screwed his courage up, and spoke. "So, Adayn Christopher, will you be my girlfriend?"

"Girlfriend?" she said, a laugh in her voice. She fell into his arms again, put her lips next to his ear, and whispered, "Jim, I want to screw your brains out." He almost fainted right there. She kissed him again. Her body curved against him, and her thigh pushed against his erection. Oh, God, he thought. They spent a few fun minutes kissing while the APC rumbled across the countryside.

"Hey," Adayn said eventually, "Where's my little Watchmaker?"

"She's back at the city working on damaged suits." She suddenly looked at him askance.

"Jim, where's *your* suit?"

* * * * *

Chapter Thirty-Four

The APC ground across the fields throwing up clods of dirt behind it as it went. The six big wheels, all independently driven, could cover almost any terrain.

Jim helped himself to some light combat armor from the APC's locker, as well as a shoulder-fired laser rifle. Prior to that, he'd only had his C-Tech GP-90. It had proved a good gun, but it would be useless against an armored trooper. Besides, he technically owned all this stuff.

For safety's sake, he had Adayn armor up as well. It was a combat zone, and now that he had a girlfriend he didn't want her getting shot. She'd tried to look angry at him for losing yet another combat suit, but she couldn't help smiling whenever they made eye contact. Their new relationship had the same effect on him. Of course, since he'd never had a girlfriend before, he wasn't sure how to act. And her plans for him...oh, wow! He hadn't felt this nervous since his first combat in a CASPer.

The rear of the APC was mostly empty, with only the two suited troopers back there. Ordinarily he would have had a larger crew accompanying him for such a foray while hostilities were still underway, even if the action was some distance away. Momentarily safe inside the APC's thick armor, Jim basked in the glow of knowing that Adayn felt the same about him as he did about her. Adayn caught a glimpse of his goofy grin out of the corner of her eye, turned toward him, and asked, "What are you smiling about?"

"We're on an alien planet, in a lone APC, with an under-strength squad, and combat is raging over our heads...and all I can think about is how happy I am." Her grin back made it all worthwhile.

The drive to the second downed piece of *Traveler* took less time than the first, even considering their greatly reduced speed across the rough terrain. While fast by APC standards, the M-336's top speed was just under sixty mph, about half that of the Toboo. The APC also had military-grade sensors, so they knew they'd found another piece of *Traveler* more than a minute before it was in visual range. It turned out to be cargo hold Number One – the one that had once held the company's heavy weapons. Unfortunately, this one had not landed as gently as hold Number Two.

One or more of the parachutes had failed, and the hold was partially crushed. He had the two troopers use their suits to tear it open. Inside they found a mess of titanic proportions. None of the heavy energy batteries had survived. It was pure luck that none of the huge laser chemical tanks had ruptured and mixed in the atmosphere. Jim climbed in for a brief look himself and saw why this section hadn't made it down. A massive chunk was torn from one side. It had been hit during the battle in space. Adayn looked over the mess and said she thought they could use some of it.

"Hargrave," he called over the radio.

"Go, boss."

"Check with Grato and see if we can use some of the city's equipment haulers. I found our heavy weapons. Or, at least, what's left of them. Still, there may be something worth salvaging." Hargrave said he would, and Jim transmitted the coordinates before setting off for the final site.

Unlike Number One, Cargo Hold Number Three had come down in perfect shape, just like Two. He immediately felt guilty and regretful, wishing it had been this one that splattered its guts all over the landscape. Inside were the pair of Raknar he'd traded for that were accidentally shipped back to them on Karma by the feckless logistics team on Earth. Several huge pallets held the other mis-delivered junk from the museum.

While Jim stood in the hold looking at the worthless piles of ancient junk, he heard back from the city. The first two dropships had been turned around and were back in the air, greatly widening the sensor ranges of the city. The transports that had landed were huge, and they were disgorging mercs. Lots of them. Hargrave estimated no more than two hours before a ground assault was mounted.

"Who are the mercs?" Jim asked. There was no immediate answer.

"It doesn't really matter," was the reply.

"Hargrave, tell me. Now."

"They're Tortantula."

"Fuck," Jim said.

"Yeah. I'm trying to figure out the best way to deploy our forces, but we just don't have enough. We weren't supposed to be the defensive garrison unit. If they come straight in, we have a chance. But the Tortantula never do. They prefer an envelopment strategy."

"Doesn't anything scare them?" Jim asked. He already knew a lot about the spider-like race. They were the most feared merc race in the galaxy. They'd killed thousands of humans during the Alpha Contracts, not long after first contact. They were bloodthirsty killers with a true love for slaughter and a reputation for giving no quarter whatsoever. They never turned down a contract if battle was involved.

"Not that I've ever heard. They're spiders. Maybe if something big enough stepped on them?" Hargrave's gravelly laugh came over the radio, and Jim rolled his eyes, even as those words lit a fuse in his brain. *Could they?* He looked back over his shoulder. Perhaps they could...

"Send some transports here too," Jim ordered.

"There really isn't time to bother with that stuff," Hargrave insisted.

"Humor me," he said, then decided to nip any further disagreement in the bud. "Okay, if that isn't clear enough, let me make that an order. I have an idea."

"Okay," Hargrave relented, "but I hope for all our sakes it's a damned good one."

The two Cavalier dropships equipped with long-range sensor suites flew a continuous circuit around the city, as high above and far away as was safe. They had staggered flight times so that, even during the minutes it took to refuel, at least one of them was still in the air. The data was streamed live to defense headquarters.

Many merc races would do everything they could to stop this kind of aerial surveillance. The Tortantula didn't give a fuck. They used heavily-armored transports and generally made a practice of arriving on planet in overwhelming numbers. Once on the ground and under defenses, they swarm-attacked, killing indiscriminately. Each Tortantula wore a type of unpowered combat armor mainly designed to protect their soft spots. Not that there were many of those. They were already tanks, after all – twelve-foot-wide, ten-foot-tall, six-foot-long, ten-legged, many-fanged killing machines.

"This is not good," Jim said, watching the enhanced video as the Tortantula unloaded from their transport. It reminded him of a time on his family's farm when he was a kid that he had watched the ranch hands pour acid onto a nest of fire ants. The way they came boiling out of the ground...Jim shuddered. These weren't ants, however; these were huge, murderous aliens with a propensity for eating those they conquered in battle, and executing the wounded.

He left the Command Center and made his way down to the huge equipment hangar. The defensive installation was designed to hold several companies of mercs, all working to defend the high-value target. As the Cavaliers were the only ones there, it had a lot of extra room. That was just as well because this hangar, originally intended to house a dozen dropships, was dominated by the hulking forms of the two giant Raknar, or as Jim thought of them, mecha.

"How we doing?" he called out as he got closer. There was a team of ten working on the closer of the two. Roughly human in shape, but without a head, the Raknar stood almost one hundred feet tall and forty feet wide at the shoulders. With arms that were longer and legs that were shorter, proportionally, they more closely resembled King Kong than any person he'd ever seen. It would only take a slight bend at the waist for them to touch the ground with their hands. Both were brightly colored in unique paint schemes, but even though some new paint had been added from time to time, most of it was now faded with extreme age. Adayn poked her head out of the nearer one and waved.

"Hey sexy!" she called out. Jim felt his cheeks burn and blood quicken. Damn it, she needed to stop that. Several of the men wolf-whistled, and he bristled. The mecha didn't have built-in ladders, and the armor resisted any welding methods they had tried so far. Adayn said it was some sort of carbon ceramic. Either way, the work team had gained access via hanging ropes over the shoulders and tying them off on mounts once meant for weapons. Both were currently unarmed. Adayn climbed down to meet him.

"I thought you were working on the blue one?" he said, pointing to the one further away. Its overall paint scheme was blue, while the closer one she'd just been working on was greenish.

"Blue proved problematic for the computers," she explained. "There is some kind of growth all through it. Like...a slime mold crossed with a lichen. Whatever it is, it's worked its way inside the control panels and every other part of it. Green over here is clean. There's some residue – looks like it was filled with the snot at one time – but it got a thorough cleaning at some point."

"Where's Splunk?" Jim asked.

"Oh, my little Watchmaker? She tinkered with Green for a few minutes, then went back to Blue. She really likes that one, for some reason."

"So, Green is running?"

"It's like I said," she explained, "we've got the interface that some aliens jury-rigged working well enough. We've charged the capacitors. You'll be able to make it walk, move around, maybe even get in a punch or two, or some kicks, but its balance is dependent on those two gyros we pulled from stores. We can't find anything in its guts that can make it walk like the bipedal mecha we've developed on Earth, or even like anything we've seen developed elsewhere in the

Union." She turned and looked up at the huge thing. "It doesn't even have normal joints, like a CASPer or cargo loader. Too big. Any metal-on-metal connections like that would experience so much stress they would have to be made of diamonds or neutronium to handle the strain. It's all super-powerful magnetic couplings with carbon nanotube cables to keep the arms and legs from falling off if the magnetic couples fail."

"Like a weird marionette," he said. She cocked her head and considered before nodding.

"Yea, I guess you could say that."

"What about firepower?"

"We're mounting a pair of rocket launchers on the shoulders. The mounts aren't too dissimilar. And we've got flame units on both arms. You'll be able to dole out a lot of hurt, for about ten minutes."

"What happens then?" he asked.

"The capacitors will be shot, and you'll probably faceplant."

"Swell," he said and looked up again.

"This was your great idea?" Hargrave asked as he walked over. He already had his haptic suit on, helmet under his arm.

"We only got two CASPers working," Jim said, "and I'm the worst pilot. No need to pretend I'm not. But I'm a gamer," he pointed up at the Raknar, "and that's a big goddamned game machine."

"This isn't no game, son," Hargrave cautioned him. "You roll out of here in that thing..."

"And I'm hoping they'll shit themselves and run for it. From what I've read, these Raknar haven't walked onto a battlefield in eons. But when they did, they were unstoppable." He looked back at Hargrave. "Yeah, it's a risk. But maybe it could turn the tide. Or at least buy us some time until backup arrives. The fight is still going on up there, after all."

"That it is," Hargrave said. Jim could tell he didn't like it and might even be regretting having allowed him to take command. Be that as it may, Hargrave had been willing to take a chance on his leadership, and Jim was determined not to let the old man down.

"*Phoenix 6* to Command," the radio in his ear spoke.

"Cavalier Actual, go ahead," Jim said.

"The spiders are on the move, sir. ETA 10 minutes."

"Acknowledged," he replied and raised his voice. "Here they come! All hands to the defenses as planned." He looked at Hargrave who had a look on his face that betrayed his grave reservations about the current plan. It could all go sideways in a matter of seconds if the older man didn't back him up. But what else could they do? Jim didn't have a suit. He either stayed here and quarterbacked the fight from a chair or went out in the huge mecha to do what he could to turn the tide. "I got this. We can do this. But I need to know you're with me. Are you?" he asked with quiet intensity. Hargrave noticed something in Jim's eyes he hadn't seen before – something that made him want to stand a little straighter.

"Lead the charge, Commander," he said and ran to his idling CASPer. The rest of his platoon had come up while they were speaking. In a few seconds, Hargrave climbed in, and all ten of them were loping away toward the northern defense. Jim headed for the improvised ladder. Adayn met him at the bottom.

"Don't try to talk me out of this," he told her. "I know this plan is completely insane, but it's our only shot." She stood on her tippy toes and kissed him lightly on the lips as she placed a small device in his hand. She stepped back, and he held it up to take a closer look, turning it over, trying to figure out just what it was. It was made mostly of plastic but had a plug and several padded contact points, shaped like an old-fashioned crown or royal circlet.

"It's a make-do haptic link," she said. "You can supplement and tweak the feedbacks through your pinplants, but it's going to be really loosey-goosey." He nodded. "This genpack," she said and pointed to a robotic power unit, "will shadow you to the gate but it's programmed to disengage and stay there. Having a portable power unit shadowing you around the battlefield won't help the illusion that you have a fully functioning monster robot."

"Got it," he said. "Look, I just wanted to say..."

"Save it for afterwards, lover boy," she said. "Just keep them off you, and avoid the heavy weapons. I doubt they have anything portable that can hurt that thing. So be smart; I know you can win this."

"See you soon," he said and started climbing. Then he stopped and looked back. "The speakers work?" She shook her head and laughed.

"Tied into the pinlink. Have fun with that." He nodded and climbed. At the top where the armored door to the cockpit stood open, he looked for Splunk, but she was nowhere in sight. "Where are you, Splunk?" he called out. She chirped from the blue Raknar, standing on its shoulder. "This one, silly!" he called. "We can't get that one cleaned up."

"Come, fight...<*Pree!*>" she trilled back.

"Splunk, damn it, we don't have time!" Her huge ears lay back flat against her head and she looked from him to the blue mecha and back again, unsure and clearly distressed. "Please! I have to go!" He climbed inside and started connecting haptic relays. The cockpit was like an apartment compared to cramming his huge frame into a CASPer.

It was obvious the operators had not been human, but it was also obvious they had been humanoid, with two arms, and two legs. The operator stood on a platform and was strapped into a harness from behind, which would then rise slightly and suspend him/her in open air where their motions could be interpreted by the Raknar's control systems into movements.

Of course, Jim wasn't the right size or build. Adayn improvised the harnesses so that it wasn't entirely uncomfortable. A pair of control panels were a few feet in front of him, just within reach while being far enough away to avoid being hit by the operator.

He flipped switches with labels written in permanent marker that read "Main Power" and "Primary Walk Motivator." He'd recorded the startup sequence in a file on his implants.

Jim reached the "Close Cockpit" step and stopped. Because the Raknar didn't have screens like the inside of the CASPer suits had, his techs had set up four small displays, gluing them to the inside of the control panels with epoxy. He didn't have time to wonder how they'd run the damned things without any way of seeing outside. He could see Splunk was gone from Blue. Come on, he urged as his hand hovered over the cockpit control, I have to go! A second later she leaped inside.

"About time," he said and closed the cockpit.

"This, wrong...<*pree!*>" she said as the cockpit ground closed with a WHUMP and sealed.

"Yeah," he said as he took the first hesitant step. The movement was delayed by half a second, resulting in a terrifying stutter step. "Whoooa...Nelly," he gasped as he struggled to stay upright using his implants to adjust the haptic responses. The human-manufactured computer fed data to the alien control system and the two found a point of agreement. He managed to stay on his feet and took another thunderous step. The power cables trailed to the power unit which hummed to life and followed him, keeping the capacitors in the green. "Here we go," he said. Splunk settled on a piece of inactive equipment to his right, fiddling with it absently and warbling nervously.

* * * * *

Chapter Thirty-Five

The Tortantula came at them in a wide front a dozen deep, just as Hargrave had predicted they would. The industrial complex that refined and stored the F11 was more than a mile wide and the Tortantula line stretched beyond its edge, with only a yard or so between each alien mercenary and the armored combat vehicles interspersed among them. They all wore armor and carried multiple ranged weapons, explosives, and blades on most arms. They could navigate the broken terrain easily at more than thirty mph, making the accompanying combat vehicles struggle to keep up. Seeing them pour over the land, swarming toward the city less than two miles away, only reinforced in Jim's mind their similarity to an army of ants.

When they passed the one-mile mark, the city's defenses opened up. The remaining missiles flew and directed energy weapons began firing. The Tortantula's armored combat vehicles used interlocking shields and laser counter-missile fire to blunt the attacks. In places, the defensive fire penetrated, and the massive aliens were blown to pieces. Others came from behind to fill the holes in the lines, driven to a killing frenzy by the deaths of their companions. Once they were within a thousand feet, the Cavaliers joined the fray.

Most of First and Second Company fanned out to either side with the APCs giving fire support. They raced out of the city to meet the oncoming Tortantula forces. Each trooper carried as much firepower as their suits could handle, and they spent it with reckless abandon. Missiles, energy beams, and projectiles arced back and forth with blazing tracers as the two mercenary units tore at each other. The Cavaliers fought furiously to keep the enemy from rolling around and behind them while the Tortantula only sought to punch through. It only took the enemy a minute to realize their adversaries had sent almost all their might to the sides to avoid an encirclement. In response, the spiders immediately formed to the center and shot right at the city's eastern gate. When they were only 100 yards out, the gate amazingly opened to welcome them.

The hundred-foot-tall Raknar strode out through the opening gates like Leonidas leading the Spartans against the Persian army. The Tortantula spearhead didn't immediately react to the huge mecha, even as it picked up its gait to a trot as the cable connected to its waist disengaged and the doors began to swing closed behind it. Only when weapons fire from the emplacements around the door stopped did the enemy realize something had changed.

Jim was still fighting the haptic feedback controls; they didn't want to stay in place, although the loping motion of the run helped. As long as he didn't have to stop suddenly! He spared just enough action from controlling the headlong rush to trigger an audio file in his pinplants and play it over the external speakers. The voice boomed over the battlefield.

"...let's do this. Leeeerooooy......*Jenkins!*" Jim triggered the shoulder-mounted missile racks, which unfortunately began to unload in a non-stop rippling wave, instead of the one at a time he'd expected. As the missiles flew, the soundtrack switched to a blasting version of Drowning Pool's *Let the Bodies Hit the Floor.* The spiders were...surprised.

The Tortantula advance slowed to a stop, the rear elements bunching up against the lead as the missiles tore into their ranks. The two armored shield transports directly in Jim's line took multiple hits and went up in stuttering fireballs of debris and personnel. Dozens of spider troopers to either side were vaporized, and many more blown dozens of yards into the air. The front line tried to back up, their multiple eyes looking up in sudden horror at this terrifying mechanized creature of legend lunging at them.

Jim wanted to charge right through, stomping and kicking as he went. Instead he caught a foot on what was left of an armored transport and almost went flying.

"Shit, no!" he yelled and worked the body's controls through the haptic system and manually inside the pinplant relays. He got his feet back under him, but turned slightly to the right as he fought for control. The giant suit tipped backwards, still hurtling at over twenty mph, and he put an arm back to catch himself. The palm of the three-fingered hand hit the ground and dug a six-foot-deep trench as the mecha did an unbelievable slide like a runner going for home plate. Tortantula troopers were pulped under the mass, dozens turned to multi-color goo while more were smashed into each other or thrown into the air.

He managed to not end up on his back by catching his leading foot under a massive pile of Tortantula bodies, bringing him to a bone-jarring stop and jerking his mecha back to its feet. He stood there for a long second, both exhilarated by what he'd just done, and amazed it had worked.

"Yeah!" he yelled as the heavy metal continued to blare over the speakers. "Holy fucking shit!"

"Kick, ass...<*skaal*>" Splunk agreed.

The momentary shock of the maneuver wore off as the thousands of alien mercs realized it wasn't a vison from their personal hell come alive for vengeance, but a machine come to do battle. And in an instant, they loved it. They all wanted to kill it, or be killed by it. The hundred-foot-tall fighting machine gained almost instantaneous demigod status. Jim had studied the Tortantula in detail when he took command of the Cavaliers. He knew he'd have to face them sooner or later. He understood what motivated them and made them tick as fully as any human could. They were more like a human psychopath than anything else. They were devoid of empathy and loved combat for the pure exultation of it.

Jim knew something when he got in the Raknar, something he didn't tell Hargrave or he'd never have allowed this plan. He knew the Tortantula would see the ancient battle robot as a chance to engage a living legend in combat. They'd throw everything they had at him. And as Napoleon Bonaparte said, "Never interrupt your enemy when he is making a mistake."

"Come get some!" he screamed, and the Tortantula flowed at him. In their mad dash to get at him, they fought each other, huge insect bodies bounding and climbing. They became a living, writhing nightmare wave growing and reaching for him. Jim pushed both arms out and bellowed a war cry, triggering the flame units and sweeping them back and forth. Two-thousand-degree fire engulfed the wave, and Jim stepped forward to meet it.

"Oh my god," Hargrave said as he watched on his CASPer's screen. He should have *known* the crazy kid would try something like this. He desperately needed to prove himself. In that moment, he knew Jim was truly his father's son – more guts than brains. The wall of squirming nightmare spiders must have been three stories tall when Jim unleashed the flame units, setting it on fire as he waded into them. It was a vision straight out of Dante.

"Sweet Jesus," one of the squad leaders hissed over the command network.

The mecha swung, kicked, punched, and stomped as it moved into the fireball of burning Tortantula. Weapons fire exploded from all directions, raking across the machine's impenetrable armor in showers of flashing sparks. Despite the chaos in every direction, Hargrave watched the war-machine-come-to-life move gracefully, as if in a ballet, sending dozens of the huge spiders flying with every punch and kick. A clenched fist swung low and hit the ground as he turned, and the arm came back with twenty Tortantula troopers clinging to it. He held the other arm out, palm open, and brought to two together with a thunderous clap, crushing some and dislodging the rest.

"The kid's in the groove!" Hargrave crowed, pulling up the battlefield virtual space on his HUD. Amazingly, not only had most of the Tortantula force turned inward toward Jim, ALL of them had. Every one of them was racing toward the berserk Raknar like moths careening toward a bonfire. And they were dying in waves. "Go, go, go!" Hargrave silently willed. "You were right – you got this!"

"Shit, shit, shit!" Jim cried out as the makeshift computer system threatened to fail, and he danced around like a lunatic just trying to stay on his feet. Several haptic relays had come unplugged, helping him understand why the CASPers were so snug inside. Splunk was clinging to a power conduit, her eyes closed as the cockpit was continually smashed from side to side by the mecha's careening movements. If it hadn't been for the crushing mob of insane spiders trying to claw their way onto him, he'd have fallen over a dozen times.

Jim tried for another punch and drove his fist into the ground instead. Pulling it free, he found it covered in troopers. They started skittering up the arm toward him.

"Blech!" he blanched and slammed his arms together. He used far too much force, and the reverberations of tons of metal smashing together echoed up the superstructure and into the cockpit, making him see stars. At least the damned spiders were off his arm! Now, more were climbing up his body.

Jim stole a quick glance at his status board. Less than two minutes of power remaining, missiles gone (that had been a fuck-up), and flamethrowers were down to ten percent fuel. The endgame was here. He triggered the flame units and twisted his right arm, raking it up and down his own body. He swept his left arm back and forth as he turned the mecha into a whirling dervish of flaming spider death. Hundreds of Tortantula were set ablaze as the burning gel dripped from his armor. He felt the heat rising up through the internal structure and a warning light came on. The translation computer said there was a fire in the lower legs.

"No shit?" he asked as he felt the balance begin to deteriorate. No, there was a fire inside the thing. "Oh, that's not good."

"Fire, stop...<*cheek!?*>" Splunk asked.

"Yes, try and stop it!" Jim said as he brushed a dozen arachnids off his mecha's waist. Splunk jumped down and through a hatch just behind him. Jim felt a wash of heat as she opened it, and smelled burning plastics. His balance was deteriorating fast. Then something hit him with a resounding "BOOM!" and he was knocked back to land on the Raknar's mechanical ass with a crash, crushing still more Tortantula. He scanned the screens and saw a tank. He didn't even know the spiders used tanks.

"BOOM!" the behemoth's gun spoke again, hitting Jim in the left shoulder. The status board screamed and he heard the scrape of rending metal. Immediately the entire machine shifted to the right. He glanced at the left view screen. The Raknar's left arm was lying on the ground, and the tank was closing in for the kill.

"No, fire...<*skaal*>" Splunk said as she crawled back into the cockpit. Well, that was something at least. He was down to a minute of power as the tank fired again. This round hit in the lower chest, ringing the armor like a bass drum and making Jim cry out from the horrendous reverberations.

"To hell with this," he said as the last of the power began to go. He threw himself forward, and with the squat legs pushed back upright. The next shot from the tank went between his legs as Jim turned and scooped up the arm. "Mess up my toy, will you?" he bellowed and activated another soundtrack. Carmina Burana blared over the remaining speakers as he stagger-stumbled a foot or so to the side, making yet another shot miss, then pushed forward, heading directly for the charging tank.

Dead Tortantula troopers lay in piles and drifts as he stepped forward, crunching them under his multi-hundred-ton bulk like they were bubble wrap. The tank tried to rotate its huge barreled energy cannon up to target him, but he closed too quickly. Holding the severed left arm in his right hand, Jim swung it down onto the tank with a thunderous "Clang!" sending secondary weapons and ceramic armor plates exploding in every direction. "You broke my mecha!" he yelled as the music roared. He swung again, and again, completely unaware that all around him energy weapons and missiles were lashing into the enemy.

The arm separated at the elbow and Jim tossed it aside, slamming his only remaining fist into and *through* the armor of the tank's turret. He closed the hand around something inside, and pulled with everything he had. The tank's internal structure bent, and gave. Inside, something failed, and the tank exploded.

The blast blew Jim's Raknar up and back. More than 1000 tons of battle machine lifted into the air, arced, and crashed to the ground into piles of dead Tortantula like a giant felled. Inside the cockpit, Jim was cushioned well, but still got bashed pretty badly by the impact. Dangling from the harness like a bug on a pin as the Raknar slid through a puddle of liquefied spider, the power display read zero, the music moaned to a stop, and the great war machine shut down, its energy completely expended. The other arm was blown to bits at the elbow, and another blast tore away half of the machine's pelvis, but that didn't matter. He wasn't going anywhere anyway.

"I'm dead," Jim said, shaking his head to clear the stars. He wondered where the techs had stashed his personal weapon as he heard feet on the outside of the machine. He hurt from head to toe and was physically and emotionally spent. "Fuck, that was fun," he laughed as he watched the cockpit being opened from the outside. He smiled as fate came for him.

"That was a hell of a show," Hargrave's voice came over a speaker as Jim looked up at a battle-scarred CASPer. It reached down carefully and held out a hand. "You coming out of there, or do you need some more time to mourn your dead toy?"

"Hargrave!" Jim said, releasing his restraints and taking the proffered hand. The suit lifted him like he was a child. Splunk jumped and caught his haptic suit as he was lifted out, catching a ride. "But how?"

"That was the greatest diversion I ever saw," Hargrave said, and sat Jim down on the smoldering ruins of his Raknar's chest. The machine rested in the middle of the blasted landscape covered in mounds of dead or nearly dead Tortantula troopers.

Everywhere he looked there were piles of crushed, split, blasted, and oozing spiders. It was a kaleidoscope of carnage. Some twitched or moved spasmodically. Most didn't. The smell of charred spider and smoke assailed his nose as enemy heavy equipment and defunct tanks burned.

The Cavaliers' CASPers were moving through the field, finishing off the few enemies that remained mobile. "I know you intended to take as many of them with you as possible, but once they went crazy on you, they didn't even see us encircling them. It was a slaughter."

A series of explosions rolled over them from the east. Far away, the Cartwright's APCs were blowing the shit out of the now defenseless grounded Tortantula transports. The company's dropships circled, providing air support as the mopping-up proceeded.

"Oh," Jim said, almost disappointed that his noble act hadn't quite worked. But it had, actually. Right?

"Don't look disappointed," Hargrave laughed. "You must have smashed half their force. All we did was clean up. They went plum apeshit on you. It was amazing. We have some great video too."

"So, we won?" Jim said, shaking his head and regretting it. He tasted blood, too. Somewhere during all the craziness he'd bit his tongue.

"More or less. I think we can hold now. It's obvious that was their main assault force." Hargrave's suit arm patted the mecha. "Man, that was amazing what you did. Excellent control, son."

"More like out of control," Jim admitted. "I felt like Buster Keaton out there."

"Whatever it was, you did it."

"Hargrave," Adayn's voice came over the radio.

"Go ahead," he replied.

"We have another transport landing. It's huge and landing with heavy fire support at the F11 processing plant ten miles to the east."

"I knew this was too easy," Hargrave said, shaking his head. "Defenses?"

"Manned by locals," Adayn reported. "It fell almost immediately." The cockpit on Hargrave's CASPer popped with a hiss and pivoted upwards to show the older man removing his helmet and wiping sweat from his face with a towel.

"We're screwed," he told Jim. "With a set defensible position, they can land everything they want and start lobbing heavy missiles at us until the shields fail."

Jim considered. The dead Raknar's arm was cocked across the mecha's body, so he sat on the charred stump of armor that protruded from it. The others troopers in Hargrave's platoon all waited and watched. The smell of smashed and burned spiders was...oppressive. Splunk hopped off his shoulder and darted into the mecha, returning a moment later with Jim's survival pack. He knew what she was after.

"I'm beginning to think you have an idea," Hargrave said. Jim grinned and patted the dead machine.

"This worked better than I hoped it would."

"Sure," Hargrave agreed, "it was impressive...in a masterpiece-of-luck-and-mayhem sort of way."

"I'll give you that," Jim said. "However, with what we learned from this one, I bet we can do better with the other."

"You must be crazy," Hargrave said, shaking his head.

"You said it yourself; if we let them continue to occupy that facility they'll eventually just come and get us." Hargrave nodded. "So, you have a better idea?" Hargrave just stared. "Right, then. Get me back to the hangar. We have work to do."

* * * * *

Chapter Thirty-Six

The best estimate was they had six hours before the enemy had all their equipment in place at the processing facility and were ready to begin their attack. They couldn't be sure because the dropships were fired on if they got close enough to get a decent view. What they did see was confusing. There weren't any huge missile launchers going up or massive land cruisers being assembled. An area was cleared and some sort of encompassing energy shields were being installed. They looked like the same kind that protected the city the Cavaliers were now defending, only instead of using them to hold the processing center, they were being set up to surround a much smaller area.

"Whatever it is, it can't be good," Hargrave insisted. There also appeared to only be a small contingent of Tortantula there, and they were acting as a garrison unit, not assault. "Damn strange," he said.

Jim had just enough time to get some nanite treatment for his bumps and bruises, grab a protein bar, and he was back in the hangar. Adayn gave him a brief hug and said he'd been fantastic. He said he felt like he'd been a complete moron.

"My warrior geek," she laughed and gently touched his face. "Jim, you got into that thing without ever having used it once, went out there against a thousand giant spiders, and kicked their asses. Tell me how that was being a moron?" He looked sheepish and grinned. "Yeah, so shut up and come look at Blue."

Now only one Raknar took up the hangar, and it somehow looked lonely all by itself. Jim felt a bit sad for killing its companion. The two had stood a silent watch outside a building for untold thousands of years until they were sold to him to pay a debt, and he went and used one as a distraction and wrecked it in the process. It seemed a terrible waste of a piece of history.

Its cockpit was open, looking like a headless gorilla with its chest split open. Adayn walked over toward one of the equipment carts and picked up a computer slate. Jim looked at the thing in amazement, at what they'd been doing. He'd expected them to slap some missiles and such on it, like the other one. What they had done is not what he'd have imagined in his wildest dreams.

"Is that what I think it is?" he asked pointing to the Raknar's left arm. A team of mechanics were working furiously there with plasma torches and improvised steel attachments. They couldn't weld to the Raknar's hybrid armor, so they were attaching it via bands around the arms that locked into previously empty weapons points.

"Yes, it is," she said with a huge grin.

"Will it work?"

"Oh, absolutely!" She pointed and an overhead crane was cautiously maneuvering another into place on the other arm.

"Holy shit!" Jim gasped as he saw what they were attaching across the chest. "Where did you get those?!"

"We fabricated them." She pointed at the long object the cranes were lowering. "The problem was the mechanism. We had to do some quick and dirty modifications."

"We only got those because we signed a contract with the Smithsonian Trustees," Hargrave said from behind them. "When the federal government defaulted we took a bunch of stuff to keep it safe for history. They're going to be pissed when they see what you've done to 'em." Adayn smiled sheepishly. "You honestly think he can employ them?"

"Based on what I saw out there before," Adayn said, "yes. The mecha has the strength and mobility. The weight of both and the ammo is only about five percent of the total mass. Shouldn't be an issue. One hell of a kick, but the effect should be devastating."

"On him or on the enemy?" Hargrave asked. Adayn made a dismissive gesture.

"Let me worry about that. Your team is being rearmed in the next hangar," she said.

"See you in a couple hours, son," Hargrave said and clapped Jim on the shoulder before heading out.

"Come on up and look inside," she said. Jim watched her start up the ladder, enjoying her "Southern exposure." Halfway up she stopped and looked back at him purposefully. "You enjoying the view?" His face burned red hot. She gave him the most unusual smile and went back to climbing, her hips going back and forth in an almost exaggerated swagger. Wow, he thought and almost slipped off the ladder.

At the top, she perched that cute behind on the edge of the cockpit to allow him to slip past her. As he went by she leaned closer, forcing his arm to slide over her breasts. He shivered visibly.

"Are you trying to drive me nuts?" he asked as he stood in the pilot's rest.

"Just trying to remind you about what's waiting afterwards," she said innocently. "I'd give you a hand job, but everyone is watching."

"Adayn!" he gasped, and she giggled. "Maybe just show me what you wanted...hey, this thing is still covered in goop!"

Inside the cockpit the strange mold/slime was still everywhere. The places where it had overflowed out of the control panels were cleaned up now, but it was still in little puddles within crevasses and in depressions next to each system panel. There were even places where it looked like gauges were missing, and there was just a glass window full of slime! Most was a bluish hue, but other colors were present as well. How could the machine even run with that stuff? He'd be electrocuted.

"That's what I wanted to show you," she said and reached out a finger to dip it in the crud. "This stuff is a lot more complicated than we thought. Did you know it's superconductive?"

"Jesus," he said, "that makes it even more dangerous!"

"Yeah, except sometimes it's the perfect insulator. It's also able to move. We tested it, and the stuff responds to electrical stimulus. It appears to have qualities of a plant, and an animal as well! Jim, this might sound crazy, but I think this stuff is part of the Raknar."

"You're right," Jim agreed, "that sounds crazy."

"Ha ha," she said. "Look, Green was modified by someone before. All the goop was gone and they'd installed artificial interfaces with the operating system."

"Yeah, that's why I could operate it at all."

"No, it was never intended to work that way." She opened a panel. Inside it looked like a science experiment. There were some obviously high tech electronic components, and there were also what looked like old fashioned vacuum tubes, only they were full of the slime. All of them were different colors and some glowed or bubbled. There were tubes that pulsed full of the slime and what looked like a slowly moving waterfall of it in the back of the panel.

"Okay," Jim said as the Raknar rocked from the assembly work outside, "say I believe you and this electroslime is what makes the damned thing work. How much power does it consume?"

"Oh, more than Green did," she said, referring to the dead Raknar lying out in the field of combat.

"Great, so I only get five minutes of battle? Adayn, I must get this thing *ten miles,* and still be able to move and fight! How am I supposed to do that on batteries that only last five minutes?"

"Blue here doesn't have those kinds of batteries at all," she explained. "The batteries in Green were added by the same people who modified the operating interface."

"You aren't exactly filling me with confidence," he complained.

"Humor me?" she asked, and he nodded. "You don't need the batteries, because this one has main power." She held out her slate to him and it had an image of the lower chest open and inside was a compact fusion power plant. A long whistle passed his lips. Except it looked black and cold.

"It's offline," he pointed out.

"Yeah," she said, "tanks empty, no F11. I don't think it's been operative for thousands of years."

"So, what good does it do us if it's ancient, out of hydrogen and F11?"

"Well, there are a few million gallons of F11 a couple hundred yards over that way," she said and hooked a thumb toward one of the nearby F11 storage bunkers, "and we're going to try and do a hot start of the fusion core."

"I seem to recall a hot start is dangerous."

"Extremely," she agreed.

"And this reactor hasn't been run since humanity was learning to use math?"

"About," she said.

"And if it fails during startup?"

"BOOM!" she said and mimicked a massive explosion with her hands. Down on the ground technicians were wheeling in a reel of superconducting cables that would feed immense power into the Raknar's fusion core to jump-start its long dead heart. As the magnetic containment field constricted the hydrogen to unthinkable density, fusion would initiate in a self-sustaining reaction. The magnetic containment vessel would be surrounded by F11 gas, controlling and dampening the reaction. This operation was usually done slowly over many hours, sneaking up on that initial fusion reaction. It caused less strain on the containment field.

A hot start didn't take the careful road. You dumped fuel into the core and shoved. The results would be a fusion reaction in seconds, instead of hours. However, if the magnetic containment couldn't take the massive energy flare as the core started fusing, that fusion reaction would escape. It never happened during normal startup, systems would detect any abnormality and stop the startup. But in a hot start, it all happened in a headlong rush of events as fuel was force-fed into the reaction chamber. If something went wrong, it would not be the magnitude of a fusion bomb, exactly, but there would be enough material for a sizeable explosion.

Jim swallowed hard as he looked down. The fusion reactor would be about three yards down, about as heavily armored as he was in the cockpit. A tiny sun, just under his feet. It was both frightening and exhilarating at the same time. So much danger and so much power. Terawatts of power at his disposal. She looked at him expectantly.

"It's kind of a shame we didn't salvage some of the MinSha energy batteries," Jim said. "We could have mounted one of them on this thing!"

I t was four hours after their victory against the Tortantula before everything was ready. The CASPers were all rearmed and repaired. Only five had been lost in the crazy battle, and there were no deaths amongst his men. So far, he'd been incredibly lucky after their losses in space. The work on Blue was finished, as well. Jim had dubbed it Dash, and took the now somewhat less-than-vintage little pony from his personal gear and hung it from a strap in the cockpit. The toy was battered and dirty, but the tail was still a brightly colored rainbow. Splunk returned from one of her explorations of the inside of the Raknar to look at the pony hanging there.

She cocked her head from side to side, ears up with curiosity as she took its full measure. She'd seen his collection more than once. A different pony sat on his desk back in Karma station. She'd never really had anything to say about them before.

"Pony, good...<*cheek!*>" she asked.

"Dash?" Jim asked and pointed at the toy. "Oh, she's a wild child, kinda like you. But she doesn't shy away from a fight. She's been my mascot ever since I put on the uniform." He looked at the little Fae and shrugged. "I can't entirely explain," he told her.

"Dash, good...<*skaa!*>" she proclaimed. This time Splunk didn't find a comfortable place to hang, she scrambled onto a little shelf behind Jim's head. He'd examined the shelf several times in annoyance. It intruded on his head space slightly and he had been considering getting rid of it. Behind and around the shelf were membranes full of the electroslime in every color imaginable. They glowed slightly, casting Splunk's brown fur into strange multicolored hues that changed as she looked back and forth. She seemed right at home, and he was glad he hadn't had the shelf removed.

"We're getting ready for start-up," Adayn yelled below.

"Clear the room," he ordered.

"It's better if we're here," she complained.

"Bullshit. You can do this remotely. The only one who needs to be here is me." There was a chirp behind him. "Oh, and Splunk. Now get," he said, "that's an order." She wasn't happy, but she went. A minute later she was on his radio as he finished plugging in his suit. The improvised inputs to this Raknar's sensors seemed even more Mickey-Mouse than they had in Green.

"We're set," she said, "the elSha say power is at our disposal." The little reptilians had been willing to give them the 250 gallons of F11 the Raknar needed to have a full charge, even though the gas was worth half a million credits. Clearly what they stood to lose was substantially greater. He surveyed the human computer readouts in his head, sent via the interpretive programs that looked at alien displays and bubbling tubes. Fuck, what a monstrosity.

"Everything looks good here," he said, *for the set of a Frankenstein film*, he added in his head.

"Okay," Adayn said, "startup in 5...4..." Splunk hopped down and through the floor hatch. "3...2...1...*engage!*"

A jet of super-compressed pure hydrogen was injected into the core at the same time as gigawatts of power surged into the Raknar's long cold reactor, creating a geometrically perfect sphere around the hydrogen, and *squeezing*. A tiny discontinuity in the containment field allowed a constant stream of additional fuel to be injected as the field compressed. With nowhere for the hydrogen atoms to go, they were crushed closer, and closer, and closer, until, with a brilliant flash of energy release, they began to fuse.

All this happened in the span of two panic-filled seconds. That and a slight discontinuity in the containment field that, by all practical reasoning, should have failed and blown the mighty war machine and a third of the city to hell and gone. Only it didn't. Something caught it, and corrected the imbalance in a microsecond. The only result was a little gasp, and a sigh from Adayn.

"What?" Jim asked as the mecha began to vibrate and thrum with power.

"Nothing," she said as she scanned a thousand readouts repeatedly. "For a second I thought..."

"What?" he demanded again, fearful he was about to become disassociated atoms.

"It must have been a transient reading," she explained. Jim felt small hands and Splunk came racing up his leg and side, landing back on her perch. "The reactor is reaching normal operating temperatures," Adayn continued. "We have clean, stable fusion. It worked." Jim breathed for the first time since she said *engage*.

All around him alien displays and electroslime pulsed and glowed with power. The ancient machine, inactive for untold centuries, was returned to life. Techs were running in, scrambling up the gantry in front of him, and removing the cables and fuel feeds that remained attached. The computer feed in his pinplants said he had several megawatts of idling power at his disposal. The power plant was operating at about two percent. He activated his radio.

"Hargrave, you ready?"

"Fuck no," the second in command of the Cavaliers grumbled. "But we're going anyway!"

"You're goddamned right we are," Jim said, then switched channels to Adayn. "Clear. I'm going out."

"See you soon," she said as the huge hangar doors swung wide.

* * * * *

Chapter Thirty-Seven

Galrath had decided he was going to be there personally to witness the Acquirers putting an end to Wathayat's little venture on Chimsa. Besides, since Project K was his brainchild, it was only right that he be there to see it brought out of the shadows. And still, the humans were there.

He'd watched from a guild cruiser in orbit as the humans snuck up on and mauled the MinSha special assault company he'd sent to take the depot city brimming with F11. They'd fled with their tails between their legs, so he'd sent in the elite company of Tortantula. More than enough of the ten-legged psychopaths to finish off the disorganized and ill-equipped human mercs. Instead the humans trundled out an actual working Raknar! Where in entropy had they found that thing?

Of course, the truth was, there were hundreds of them lying around the galaxy. Many in museums or as corporate and guild doorstops. He'd even seen a few that could walk, and that's about it. But no, Cartwright's Cavaliers had one that could fight! And there was nothing the Tortantula liked more than an insanely violent and destructive fight to the death. Challenge accepted. Of course, the 100-foot-tall mechanical slaughter machine ground them to sticky green-hued goo.

He had convinced the remaining MinSha to intervene with an assault tank, after a sizeable credit transfer to their account. The Raknar took it out, too, but not until after the tank finished the Raknar.

At least that was out of the way, so he could now land his Project K transport, although he didn't risk landing too close to the city where the F11 was stored. The humans still had assets, and their defense of the city was impressive. He had to find out who built those defenses; it might be worth contracting with that company in the future, once the Acquirers controlled the F11 trade. The remainder of the devastated Tortantula company, as well as a unit of his fellow Besquith, were deployed to defend the perimeter around the processing complex until the moment was right.

With the special transporter down, and the energy pen set up, Galrath ordered his special weapons unloaded and their operators prepared. In a few hours, it would all be over. He stood outside the ramp to his ship and listened to the earth-shaking shrieks and howls reverberating through the hull of the transport. Galrath bared his teeth in anticipation. The slaughter would begin soon. The new order was about to be born. The ramp lowered on the transport, and they unleashed the nightmare just as the alarm sounded.

"No," Galrath said as he looked at the displays. Another Raknar was striding across the lightly forested plain directly toward them. "That isn't possible!"

* * * * *

Chapter Thirty-Eight

Jim was both excited and terrified in equal parts. Operating the mecha, now driven by practically unlimited fusion power, was like trying to control a hurricane. The powerful legs surged him forward with such force that the machine looked like a man running in low gravity. Each footfall was like an explosion, tearing up dirt, rocks, and small trees, sending them flying in a fan of destruction in his wake. From a distance, it looked like a high-speed snowplow crashing through drifts. The feed into Jim's pinplants said he was running at close to forty mph.

Unfortunately, that much power and speed made controlling the contraption more complicated than the other one had been. If Jim hadn't operated the green one, he would never have made it ten steps in Dash. Even so, his pinplant processors were all but completely overwhelmed with the volume of staggeringly complicated processor cycles needed just to make the legs churn at his torso to balance his headlong rush into battle.

"Whoa, Jimbo!" Hargrave called over the radio. "Slow the fuck down!"

"I can't," Jim said, but he tried to anyway. He almost fell face first at forty mph, something he knew that, regardless of how tough the mecha was, would probably rip it to pieces. He kept its feet down and torso up through sheer force of will. His speed dropped to thirty mph. Behind him, sticking to the road and the cleared sections of terrain, all the Cavalier's APCs raced to keep up. They were fully loaded with firepower and CASPers, with even more troopers hang-ing off the sides and top. It looked like a scene out of *Mad Max and the Psychotic Calcutta Taxicab Attack*. Jim had put all their cards on the table.

The processing plant with its thick containment walls was com-ing into view, and as soon as it did, the missiles began to fly. Appar-ently, his arrival had made quite an impression. In a flash, missiles were raining down around him, and some on him. The warheads that could send a CASPer-suited trooper to the afterlife with a single hit exploded against the ancient mecha armor without any effect. He felt the impacts and expected warnings to appear on his status board for damage. Nothing happened. *Now if I could just fight and run*, he thought.

He felt a tugging on his haptic helmet from behind. For a mo-ment, he didn't know what it was. Had he caught his helmet on something? It was taking all his concentration to steer the monstrous machine with only the trio of monitors affixed with epoxy to the front of the cockpit. He finally saw the long, delicate fingers of Splunk trying to pull his haptic helmet off.

"Splunk, what the fuck?"

"You, me...<*akee!*>" Splunk insisted. Jim blinked. He didn't know that word: ah-KEE. More missiles hit, and a few hyper velocity projectiles. It reminded him of rain. Wait, he did remember hearing Ah-KEE once before. The night he'd had the sex dream about Adayn. Now Splunk was fumbling at the straps of the helmet, work-ing them loose.

"Splunk! Stop that!" he said and shook his head, and almost tripped on a light post. A massive energy beam passed over his shoulder with a crackling "SNAAAP!" playing static electricity up the side of his Raknar like a Van de Graaff generator. "SHIT!" he barked trying to turn. The set foot dug in and he went flying.

Jim figured that was it, but he still tried to control the fall. He tucked the machine's shoulder and landed with an earth shaking crash, taking a hundred yards to skid to a stop. Though the safety straps kept him from being smashed against the side of the cockpit, they did not prevent him from being jerked around like a yoyo on a string. His anger at Splunk dissipated immediately. If she hadn't been messing with his helmet, that blast would have burned him like cheap toast. Splunk had just saved his life. He shook his head, and when he opened his eyes he saw the monitors were all broken loose from their mounts and shattered. He was blind. A further check with his pinplants showed the improvised haptic system was down. So, he was crippled, too.

"Well," he said, "that's that." He started pulling out the haptic plugs and reaching for the reactor controls to safe it when Splunk spoke again.

"Kick, ass...<*skaa!*>"

"We can't," he said as he started the reactor shutdown. She shook her head and took his hand.

"No, Jim...<*akee!*>"

"I don't understand what you want," he said and pointed to the broken computers. "Everything is broken."

"That, junk...<*pree!*>"

"But we needed it to run this thing!" Jim tried to explain.

"No, us...<*akee!*>" She leaned closer and unhooked his helmet like she'd been trying to do before. This time he let her. The Raknar rocked as missiles landed around it. He needed to get out of here before they got the range. Splunk reached for his head, almost lovingly, her fingers feeling along his skull, under his hair, until she found his pinlinks, the data connections that led right into his brain.

"<*akee!*>" she said, and contacted the pinlinks. "Join me," he heard, and his consciousness exploded.

J im spun into a fathomless void, his mind spread open like a spiraling galaxy. In a moment he was everywhere, and nowhere. He felt the wind of eternity on his soul, and the heartbeat of Creation. Only he wasn't alone. A presence as strong as his own was there, sharing the same space in the universe. It was Splunk, only her name was much, much more than what he'd given her. Time stretched to the infinite as he took a thousand years to appreciate it fully, and still didn't have the full meaning of it.

"We must fight now," he heard.

"Why?" he asked as Creation wheeled around them.

"Because it is what we do." In a tiny corner of the universe, he could see a battle taking place. It seemed so insignificant, so meaningless in the grand scheme of things. Yet it had...something else. The battle was a moment in time that another thousand moments all depended on. Somehow that tiny battle had a billion lives balancing on a knife's edge of annihilation. His actions in this moment controlled how the knife fell.

"Okay," he said, and instantly he was drawn down into himself again. Only, he wasn't himself. He was a 100 foot-tall, 1,000 ton Raknar. Not inside it, he was it, and it was him.

"<*Now we fight*>," his other half said.

* * * * *

Chapter Thirty-Nine

J im rolled sideways away from the spread of energy beams aimed where he'd been lying. The deadly energy raked the ground, vaporizing great sections of it, but he was untouched. Jim extended the roll and came to his feet, the previously retracted blades in the balls of the feet extended, chewing into the earth and bringing him to a fast stop before retracting. He came into a crouch, the power of the great Raknar coursing through him.

"Oh, yeah!" he said, his voice echoing out over the battlefield. He laughed and raised his arm, pointing at the Besquith energy cannon poking out over the top of the wall less than a half mile away. Ten tons of layered, rolled, alloy-steel barrel lined up with the target. He didn't aim the gun; he didn't need to. It was like pointing his finger. He knew it was going to go where he wanted. It didn't even matter that it wasn't a weapon ever mounted on this Raknar. It was now as much a part of him as his own hand. He triggered the firing mechanism. "Eat it," he said.

The barrels were sixty feet long, the entire length of his arm. Mounted entirely on the forearms. When he straightened the arm, the breech locked against the upper arm into a support set there and the barrel extended ten feet past the hand. It looked unwieldy, but the Raknar, through him, compensated easily. The firing mechanism ignited the charge of the 16"/50 Mark 9 gun. The final generation gun mounted on *Missouri* during its brief recommissioning in the early twenty-first century was much lighter than its predecessor;

thanks to advanced alloys, it only weighed 20,000 pounds. The projectiles were almost a ton each. Adayn, with the other Cartwright's mechanics, had quickly improvised casings and propellant that would have left those twenty-first-century naval armorers with their jaws hanging down. When Jim fired, the chamber pressure was the maximum the breech was capable of handling.

"BOOOM!" the gun roared, the shockwave blowing the leaves from trees for hundreds of feet. The Raknar's entire body was required to manage the recoil, the arm rode up and back, and the blades on the feet popped out again to keep the mecha from skidding backwards.

The sixteen-inch projectile left the gun barrel traveling at just under 3,000 feet per second, or more than 2,000 mph, and reached the target in 1.6 seconds. The projectile itself was a creation of Adayn's, crafted from pieces of armor salvaged from the other Raknar. The hybrid steel/ceramic/carbon projectile hit the energy shield protecting the enemy weapon with half a billion foot-pounds of energy. The shield integrated into the energy cannon was meant to stop energy attacks. The ballistic energy of a small family car traveling at five times the speed of sound was far beyond what it was designed to handle. It didn't matter than the shell was harder than most known materials. It could have been made of pudding. The shield flashed off less than a picosecond after impact to avoid exploding. The shell wasn't slowed by even 500 feet per second.

The projectile hit the gun itself as it was traversing to track the Raknar. It had a computerized detonator programmed to explode a thousandth of a second after contact with any hard surface. It correctly recognized the shield was not a hard surface. The gun, on the other hand, was made of alloys and counted. After traveling a foot or so into the energy cannon's complicated guts, the detonator fired and 500 pounds of K2 went off. The blast amounted to a ton and a half of dynamite, in addition to the energy of the cannon's charging coils, and it blew a sizeable chunk out of the wall's top and turned the gun crew and power system into a crater.

Now with a better feel for how the gun interacted with the Raknar, Jim dropped to his left knee, raised the left arm, locked that barrel into place, and fired. "BOOOOM!" The second energy cannon ceased to exist just as spectacularly.

"You want some more?!" Jim laughed, and was instantly on his feet and jogging. He cocked both arms at the elbows, pointing hands at the sky and released the breeches. The empty 200-pound casings fell to the ground, still smoking. As he ran, he reached with his left to the bandolier across his chest and slid another round out, pivoted the right arm, and dropped it into the breech, which automatically rotated closed.

His awareness of the battlefield was perfect. He could see the final two energy cannons desperately trying to target him. One had a ten percent chance of scoring a hit, so he brought the right gun up and destroyed it. "BOOOM!" the cannon roared. He allowed the recoil to spin him to the right, pivoting again on his left foot to change directions. The thousand-ton mecha skidded as it turned, right through the middle of the main road between the processing plant and city. The foot tore up reinforced concrete like it was turf on a golf course.

He lowered the body and rushed toward the doors, now less than a thousand yards away. Part of his mind – the part that was neither Jim nor Splunk – lamented that the Raknar's flight pack and energy sword were missing as both were better options for breaching a facility like this, but the guns were serviceable. He reloaded both as he fell below the arc of the only remaining energy cannon. At 200 yards from the door he did a little bunny hop, leveled both guns at the door, and fired. "KABOOOM!" they both roared. The titanic back blast of the guns' firing canceled almost all his forward momentum, and he landed with a slight stutter step as the huge doors disappeared in a fireball.

A thousand yards behind, nearly two companies of CASPers on board their APCs came to a stop as they watched an unbelievable spectacle. Hargrave winced in anguish as Jim, super-powered by the fusion plant, went racing across the battlefield, then caught his foot on a lamp post and did a pratfall within sight of the walls. When the enemy energy cannon popped up, he knew Jim was dead. There was no time to order a strike by the dropships.

As the enemy fired, Jim's mecha rolled easily out of the way, and to its feet. Then it went wild. He wasn't moving with those hesitant, stumbling moves anymore. Now it was like Jim *was* the machine. Somehow, it was like they'd merged. Jim performed an incredible side slide, raised the damned battleship cannon that had been accidentally shipped from Earth, and fired. Even from as far back as they were, inside his CASPer, Hargrave could *feel* the gun blast. The energy cannon was obliterated and almost half the wall next to it!

Jim dropped the mecha to a knee and blew another cannon to hell. After that the entire line of APCs came to a stop to watch in stunned amazement as their commander fired the huge guns over and over, running up to the gates and firing both guns in midair, using the recoil like a brake to stop himself. Hargrave realized everyone had stopped as Jim strode into the processing plant defensive wall like he owned the place.

"What's everyone sitting here for?" Hargrave asked. "Attack, attack, attack!" The force catapulted forwards.

Let's end this, Jim thought as he walked through the shattered gates and into the processing plant. He loaded the last two rounds he had for the battleship guns as he strode. The action was smooth, as if he'd done it ten thousand times before. A part of his mind struggled to remember that he was not this machine, he was a man. But he laughed at the thought as he walked inside.

His new powerful awareness took in everything about the inside of the defensive wall as soon as he passed through it. The charred and smoking remains of the three energy cannons he'd destroyed, the ranks of Tortantula mercs waiting for him, and the dozen tanks coming around the corner of a series of huge gas separator towers a mile away. Everything seemed suspended in time as a dozen scenarios played out in his mind's eye. As the first tank came around the corner and tracked him, the Tortantula surged into action, and Jim moved.

The left-hand gun came up and fired over the Tortantula running toward him. The shock wave of the gun killed a dozen. The projectile was aimed down the avenue at an average-looking storage tank, which Jim's sensors showed held an incredibly volatile chemical. The round passed into the storage tank and exploded, then a secondary explosion vaporized all the chemical-filled tanks around it, and it turned the approaching tanks into burning wreckage.

The Tortantula rained fire and rushed him, climbing him rapidly to attack the cockpit. Jim sidestepped and ripped a huge beam from one of the shattered energy cannons and started crushing them wholesale. There were hundreds, not thousands this time, but they were better prepared.

He felt the sting of damage to his left knee, and several well-placed rockets scored hits in articulation points on his torso. While he was spinning away from the hits, several dozen bloodthirsty arachnids raced in and attached heavy alloy cables to his legs. *That,* he was not expecting! The cable was attached to the wall, and quite strong. Strong enough that he was caught completely off balance and fell against the last energy cannon tower. The Raknar was much heavier than the tower, which instantly collapsed like a house of cards, half of it coming down on him as he went to the concrete ground in a heap.

"Great, now what?" he said as he tried to roll, and the cable stopped him. He ended up lying on the mech's front, almost spread-eagled. In a flash, the Tortantula swarmed him. "Not good! Not good at all!" He could see several carried specialized breaching charges.

The left cannon was spent, so Jim triggered the release. Explosive bolts fired and the ten-ton piece of steel fell free, enabling him use the hands. He half-rolled to the right and swung. The spiders tried to dodge, but how do you dodge a small building being swung at you? Crushed and mangled enemy troopers flew in every direction. He noticed two Tortantula heading toward him with a demolition charge and swatted at them like flies, but ten more were rushing him from the other direction.

"This is it," he said. At that moment, dozens of CASPers soared over the battlements on their jumpjets, weapons blazing. Missiles flew, lasers blazed, and projectiles tore into the unsuspecting Tortantula like a chainsaw. Faced with ignoring the withering attack from the suited Cavaliers or continuing their assault on Jim, the enemy turned on the Cavaliers.

Suddenly free, Jim sat up and reached down, chopping the cable tied to his leg with ease. He got back on his feet and turned to see what he could do to help his comrades. The difficulty was...given his size, he was as much a danger to them as to the enemy. He had to move forward; something was calling to him.

His new self, the one that was more combat machine than human being, saw the obviousness of it. The light-armored troopers now tagged as friendly were in just as much danger of dying from his attacks as the enemy. Still, he hesitated. Two of his troopers were felled almost immediately by the powerful lasers mounted on the Tortantulas' assault armor. The beams simply punched three-inch holes right through the suits.

We go, a voice echoed at the edge of his consciousness. *Our enemy waits!*

And he was off, jogging down the main avenue. As he closed on where he'd destroyed the tank farm, the ground was still covered in pools of brightly burning liquids. Several of the Besquith tanks had turned into funeral pyres. He jogged, each step throwing up divots of concrete, and slowed to turn the corner, the retractable blades coming out again and digging great furrows in the road. With a glancing blow, his shoulder gouged a hole in an already ravaged, burning tower. Because of the sudden change in direction, only one of the particle beams hit him.

The blast was powerful, and hit him in the left thigh. The kinetic impact of the weapon and the armor exploding knocked him back into the crumbling tower with enough force to collapse the structure on top of him. Hundreds of tons of metal piping and steel skeletal structure shattered and pummeled him as it fell.

The advantage of being mentally linked with the Raknar was that he was the mecha. He was strong and fast, and he felt invulnerable. He could feel through the Raknar, it was an extension of his body. It also meant when it was damaged, he felt it as physical pain.

"Argh!" he cried as the energy beam seared into his leg. Then, "Oh, crap," as the tower began to collapse on him. Jim tucked into a ball, protecting his torso and right arm as beams and burning debris slammed into him like multiple hammer blows.

Three Besquith tanks had survived the conflagration of their comrades when Jim detonated the storage tanks. They were all far enough away that the blast didn't affect them, and none got covered in burning fluids, certain death for tanks even in the twenty-second century. They had all waited in a line abreast until Jim came around the corner, and then they had opened up. When the Raknar was blasted back into the structures they thought they had finished it.

"Move forward," the highest-ranking commander of the three surviving tanks said. "Watch for movement."

"Why not just fry the whole area?" one of the other commanders asked. "We've already lost 8 of our best tanks! A fully operative Raknar is almost impossible to destroy!"

"How would you know?" the last commander asked mockingly. "Children's stories told to our puppies? You are a fool."

"Enough," their senior snapped. "We are paid to help secure this installation, not annihilate it! Besides, we will be at point-blank range. Should it emerge from the debris, we will be ready."

The three massive tanks rolled forward slowly, each riding on six large uni-balls. They would have been almost silent except the roadway was covered in rubble and what was left of their comrades. They had to push through the debris, which squealed in protest as they moved and crunched over it.

As the point tank got within fifty feet of the collapsed building which marked what they hoped was the burial ground of the entropy-cursed Raknar, they all trained their powerful particle accelerator cannons on the site. Capacitor coils hummed with full charges, and the crews snapped their long muzzles in nervous tension.

"Nothing is moving," the commander who had wanted to destroy everything complained. "How can we be sure it is there?"

"Fine," said their senior. "Spray the debris with bullets, but no energy weapons!" He ordered the least senior among them to do the task. Inside that tank, the commander cursed his luck and ordered his vehicle to slide forward. He popped the commander's cupola and gimbaled the electromagnetic autocannon up to face forward. Designed to keep light infantry at bay or deal with unarmed vehicles, the gun held a 500-round magazine. As he triggered a burst, the gun's coils gave the customary high-pitched ratcheting squeal as hypervelocity rounds whanged off and through much of the tower's debris, ricocheting around frighteningly. The few that came back toward him bounced harmlessly off the tank's glacis armor, but he knew if any found him, his guts would rain into the tank.

"There is no response," he proclaimed over the tanks' shared channel. "Perhaps a round of cannon fire?" As he waited for his superior to make up his mind, the sound of tortured metal reached his ears. He looked up just in time to see a foot nearly the size of his tank coming down at an astonishing speed. His death was considerably quicker than it would have been if a ricochet had found him.

The other two tank commanders watched in horror as the Raknar jumped over the building and landed on the first tank. Like a firecracker stomped by an elephant, there was a "Phwunt!" and a little debris, but most of the explosion and pieces were crushed almost a yard into the ground as the 1,000 tons of Raknar settled and turned.

They'd been aiming at a point in front, and hadn't expected their enemy to appear above them. Both tanks' uni-balls squelched as they were put in reverse, and their turrets whined as they tracked upwards. Jim did not feel like being subtle. He simply jogged forward, kicked one of them over the next line of industrial buildings and stomped the last one. His path was now clear to the mysterious landing area.

* * * * *

Chapter Forty

Jim came to a stop one turn away from the center of the complex, where his long-range sensor equipped *Phoenix* had seen the ship land. He could see the massive curve of its bulk over a line of processing machinery. He stopped and checked his status. Everything felt okay. He had several small injuries, the leg being the worst of them.

We are fine, a voice whispered in his mind. *The ancient adversary awaits.*

Ancient adversary...? What did he remember reading about the Raknar? His awareness that he wasn't alone cut off his train of thought. CASPers were landing all around him, on the buildings, pipes, and storage tanks. They would want to communicate with him. How did they communicate? Radio, he thought, and concentrated on how radio worked, and a second later he heard Hargrave's voice.

"You okay kid?"

"Sure," Jim answered, feeling like he was speaking through a dream.

"You don't sound normal, kind of like you're in a fishbowl." Jim didn't answer. What had he been just trying to remember? "You're kind of shot to shit too."

"I'm fine," Jim repeated. "The adversary awaits."

"Hold on there, Jim, you—" Hargrave cut off as the Raknar started forward at a brisk pace. "Damn it," Hargrave barked. "First Platoon, on me!" he ordered and triggered his jumpjets.

Jim rounded the corner, and the center of the complex came into view. The largest open area in the complex, it was where the shipments of unprocessed gas were delivered. As such, there was more than enough room for an enormous space tanker. The transport grounded there wasn't a tanker, though. It didn't look like any kind of ship Jim had ever seen. Part tanker, part transport. Almost a quarter of the side facing him was split open, half pivoted upwards and the other down. The lower part created a ramp.

They are there, Jim heard. *The adversaries.*

Jim felt his pulse quicken and was suddenly aware he was increasing power to the Raknar by pumping more fuel into the fusion power plant. He increased his walk to a jog. As he got closer, he could see there was a force field shimmering around the huge transport. Next to the transport, a cruiser was also on the ground, but there wasn't any sign of ground defenses or a response to his presence.

The shield would be the problem, his mind analyzed as he closed rapidly. There was only a twenty-five percent probability that physically colliding with a shield of that order would cause it to drop, the remaining probabilities were a partial drop or he'd just bounce. All those probabilities resulted in serious damage to himself. The cannon should bring it down, but then he was reduced to fighting hand-to-hand, and the little voice in the back of his mind said there was something very nasty waiting for him inside. He was considering other options when the shield suddenly dropped.

The move caught Jim off guard, and he slowed. He was walking when he came to the end of the street, and the entire open area was in view. Roughly a mile across and bowl shaped, the space was designed to host several tankers landing at the same time, though the huge, unusual one was twice the normal size. Various mechanisms dotted the perimeter with hose-handling robotics designed to ease the offloading of liquid cargoes. Shield generators were placed in a rough circle, with the downed transport to the far side of that circle, opposite where Jim entered.

He knew he wasn't alone. Some inner sense told him something else occupied the open depression. Another two steps, and he passed into the central area, and the shield came back on.

"Fuck," he said and cursed himself for not recognizing a trap. Still, the power had to be coming from somewhere, so he raised his right arm and felt for the center of the huge ship's fusion core. A single sixteen-inch round should put an end to it. Movement caught his eye. Something was inside the ship. He turned his attention to it, and gasped.

At first, Jim didn't think it was real. How could such a thing take animate form? Half centipede with two sets of serrated claws, the thing rolled out of the ship on hundreds of legs and reared up, up, and up until it was 100 feet in the air, its glistening red eyestalks level with his own head. At least that much or more remained on the ground bracing the part that rose to oppose him. Its entire length was covered in thick brown armor plates. Segmented mouthparts broke open in what could be called a head, and it screamed a nauseating challenge that tore at his mind like gauntleted fingers on a chalkboard. Claw-like pincers snapped as it turned and moved lateral to him, in front of the transport.

"You've got to be shitting me," Jim gasped.

At last, the adversary! His new self spoke from deep within his being. My God, he thought, is that what the Raknar were meant to fight?! Then the word came to him at last: *Canavar.* This was a Canavar – a giant mutated creature. Not the spawn of some devil as his Earth-based mythos had tried to suggest. This creature was the product of ancient sciences and had once been responsible for a war that nearly scoured society from an entire galaxy – a monster that still haunted the nightmares of a thousand races, that was used to frighten and horrify children to this day. They were the ultimate terror weapon of an arms race long past, just like the Raknar were the ultimate weapon that defeated them.

It screamed that soul-scraping scream again, then began racing toward him. Jim took a couple of steps back and smashed into the unyielding force field. The Canavar turned from its blazing headlong rush across the landing area, now an arena of mortal combat, its body turning sideways in a blur as it lashed out at him with a segmented tail that held a shining spike. Jim, too stunned by the thing's appearance to fully implement the defensive actions that came into his mind, instead went with direct action. He raised his right arm in a cross body block.

"WHANG!" the stinger crashed across the gun barrel in a magnificent explosion of sparks and with enough force to push his arm back into his chest and stagger him backwards. He could see a gouge taken out of the gun barrel at least two inches deep! Damn, had that compromised the barrel? The tail stinger was obviously not bone or chitin. The creature screamed and circled back a few hundred yards away, regarding him.

"Fuck this shit," he said and leveled the gun. Its eyestalks stared at the barrel in uncomprehending malevolence. "BOOOM!" The sixteen-inch projectile slammed into the segmented body just behind the second set of claws, and exploded. Foot-thick chitinous armor, bodily fluids, and viscera exploded in a tidal wave of gore for hundreds of yards in every direction. It looked like a thousand tons of spilled 'ocean surprise' soup splashing down. A claw bounced off his chest, and gore dripped from the force field like paint from a wall. He took a few steps forward to the edge of the pool of bodily fluids and pumped an arm in the air. "Eat that!"

Yes! His other self rejoiced at the macabre scene. A second later another Canavar slammed into him at full speed. The Raknar was knocked off its feet and sent careening into the base of the force field. He felt as if he'd just been hit by an enormous bus and sent flying into a brick wall. The energy field was unyielding. Metal protested, and Jim was distantly aware his body had been slammed against the back of the cockpit with bone-breaking force. Worse, his head hit Splunk, knocking her unconscious and severing the connection.

Like being ripped from a splendid dream by having a bucket of ice water thrown in your face, Jim was rudely returned to his normal level of consciousness sputtering and gasping. He didn't know where he was for a full second, and his head hurt like someone had jammed an icepick into the base of his skull. The last half hour linked with the Raknar was an altered-state experience, both completely real and surreal at the same time. He was now locked in the almost-dark interior of the mecha, glowing electroslime apparatus all around him, and had no ability to control his surroundings.

The Raknar gave a mighty groan, and he screamed as the machine was picked up bodily and thrown. He could only guess how as he suddenly felt weightless and spinning.

"Oh, this isn't good," he said as the machine hit something hard. Luckily for him, it hit front first, allowing more room for the support straps to absorb the impact. That kept his face from smashing into any of the controls or displays. It felt like he'd torn skin in at least a couple places from being jerked by the impact against the straps.

He turned as best he could, suspended half-sideways in the straps, and found Splunk still on her shelf. She appeared to be wrapped in what looked like bands of multicolored spaghetti, her ears down and head lolling to the side. A little pink blood was dripping from her nose slit.

"Splunk!" he yelled and twisted enough to get a hand on her. It took an agonizing second, but he finally felt her little chest rise. "Oh, thank God," he said and gently shook her. "Come on, wake up. We're getting our asses kicked." The Raknar jerked, and it felt like he was being dragged somewhere as he worked in vain to wake the Fae up.

* * * * *

Chapter Forty-One

Hargrave and his platoon leaped clear of the careening Raknar just in time before it hit the shield backwards with a flash of resisting forces and slid to land on its ass with a thunderous crash. The fucking centipede-scorpion thing – the second one – rushed in and grabbed the mecha with two claws, contorted its body like a snake and did a sort of alien judo throw, sending the machine holding his boss hurtling a quarter mile across the arena to slam face-first into the reinforced concrete landing tarmac. Bits of concrete and debris flew up, and the machine skidded through bits and pieces of the first monster. As if things couldn't get any worse, a third was now crawling out of the damned ship too! Okay, jumping on the back of the Raknar might not have been the best idea, but when Jim, acting weird and dreamy, just started to walk off, it was all he could think to do.

"Sit-rep?" he called to Sergeant Blackard in his platoon.

"Crenly is gone," the Sergeant replied immediately. "He got hung up and turned into paste against the shield, the rest of us are fine and on your six, sir." Hargrave slewed his view and spotted the other eight CASPers, all kneeling behind the gore covered carapace of the dead…he couldn't keep calling it a centipede-scorpion, especially since there were now two more of them! Okay, fine, Scorpede it was! Whatever, better than Centipion.

He moved over to them, and tried to keep low. The two Scorpedes were circling the downed Raknar, which wasn't moving after that crazy throw. Something must have been damaged. They needed to help him, but how? The other platoons were outside the shield, and the generators were all inside. Besides, they were protected by their own shield as well. He looked over toward the transport. That was surely powering the shield. If they could get it down, then the entire company would put a hurt on these monsters. They still had most of their heavy ordnance, even with their previous losses. How tough could the monsters be?

There was an earsplitting sound of metal rending and he looked over to see the two Scorpedes trying to pull the Raknar apart. Okay, that's got to stop.

"First Squad, on me," he called. "David," he said to the sergeant, "take Second Squad. See if you can get those Scorpedes off Jim."

"Is that what they're called?" the sergeant asked.

"It is now. Try not to get eaten!"

"Oh, without a doubt. Come on, shovelheads," he yelled. "You heard the boss!" The three remaining troopers fired jumpjets and roared away.

"Alright men," he said to his four troopers and pointed at the transport. "Let's go see if we can get this damned shield down!"

He immediately decided it was better to run than jump. He wanted all the attention on the other squad so his men could get inside unnoticed. He hoped there weren't more of those fucking things inside the ship. Looking at their size and the ship, he doubted it.

It was the better part of a mile and they took about a minute to cover it. Halfway there, he saw the flash of rockets and knew Blackard was making a nuisance of himself. The Scorpedes screamed, and he spared a glance in their direction. Both had dropped Jim's limbs and were in hot pursuit of the CASPers who were leaping around and raining rockets and grenades on the beasts. He could see the explosions leaving angry black patches on the creature's hide, but not much else. He wondered if the whole company could do anything to them.

They reached the ramp of the massive transport at last. All five of them settled underneath where it joined the body of the ship, about forty-five feet over their heads. Hargrave snatched a snooper ball from his belt and lobbed it overhand upwards, toward the door. At the top of its arc, the drone came alive and arrested its fall, spun in a circle to orient itself, then shot upwards, into the ship.

Inside his suit, Hargrave watched the drone feed on a little side screen. The interior of the ship was nearly one massive cavernous space broken into...stalls? Some kind of berth where the Scorpedes must have been kept. He was looking at some of the personnel moving around when he realized there were not three stalls, but four. Fuck, fuck, fuck.

He took control of the drone and sent it flying right down the center of the ship, slowing and looking in each stall as he went. There was a lot of activity near the end, in the last stall. Aliens of a half dozen races were there, all standing around a gantry placed over the back of an inert Scorpede. One of the aliens had on a suit with a passing resemblance to a haptic suit, holding a bunch of cables in one hand, and was yelling at the others who were all using various instruments or doing other unknown tasks.

Good, Hargrave thought, having trouble with one of your damned monsters? "Come on," he said to the squad and fired his jumpjets. He did a perfect leap and landed lightly on the edge of the cargo door without having to use the jets to level the landing. His squad did likewise. Once inside he moved to the side and shared the feed with them.

"I think those fucking monsters are operated," he told them, "just like that Raknar Jim is running." They all exclaimed in disbelief. "Yeah, I know, sounds stupid. But look at the feed." Now the one in the suit was bending over, half its body inside the body of the Scorpede. The drone wasn't close enough to see how it was getting inside. Hargrave guessed an access hatch was installed.

He remembered the first time they had buttoned him into a CASPer. The claustrophobic, helpless feel it gave you at first, and tried to imagine being inside a breathing animal. Especially a fucking insect? He shuddered, the suit shuddering in reply.

"Whatever the case, two of those things are bad enough, we don't need three of them out there. We're going to cause a small malfunction." The others laughed. He knew they'd like that plan.

As silent as a three-yard-tall armored trooper could be, the squad made its way down the cavernous interior of the transport until they were across from the Scorpede and its flurry of workers. There Hargrave took a few seconds to examine the stall and how it held the monster in place. It looked to him as if the rider was in a hole dug just behind the beast's "head." Powerful restraints, spaced every twenty-five feet or so, held the creature in check. There was also one robotic arm added to each claw. This didn't speak to him of a domesticated creature, but rather of a dangerous animal barely kept in check. A feral grin cut his grizzled features. He sent target data to the others in his squad who quickly acknowledged.

The aliens working on the monster suddenly became very excited. The one in the haptic suit clapped another on the back and began to climb into the hole in the monster's back. Game time, Hargrave thought.

"On three," he said. "One...two..." He triggered his jumpjets and soared up over the workers. Several looked up in confusion at the "WHOOSH!" of the jumpjets and tracked the CASPer soaring over their heads. "THREE!"

All four of his troopers fired at the same time. Armor-piercing rockets lanced out, several from each. All the restraints were hit except one holding a claw. They'd been fabricated to keep a Canavar controlled, not to shed armor piercing rockets. They were either blown loose or substantially damaged. The creature shuddered from the stimulus.

About fifty feet above the Canavar, and at the apogee of his flightpath, Hargrave gave a little wave to the technicians prepping their charge for combat. Hargrave chuckled as he fired a single rocket.

Inside the Canavar, the linked operator was plugging in his relays and situating himself in the mushy, fleshy areas just behind his mount's ventral nerve ganglia. All the bio-feedback monitors that controlled the creature were in the green, mood-altering chemical levels were ideal, and he was ready for action. He was just about to signal the crew to button him in when Hargrave's rocket flashed through the open hatch and blew up between the driver's legs.

The Canavar's interface and controls were destroyed, along with a fair amount of nervous system feedback. So, in addition to no longer being able to be controlled, even if the operator wasn't blown to gooey, smoky bits, the animal could no longer feel with its limbs. That didn't mean it wasn't in pain, because it was. More pain than it had ever felt before.

422 | MARK WANDREY

The monster howled and reared. All the restraints exploded in a staccato cracking line as it flexed its seventy-yard length, legs thrashing, scoring steel from the hull and its stall. The technicians – those not unlucky enough to be right next to the operator's hatch when it exploded – all screamed and ran. The Canavar reeled, still held by one claw, and the technicians were sent flying in every direction. They were already up almost fifty feet in the air on the gantry where the operator mounted, so it was a long way to the deck.

Eyestalks panned from side to side, looking for the source of the pain that was drilling into its brain. It tried to move and could not as its one claw was still restrained. It wrapped half its immense length around the structure of its stall's support and pulled. The restraints were not individually stronger than the Canavar; they were designed to work in concert. Any pair was more than enough, however, and they were all mounted to key support points within the ship's interior structure to further burnish the strength as best as possible. As the Canavar's powerful body flexed, the restraint didn't give, the connection did.

With a bang loud enough to be heard outside, the restraint tore away with a ten-foot section of hull and all the cabling running through that section. A second later a gout of flame issued from the hole, energetic and indigo blue. Now free, the Canavar uncoiled, rose, and screamed a challenge, dripping fluids and former operator parts from the hole in the back of its head.

"Dave," Hargrave called.

"Go, sir."

"There's someone inside those things driving them."

"Sir?"

"Trust me. I know it's crazy, but look for the door behind their heads and target that area." A roar echoed over the radio, and he didn't hear anything back from his man, so Hargrave assumed Sergeant Blackard had it under control. The Canavar was thrashing around the hold looking for something to punish for the pain it was feeling. He decided to give it a target. "Men, on me!"

Jim figured he was done for as it felt like the two Canavar were trying to tear his Raknar limb from limb. Splunk didn't look like she was critically injured, but she wouldn't wake up. He didn't know what to do. His eyes strayed to the medkit hooked to the bulkhead not far away. He snatched it and jerked the package open. There were some basic dressings and two nanotherapy injectors. The nanites were designed for most races in the galaxy, though there were exceptions. The question was whether Fae was one of them. While negative side effects were rare, they did happen with some species – generally ones who were not listed in the medical database. His inability to find the Fae meant they weren't listed. Jim inserted the needle into her tiny forearm and released a single dose then dropped the dispenser on the floor.

The Raknar shuddered, and he heard explosions echoing through the hull, closely followed by one Canavar roar and then another. He looked down at Splunk, who was looking up at him.

"Okay, Jim...? <*cheek!*>"

"Am I okay? Forget about me, are you okay?" Another series of explosions, and the Canavar howled sounding really pissed this time.

"Splunk, okay...<*akee!*> We, kill...<*adversary!*>"

"You bet," he said and settled into position again. He felt her delicate fingers in his hair. "Akee," he said.

"Yes, Jim...<*akee!*>" she replied, and found the points. A second later, he was the Raknar again.

"<*Let's do this*>," they said.

* * * * *

Chapter Forty-Two

Jim got to his feet and felt the damage to his leg as pain, and the damage to his motor centers as a slight sensation of dizziness. But he had plenty of power, and the Canavar were distracted. Amazingly, there was part of a squad of CASPers inside the shield with him now, and they were giving the monsters holy hell. The small, dashing combat suits were like flies to the seventy-yard-long centipede nightmares, but they were flies with stingers.

As he watched, one made an insane leap just as the Canavar shot toward it, mouthparts open to crush it to oblivion. The trooper cleared the eyestalks by feet, spinning in midair and firing a single rocket, obviously intended for a specific target. The missile struck, and it looked like it did some damage! The beast roared and flicked the rear half of its body, and the trooper was swatted from the air like a fly. His suited body spun wildly and slammed into the force field before sliding to the ground.

"That one," Jim said as he moved forward, "while it's distracted." He was weaponless, outnumbered, and damaged. This was no time for subtlety. He let the complex combat system that was part of his brain predict the movements of the Canavar as he closed. As he walked he triggered the release of the right battleship barrel. The explosive bolts popped and it began to fall. He caught it in his left and flipped it around, added his right hand to the grip, and swung it. The plan was perfect, just as he walked within range, the one that had killed one of his troopers turned and lifted its head to follow another trooper in flight, putting itself at the perfect height.

"Batter up, bitch!" Jim snarled and swung for all he was worth. The Raknar's fusion-powered "muscles" pushed the bat handle in a rotation that, had it been a human-sized player, was about 115 mph at the swing's maximum extension. However, because the *Missouri*'s gun barrel was more than twenty times the length of a regulation baseball bat, the tip of the bat/barrel (being the gun's two-ton breech mechanism) was, when it hit the Canavar, travelling in excess of Mach 2.

"Craaack!" went the sound barrier. "*CARRUNCH!*" went the Canavar's torso. The sonic boom of the approaching weapon gave the monster just enough warning to slide to the side, making the impact strike its left side, pulverizing one of the pincers in a spray of chitin and goo.

The Canavar screeched in pain and lashed out with its deadly spiked tail. Jim had foreseen that as a high probability should his strike not get a kill. He side-stepped and back-swung the gun barrel. It didn't have nearly the force or speed as the first swing, but it didn't matter. When 20,000 pounds of hardened steel hit the extended tail, the alien creature's armored carapace shattered, and the tail tip went flying.

As that Canavar screeched in agony from its serious injuries and backed away, the other monster realized the CASPers had been a deadly distraction. It launched itself at Jim like a bullet, low to the ground with its legs churning. Its tail tip was raised and pointed over its back as it approached, a 200-foot-long ribbon of living, armored, alien nightmare with a killing spine poised for battle.

With a nearly perfect sense of his surroundings, Jim saw it coming, but he waited until the last second before half-turning to his left and swinging the barrel again, this time like a golf club. The Canavar tried to change direction, stop, do anything. The ground was hardened ferroconcrete which provided very little traction, and physics was a stone-cold bitch. Sparks and shards flew as its legs dug at the ground. The barrel again boomed as it broke the speed of sound, and there was a thunderous, earth-shattering crash as his weapon struck home. The Canavar's head and first twenty-five feet of its body half-split, half-splattered into a wet, chunky explosion of guts, brains, and tiny bits of operator. All four claws went flying, and Jim hopped back as the rest of the body flew crazily past him in a spinning, rolling, out-of-control death spiral into the side of the huge transport.

Die adversary! His other self exulted. Unfortunately, his celebration was premature. The remaining Scorpede rushed up from behind while he'd been avoiding the other one and jumped on his back. Jim tried to spin away, losing the cannon which crashed to the ground at his feet. The Canavar's mouth segments tore at the top of his chassis, not far above his head, trying to rip open the armor. Pain registered as armor plates parted, and a sliver of sunlight came through above his head. He pounded at the thing and only managed to get a hand on one of the pincers.

"Jim, throw it at the ramp!" Hargrave's voice came in over the radio. He spun, reached up with the other hand, took hold of the claw, and *jerked!* Either the Canavar was coming off, or the claw. It was the entire monster. It wasn't much of a throw; the thing was twice as long as he and weighed almost as much. It spun and managed to land almost on its feet while Hargrave and his squad rocketed out of the hold, soaring over its head.

The Canavar's eyestalks followed the flight of the five CASPers and was about to turn toward them when the fourth monster came tearing out of the ship and down the ramp. It was in a headlong rush of unspeakable rage, chasing the tiny racing suits. Driven to the point of insanity by the pain in its brain, it attacked the first thing it saw, which was its brother. The two collided and instantly rolled into a ball of clawing, biting, stinging fury.

Jim backed away as the two monsters tore into each other. Claws, pieces of chitin, and bodily fluids flew for hundreds of feet in every direction. It was like watching a lobster thrown into a blender. The fight only took about thirty seconds. Despite the brain damage to the last Canavar, it was fresh and uninjured, while the other had been ravaged by the Raknar. The third Canavar lay in twitching ruin as the final one, now missing a claw and leaking fluid in several places looked for another target. The last thing it saw was the breech of a ten-ton battleship gun arcing into its head. Jim stood over the monster and pounded.

"Crunch, crunch, whang, crunch!" Jim pulverized the last beast into gooey pieces. Finally standing upright, he inspected the gun barrel. It had a noticeable bend where the second monster had almost finished him with its tail spike. The Canavar on the ground moved, and Jim stomped on the bigger parts a couple of times for effect. *Now* it was dead, he figured.

"Boom!" fire and debris erupted from the side of the transport, and the shield failed.

Galrath watched in stunned disbelief as Project K, the culmination of decades of research, was systematically shot, pounded, baseball-batted, golf-swung, and curb-stomped to death. One damned museum piece had not only devastated all the mercs he'd brought with him, but killed all the Canavar he'd managed to breed in the twenty years of the project.

"Get me out of here," he snarled and snapped at the captain. "Entropy take that damned thing!" he exclaimed, pointing at the Raknar. He'd been bragging a short time ago to the cruiser captain about how the Canavar would use the Raknar for sport – a great test of their abilities. When the cursed machine blew the first Canavar to bloody bits, he'd been stunned into silence.

Hope returned briefly when the machine seemed to be disabled, and the humans' powered suits arrived. His creations could deal with those easily enough. Only they hadn't. The little things were tough and fast, and they managed to sting the big Canavars. He'd called the last one into action, the one having trouble with the bonding process. The rest...was not worth remembering.

"Get us into the air," he ordered, "and we'll obliterate them from ten miles up. Shields as soon as we clear the ground!"

The captain had had enough of the arrogant Acquirer and his crazy schemes. If he'd had time, he would have ordered his mercs to toss him out to be eaten by his own monsters. However, with the Acquirer's ground forces destroyed, staying on the ground could well cost him his ship. Or worse, that Raknar could decide the precious cruiser was just as valid a target for its wrath as any. Yes, leaving was a good idea. He gave the order, and the cruiser's ascent/decent engines roared to life, just as the Canavar transport's near side blew out in a gout of flame, and the shield fell.

"Hurry!" Galrath yelped in very un-Acquirer-like fear as the Raknar turned to regard the ship. The captain and most of the bridge crew were so preoccupied watching the thirty-yard-tall killer robot they failed to see the dozens of ten-foot tall CASPers bound onto the stricken transport, and up onto their cruiser. The shields came on and Galrath laughed.

"What are you going to do now?" he yelled, as if the Raknar could hear him from inside a roaring space ship a mile away and climbing. "Your gun is broken, and you cannot fly! I will rebuild. We still have the embryos, and the next generation will be even bigger and more powerful—"

Galrath was cut off as the cruiser lurched violently and slowed its ascent. Alarms began to howl, and the bridge crew worked furiously, calling out damage reports.

"What is happening?" he demanded of the captain, who ignored him and fought to save his ship.

"Primary lifters 3, 5, and 9 are destroyed!" his pilot called out in a panic.

"Lateral thrusters," the captain yelled. "Get us away from them; they're penetrating our shields somehow." The great cruiser angled away from the processing center, no longer climbing but slipping sideways. On the exterior of the ship, Hargrave reached the top of the superstructure and found what he was looking for. He yanked his last grenade from his belt, set it for a five-second delay, and dropped it into the howling lifter intake.

"Get the shields down," he ordered the troopers who were all over the outside of the ship. Seconds later, explosions pocked the surface and the shields flickered out. Another second and his grenade went off deep in the bowels of the jet-ascent engine. The ship began to pitch violently.

"Everyone clear," he called, set his angle, and rocketed off the crippled ship.

Galrath grabbed the arms of his chair on the bridge as the ship rolled over on its side. The crew fought to use the ship's secondary thrusters to right it, but they were unable. The ship rolled all the way over and accelerated toward the ground. Everyone on the bridge was too busy to see the tiny human combat suits leaping away on the viewer, their mischief done.

"Humans," Galrath growled as the ship plummeted out of control. They were more than a mile away from the processing center now, but he could still see the 100-foot-tall Raknar standing, watching the ship crash. As the ground rushed up, the Raknar raised one hand, made a fist, and elevated its middle finger. The ship slammed into the ground and exploded.

* * * * *

Chapter Forty-Three

Jim sat in the ground car sipping a bottle of water, wishing it were an ice-cold Coke, as one medic looked him over and another examined Splunk. He'd given himself a massive gash in his head and never even noticed it. They said the nanites had worked fine on the Fae, and she had no signs of injury at all. One of the troopers had given her an entire package of beef jerky, and she was busily chewing and trilling happily.

The elSha were at the processing plant evaluating the damage while Hargrave argued with administrator Grato about the contract details. The elSha wanted to take out the cost of repairing the processing facility, but Hargrave kept insisting that, since the Cavaliers were tasked with defense of the tank farms and city, the processing facility was considered collateral damage. The biggest thing in the Cavaliers' favor was that reinforcements had arrived in the form of two merc units: one space defense and the other light assault.

With the loss of most of the ground units, the surviving aggressors had withdrawn, so the system was once again secure. Jim glanced down at the slate which held the unit's TOE, Table of Organization and Equipment, as well as the personnel muster. It had been a costly, bloody affair. In addition to the loss of *Traveler*, they had twenty-one dead troopers and fourteen injured. Support personnel were eleven dead, two injured. And the crew of *Traveler*, all fifty-two, were missing and presumed lost.

Now that the space around Chimsa was secure, a search was underway. It had only been twenty hours since the ship was lost. The problem was that merc ships, as a general rule, didn't use distress beacons. Many races did not consider it dishonorable to splash an escape pod, so better to be safe than sorry.

Adayn walked back from inspecting the Raknar, a swagger in her step, and a grin on her face.

"So, give me the news," he said.

"It's in pretty good shape, considering. I think we have enough parts from the other to fix this one. If you want, of course."

"Absolutely," he said and glanced at Splunk. The little Fae looked up, mouth stuffed with cured meat, and nodded her head. "See, there you go." She gave a thumbs-up to her team who waved and went back to work on the Raknar. Gonna cost a shit load of credits to get it home without a ship, he lamented. One of their support people brought him a packet of field rations, and he dug in, surprised by how hungry he was. Splunk sidled over to investigate.

"They should pay more attention to their contract wording," Hargrave said as he walked over, an ear-to-ear grin on his face.

"No penalty on the processing center I dinged up?"

"Dinged up? Kid, you went through that like a bull in a china shop." He looked serious but his eyes were twinkling. "No, they can't fine us. They hired nine merc companies, and we were the only ones to make landfall. That sort of collateral damage is in the contract." He glanced at the elSha administrator and a bunch of his assistants. The tiny reptilians were already busily planning repairs. "They didn't have it in them to bitch too much anyway. The storage facility was untouched and full of F11. Between that and the other mercs being no-shows, we hit the motherlode."

"What do you mean?" Jim asked and finished his meal, minus several key bits of meat to his partner.

"Well, like many of these ground assault/defense contracts, there is a bonus based on combat action. That's generally split between the participants."

"Holy shit, so we get it all?" Jim crowed.

"Not quite. The space-based companies get their cut. They did their job, just didn't have enough backup. But even with that in mind, yeah, we get a *big* extra payday." Jim smiled and nodded, then sobered when he remembered the rolls of the dead.

"Be sure that all the casualties are paid out a percentage of the bonus, and that the survivors of those who died receive their full death benefit." Hargrave nodded – his respect for the kid was growing daily. Many companies didn't do it that way, but it had always been Cartwright's practice. He was happy to see Jim carrying on the tradition.

Jim raised his voice. "Okay, team; let's get this policed up and move it all back to the garrison. We're still on contract here!" When most of the men had set about the task, he took Hargrave aside and spoke in a lower voice. "What about the damned Canavars?"

"What about them?" Hargrave asked. The planet wasn't very hot, but already the titanic carcasses were beginning to smell. A couple thousand tons of dead insectoid monster were bound to do that. Thousands of rotting spiders added to the stink in a most unpleasant manner. Not far away a couple of heavy equipment operators were looking from their front loaders to one of the carcasses and back in stunned disbelief.

"Hargrave," he said incredulously, "those things haven't been seen in the galaxy for more than twenty-thousand years! The last time they appeared, it caused an interstellar war that ruined the previous government and killed billions." Hargrave turned to look at the macabre scene.

"Huh," he said noncommittally and shrugged. "What are you saying we should do about it, boss? We're just mercs."

"I think we should document this and send a message to the guild about it. The Union needs to be informed that someone out there is breeding Canavar. You can't just buy a pack of monster seeds and grow them in your backyard. The history I read said they were produced on a planetary scale." He pointed at the nearest one, the one he'd killed with the golf swing. "It took years – maybe even decades – to grow something this big. Decades and huge facilities." Then he pointed at the still-burning transport. "And that ship was custom-made to move these fucking things."

"Okay," Hargrave said in a mollifying tone, "I see your point. But do we really want to get involved in this?"

"We already are," Jim said. "And if the shit hits the fan about this on a major scale..." he looked around and retreated, "well, more major than this, I want everyone to know for damned sure that Cartwright's Cavaliers didn't have anything to do with them beyond ensuring they were completely destroyed."

"Smash, adversary...<*skaa!*>" Splunk said and smacked one little hand into another.

"What she said," Jim said and rubbed her ears. The Fae trilled affectionately.

The barracks were mostly empty. Designed to accommodate many merc companies at once and only holding the Cavaliers now, the space seemed to echo. Another company would be landing within 24 hours to relieve them for a week while they did necessary repairs and got medical treatment for their injured. Jim's office was standard fare in the Union for a merc commander: a room with a desk and a couple of chairs, a private bathroom, and a small bedroom. Of course, most of what he'd owned had been aboard *Traveler*. All he had now was a small day bag he'd kept with his CASPer, something most mercs tended to do, and a habit he'd picked up from them. Now he knew why they did it.

He'd placed his meager possessions in the office and made a comfy spot in a desk drawer where Splunk could crawl in to sleep when his door flew open. Hargrave came rushing in.

"You won't believe it," he said.

"At this point, you might be right," Jim said, "but tell me anyway."

"The commander of the Nightbirds just contacted us," he panted, half out of breath from running to tell the news. The Nightbirds were the space-based defensive merc unit that had just arrived in system a few hours ago, "They found survivors."

"Excellent!" Jim said and slapped his desk. Splunk grumbled from inside and he soothed her. "Any details?" Hargrave handed him a slate and Jim scanned the list, his eyes growing wider and his grin broader. "Holy shit, that's most of them!" He checked some names. "No one from the bridge of *Traveler*?" he asked. Hargrave looked down and shook his head. Still, most of the rest of the crew was there. Captain Winslow had done what every captain strived to do, keep most of his crew alive, even if it meant he went down with the ship.

Jim sat in his commander's chair, nodded and grinned a little. It could have been worse, so much worse. Hargrave came forward and held out a hand. Jim looked a little confused then stood and shook the hand.

"Well done, sir," Hargrave said.

"What was that for?" Jim asked.

"You're the Commander of Cartwright's Cavaliers," Hargrave said and winked, "and you deserve it. Your father would be proud of you." And he left Jim alone to smile and count his fortunes.

It was a couple of hours later, and fatigue was finally catching up with him. Listening to Splunk's gentle snores in the desk drawer wasn't helping. His desk had several monitors running showing captured images of the Canavar, both assembled and disassembled. One particularly spectacular shot was the instant before he fired the battleship cannon and blew the first one all to hell. He smiled, thinking that would make a great poster, then scowled as he thought about the message he needed to send to the mercenary guild. There was a gentle knock at his door.

"Come," he said and the door cracked open followed by a lovely woman's head. "Adayn!" he said, his scowl turning into an ear-to-ear grin.

"Got time to see me, Commander?" she asked.

"Of course," he said and used an expansive gesture to welcome her into his incredibly spartan quarters. "I was just going over the pictures we have of the Canavar." She closed the door and crossed over to his desk. He was intensely aware of just how shapely she was, and how she kept her waist-length ponytail carefully braided so it didn't get in the way of her armorer's work. Several buttons of her uniform tunic were undone and showed off a modest amount of cleavage and a black, lacy bra. She spoke as she walked.

"The men say we'll have your Raknar operational inside forty-eight hours. We're even looking to see if we can salvage some of the weapons from that downed cruiser, to fit on your new toy." He nodded absently, the swaying of her hips had pulled his eyes like a snake charmer. He swallowed and felt his blood racing. Suddenly he wasn't at all tired. "All the CASPers we can field will be ready about the same time," she finished and put a slate with the data on his desk. "Can I see?" she asked. He nodded, keenly aware that his extra chin kept nodding for a moment. He tried to suck his considerable gut in a bit as she came around the desk instead of turning to the display, but it was a hopeless endeavor.

Adayn looked through the various displayed images, leaning over his desk to tap at them for different views. Her breasts were inches from his face. Jim felt faint. He was breathing hard, he realized, and he forced himself to calm down. She clicked again and the poster image came up.

"Wow," she said; "that's spectacular!"

"It sure is," he said. She turned to look at him, then down where he was looking. "Are you staring at my boobs, Commander?"

Jim turned three shades of red, then immediately blanched, sliding his chair back and jumping to his feet.

"I'm s-sorry," he said and looked away. "That was uncool."

"You remember what I said to you when we met after the crash?" Much like when he had first fired the battleship cannon, an explosion in the back of his mind rocked his being. He staggered a little and fortunately ended up against the wall before he could fall over. He couldn't speak so he just nodded. "Well, I've been thinking about that..." He deflated like one of those big inflatable animals they use to advertise businesses on Earth when the power is unplugged.

"Yeah," he said.

"It's just that..." she started.

"You don't have to say anything," he told her, managing through a herculean effort to summon up the most half-assed smile any man who'd just been turned down had ever managed in the history of men and women. "It was an emotional moment; you might have spoken off-hand."

"No, I..." she started but he held up a hand.

"No harm, no foul." He shrugged. "I mean, I'm a nineteen-year-old kid, and your Commanding Officer. I know you're much older, and there isn't much I can offer you anyway. If you..." he choked a little, ". . . want to go, I understand."

"Oh," she said and nodded. Without saying anything else she went back around the desk and to the door. Jim felt like his heart was tied to her belt, and slowly being pulled out. She reached the door, grabbed the handle, and turned the lock. She turned around and walked right up to him. "Jim, you have everything I want, and I don't care that you're only nineteen, and I don't care that you're my Commander." He looked down at his figure and sighed. "And I don't care that you're a big guy."

"I'm fat," Jim said plainly, "it doesn't hurt anymore to hear it."

"That's a lie," she said and came over to touch his cheek gently. "That's a lie. It hurts you every time because people want it to hurt you. They don't understand, and it's a weapon, and you are tired of being hurt." He gave a little choked sound and realized he was crying. "You are the kindest, most interesting, loving man I've ever worked for. Merc commanders seldom love their men like you do. When you saw that lost manpower report, I could see the pain it caused you."

"I got twenty-six men and women killed," he said, now crying even more and hating himself for it.

"No, dammit, you saved over 200! You and Captain Winslow, and you don't do him any honor acting this way." She leaned closer and wiped his tears away with her hand. "There is nothing wrong with you, Jim." Her lips brushed his, and he shuddered. Her arms went over his shoulders, and he stiffened in surprise. "Absolutely nothing," she said and kissed him full on. He knew the basics but had never done it before, so she gently guided him. His hands reached slowly to her waist, and she pressed even closer, encouraging his touch. When her tongue touched his lips, he opened his mouth and felt like he was flying as their tongues intertwined.

He realized she was breathing hard when she took his right hand from around her waist and put it on her breast. It was warm and giving, like he thought it would be. He could feel her nipple, hard under the bra. Oh shit, oh shit, oh shit. Being shot out of a dropship in his CASPer was the bravest thing he'd ever done in his life, but it was nothing compared to the effort it took to move his hand and slide it inside her bra and cup her breast. She moaned and rubbed against him.

All too soon she broke away, but took his hand and pulled him toward the tiny bedroom. He was shaking worse than when he'd been trying to put on his survival suit, nearly freezing to death on Kash-Kah. She looked back at him. The look on her face was beatific and inviting. It spoke of wonders undiscovered and desire for him.

At the door to his quarters, she stopped and slipped her tunic off, removing the bra as well in a move that left him almost as amazed as the view he now had. She held out her hand to him.

"I've never done this before," he admitted. She giggled a little and blushed. She actually blushed.

"It's okay, baby," she said as he took her hand. "I have. Come on, this is going to be fun. I promise." She guided him into the bedroom and flicked off the light. "And I'm thirty-two years old."

Back in the office, a pair of dimly glowing eyes watched the closed bedroom door as gasps of delight and moans of pleasure came from inside. The sounds were strange, but the emotions were comforting. Satisfied that all was well, Splunk settled back into the comfy drawer and drifted off to sleep.

* * * * *

Chapter Forty-Four

Six months later, Cartwright's Cavaliers arrived at Karma. Jim had managed to save almost a hundred thousand credits by bumming a ride with the Nightbirds who were heading in the same direction they were. It was an unspoken agreement between Earth merc units – you don't leave your fellow humans stranded if you have room. Besides, their unit had blood between them.

"Thanks for the ride, Commander *Shoji-san*," Jim said. He shook the man's hand, then bowed. The Nightbirds' commander returned the bow, lower and longer than Jim had held it.

"It was our honor," he said in passable English with a thick accent. "Your father saved my brother once. *Yoru no Tori* is at your service, you only need to call!" Jim thanked him again, checking his pinplants to see that *Yoru no Tori* meant night bird. Ah, a literal translation.

It had been an enjoyable trip, and the food was wonderful. The best part had been that their transport had a massive gravity deck that included a sauna and hot tub! What a great ride. As he walked into the station and scanned his ID into the automated customs system, Adayn ran up and took his hand. He smiled over at her as she entered her data as well. Splunk rode on her shoulder as often as his. Splunk had instantly accepted her, even when she moved into his quarters a week after that first night. The Fae was already in the station's computer, registered as a pet. The system scanned Splunk, recognized her bio signs, and admitted them.

It was good to be back on Karma station. His quarters were familiar, and they were finally able to unwind completely. After meeting with his senior staff, Jim decided to give the company sixty days leave, owing to their need to return to Earth and bring in new equipment. Not to mention, they needed a new starship. That turned out to be one of the first things to be dealt with.

Two days after getting back, Jim and Hargrave traveled to Bartertown. The city hosted the regional headquarters of the Mercenary Guild, and he wanted to hand-deliver the message so he could be certain it reached their headquarters on planet Capital, where the minimal Union government sat. Hargrave had tried to suggest he wait to send that message until they knew more about the mystery of the Canavar, but Jim felt strongly that time was of the essence. So, they walked into the Grand Hall of the Mercenary Guild on a bright, sunny day.

"Can we help you?" asked a tiny little XenSha at the front counter. Its furry white nose twitched as it examined his uniform, apparently not recognizing it. Its ears were upright and curious, though.

"I'd like to speak with a Guild Master," Jim said. Hargrave waited a few steps back.

"Guild Masters are quite busy. Who wishes to see one?"

"Jim Cartwright, Commander of Cartwright's Cavaliers." The XenSha's eyes got a little wider as it finally placed the patch on Jim's breast pocket.

"And the business?" it persisted.

"That's between myself and the Master." He leaned closer. "You can stop fucking around. It says in the charter that any commander of a mercenary company in good standing can speak to a Guild Master any damned time he wants. So, call one, now." The XenSha looked like Jim had just read off a recipe for XenSha stew.

"There is no reason to be upset, Commander," it said and pressed a button out of view. "A Guild Master will be here in a moment."

"Pricks," Hargrave said over Jim's shoulder. "If you were a Tortantula, they'd have had a Guild Master down here before you could blink your ring of eyes."

"If I were a Tortantula they'd probably have a dozen armored troopers watching to make sure the shit didn't go crazy." True to its promise, an alien came striding down the ornate hall. Jim wasn't surprised to see it was a Veetanho.

"Commander Cartwright," the master said and bowed, her eyes covered by ornate goggles. She was a striking Veetanho. "How can the Guild serve you today?" The master led them to an antechamber and closed the door.

"I have a message for the Guild," Jim said and took out a data chip. The Guild Master looked at it curiously.

"You could have simply transmitted the message to us through the usual channels, Commander." The Veetanho made an offhand gesture. "It would be secure, of course."

"Not good enough," Jim said and set the chip on the counter. "Review the data, and then forward it to the Guild headquarters on Capital." Jim turned with Hargrave, and they both left the Guild Master staring at the chip still sitting on the desk. "I've done my duty," Jim said as they got into a cab.

A few hours later they were both in a dark and noisy bar surrounded by other mercenaries. Hargrave was drinking deeply of his favorite beer and Jim an ice-cold Coke. The wall screens in English were displaying contract offerings while others showed contracts completed. Each of those completed contracts only showed one of four different conditions: Terminated, Withdrawn, Lost, or Fulfilled. Jim's eyes quickly picked himself out of the completed column.

Cartwright's Cavaliers – Defensive Assault (1 of 10) – Chimsa [STATUS – FULFILLED]

Nine other merc companies were listed after his own, only two others listed complete, Nightbirds and the garrison company that had joined them after the big battle. The rest were listed as lost.

"To those who risked and lost," Hargrave said and raised his beer.

"To those who risked and lost," Jim echoed and sipped his Coke.

"You know," Hargrave said, "I figured after Adayn and you shacked up, you'd upgrade to something with a bit more bite to it." Jim inhaled and choked on his drink. "Oh, don't be acting all prissy. It's not like it's a secret you two are bumping uglies." Jim gave a little grin, and Hargrave shook his head. "Yeah, and you're pretty pleased with yourself."

"Don't know what you're talking about," Jim said and took a drink, but it didn't hide his huge grin.

"Well you should be; she's a fine lady."

"She is," Jim said.

"Pleased I am to see you back in my pit," a familiar voice spoke from their side.

"Pleased I am to be here, Peepo," Jim said, and inclined his head. Comparing her to the Guild Master, it was easy to tell that Peepo was not a young Veetanho. Still, he wondered how old she was.

"As am I," Hargrave said, but Jim could have sworn he wasn't as pleased to see her.

"Your contract has drawn much attention in the Guild," Peepo said. "I understand it was quite profitable."

"Yes," Jim agreed, "it was, but it also cost much blood."

"Sometimes profit and blood are close relatives," she said and nodded. Jim wondered, was she analyzing him? "Be well, Jim Cartwright," she said and was gone. He looked at Hargrave curiously, but the other man just shrugged.

"Jim Cartwright?" asked a stranger. They both turned and Hargrave gave a little start, standing up to face the new arrival. She was a human woman, quite tall and whipcord thin. She had waist length white hair loosely pulled back with a single golden cord and she was staring at Jim with the deepest black eyes he'd ever seen. She was dressed in the black uniform of a human merc spacer. A similarly uniformed Veetanho stood a respectful distance behind her. Jim's eyes strayed to the logo on her uniform with its stylized mounted lancer sporting huge wings.

"Oh," he said and hastily stood, "yes."

"It's okay," she said with a little crooked smile, "we've never met. Alexis Cromwell, Commander of the Winged Hussars." She bowed. "At your service, and this is Paka, my Second-in-Command." Jim was a little put off and surprised, but finally managed a reply.

"J-Jim Cartwright, Commander of Cartwright's Cavaliers," he said and half-turned to Hargrave, "and..."

"Ezekiel Hargrave," Commander Cromwell said, again with that crooked smile, "and Second-in-Command now, I see." She held out a hand.

"Commander," Hargrave said, taking the hand and bowing over it before gently placing a kiss on it. Jim lifted an eyebrow, but Hargrave tilted his head and mouthed *some other time* to him. "I serve the Cavaliers in whatever ways I can." Commander Cromwell gave a nod in reply.

"What can we do for you?" Jim asked. "Would you care to join us?"

"I would love to," she said. "I think our Seconds wouldn't mind an opportunity to gossip behind our backs?" Hargrave and Paka bowed out and left the two commanders alone. Around the pit, conversations suddenly changed subjects as human and alien alike realized that two of the storied human Four Horsemen commanders were talking. She ordered a nondescript wine from the autoserver and took a polite sip before launching immediately into what she wanted.

"That mission you just completed, how did it go?"

"Beyond the public status board?" he asked.

"Of course." Jim hesitated. "Son...sorry, *Commander*, if you can talk to anyone, you can talk to me. I knew your father personally. We worked together often. The Four Horsemen stick together, you know."

"I know," Jim admitted. "I think I met you once when I was very young." She smiled at that.

"Yes, I wondered if you remembered. You were maybe five?"

"Seven," he said, and she gave a little nod with a shrug. "The mission was a cluster fuck, as you can see. We were jumped immediately after making transition. We lost *Traveler.*"

"Damn," she said and shook her head. "My mother designed the refit of that ship for your father."

"Then she did a great job. We managed to save almost everyone."

"Captain Winslow?"

Jim shook his head.

She reached out and touched his chest. "I mourn for your loss."

He was surprised, but replied, "Our fates are shared," deploying the ancient ritual human mercs had adopted from their alien brethren.

"The Four Horsemen for Earth," she said, again surprising him. He'd never heard that part before. Of course, he'd never shared a merc's prayer with another of the Four Horsemen. She hadn't taken her hand away yet, so he spoke.

"The Four Horsemen for Earth."

She nodded and took her hand away, asking him to continue. He glanced around, making sure no one was within earshot, and told her everything about the mission. When he got to the end, she sucked air through her teeth and leaned back.

"So, four Canavar, eh?" He nodded in confirmation. "And you with a working Raknar. Tell me, how did you get it to work so well?" Jim swallowed. He'd not included the part about the strange link with Splunk. He was grateful now that he'd left the little alien back on Karma station with Adayn. Coincidentally, they were working on the Raknar.

"We figured out some computer interfaces. I have a good team." She regarded him coolly for several long moments, waiting to see if he would add anything more.

"Okay," she said finally, "well done. Canavar are a special study of mine, you know?"

"No," he said, "I wasn't aware any humans knew much about them." That wry grin was back. There was a lot more going on behind that smile than she was letting on.

"They're a fascinating subject," she said, then circled back to discuss the battle. "So, you destroyed them all? And that's it?"

"I did, but I don't think that's it." He told her about his belief they were being bred in number, and about his message to the Guild.

"That could have been a very good move, or a very bad one," she admitted. "I sent you a message myself a while back. I suspect now that you are here, it will catch up to you."

"Is that why you are here now?"

"Yes and no," she said. "I did want to see if you had received the message, but it can wait. I just happened to be here. I came in because I heard you were here, but I didn't see *Traveler* in orbit. Now I know why." Jim shrugged. "You know we bought *Bucephalus* in the bankruptcy sale?"

"Yes," he said in a noncommittal voice.

"And did you know it's here?"

"No," he said. "I didn't get a good look at the other ships in orbit. We came in with Nightbirds."

"Good little outfit," she said in an almost condescending tone. Of course, compared to the Winged Hussars, almost every nominally human space-based merc unit was little. "Anyway, we really don't have much use for *Bucephalus*." She made an almost frustrated gesture of dismissal. "The Akaga class is a good cruiser, but *Bucephalus* is modified for ground assault." He looked confused. "Your dad ordered it with fewer guns, more shields, and increased cargo space. That's not generally how we roll."

"I see," he said, confused about she was getting at. She glanced at him, a little annoyed. Suddenly a light went off. "Oh, crap. Uhm, we'd be willing to take her off your hands."

"Oh, really?" she said with overly exaggerated interest. "That would be lovely. What would you be willing to pay? The ship is quite valuable." Jim thought frantically. What would a ship like that be worth? He accessed his pinplants and searched the Galnet, then choked.

"I can't offer a fraction of its value," he admitted, then used his pinplants to scan their bottom line. It was quite a bit better off after they'd gotten paid by Wathayat for that gig, but still nowhere near what the *Bucephalus* was worth. "How about twenty million?"

"Hmmm," she said and Jim looked surprised. He'd expected her to laugh at him. "That's an interesting offer, however I can't afford to profit on that sale too much. You see, it would get taxed on Earth. You know...accountants." She took a slate from her belt pouch and tapped on it. "I'll sell it to you for double what we bought it for," she said and slid the slate across. There was the bill of sale where they'd paid the bankruptcy court on Earth for the ship. His eyes bugged out. "Surely, you can handle that?"

"Sure," he said and considered those incredibly black eyes. They had an oddly amused twinkle to them. Jim reached into his pocket and took out a ten credit note and slid it across to her. She tapped on the slate and his pinplants pinged him. Cartwright's Cavaliers had just accepted the transfer and mastery of *EMS Bucephalus* from the Winged Hussars, for twice the original sale price.

"Pleasure doing business with you," she said and offered him her hand. Jim stood and took it, then almost fell. For an instant, it felt like when Splunk touched him, and the two had merged to control the Raknar. It was over so fast, he wondered if it was just vertigo from standing too fast. He opened his mouth to say something, but she was gone.

"What...?" he said, shaking his head. He almost followed her, then decided he was just imagining it. Had to be. He brushed it aside the moment he remembered he had a ship again! He needed to get back to his office and start hiring a crew. He looked for Hargrave and couldn't find him, so he went ahead and took a cab back to the starport. There was a lot of work to do.

* * * * *

Epilogue

The cab maneuvered on its uni-ball drive to shoot between traffic and drop Jim at the front door of the Hilton safe and sound. It seemed human-operated cabs on Earth, especially around starports, were becoming increasingly rare.

"Twenty-nine credits," the machine announced. Jim slipped his yack into the slot and thumbed the ID to withdraw the credits. At least robots didn't need tips. Pocketing the card, he climbed out into the blustery January Houston weather. The thermometer hovered around 50 degrees Fahrenheit, and for Houston that was damned cold.

"Good afternoon, Commander Cartwright," the doorman said, holding the cab's door and touching the tip of his hat.

"Edward," Jim said and handed him a five-credit note. He still liked cash for tipping; it just felt better.

"Will you be needing anything tonight, sir?"

"I might want to go out to dinner later."

"I'll notify the concierge to be on the lookout."

"That would be great. I heard there is a new Cochkala restaurant near the starport." The tall man gave a little shudder and tried to smile.

"You merc types always have the strangest tastes," he said. "Don't go in for alien food myself, but I'll let him know to check into it." Jim thanked him and headed inside. The manager caught his attention from the desk and Jim went over to see what he wanted.

"Mr. Cartwright," he said in his New York accent, "I have a message chip for you, just arrived from the Mercenary Guild." He placed it on the desk and Jim took it. A little hologram had the logo of the Four Horsemen. So not the Guild, but one of his fellows. He'd yet to hear a peep from the Guild, and more than a month had passed.

"Thank you," he said and turned to go, but before he could get more than two steps away, the manager spoke in a hushed and urgent tone.

"Oh, sir? There's someone here to see you. They tried to insist they be allowed access to your suite, but of course I refused. They are in the bar, if you care to meet them."

"Who is it?" he asked, and the manager whispered the response in his ear in hopes that his discretion might be able to save Jim from the encounter that was waiting. "Oh," Jim said, nodding as he headed for the elevator.

"Jimmy?" he heard from the direction of the bar. Fuck. "Jimmy, my God, is that really you?" He turned to see his mother strutting across the lobby toward him.

"Hello, Mother," he said. He considered continuing on toward the elevator, but discarded the idea. He knew this would happen when the current issue of *Soldier of Fortune* came out. He was on the cover, striding down the gangway from *Bucephalus*, Hargrave and his other officers following behind. "Large and In Charge," the article headline read. When he'd left Earth all those months ago, he thought he'd looked a little ridiculous in that uniform. Now, it seemed to fit him just fine. That article might have been written tongue-in-cheek, but it was fairly flattering. Hard not to be after the series of contracts he'd won, and the millions he'd brought back.

"Jimmy, I've tried to get in touch with you, but the bitch you hired at the office won't forward your messages!" She sniffed in mock hurt. "She wouldn't even let me in Thad's old office."

She'd been an incredibly beautiful woman once. Now she weighed almost as much as Jim. At five-foot-ten-inches, tall by average North American standards, she was very large for a woman. She was light complexioned with high cheekbones, long blonde hair and striking blue eyes. His father had said she had a figure that would stop a rampaging Tortantula. Now it looked like she had one that would feed a company of Tortantula. She'd put on at least fifty pounds, and it looked like a lot of it had been from drugs and booze. She looked hard-used, and her clothes were not the usual pristine high-end brands she'd stuck to exclusively when he was growing up. The handbag appeared to be a knockoff, too. He dimly wondered what she'd done with the money.

"That's because you aren't allowed near the company," Jim told her. "Try to get into the offices again, and I'll file a restraining order."

"Jimmy, is that any way to talk to your Mom? I mean, really." She tried to blow it all off. "Anyway, look at you!" She said and inspected his uniform. The golden eagle of commander favored by the Four Horsemen leaders, Cavalier logo on his chest. "You've lost weight!" she said.

"Some, yes. Been working hard," he told her, unable to pass up the compliment.

"Great, so why don't we have dinner. You can catch me up on what's happening! I need to know everything."

456 | MARK WANDREY

"I don't have time, Mom. We're hiring a few hundred new people, and frankly...I don't want to see you." She had been looking annoyed until the last, then she looked worried.

"Jimmy, why are you being this way?" He heard the elevator open behind him.

"Maybe because you almost destroyed the Cavaliers, stole millions of credits, caused us to lose billions, and then went on a two-year bender to spend it all?" She looked sideways and snorted. "Don't even try to say you didn't. Come on, Mom, look at yourself! Do you have any idea what I went through trying to save this company?"

"You look fine," she said. "I saw that article. You bought the ship back, ordered a bunch of guns..." He glared at her. She seemed to notice something behind him but went on. "Can't you spare some time for your own mother?"

"Where were you two years ago when I had to live in a dump and do software work just to survive? I studied for years to run the company, and you ruined it."

"It was all just a misunderstanding," she said, then her face darkened and she yelled past him. "Excuse me, but this is a private conversation!" Jim felt a hand slip into his arm and Adayn was by his side, comfortable and familiar. He felt his confidence soar. "W-what...I mean, who is this?" she asked, trying to sound sweet and interested when her body language was fearful at best.

"Adayn Christopher," she said sweetly and held out her hand. Jim was impressed, he could feel her tension. She was a much better actor than his mother.

"Elizabeth Cartwright-Kennedy, Jimmy's mother."

"I know who you are," Adayn said.

"And who are you exactly?"

"She's my girlfriend," Jim said levelly.

"Girlfriend?" his mother said, somewhat incredulously. "What is she, twenty-five? After his money, are you?" Jim felt his anger growing quickly. Adayn moved out from his side a bit so Jim's mother could see her uniform, identical to his except sergeant's chevrons on her shoulder with a "T" under them for technical. His mother had been about to say something harsh when she finally saw the uniform and came up short.

"Oh," she squeaked. "Can we just..."

"What do you want, Mother?"

"I just wanted to catch up," she said in a small voice. Jim cocked his head. "Maybe see if you could loan me a few credits?"

Adayn sensed his resolve and half-turned, pushing the elevator call button for him, and Jim turned with her to wait for it.

"Jimmy Cartwright," his mother said in her best mom voice, "you can't just walk away from me!" The elevator arrived and opened. He walked in with his lady and turned around. His mother was standing there, easily summoning crocodile tears to her cheeks. He smiled to her.

"I don't have to," he said, "you walked away from me, years ago." The doors closed on the stunned look she gave him.

In his room Jim dropped into a chair and sighed. Adayn came up behind him and massaged his neck and patted his back. Jim wasn't feeling emotional, and that surprised him. He just felt drained.

"You handled that well," she said.

"Thanks," he said. "Tomorrow I need to go to the courthouse here in Houston and file a restraining order."

"You think that's necessary?"

"Absolutely," he said. "Anyway, don't worry about it. I'm actually surprised she isn't wanted by the law." Adayn leaned over his shoulder, her arms encircling his neck. He turned his head and nibbled her neck playfully. "We have some time before dinner..." he said, letting the suggestion trail off.

"Oooh," she said and kissed him.

Later as they were heading down to the lobby to go to dinner, Jim's thoughts turned to Splunk. The little Fae had taken off on one of her explorations just when they were ready to leave Karma.

"I hope Splunk is okay."

"I'm sure she's fine," Adayn said and straightened the tie on his formal uniform. "You remember how she'd take off for days at a time on that station." Jim shrugged. "She's probably taking apart everything in the place and seeing how it works." She was probably right. Besides, Earth customs likely wouldn't allow her on the planet anyway.

L ight years away on Karma station, the administrator was dealing with a flurry of complaints. A crime wave was underway, and he had no clue who was responsible. Parts stores of a dozen merc units had been raided. Nothing big, just a part here, a part there. Everything imaginable from carbon fiber reinforced beams to optical data cable. Law enforcement was watching the docks day and night, waiting for the thieves to try and unload the goods. Yet, nothing had shown up. Yesterday, two obsolete fusion cores were discovered missing. The administrator shuffled that report to the side. They were obsolete cores used on an ancient design of gunboat. Who would steal something like that?

The station was vast and ancient, with miles of corridors. It had first opened thousands of years ago and been rebuilt and expanded several times. There were even several bays, on the inner ring where gravity was low, that had been lost during those expansions. New walls were added, tunnels closed off for structural improvements, and the existence of the bays forgotten. Unable to be used in any practical manner, they had supports or power conduits running through the center. They were not on most maps anymore.

The Fae slipped from the ventilation shaft into one of those huge, abandoned bays. Taking a second to orient in the near zero-gravity while controlling her prize, she leaped across the open space and expertly landed. In one corner of the bay, constructed from scrap lightweight wall panels, was a small living area.

Complete with its own heating and an autochef which was on the station administrator's theft report log, the quarters would barely have been sufficient for a single small adult human. The Fae pulled open the door and looked inside. Nine sets of large, light reflecting eyes gazed back at her.

"You, find...<*cheek!*>" asked one of the occupants.

"I, found...<*creet!*>" The lighting level was increased slightly via an assortment of office and living quarters lamps, all of which were also reported as missing. All ten Fae gathered around to examine what the new arrival had brought. When another of their number arrived through the door, they all respectfully made room for her to see as well. Since she'd brought them all together, they'd decided she would lead.

"Where, find...<*cheek!*>" Splunk asked.

"Besquith, ship...<*proo!*>" They all chittered in delight. Splunk pointed and it was stored in its special place. The living space was jam packed with storage places, now almost all full of various tools, electronics equipment, and gadgets. In one place was a collection of jars all holding tiny amounts of greenish goo. A series of lights casting a blue-white light caused the goo to gently sway and pulse.

"We, ready...<*skaa!*>" Splunk said.

"<*AKEE!*>" they all intoned together.

Splunk turned her head and looked far, far away. She could feel him through their connection. Distance would make no difference. He was working toward their mutual goal, though he had no idea that they shared it in common. The other Fae went about their various tasks, and Splunk went to help. She trilled happily as they worked.

# # # # #

ABOUT THE AUTHOR

Located in rural Tennessee, Mark Wandrey has been creating new worlds since he was old enough to write. After penning countless short stories, he realized novels were his real calling and hasn't looked back since. A lifetime of diverse jobs, extensive travels, and living in most areas of the country have uniquely equipped him with experiences to color his stories in ways many find engaging and thought provoking.

Sign up on his mailing list and get free stuff and updates!
http://www.worldmaker.us/news-flash-sign-up-page/

Caution – Worlds Under Construction

Titles by Mark Wandrey

A Time to Die

Earth Song: Twilight Serenade

Earth Song: Etude to War

Earth Song: The Lost Aria

Earth Song: Sonata in Orionis

Earth Song: Overture

* * * * *

The following is an
Excerpt from Book 2 of the Revelations Cycle:

Asbaran Solutions

Chris Kennedy

Available from Seventh Seal Press

January 13, 2017

eBook, Paperback, and Audio Book

Excerpt from "Asbaran Solutions:"

Planet Moorhouse, Kepler 62 System

"This is bullshit," Sergeant James Wilson said. The tall, dark-haired trooper spat, the betel nut chew making his spittle a bright crimson on the sun-bleached sand.

"What's bullshit?" Private Dave Daniels asked, his pale brows knitting. "This is only my second contract, but it seems like pretty good duty to me. Walk some fence line, guard a mine, and get paid a ton of credits? Seems pretty soft. No one's trying to kill me, and I can go down to the bar after my shift. Sure, the locals look like ant-eaters, but they pay well enough so I can afford some of the over-priced beer they've imported."

"Naw, that ain't what I'm talking about, at all," the sergeant replied. He spat again. "Don't get me wrong, I enjoy not getting shot at as much as anyone. Having actually been hit a couple of times, I may even enjoy it more. What I'm saying is that this whole contract's fucked up."

"Why's that?"

"Do you see the bird on our crest?" Sergeant Wilson asked, pointing to where the Asbaran Solutions company flag hung limply from the staff in the humid, breezeless air.

Private Daniels nodded his head, then wiped the sweat from his eyes the motion caused. "Yeah. There's a bird with the company's motto, 'Kill Aliens. Get Paid.'"

"Do you know what kind of bird that is?"

"Nope; it looks like some sort of griffin."

The sergeant stopped and glared at the junior enlisted. "Do they not teach unit history at basic any more, or are you just too fucking stupid to remember? It ain't no damn griffin, boy; it's a huma bird."

465

"A huma bird?"

"Yeah. It's a type of bird that never lands; it lives its entire life flying above the clouds where you can never see it."

"Wow, that's pretty cool. I've never heard of a bird like that."

"That's because it doesn't exist, you dumbass," the sergeant said, cuffing the private in the back of the head. "It's myth-o-logical. The point I'm trying to get through your stupid fucking head is that us Asbaran ain't for sitting around guarding shit. We're mobile; we strike from above and crush our enemies. We don't hang around waiting for them to hit us while we're sitting on the damned toilet in a guardhouse on some godforsaken planet at the ass-end of the galaxy." He spat; another red stain marked his passage. "If the Founder could see us now…"

"What? What would he do?"

"If the Founder could see us now, he'd probably come back and kill every single mother fucker in management. This ain't how we're supposed to be used. It don't play to our strengths…*and it just ain't right!*" He sighed. "It ain't what I signed up for anyway." He spat again, hitting his first mark dead center. "I signed up to be up there," he continued, pointing up to the sky.

Daniels looked up to where the sergeant pointed and squinted. "Hey, what's that?" he asked. "There's something up there."

Sergeant Wilson looked up. A miniature boomerang shape could just be seen, silhouetted against the clear green sky. "Fuck!" he grunted as he broke into a run back toward the shelter. "*Incoming!* Get under cover *now!*"

He had only covered half the distance to the bunker when he heard the tell-tale shriek of the banshee bombs, and he knew they weren't going to make it.

* * * * *

Find out more about Chris Kennedy and get the free prequel to Asbaran Solutions, "Shattered Crucible" at:

http://chriskennedypublishing.com/

* * * * *

The following is an
Excerpt from Book 1 of The Kin Wars Saga:

Wraithkin

Jason Cordova

Available Now from Theogony Books

eBook, Paperback, and (soon) Audio Book

Excerpt from "Wraithkin:"

Prologue

The lifeless body of his fellow agent on the bed confirmed the undercover operation was thoroughly busted.

"Crap," Agent Andrew Espinoza, Dominion Intelligence Bureau, said as he stepped fully into the dimly lit room and carefully made his way to the filthy bed in which his fellow agent lay. He turned away from the ruined body of his friend and scanned the room for any sign of danger. Seeing none, he quickly walked back out of the room to where the slaves he had rescued earlier were waiting.

"Okay, let's keep quiet now," he reminded them. "I'll go first, and you follow me. I don't think there are any more slavers in the warehouse. Understand?"

They all nodded. He offered them a smile of confidence, though he had lied. He knew there was one more slaver in the warehouse, hiding near the side exit they were about to use. He had a plan to deal with that person, however. First he had to get the slaves to safety.

He led the way, his pistol up and ready as he guided the women through the dank and musty halls of the old, rundown building. It had been abandoned years before, and the slaver ring had managed to get it for a song. In fact, they had even qualified for a tax-exempt purchase due to the condition of the neighborhood around it. The local constable had wanted the property sold, and the slaver ring had stepped in and offered him a cut if he gave it to them. The constable had readily agreed, and the slavers had turned the warehouse into the processing plant for the sex slaves they sold throughout the Dominion. Andrew knew all this because he had been the one to help set up the purchase in the first place.

Now, though, he wished he had chosen another locale.

He stopped the following slaves as he came to the opening which led into one of the warehouse's spacious storage areas. Beyond that lay their final destination, and he was dreading the confrontation with the last slaver. He checked his gun and grunted in surprise as he saw he had two fewer rounds left than he had thought. He shook his head and charged the pistol.

"Stay here and wait for my signal," he told the rescued slaves. They nodded in unison.

He took a deep, calming breath. No matter what happened, he had to get the slaves to safety. He owed them that much. His sworn duty was to protect the Dominion from people like the slavers, and someone along the way had failed these poor women. He exhaled slowly, crossed himself and prayed to God, the Emperor and any other person who might have been paying attention.

He charged into the room, his footsteps loud on the concrete flooring. He had his gun up as he ducked behind a small, empty crate. He peeked over the top and snarled; he had been hoping against hope the slaver was facing the other direction.

Apparently Murphy is still a stronger presence in my life than God, he thought as he locked eyes with the last slaver. The woman's eyes widened in recognition and shock, and he knew he would only have one chance before she killed them all.

He dove to the right of the crate and rolled, letting his momentum drag him out of the slaver's immediate line of fire. He struggled to his feet as her gun swung up and began to track him, but he was already moving, sprinting back to the left while closing in on her. She fired twice, both shots ricocheting off the floor and embedding themselves in the wall behind him.

Andrew skid to a stop and took careful aim. It was a race, the slaver bringing her gun around as his own came to bear upon her. The muzzles of both guns flashed simultaneously, and Andrew grunted as pain flared in his shoulder.

A second shot punched him in the gut and he fell, shocked the woman had managed to get him. He lifted his head and saw that while he had hit her, her wound wasn't nearly as bad as his. He had merely clipped her collarbone and, while it would smart, it was in no way fatal. She took aim on him and smiled coldly.

Andrew swiftly brought his gun up with his working arm and fired one final time. The round struck true, burrowing itself right between the slaver's eyes. She fell backwards and lay still, dead. He groaned and dropped the gun, pain blossoming in his stomach. He rolled onto his back and stared at the old warehouse's ceiling.

That sucked, he groused. He closed his eyes and let out a long, painful breath.

* * * * *

Find out more about Jason Cordova and "Wraithkin" at:
http://chriskennedypublishing.com/imprints-authors/jason-cordova/

* * * * *